Praise for *The Crooked House*:

'*The Crooked House* hooks the reader through the gut from the first dark page, driving you on in a lather of fear and excitement until the great reveal. The author's bleak estuary flatlands are every bit as menacing as the Cornish crags of Daphne du Maurier: this is geography as psychodrama, calling the survivors home for a day of reckoning'   **Rowan Pelling**

'*The Crooked House* is a terrific, powerful and unsettling novel, beautifully written; I read it with my heart in my mouth.'
                                                    Jill Dawson

'Any novel by Christobel Kent is a pleasure to savour, but *The Crooked House* is almost indecently good. A psychological page-turner imbued with depth and humanity. *Broadchurch meets Rebecca*. I loved it'   **Allison Pearson**

'A gripping thriller, beautifully unfolded, with gorgeous, evocative writing that builds to a shattering climax. There's an eerie sense of place that cleverly captures the particular claustrophobia that wide open spaces can provoke'   **Erin Kelly**

'Oh my goodness – what a book! Such evocative writing; such a brilliantly visual book, and so beautifully tense . . . just glorious'   **Clare Mackintosh**

'I thought it was a brilliant read, dark and vivid and almost unbearably suspenseful with a sense of menace and claustrophobia as the local community clings to its secrets'
                                                    Cath Staincliffe

The
CROOKED
HOUSE

Christobel Kent

SPHERE

First published in Great Britain in 2015 by Sphere

1 3 5 7 9 10 8 6 4 2

A CIP catalogue record for this book is available from the British Library.

Hardback ISBN 978-0-7515-5750-3
Trade Paperback ISBN 978-0-7515-5697-1

Typeset in Bembo by Palimpsest Book Production Limited,
Falkirk, Stirlingshire
Printed and bound in Great Britain by Clays Ltd, St Ives plc

Papers used by Sphere are from well-managed forests
and other responsible sources.

MIX
Paper from
responsible sources
FSC
www.fsc.org   FSC® C104740

Sphere
An imprint of
Little, Brown Book Group
100 Victoria Embankment
London EC4Y 0DY
An Hachette UK Company

www.hachette.co.uk
www.littlebrown.co.uk

To Ilsa, for her beauty, love and courage

Acknowledgements

I'd like to thank my impeccable, surefooted editor Jade Chandler of Sphere, Richard Beswick of Little, Brown for his unstinting friendship and literary insight, Sara O'Keeffe of Corvus, without whose clear-eyed support and strategic genius this book would never have been begun, and Victoria Hobbs, the bravest literary agent, critic and champion a writer could ask for. But most of all my husband Donald, who has believed in me since 1981.

Thirteen Years Ago

When it starts again she is face down on her bed with her hands over her ears and she feels it more than hears it. A vibration through the mattress, through the flowered duvet, through the damp pillow she's buried her face in. It comes up from below, through the house's lower three storeys. *BOOM*. She feels it in her throat.

Wait, listen: one, two, three. *BOOM*.

Is this how it begins?

Leaning on the shelf over the desk, wooden letters spelling her name jitter against the wall. They were a present on her seventh birthday, jigsawn by Dad, E.S.M.E. The family'd just moved in, unloading their stuff outside this house they called the crooked house, she and Joe, as the sun went down over the dark marsh inland. Creek House to Crooked House, after the tilt to its roofline, its foundations unsteady in the mud, out on its own in the dusk. Mum was gigantic with the twins, a Zeppelin staggering inside with bags in each hand. *We need more space now*, is how they told her and Joe they were moving. It was seven years ago, seven plus seven. Now she's fourteen, nearly. Fourteen next week.

1

Ah, go on, Gina had said. *Just down it.* Then, changing tack, *You can give it me back, then.*

Esme's been back an hour. She isn't even sure Joe saw her pass the sitting-room door, jammed back on the sofa and frowning under his headphones: since he hit sixteen he's stopped looking anyone in the eye. The girls, a two-headed caterpillar in an old sleeping bag on the floor, wriggled back from in front of the TV, twisting to see her. Letty's lolling head, the pirate gap between Mads's front teeth as she grins up at her, knowing. She mouths something. *Boyfriend.* Esme turns her face away and stomps past.

Mum opening the kitchen door a crack, leaning back from the counter to see who it is. Frowning like she can't place her, she gets like that a lot these days. *What are you doing back?* Esme doesn't answer: she is taking the stairs three at a time, raging.

Outside the dark presses on the window, the squat power station stands on the horizon, the church out on the spit that looks no bigger than a shed from here, the village lights distant. Make all the noise you like out here, Dad's always saying, no one can hear.

Hands over your ears and never tell.

On the bed she lies very still, willing it to go, to leave the house. Whatever it is.

Her hands were already over her ears, before it started. Why? The boom expands in her head and she can't even remember now. All she knows is, she was standing at the window, now she's on the bed.

She grapples with detail. She heard a car. There were voices below in the yard and, after, noises downstairs. Something scraping across the floor, a low voice muttering and she didn't want to deal with it, with his questions; she flung herself down on the bed and the tears began to leak into the pillow. She would have put on her music but she didn't want him to know she was back.

Now. A sound, a human sound, just barely: a wounded shout, a gasp, trying to climb to a scream that just stops, vanishes. And in the silence after it she hears breathing, heavy and ragged; up through three storeys and a closed door, it is as if the house is breathing. And Esme is off the bed, scrabbling for a place to hide.

BOOM.

On the marsh behind the house there are the remains of an old hut with a little rotted jetty. The tide is beginning to come up, gurgling in its channels, trickling across the mud that stretches inland, flooding the clumps of samphire and marsh grass and the buried timbers. Behind her the house stands crooked in the wind freshening off the estuary.

The lights of the police cars come slowly, bumping down the long track, an ambulance, the cab lit. It is three in the morning but the inky dark is already leaching to grey behind the church on the spit. One of the coldest June nights on record, and it takes them a while to find her. She doesn't make a sound.

Chapter One

Alone in the bed Alison sat bolt upright. She had trained herself not to gasp when that happened, long before she woke next to anyone, long before there was anyone to ask her what had scared her. But she couldn't stop the jerk upwards, as if she had to break through the surface, as if water was closing over her. Paul had never asked, though: it was one of the reasons she was still here, eight months on.

Not the only reason. She could hear him in the next room; she leaned down and groped for her glasses – no table on her side of the bed, they were entangled in the bedclothes on the floor – and the bright room swam into focus. Better.

In the small old-fashioned kitchen, Paul was making tea: she could hear the kettle spit and gurgle, coming to the boil. She liked everything about Paul's flat, a modest three rooms in a white-balconied grey-brick tenement above the comforting roar of a main road. A white-painted mantelpiece, bookshelves, two large windows, the kind of desk you found in council offices. There would have been fires in these rooms once, and a maid to lay them, someone to sweep the big chimneys that ran down through the six floors. It would be nice to live here.

It was out of her league. Alison rented a bedsit south of the river, not much more than a useful box; a bed and a foldaway kitchen and students for neighbours, although her room had a view of a tree. She liked it enough: she went back most nights still, on principle. Increasingly though, she didn't know what to do with herself there – it had got untidy, downgraded to storage, a place where she dropped stuff without bothering to put it away. Now she shifted her gaze from Paul's tidy desk – the pile of books, laptop, card index – to the mantelpiece. A couple of Japanese postcards, a pewter bowl, an old mirror framed in dark wood. An envelope leaned against the mirror, his name on it in big cursive script, heavy paper.

He was in the doorway watching her.

From the start there'd been that something about him, some natural reticence or perhaps just his age, that meant that other, secondary panic didn't set in. Over the second meal out, after the first visit to the cinema. The strategies didn't start building themselves in her head, for what to say, when he asked. About her life. About where she came from. About her family.

'What's that?' she said now. She stood up and took the cup he held out to her.

Before Paul they'd been boys, scruffy, well-meaning, lazy. They'd hardly qualified as relationships: more mates, easy to close the door on quietly in the early morning, tiptoeing off to take her place in rush-hour traffic, to breathe a sigh of relief. Paul was more than a head taller than her so she had to look up to see in his face; he set his hand lightly on the small of her back and looked down. She took in all the detail of his face at once, as she'd got used to doing, gazing straight back into his light eyes, seeing him smile, seeing him approve her without thinking.

She had half an hour before she needed to get going. 'What's that, then?' she said again, and pointed. He followed her gaze

6

and, removing his hand from her back, reached for the card on the mantelpiece. He held it out.

Dr Paul Bartlett, it read, handwritten, real ink on vellum. No address, therefore hand-delivered. Something crept in between them.

'Well, open it, if you're so curious,' he said, stepping back. She was aware of his eyes on her back as she took the envelope: it felt substantial. Inside there was an embossed card, gold-edged.

Dr and Mrs . . . Request the pleasure . . .

'I'm to be a best man,' he said. 'Can you believe that?'

'Morgan Carter,' she said. 'Have I met her? I have.' She stared at the script. *At St Peter's on the Wall, Saltleigh*. The line before her eyes wavered, the line of a silver-grey horizon, the church on the spit in a freezing midsummer dawn: something jumped in her chest. Her lungs burned as if she'd been running.

'June,' she said, the first thing that came into her head. 'Nice month to get married.' The words sounded strange, mumbled. She handed it back to him.

'Got to get to work,' she said, ducking his gaze. He set the card on the mantel and took her by the wrists. Gently.

'Come with me,' he said.

Chapter Two

The story was, her parents were dead, she was an only child, she'd grown up in Cornwall.

Paul's parents were safely dead too, she'd checked on that one, slyly, slipping the question in in passing. He'd hardly looked up from his book: heart attack and cancer five years apart. But twenty minutes later he'd put the book down and said, taking her hand, maybe it's my age. But look at what you go through with old parents and . . . being an orphan seems easier. The thought seemed to sadden him, but then he picked the book up again and went on while she watched him, surprised by a lingering sense of having been comforted.

It was odd how few people even asked, and if they did, they weren't really that interested in the answer. She'd read somewhere that the key to a successful lie is that it should contain elements of truth. She chose Alison when the police and the psychotherapist appointed by social services talked to her about changing her name, because there'd been five Alisons in her year – anyone could be an Alison. Esme stood out, it said she wanted to be noticed. She didn't want to be Esme. She wanted to be invisible.

Esme had had a clock in her bedroom, with a loud tick. Joe used to complain about it keeping him awake on the floor below; about the alarm she set for seven every morning. She didn't know if it had gone off that morning because she never went back to the crooked house after the police took her away, but she had watched the clock those long hours from where she crouched behind the door. While she waited, she had listened to the tick, cringing, thinking, *Joe*.

BOOM: ten forty-two. And then nothing.

She told herself: everyone's gone to bed, even though the silence said otherwise. No pleading for a story or a kiss, no thump of music from Joe's room, just a creaking and settling of the house in the wind. The hot water going off, on its timer. The lights all still on, flooding up the narrow stairs.

Her family.

The clock says one a.m. when she comes out, on cramped stiff legs, unclenches her fists.

She sees Mads first, sees her from the top of the stairs and scrambles to get down, sliding on the stair carpet. The girl is tangled in the soaked sleeping bag, half through the sitting-room door. On her knees Esme scrabbles to pull her free, her hands slippery with blood, she can smell it, like iron, and she can feel the other weight all the time, Letty still down there inside the wadded nylon. Dead weight. Esme sobs in her throat, her arms grappling around her sisters. *Stay.* Mads's head lolls back again, her eyes don't see. *Don't leave me.* Esme stares and stares, she can't let go. She tries to pull them up into her lap on the stairs, the door into the sitting room swings open and there is Joe, looking at her from the sofa.

She says something, she doesn't even know what she's saying. Something like, *I can't, I can't*. A moan. Joe is dead. He has his headphones still on and his eyes are looking at her but he is dead. Underneath him the green velveteen sofa with fringing that came from her grandmother's house is black with blood. One of his shoes is off.

Her mother is on the floor in the kitchen face down, one bare leg twisted under her, her skirt riding up, her best skirt. A plate is smashed on the floor beside her. She is dead.

Her father is in the hall.

Chapter Three

She'd met Paul at a small gathering in the neon-lit open-plan offices of the independent publishing house whose accounts she worked on, a launch party for a book about the Second World War in Italy. It was a democratic sort of place, so all members of staff were allowed along, plus the offices were so small it was pretty near impossible to exclude anyone, if they'd wanted to come. The author was a bullying military historian called Roy Saunders: he stood in a corner of the room holding court, booming across the desks. Groups formed circumspectly, drifting away from him.

She'd been in London four years and had spent her share of evenings in wine bars, with trainee doctors, boys in IT, even an artist, or that's what he said he was. None of them had stuck. Alison just found herself discreetly backing off each time, mostly they got the message. One had gone on calling, asking her what was wrong with him though she thought she'd been kind, she'd said nice things about him . . . and in the end she'd changed her number.

She hadn't even planned on staying for the launch – the

whole point of working in accounts was that it was a back-room position, a below-the-radar position – but Rosa, a new assistant in editorial, had begged her, in solidarity. It didn't take long before Alison worked out the real reason – the girl had screwed up an author payment. Alison was showing her how to get out of trouble, Rosa almost in tears of gratitude. 'I'll write the email for you,' Alison was saying.

She hadn't seen him approach: he was at her shoulder when he spoke and she had to turn to see him. Tall, maybe fifteen years older than her, he asked her name, abrupt but not rude. He was a friend of the author's, he said, and held out his hand. *Paul Bartlett*. Behind her Rosa was gone. The next morning the girl said, slyly, taking the scribbled note Alison had prom-ised, you looked like you wanted to be alone.

They didn't even go for a meal; he took the glass of warm white wine out of her hand and set it down. 'It'll give you a headache,' he said, 'don't you think?' and gave her that almost-smile she now knew, shy, diffident, determined. He was right: she looked at the glass and the bottles of wine on the recep-tion desk and the others talking between the desks under the striplighting and she reached for her coat. His arm came around her, light and strong, and she felt the warmth from him.

His flat was five minutes away. Inside his front door, in the dark, he took her breath away by how ready he was, how insistent. As the door closed behind them her bag fell and he put his hands on either side of her thighs, raising her skirt, making a soft sound that frightened and excited her. He took hold of her forearm to keep her in position, brushing her hair aside from her face under his, didn't let go until she'd come. It seemed that nothing so deliberate had ever happened to her before, it was like a white light inside her head, flooding the chambers. For seconds, whole minutes, she was cleaned right out. The rubbish crept back, of course, a muddy tide, but for the interval she gazed on nothing. He watched her, intent in

12

the gloom, for a moment and only then did he release her arm. He put a hand to her cheek and rested it there.

Afterwards he made her a sandwich in his kitchen, ham and mustard and lettuce and butter, meticulous while she sat on his sofa with her bare feet under her and examined the titles on his bookshelves. *Paris Under the Occupation.* Sartre. Céline. Her heart pounding with panic, knowing that there must be a right thing to say or do to make this continue, not knowing what it was. She shivered suddenly, the knife clattering on the plate, and he sat down beside her. Warm. When she'd eaten the sandwich he asked her if she wanted to stay the night, and the next morning when he gave her a cup of tea he said he'd see her after work, if she wanted. The university building where he worked was in the next street from the publishing house's offices. It was like suddenly inhabiting a village; she only had to walk around the corner and knock on his door. He always said yes.

'Morgan Carter? She's a cow.'

Kay – five years older, severe dark haircut and boys' trousers with her hands shoved in the pockets – knew everything about everyone, and was as ready with her judgements as if she had them waiting in a card index. She worked selling the company's books abroad: she brought in money, so Alison had dealings with her regularly. She had an abrupt dirty laugh after a couple of drinks and Alison had the feeling she was one of the few Kay hadn't got a card on in her index; for some reason she relaxed her vigilance for Alison. Alison couldn't really afford to relax hers in return, but Kay didn't pry – or at least, she hadn't yet.

They had stopped in the alley, a snaggled row of eighteenth-century houses, outside a shopfront. Without looking Alison knew it was an underwear shop, expensive but pornographic, because they passed it every day on the way to buy lunch. It couldn't have been further, this crowded pocket of central London, from the small village in Cornwall where her aunt Polly still lived and where Alison had done some growing up, if not all of it – that was one of the partial truths she told.

Her aunt had driven across the foot of the country thirteen years ago, rocky west coast to muddy east, in her small battered car with cat hair on the back seat. She'd left Cornwall at seven that morning, not even pausing to pack a bag, and had arrived to find Alison – Esme – in bed at a foster placement, a policeman still in their kitchen. She had fought for Esme: she had wanted to take her out of bed there and then, fought for her angrily. Sometimes – rarely – in the succeeding years Alison found herself forced to think that they were alike, she and Aunt Polly, raging away, refusing to be cast out. That little gap adolescence had set up between Alison and her mother, magnified in Aunt Polly, who hadn't spoken to her sister in years.

Upstairs, befuddled with a sleeping tablet she'd been given by the duty doctor, Esme had heard her aunt's voice raised and knew it, from far off, although she couldn't make sense of what they were saying. She hadn't seen Polly – her mother's sister – in a long time: seven or eight years. Her father would mutter about her record with men, her cats and her spinster humourlessness. They'd fallen out over something, and it was too far to come, from Cornwall to Essex – except in emergencies. A day later, Polly had won the right to have Esme in her care, through the grim determination that would be the hallmark of their years together.

At home now in Alison's top drawer, behind the folded bras and rolled knickers, was a scarf of her mother's printed with scenes of Amalfi, orange trees and tumbling villages, real silk, gold and yellow. Polly had gone in to the house to get some of Alison's things, and when they unpacked in Cornwall there it was, on the top of the pile. *I didn't know what to get*, Polly had said, fierce. *Just something of hers. Her drawer had been all turned out — but the policewoman said it would be all right to take it.*

By then the police had gone through everything, she supposed. Alison never knew, never asked, what happened to the rest of it. The pots and pans, the few bits of cheap jewellery, the tatty furniture. The house. As with everything, if she'd asked Polly would have answered her, but nothing was volunteered. And Alison didn't want to know. She wanted to walk away from it, because every time she thought of anything – the china dish her mother would put her earrings in before bed, Joe's posters, the twins' ratty soft toys – she felt a commotion set up in her head, things asking to be seen, to be remembered. But she hung on to the scarf.

Four years, Alison lived with her aunt. When she finished school she left for university in a northern city to study maths – to Polly's bewilderment, Polly who like her mother was flustered by maths, which perhaps had been why Alison chose it although she also had a facility that must have passed down to her by some meandering quirk of genetics - and never came back. It wasn't that she didn't like Polly – she loved her, in her way – but it was just too tragic, the two of them tied together in the damp cottage. Alison had no intention of being tragic.

Alison had her back to the window display that featured mannequins bent over a table top; Kay had half an eye on it, eyes dancing.

Almost a week had passed since Alison had taken the invitation off the mantelpiece, and she and Paul had barely seen each other. That night she'd got straight on the bus across the river and let herself in to her bedsit, trying to ignore the musty smell. A bulb had gone. The next day she phoned him from work and told him she was going away for the weekend but instead she bought cleaning products, things for dealing with limescale and stainless steel and tablets for putting down the loo. She unearthed dusty tights from under the bed and bleached the basin and threw away some broken crockery. She spent Sunday looking out of her window at the tree, tall with small luminous pale green leaves; in the autumn they would turn bright yellow. The sun came out and she cleaned the windows with vinegar – Polly must have taught her that trick. She didn't think it had been her mother. She read novels until midnight, and the next day she was back at work.

Have fun, was all Paul had said when she'd told him she'd be away for the weekend. She could hear the tension in the high pitch of her voice as she told the lie, but maybe he thought she was just sulking.

'A cow,' Alison repeated now. 'Yes.' Because she *had* met Morgan Carter, even though when she'd said as much to Paul she'd been on mumbling auto-pilot. In a pub, before the theatre one evening, by chance they'd sat down next to her at a crowded table and she'd immediately been all over Paul, a cloud of perfume and blond hair. With a man – possibly her husband-to-be although, it occurred to her only now, Paul had hardly seemed to know him – sitting next to her, a quiet type who'd let her get on with it. They must have even been introduced, for Alison to have the name in her head, though she couldn't remember Morgan Carter addressing a word to her.

'She's one of Saunders' exes, I believe,' Kay said. Roy Saunders, the hectoring military historian, not at all the quiet type. Then, curiously, 'Why d'you want to know?'

'She's getting married,' said Alison, and half turned. The window display came into view. The mannequins were made of some hard white shiny material: strapped and bound in silk and lace, bent across the table top they stared out into the street. 'Paul's going to be best man.' Perhaps she'd appointed him. Morgan.

'Very respectable,' said Kay. 'So will that be your first outing as official girlfriend?'

'I'm not invited,' said Alison.

Kay raised her eyebrows. They looked in the window together, the mannequins staring moodily back, and in defiance Alison stepped up to the door and pushed it open. It was a week and she hadn't spoken to him; he hadn't phoned, and nor had she.

'Like that, is it?' said Kay. 'Yeah. Morgan Carter. She's not nice.'

'It's complicated,' said Alison.

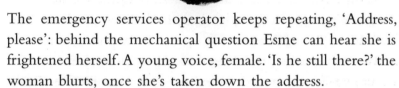

The emergency services operator keeps repeating, 'Address, please': behind the mechanical question Esme can hear she is frightened herself. A young voice, female. 'Is he still there?' the woman blurts, once she's taken down the address.

'Creek House, there's no number,' Esme says, 'it's just down the end of the track, everyone knows.' Only it's two in the morning or something, there'll be no one to ask directions of.

The dark beyond the door seems crowded, whispering, as if there is an invisible mob pushing to get in to where she crouches, the phone pressed against her chest, under the coats hanging in the hall.

She is looking at her father's leg raised up towards his chest where he lies, face down, just inside the front door. There is a gun, a shotgun with a rusted stock and a long barrel, a thing Esme has never seen before, not this one, not any gun. Both hands reaching down to the trigger, one big blunt forefinger slipping off. Blood. She has positioned herself so she can't see his face, on its side in the blood that soaked half the oval hall carpet. He is unshaven, stubble coming through half white against his reddened skin. A raw mark on the back of his neck.

17

When they arrived at the crooked house his skin was smooth and tanned, he was slight and strong.

'Is he still there?'

'They're all dead,' says Esme.

'Someone is coming,' says the operator, urgently. 'They're on their way. Someone will be with you soon.'

'They're all dead.'

They call for her when they come but she doesn't answer.

Stepping around him, not looking down, she hears something. The faintest wheeze, a bubbling in the membranes of the throat, and she flies through the front door, which bangs back as she passes through and catches her on the temple – but it doesn't slow her down.

'This one's not dead,' Esme hears them shouting inside the house, from where she is crouched on the edge of the mud behind it. She can't move.

Her father is alive, but he won't ever speak again.

The bruise the door left on her temple is still there a week later. As it fades she can't recognise herself in the mirror: she stares, but in her aunt's bathroom a stranger looks back at her from behind her eyes. Alison.

Chapter Four

In the underwear shop Kay was handling the merchandise, holding something up that dangled straps and buckles, more apparatus than lingerie.

'Complicated,' said Kay. 'Isn't it always? But he said he wanted you to come?' She stroked a slip, dark-red satin and lace, wistful. Alison couldn't imagine her in it, Kay who only ever wore clothes like school uniform to work. But what did Kay dream of? Who knew what anyone dreamed of, and just as well.

Alison couldn't begin to explain how complicated, not to Paul, not to Kay. She'd never told anyone, and she never would: she didn't have to. It had been a decision made long ago, easily, it was the simplest way. Her aunt had agreed: the therapist Alison had seen for three years in a Portakabin at the local hospital had been less easy with the decision, had asked her — they weren't allowed to tell you, only to ask — if she thought there might come a time when she had to talk about it, a time when she had someone she could trust? For the sake of a quiet life Alison had pretended to agree, but she knew that time wouldn't come, that there existed no such person. The therapist herself was a worn-down woman with an alcoholic's face, puffed and red – even at sixteen Alison could see what listening to people's horror stories had done to her.

Alison had read the address on the stiff gold-edged card, and it had ballooned inside her, a horizon, houses popping up along a road, a whole landscape. *St Peter's on the Wall, and afterwards at The Laurels, Dyke End, Saltleigh.* With Paul looking at her, puzzled, she'd had to close her eyes so he wouldn't see. In the dark behind her eyelids she had felt sweat bead on her upper lip, terror mixed with queasy longing. She had felt for a moment as if she might actually be sick.

'He tried to persuade you?' Kay's eyes were watchful behind the slip's lace, that she was holding up like a veil for the lower part of her face like a desert bride.

He had tried very hard: he might even have thought he'd succeeded. She'd kept her eyes closed and could feel him stroking her hair gently, as if she was an animal that needed calming, where they stood beside the mantelpiece.

'She'll have written the guest list a year ago,' he said easily at her ear. His lips were on her cheek, just brushing it. 'She'll have got some underling to write the cards.' Then he stepped back and Alison opened her eyes, smiled carefully.

'But still,' she said. 'You know. It's embarrassing, it's . . . I don't want you to ask her if you can bring me. They have seating plans, all that, I'm sure they need to keep numbers down. Why not just leave it?' She shifted, disguising a tremble. 'It's just a wedding. One day in our lives.' He wasn't smiling, though. Was he testing her, was she the kind of shrill woman who'd set up a complaint about not being invited? She could get through that test.

'I won't even need to ask her,' he said. 'She'll be mortified. She knows we're together.' He had set the card back on the mantelpiece, and Alison, still naked from bed, had wrapped her arms around herself. Mortified? From what she remembered of the woman they'd met in the pub, it seemed unlikely.

'I mean it, Paul,' she said. 'Don't.' He didn't answer; she had gathered her things and gone to work. A week ago.

Now Kay was looking at her.

'Cow,' she pronounced. 'Like I said. She obviously did it on purpose, to cause trouble. She's met you, right?' Alison frowned, nodding. Kay shrugged. 'You're competition.'

Alison frowned more fiercely, pushing her glasses up her nose. 'Don't be stupid,' she said sharply. 'Have you seen her? I'm not competition.' Kay just laughed.

'She's done it, too,' she said. 'Hasn't she, though?'

'Done what?'

'Caused trouble between you.' She dropped the dark satin into Alison's hands and for a moment its cool, slippery weight stirred up a thought of Paul, a desire to see him. 'Are you going to let her do that?'

The saleswoman stepped up smartly as if on cue, a haughty foreign girl with high-arched eyebrows and breasts cantilevered under her uniform, barely containing her impatience. 'You try this, madam?' she said.

She left it another day, though – and she didn't phone him even then. Instead, after work, she wandered through the scuffed institutional corridors of his department, past students not much younger than herself, when she knew his teaching would have finished for the day. Of course, Paul might not be there, it was that kind of job, not a nine to five. But he was there, glasses on, frowning down at a sheaf of papers. He pushed the chair back and smiled, delighted. Not triumphant – if he'd given her any indication that he'd been playing a game with her, she'd have been out of there without pausing for breath. But he just looked relieved and happy, sitting there in his shirtsleeves, and then he was grabbing his jacket with one hand, her arm with the other.

21

It was warm out, and the streets were swarming with workers just released and in high spirits. The trees were in full leaf as they walked through one square and then another. Paul talked about nothing, about his weekend — he'd walked by the river, seen an old friend — about his students. Not pausing until they reached a corner she hadn't known existed, up an alley that led nowhere, a tiny French-looking bar no more than a hole in the wall with some wicker brasserie chairs and two zinc tables.

He knew a lot of places. Paul had been born in London. He'd told her once, a rare moment, in some restaurant after more wine than they usually drank, that when he finished school and came back to the city to attend university and saw the crowds and the secret streets he could disappear into, it was like life starting. She had just nodded, not telling him, *That's just how I felt.*

He sat her at one of the tables and went inside.

Alone on the pavement Alison tried to go over what she'd planned to say if the wedding came up, but it evaporated. Perhaps he wouldn't mention it at all, she decided. She was wrong. He emerged holding two glasses and Alison realised she'd been holding her breath.

'Morgan says she couldn't bear it if you didn't come,' he said, setting the glass down in front of her. It was champagne. She sat very still; it was as if her thought processes had slowed, she needed to get out of this. There was a clamour in her head, *No, no, no, no.* She put the glass to her lips, drank. All right, she told herself, as it hit. Alcohol on an empty stomach: the best kind, Kay would say. Calm down. Pretend it's no big deal.

'I told you she'd be mortified,' Paul said, looking at her earnestly. He sat back in the wicker chair. 'She gave the list to some company months ago, like I said. It's not like we see each other much, she had no idea.' The barest trace of a side-long glance to look for her reaction.

She smiled, straining not to show what she felt. 'That's nice of her,' she said, sipping.

Thinking, Isn't there a form of words? *Plus one.* Then reminding herself, she didn't want to have been invited. She didn't care what message Morgan Carter wanted to send. The wedding was in a month, at the end of June; there wasn't a detail she had forgotten from that gold-edged invitation. There would be time to think of something.

And with that thought, with the memory of the silhouette of the church on the marsh, something else entered the equation too, swimming in on the champagne. A kind of exhilaration, a kind of bravado: I could do it. I could go back. I could show them. And a kind of longing, because Esme was there, buried somewhere, or wandering on the marsh; Esme who'd swum in the grey salt estuary warmed over the mud, who'd played hide and seek with her sisters between beached dinghies. Alison felt hard, turned to stone, when she remembered that girl.

'So, you'll come?' said Paul, his hand out on the table, fingers at the stem of his untouched glass. He's trying, she thought with a kind of wonder, he's trying to hold on to me, he wants to play it right. And if I say no? It occurred to her that he had probably already made his decision. He was like her – or like she'd been before she met him: a solitary. He'd walk away. It was how Paul was made. It was, she realised, why she kept coming back, knocking on his door. She felt sick, all over again.

'Of course I'll come,' she found herself saying. 'Yes.' He raised his glass to her empty one then, and the champagne-euphoria drained out of her system as quickly as it had arrived. Too late.

'Did you know your father had a gun?'

She'd shaken her head, no. No, no, no. Her father was a

joiner and cabinet-maker, he had a workshop in part of an old sail-loft in the village, it was neat and cosy. A whole wall of tools, some bright, some dull: rawls and gouges, chisels and adzes, he told her the names. She remembered the feel of their worn handles, hung in size order, another wall of little drawers, stacked rough lengths of wood, maple and ash and oak, just ordinary-looking until he turned them into something else. A cabinet with bottles of tints and varnishes. Her father humming, dreaming. No gun.

Joe didn't want to follow in his father's footsteps, he wanted to be in a band, always off at some gig, hitching home at two in the morning. It was Esme who'd sit in the workshop with her dad when she came home from school – or at least she did at the beginning.

The policewoman talked to her in the front room of the foster family's house. She could still remember the swirled carpet, the layered net at the windows and the smell of their kitchen. Not a bad smell, just different, someone else's cooking: they had a microwave and shiny red units. They'd bought fish and chips, the first night, the anxious foster parents and Aunt Polly at the table between the red cupboards, watching Esme eat. She hadn't got even halfway through it although it had always been her favourite. The batter like glue in her throat. Polly kept her coat on and her bag on her knee as if they were about to leave, although the police didn't let them go for a week.

'In the pub he was asking for a gun, for rats, apparently.' The policewoman's voice was soft, concerned. 'Do you remember there being rats?'

Uncertainly Esme nodded. 'Mum and Dad had a row about the rats,' she said. 'She wanted to call someone. An inspector.' She'd never seen them, though she'd heard her father tell her mother that one had been in the bin when he'd taken the lid off. 'He didn't want an inspector.'

'That was all the row was about?' The policewoman's voice made her feel sick, suddenly. She held still.

At the beginning, when Esme would come into the workshop, down the path from the bus stop, past the little marina, with the salt wind off the marshes in her face after a day in stifling classrooms, there would be something taking shape in the little wood-lined room. The sail-lofts were tall, on stilts for the spring tide to come up under them, steps up to windowless rooms, one above the other, her father's the first. She remembered a table with different kinds of wood in the top, and her mother coming down to see it when it was finished, running her hand over it, standing close to him.

The woman was watching her.

'They loved each other,' Esme blurted. 'They didn't have rows.' Her eyes starting out of her head, trying not to remember.

Everyone's parents had rows.

'You'd been out,' the policewoman said softly. 'That evening. That's right, isn't it?' The policewoman had come to the house with a man, a male police officer. He was making tea in the foster family's kitchen and when she asked the question he was coming back in with two mugs, brimming. Joe always made tea too full, you burned your hand taking it off him. Lazy, Mum always said. A good way of not getting asked to make the tea.

'Yes,' Esme said, submissive as if she was in a teacher's office. 'I was supposed to be sleeping over at Gina's.' She'd told them this three, four times.

The policewoman took the tea, winced. 'Why did you come home?' Her voice was light and quiet. Polly on the sofa stirred, shifted forward to listen.

'We fell out,' Esme said, looking into the policewoman's face. Why did she keep asking? Esme hadn't spoken to Gina since it happened; days passed, four, then five, and no one was in touch. 'I hadn't brought my hair straighteners.' It sounded

25

stupid. 'We were going to do makeovers.' The policewoman smiled and Esme suddenly wanted to shove her, to jump up and run out, to keep running. She fixed her eyes on the tea.

'Did you see your father when you got home?' said the woman, very quiet now.

Esme was still, hunched. 'He wasn't there,' she said. The policewoman waited. 'I think he was at the pub.'

Because he always was. Usually he was there till closing time: ten was early for him to come home. She wasn't going to tell the woman that, though. There were other people the police could ask.

Throughout that week the police kept Esme with the foster family, always gentle but always insistent. Always the same questions. Once Polly went in to the police station, leaving her in the car outside, and she heard a door slam. She heard Polly shouting, 'She's only a child. Can't you see what you're doing to her? You think she did it?'

Did they? She was the only one left.

'So,' the policewoman said. 'It's possible your father didn't know you were in the house.'

If he'd known. If he'd known. What did they think? That he could hold a gun in her mother's face, murder Joe on the sofa, dreaming with some band still playing in his ears, he could pull the trigger on the live small bodies of her sisters, but not her?

If he'd known, you'd be dead too, said the policewoman's eyes.

Chapter Five

Alison dreamed of the marsh for the first time in ten years. She dreamed she was waking on a boat, climbing up through a hatch and there was the wide expanse of mud silvered in the dawn, the birds stalking the creek on long legs and the power station's cooling wall breaking the surface out in the estuary, as low and dark as a submarine. The little Saxon church stood on the horizon, no bigger than a hut, no more than a sharp black silhouette.

Then a man pulled her down, thick furred arms wrapped round her legs and pulled, into the hold of the boat. Diesel and rope and wood.

She woke, in her own bed, alone, and for a moment it was as though she couldn't remember how to breathe.

She had cut down the nights she saw Paul – he didn't seem to have noticed, although perhaps he was gentler when she did see him, more attentive. They went to see an Italian film at an old cinema in Mayfair, leaning against each other in the red velvet seats, below them the cinema almost empty, and he stroked her as he had before, for a long time, until she wondered if he even knew he was doing it. He didn't mention the wedding again, and although it was her plan to devise an escape from it, nor did she. The next time she came to his flat, loosened up after a drink with Kay, he was quietly ruthless, moving very quickly, holding her down. Which she liked.

Afterwards, when she pulled herself upright, feeling as though she was coming up for air, her eyes wide, a smile broke across his face and he kissed her.

Something had changed, it seemed to her. She didn't want to look too closely at it. It didn't feel like a change for the worse; it wasn't exactly trouble Morgan's wedding had caused, more like intensity: the stakes had suddenly jumped higher. She had discovered that Paul wanted to hang on to her, and he – he knew she was hiding something. Kay had said, once, men like secrets. They don't want to know everything about you, you have to hold stuff back.

At work, Rosa, the long-limbed, glossy-haired girl from editorial who'd been witness to their first meeting, had been asking questions. People did, now and again: it always brought Alison to the alert but she had strategies. Alison wondered about the way the girl looked at her, a couple of years younger and not long out of one of the grand universities. Rosa knew Paul – or knew of Paul – through her supervisor: it seemed to be how she'd got the job, being a friend of a friend of an author. There was something about Rosa's interest in her and Paul that made her uneasy. A girl prone to hero worship, was what Alison thought, from the big swimming avid eyes. That'd teach Alison, for helping her out.

So Rosa had tagged along with Alison and Kay for a drink one night, Kay giving her one of her looks when she asked, a sidelong look down her nose that went unnoticed, apparently. Rosa was pretty, with long dark hair and smooth golden skin: her mother was Brazilian, her father was wealthy. She started by talking, too much, about her flat in Pimlico, visits home

28

to the country at weekends, her mother's mail-order company, her brother's job in California and then she said, 'Do you get home at all?'

'Oh, it's too far,' Alison said, helping herself to a handful of crisps. Kay's quick glance didn't pass her by. To drain her glass would have been too dangerous, she'd learned that much. She crunched on the salty crisps, swallowed before her throat closed up in panic. Smiled.

'Cornwall.' She grimaced. 'And too tragic.'

'Tragic?' Rosa leaned towards her, eyes wide. Her hair swung forward.

'Schoolfriends. On the till in Budgen's or pregnant with the dodgy boyfriend. Tragic. You know.' And then Alison *did* drain her glass, and stand up. 'My round.' They were in a bar she suspected Kay of having selected for its startling ugliness, to put Rosa off. It was in the basement of the local YMCA, scratched tables and decor untouched for thirty years but mercifully dark.

'Perhaps it's not tragic like that where you came from, Rosa.'

She saw Kay smile at that: born in Croydon Kay was, like her if for different reasons, a girl from nowhere. Rosa stuck it for two more drinks, by which time Kay and Alison were jammed close in the dark, shoulder to shoulder, and talking about music. Rosa looked hurt as she stood to leave.

Thank God for Kay, she thought. But even woozy with the wine and waving Rosa off across the room, Alison didn't confide in her friend. Maybe there'd come a time when she didn't have to be obnoxious to naive, curious girls like Rosa. Maybe not.

As the wedding drew closer, Alison told herself she could always fake illness as a plan. She could even poison herself with something: old pâté or laxatives. She wanted to see Paul but five nights out of six she still made herself take the bus down through the West End, Trafalgar Square, Whitehall, over the river.

29

Her bedsit looked better for it. She had put everything away, in drawers and cupboards, under the bed, so that the room seemed one big window, filled with the luminous green-yellow tree. But as she tidied, and straightened the bed, she wished for Paul: she found herself doing everything as though he was watching her. It was dangerous.

Since the wedding invitation, too, crossing the water did something to her insides. From the top of the bus she always looked downriver, to the clustered skyscrapers that stood between her and the estuary.

He called her at work, the week before the wedding. Which was unusual: mostly they sent each other very brief, functional text messages if arrangements needed to be made, which was down to Alison's habit of holding back and Paul's distrust of mobile phones – his age, he always said, though he was only forty-odd. They did their talking in person, face to face, long peaceful silences, then he'd look up and say, 'But did you like it?' about some book he'd given her, searching her face, wanting to know, patient. Long, lazy conversations about books and movies and work, eating dinner at his big wooden table or leaning against each other on his old sofa, but silence in between. It was more exciting that way, she told herself, and messages and phone calls were for teenagers and never satisfactory anyway, but sometimes she wished for a sign, some kind of softer communication.

'I've booked somewhere,' he said. She could hear alertness in his voice.

'Where?' she blurted, knowing he meant Saltleigh, knowing he meant the wedding, but her mind abruptly, crazily, seesawing at the thought. Hotels, in Saltleigh? She could only remember the pub. It wasn't the kind of place for bed and breakfast, even, not a tourist spot, what with the mud and the power station. Before anything was said she felt herself rise to its defence, the tufted grass of the dykes and the wide grey horizon, the

30

place where you could see the sun come up over the sea. Aware of a head raised across the cramped open-plan offices, Alison turned on her chair with the phone to her ear. Her heart bumped in her chest: he would find her out. How could he not? She waited for him to answer.

'The wedding,' he said. 'You haven't forgotten?'

'No,' she said, trying to sound bright. Normal. 'Do we . . . um is there a wedding present list?'

'The wedding's on Saturday but I thought we'd go a few days ahead of time. Tuesday,' said Paul, his voice warm now, reassured. 'Make a, you know, a little holiday of it. There's a place, it's on the edge of the village, apparently, it's even got a website. The Queen's Head, an old Edwardian roadhouse, must have been done up quite recently. It looks all right, actu-ally. Look it up.'

'I'd have to talk to work — it's short notice.'

'Sure,' he said equably. 'But it'll be fine, won't it? Gerry's always telling you you need a holiday.' Gerry owned the company: he was also an acquaintance of Paul's, and of course Paul was right, that was no escape route. 'We can get you something to wear, if you like. Get a present. Do that together. If you'd like.'

'Oh, I don't need . . . I've got things to wear,' she said, thinking of what Kay would say. Her eyes would open wide, *He's hooked, all right. Wants to take you shopping?* She closed her eyes. She had talked herself out of faking illness, telling herself it would be a night. Twenty-four hours. But five nights? Her heart in its cage of ribs felt squeezed with fear, a hand in there groping for it.

'I'll look after you,' he said. 'If you're still worried about Morgan.'

'Morgan?' Now she did sound shrill: with an effort she softened. 'I'm not worried,' she said.

'I want some time with you,' he said. 'I want to get away

31

with you. All right?' And he had a point: they'd never been away together, not even a weekend. She wondered if that made her look odd to him: magazines were full of articles about romantic mini-breaks, so maybe she could assume that was what most women wanted. Women who had nothing to hide, though.

He'd never suggested anything like it before, but now he sounded hurt, on the edge of angry.

'All right,' she said hurriedly, rattled into it. 'Yes. It'll be . . . perfect.'

After he'd hung up she went online and looked up the Queen's Head, Saltleigh. The picture came up, a tall-gabled, red-brick roadhouse flanked with Leyland cypress trees, a wooden veranda. She knew it straight away, on the edge of the village; she remembered it as semi-derelict, inhabited by an ancient couple, the rooms piled with hoarded rubbish. They must have died.

She stared at the page, hypnotised.

Below it a gallery of photographs: a boat sailing in the estuary, the photo carefully angled so as to exclude the power station; a close-up of the little flint church; the row of sail-lofts. The roadhouse's paintwork was fresh, the brick repointed. How could it be worth it, Alison wondered. Who would want to come to Saltleigh for their holidays? Especially . . . and then it dawned on her. It was on the map, wasn't it? They'd put it on the map.

Family slaughtered.

How long did it take for people to forget?

In Cornwall, as the months passed, Alison registered dully that the things she'd seen, coming down the stairs of her family's crooked house, had not altered the wider world, had barely even surprised it; violence was something a man resorted to, when he was at the end of his tether. Within months there was a similar case: a man with money troubles and an unhappy marriage took his children off in a car and gassed them, and himself, while ranting to his wife on a mobile phone.

The world forgot quicker if there'd been no survivors. Although there were always relatives to milk for information, schoolfriends, work colleagues, survivors were what kept things going longer, in the newspapers. But the courts did a good job of keeping the press at a distance from Polly in Cornwall, or perhaps journalists were even decent people, because there was never a sign that Aunt Polly's neighbours, or the children at Alison's school, knew who she was. She didn't ever think she was free, though. There were people who knew, even if they didn't choose to act on it, they were out there, they kept tabs. A year on – a year to the day, newspapers working doggedly, Alison quickly understood, according to timetables, anniversaries, links – a newspaper published a picture. A photographer, disguised as an orderly, had managed to get into the rehabilitation ward where her father was being held and get off a couple of shots before he had to run.

Perhaps whoever sent the photographer had expected something more dramatic – 'rehabilitation ward' suggesting that some progress back towards human function, or release, was a possibility – but the photo only showed a humped figure in a hospital chair, hooked to tubes. His hands were like claws in his blanketed lap and his head bent sideways, eyelids half open to show a dull unfocused gleam. His chin was sore with the saliva that ran from his lopsided mouth. The photographer had got in because John Grace, Esme's father, wasn't being held in a secure unit – he was no threat to anyone: he would never walk or talk again. He had, the neurologist responsible for his care told Polly – who told Alison – some residual brain function. It wasn't that there was only random electrical activity

33

in there, but there was – realistically – no possibility of a recovery or even improvement in his condition. No doubt if he had got there as a result of a car crash or a catastrophic aneurysm there would be family sitting at his bedside, trying to get through, playing him music or holding photographs up to his face. Talking to him, and holding his hand.

The gunshot had blown away half of his brain, damaging the part governing his motor functions, and the centres of speech. He responded to sound by increased agitation, and although they tried him with various computer devices, joysticks that could be operated by a single finger, or eye movement, he showed no ability to process or answer questions.

The inquest, Polly told Alison over her shoulder one night while at the kitchen stove, had decided that although the evidence that John Grace killed his wife, son and twin daughters, and attempted to kill himself, was overwhelming, as he was definitively unfit to plead the CPS decided no public interest would be served in proceeding with a prosecution. Alison's interest would not be served. She didn't tell Alison anything else: they lived for some time without watching the television news, and Polly didn't get a newspaper. You couldn't stay away from them altogether, though, how could you? How could you know that the front-page photograph of a man in a hospital bed – the paper carelessly left in the doctor's reception area or standing on the garage forecourt – would be your dad?

They didn't talk about it. About why. She could guess – she couldn't stop herself – at the usual reasons. If she'd asked for information, Polly might have turned off the gas ring and sat down at the table and told her anything she wanted to know, although she wouldn't have liked it. But Alison didn't want to know, and when the sad-eyed psychiatrist with the drinker's face probed her gently she only hardened her position. 'I don't have to know any of it,' she said. 'Aren't you supposed to be helping me? The less I know, the more normal I am.'

34

The woman's face sagged. 'What's normal?' she said, game but hopeless. 'We don't have to be normal.'

The week after she turned eighteen, though, Alison asked Polly for the details of the unit in which her father was being held – now a secure ward, for his own protection as much as anyone else's, in the grounds of a large psychiatric hospital – and went to see him.

It was a hot day, in early July. The nurse who looked up from the reception desk at Alison's arrival and walked with her down the wide corridor, its polished blue linoleum gleaming, to the room where her father sat, showed no sign of horror or pity, for Alison or her father. She was broad and cheerful, with clean strong hands. She addressed John Grace as though he could understand her, leaning over him to adjust a tube. As if he was a human being; something inside Alison came untwisted painfully as she watched the nurse's gentle familiarity. 'You'll see his eyes water,' the woman said, straightening. 'He's not crying, it's just damage. To the nerves supplying the tear ducts. He's not in pain.'

She left Alison alone with him. As the door closed behind her Alison wondered why they trusted her not to harm him, and something weird happened, a ringing in her ears, a dizziness. She stood very still, for fear she'd fall. In the chair he didn't move; eventually she took a breath, and a step. There was a bed with a hoist over it in the corner of the room and the nurse had pulled up another chair for her, close to his. She sat. *Dad*. She didn't say it, she didn't touch his hand or ask a question or say that word, the word that would identify her. It was all she could do to contain the terrible hardening in her chest; she felt it might swell and crack and burst, it might break her open. He was alone, and he'd be alone till he died. No one else came to sit in this chair, and she would never come back. Never.

She didn't know how long she stayed. She looked at the

machine he was attached to, that had a number of readings displayed on it, a heart rate and other things. At one point he sighed, and a bubble appeared at his lips. At last she got up.

'They thought I might have done it,' she said, all in a rush, but he showed no sign of hearing her. 'Did you think of that?' His hand fluttered in his lap, wasted but still recognisable, the scar on his broad thumb where an adze had slipped. 'I could have stopped you.' Something was in her throat, threatening to choke her.

She looked into his face, and behind the slack mouth, the dull eyes and the raw skin, the hair that had been cut as he never cut it, in there somewhere was her father. Water leaked from his left eye, the side he'd lain on, the eye that had rested sightless on the bloody hall carpet. Damage.

As she turned to go she saw a closed-circuit camera above the door, a red light blinking. So they hadn't trusted her.

Chapter Six

She had her hair cut very short over lunchtime, the week before they would leave for the wedding. She walked back, crossing the square in the clean June sunshine that filtered through the big London plane trees, and a man looked up from a bench when she passed: without hair to shield her she felt conspicuous. She had put her mother's scarf in her bag that morning, to give her the nerve for the haircut; she took it out now and leaning to look at her reflection in a car window she tied it quickly, knotting the heavy, slippery silk twill at the nape of her neck. A spy, a girl from an old movie. But as she came out of the lift at work she pulled it off hastily and felt the nakedness all over again.

Her boss Gerry peered at her over his glasses, bewildered, when she crossed the office. 'Respect,' said Kay, brought to her feet behind her computer terminal, but she looked distinctly taken aback.

At thirteen Esme's hair had been long and wavy, split-ended, tangled and streaked from the sun: it blew around her face when she cycled along the bumpy track into the village. Her mother didn't want her to cut it: a week after she arrived in Cornwall Alison had taken the kitchen scissors to it in her aunt's cluttered bathroom, chopped it to below her ears and added a pack of black dye bought at random from the chemist's into the bargain. At sixteen she got glasses – she'd started having trouble reading the school whiteboard – and the disguise was complete.

'Suits you, actually,' said Kay, when she'd recovered. But the question still hung between them: *Why?* When she looked at herself in the mirror Alison found herself quite unable to say whether anyone who'd known her as a thirteen-year-old would recognise her now. She felt a little itch of uncertainty. Was this what she wanted to look like? She had no choice.

She saw Paul that evening. There'd been no shopping trip in preparation for the wedding, much to Kay's disdain; with Paul Alison had stuck to her line that she had something to wear although in fact she had no idea. And Paul had got them a wedding present on his own, he didn't like wedding lists, he said, he'd chosen something himself.

Opening the door to her now he put his hand to the thick short hair, standing up from her forehead. 'Pretty,' he said, but his eyes had darkened, looking at her.

She came past him. 'It'll grow out,' she said carelessly, not meeting his eye.

Her sisters had both had long hair too, theirs much fairer than hers, fairer even than her mother's: the memory of that hair, their light, shifting eyes jolted her, after all this time. She'd trained herself not to see her sisters: they were there, always there, but they inhabited a soft dark place in her head, hidden as though behind a curtain. When this wedding was over it would stop, these images would stop, thought Alison, letting her bag drop on to the sofa. She sat beside it. Her head felt odd, shorn, cold.

'No, I like it,' he said, leaning down over the sofa behind

her, and for a moment he let his hand rest on the back of her neck. Then it was gone, he was gone. 'I got you something.'

She recognised the logo on the box. A line appeared beside his mouth as he gave her that half-smile, looking down at her on the sofa, searching her face. Watching. No one had ever examined her before, as he did – it was as if he was memorising her.

'For our holiday,' he went on, standing, as if he'd read her mind. 'Drink?' He was by a long veneer sideboard, where he kept booze, odd bottles of foreign aperitifs made of things like artichokes. 'Damn,' he said. 'No tonic.'

She pulled at the ribbon around the box, but she knew already. There were layers of tissue, she could imagine the salesgirl with her startled eyebrows and her tight-buttoned dress folding the fine light stuff inside. 'Oh,' she said, panicked and excited at once.

Inside the shop's changing room, a thick heavy curtain behind her that muffled whatever the salesgirl and Kay had said to each other, Alison had hardly dared look at herself when she'd tried it on, but she remembered the thrill of the garment's unfamiliarity, the weight and coolness of it. It was something for an older woman, it was dressing up, it promised things. Kay had tugged at the curtain, her eyes appeared at the gap, an *oh* had escaped her, sounding almost put out and she'd pulled back straight away, out of sight. When Alison had come out and shaken her head to the assistant Kay had frowned. 'Just as well,' she said. 'I'd have had to kill you for it, looking like that.'

He still had his back to her. 'Did Kay tell you . . .' She must have done – but Alison couldn't imagine any such conspiracy. She held it up. She didn't even know what it was supposed to be, for sleeping in? Or drifting about. She put a hand to her cropped head, thinking, stupidly, wrong time to cut your hair. But she couldn't stop looking at it.

39

'You like it.' Now Paul had turned, a bottle of gin in one hand.

She looked up at him over her shoulder. 'How did you know?' she said.

'I was in Soho,' he said. 'I was on my way to lunch with someone and I saw you go in there, with that woman you work with.'

'Kay.' Something in his voice made her wonder if he didn't like Kay. Had they ever even met?

'I went back later,' he said. 'She told me what you tried on. The girl.'

'Clever,' said Alison. She thought of him talking to the foreign girl in her tight-buttoned uniform, in the dark room hung with expensive things to be worn in bedrooms. But she wanted the slip: she pulled it into her lap, *mine*.

'Thank you,' she said. Paul set the gin bottle down, came over and stroked her cheek. 'You don't mind, then,' he said.

'Mind?'

'You're a pretty independent girl,' he said. 'Woman.' She flushed.

'I don't mind,' she said.

'I'm going out for some tonic.' He reached for his wallet, and the door swung behind him.

Alison had never been in his flat alone before: she was aware of that before the door even clicked shut. Did this mean something, that he trusted her, for example? It occurred to her as she stood from the sofa and let the slip fall that one of the reasons they'd got this far was that she had showed as much respect for his privacy as he had hers. Which meant that there was plenty she didn't know.

She didn't know if it was the knowledge that he'd watched her go into the underwear shop without disclosing himself, or that he'd been on his way to lunch with someone whose name he hadn't told her, but she was curious; suddenly, greedily,

40

childishly curious. How long would it take him? There was an off-licence and convenience store at the foot of the building, with a security-grille for a window. Often a queue.

Three paces and she was inside the bedroom. She skimmed the shelves with her hand, coming away with dust; she looked at the objects on his side of the bed. An old watch with a heavy link strap, two books, both by colleagues of his, a packet of paracetamol in the little drawer. She turned. Unhesitating as a burglar, she went to the walnut chest. A single silver-framed photograph stood on it; she'd glanced at it a dozen times but had never picked it up. Nosy: never be nosy, you might get him nosy back. It was a picture of Paul, alone on a clifftop, arms folded across himself, shirtsleeves rolled. He must have been thirteen or fourteen; he stared at the camera, composed. She pulled open the top two drawers, the place everyone hid secrets.

Striped cotton boxers in rolls and two unopened packs on one side, on the other black socks, grey socks, a belt, ties, everything neat. A small box sat inside the curled belt; she lifted it out, didn't even need to open it to know that it contained a ring. A large square stone that looked to her like a diamond, a setting from early last century. His mother's? Quickly she put it back: the socks shifted and she saw something else, disguised among them. Something wrapped in a heavy woollen cloth, khaki, not clean. She cleared the socks and looked down at it nestling there, bewildered as she saw an outline that seemed ridiculously familiar. A child's toy? She picked up the small bundle, and its weight was alarming, it was too heavy to be a toy. She set it down again with clumsy hands and stared at it. Then unrolled it. It was a gun. A real one.

An old gun. She grasped for an explanation. A memento? Old but she didn't know how old: it was chunky scarred black metal with a cross-hatched metal grip, a handgun. It had *Herstal*

41

Belgique stamped above the trigger, and there were some numbers. The khaki it was wrapped in looked old, certainly. Had his father served? Now she was embroidering, a dead mother who'd given him her engagement ring and a war hero for a father. Too young to have had a father in the war. She searched through their conversations, coming up only against how little she knew. One thing she was sure of, as she heard a sound from the stairwell, was it was none of her business. A gun. He'd find her with it in her hands and there was nothing she could do.

The doorbell rang and her heart jumped, hammering. He hadn't taken his keys: she was saved.

Carefully, Alison replaced the gun in the bag and pushed it under the socks, slid the drawers closed quietly, went into the bathroom as unhurriedly as if sleepwalking, flushed the lavatory, walked out again. She picked up the slip from the sofa as she passed, to explain the rush of blood to her face.

Not a crime, to own such a thing. Or was it? Was it odd? A historian might own such a thing, a teenage boy might. A farmer or the owner of an isolated house might, to shoot rats. More of a crime to be searching through someone's drawers.

Had it been loaded?

She opened the door.

Chapter Seven

It's Gina from her childhood that she dreams of, the night before they go, or at least she thinks so. Even awake, somewhere in the recesses of her mind Alison confuses Gina with Kay; they both share the sly sharpness, the knowingness, looking sideways at her, laughing. They both tug at her with their promises of friendship.

In the years between Alison has often wondered about Gina – she thinks about her more often than she does her mother, or the twins. Joe is the worst, she hardly dares ever approach Joe in her mind, she is terrified of remembering his smile, the frayed edges of his jeans at the heel, the way he would swing himself on to his bicycle. She didn't even dream of him: it was one thing she did ask the therapist in that stuffy little room with the plastic flowers on the table, and the box of tissues. 'Why not?' The woman said, sadly, 'Your brain's protecting itself, I expect. It . . . it may change.'

The therapist never promised anything, Alison noticed that, as if she might get sued, and she never gave advice either. Always little tentative suggestions – it was one of the reasons

Alison stopped believing in her. Take up swimming, drawing, walking. The situation seemed to her to require something more extreme, not sensible civilised suggestions. It wanted some violent and dangerous therapy: jumping off high buildings with a rope around you or that kind of deep-water diving where you go down to the limits of your lung capacity and pass out. Or total denial.

Gina had looked nothing like Kay. Strong-willed and bold, she'd been tall and well-developed, breasts and everything at fourteen, too big for the crowded mess of the small terraced house where she lived with her father. When she was eleven her mother had left them for another man and her dad worked on the cargo boats, running freight around the coast for days at a time, Ipswich to Gravesend, mostly sand, he once told Esme, coming in glassy-eyed with the booze and uncharacteristically forthcoming. Esme generally steered clear when he was home. He worked sober, then drank when he came back. Social services were kept in the dark and Gina fed herself with money he'd dish out to her every couple of weeks. 'He's all right,' was all she'd say of her father. 'Better than being in care.' Esme's mother made noises but she never told on Gina.

Gina did badly at school: she could hardly write, Alison happened to know. She simply wasn't interested: partly a matter of hating every authority figure, every teacher, on principle; partly a matter of recklessness. But she wasn't stupid.

In the dream Gina was running, out along the horizon towards the little church, fast and fearless. She was running away, and Alison was behind her. They reached the end of the spit where the marsh dissolved into shingle and mud but Gina didn't stop, Alison fought through the mud after her and into the grey tide where they twined around each other, down under the surface. Under the water Gina's eyes were open. She spoke, bubbles rising from her pale lips in the clouded water.

'He's still there,' she said. 'It's still there.' And her face wavered, shifted in the water: it was Kay, it was Gina. It was someone else, someone she couldn't name.

Alison woke up.

It was eight by her mobile, and Paul was coming for her at nine. He'd never been to her place before: she looked around, trying to see it through his eyes. A little bolthole for a scared rabbit. Where once it had been an untidy burrow heaped with crumpled clothes and piled books, now it looked neurotically neat. She sighed and got out of bed. So far her suitcase only contained the slip, still folded in its dark tissue. On impulse she dropped her trainers in on top, and a sports bra, but the dark red still glowed.

Kay had been impressed. 'He actually took the trouble to find out what you wanted?' she'd said, eyebrows up under her chopped fringe. 'He didn't just buy you a bit of scratchy red tat?' And shrugged. 'I suppose that's cool.'

She'd told Kay about the gun, too; her eyes had widened. 'Jesus.' Then she'd gone quiet for a bit and finally had shrugged, unwillingly. 'Second World War's his thing? Men, though. Collecting gas masks and that stuff. A bit weird, if you ask me.' They'd laughed.

Dodging the issue of the wedding outfit she put in jeans, a shirt, a jersey, thinking, there'll be wind off the sea, feeling memory press against her. A swimsuit. She held it up, frowning, and something happened, the feel of the water from her dream and from further back flooded her senses. The memory of swimming out in the estuary off someone's battered little dinghy, out by the power station's cooling wall and the water marvel-lously, unnaturally warm.

And suddenly a face — broad, serious, a direct gaze from under a straight fringe — looked back at her from down the years. The woman who'd asked her those same questions over and over every day for a week after the murders. The

45

policewoman whose eyes had not left Esme's, unwavering in their inquiry even as the too-full mug of tea burned her hand. And with the realisation it was as if Alison had answered a ringing phone and the policewoman was there on the other end and about to speak. Alison held her breath. The murders. She had never called them that, not even in her head, because that would have made her father a murderer. She reached up into the cupboard where her dresses hung and took a handful down. One of them would do.

The police hadn't told her much of anything, during that terrible endless week, only asked her questions and dutifully she had answered. It only occurred to her much later that she could have screamed and shouted and demanded to know: also that they might not have told her anything because she could be a suspect. She had had blood everywhere when they came for her, her hands, legs, feet, even a smear on her neck, and there were bloody footprints on the hall carpet she didn't remember leaving. That was one of the things they'd asked her, over and over, which rooms she'd been in afterwards, with blood on her feet.

Alison knelt with the dresses in her hands, laying them in the suitcase, as the questions they'd asked her all those years ago rattled in her head like grit in a wheel.

Shoes. Head down, she put in a pair of sandals she liked, with fine gold straps. She'd worn them at a work do one time and a man had knelt down to look at them.

Of course the policewoman still existed, she might even be still there, behind a desk at the police station. And with a pulse of certainty Alison knew that if no one else recognised her, the policewoman would. Her doorbell rang shrilly and she crossed the landing to the front window to look down.

Below her Paul stood looking into the square, his back to the door. He had his hands in his pockets, shifting on his feet, impatient, and for a split second Alison thought about not answering. Then he turned, and looked up.

She'd delayed as long as she could in London, showing him around and registering the look of silent dismay he gave the battered hallway and the shared bathroom (a stale flannel over the sink, a ring round the bath). She moved him along, to her room. 'It's all right, I suppose,' he said dubiously, glancing inside, the yellow light reflected off the big tree. 'Well, short term, anyway.'

She stopped. 'What, until I hit the big time, you mean?' she said. An arm around her shoulders he laughed, squeezing her against him and smiling down.

'You know what I mean,' he said. 'I'm going to look after you.' And she said nothing, blinking, a secret stupid excitement inside her.

But then he was turning, briskly. 'Come on, then.'

Getting out of London had seemed to take hours, but Alison had been grateful for every crawling minute. Stuck in traffic round arterial roads, between parades of houses and trees sooty with a century of exhaust fumes, past Turkish bakeries and fried chicken shops and used-car forecourts. Creeping through the suburbs, Alison covertly observed Paul's driving, and his car; she hadn't seen either before. The car was small and sensible and so clean it might have been hoovered. Paul was a confident, slightly impatient driver, too long in the leg for the car and shifting in his seat every time they got stuck in the sluggish traffic.

His phone had rung once and although they were stationary at that point his hand had gone straight to divert it. At last the lanes had multiplied, the shops and pavements disappeared behind siege-strength walls and the sprawling outskirts abruptly receded in the rear-view mirror. Paul straightened in his seat with visible relief; Alison realised she was pushing back in hers, as if bracing herself.

By the time the estuary came into view it was evening, but not dark yet. They topped a slope and there it was, spread out, grey and silver, the low rays of a midsummer sun glinting off the mirrored cube of the power station, far out towards the horizon. Even from miles inland Alison could see that the tide was out, the meandering channels gleamed all the way to where brown water met the bruised-blue sky. If she closed her eyes she would smell the trickle of sea over mud, she would see the bristly lavender-grey plant that grew among the creeks. As they turned down the shallow incline around them the fields and orchards and hedges were luminous green in the low, flat midsummer light and she felt it, the thing she'd been resisting – not fear but the sweet yearning tug of home.

'Look,' said Paul, 'that's quite something, isn't it?' His head turned quickly to see her reaction but she only stared straight ahead, as though she was the one driving. It was like a great slow green wave pulling her down, washing and turning, her childhood a tide coming up to reclaim her.

He turned back. 'Morgan grew up here,' he said, raising an eyebrow. 'Can you imagine that?'

Five miles or so from their destination they had stopped for a late lunch. Without saying anything Paul had indicated and pulled in at a thatched pub beside a pond. The Plough: she must have passed it a hundred times as a child in the back of her parents' car. Someone they knew had even worked here, though she couldn't remember who. As she sat in the garden it crowded in on her, the bulrushes in the pond, the leaning apple tree, the swinging pub sign, all horribly familiar, bringing with it the smell of the seats in the car, the line of her mother's jaw as she leaned into the back to tell them off, her father's hands on the wheel.

When the waitress came out for their order and she was too young to have been more than a baby the last time Alison was here, she realised she'd been holding her breath, half dreading, half wanting a face she knew. Aware of his eyes on her she ate up every last crumb of her meal though it took an effort to remember what she'd actually eaten. Chicken pie, glutinous and pale, green beans. Watery coffee, some kind of cake with icing. Every time the gawping, near-wordless waitress came out with the laminated menu Paul would start to shake his head but Alison would take it from her and order something else she didn't want, just to postpone the moment. In the end Paul had jumped up and gone inside for the bill, leaving her at the table.

In the car now as they crested the last long shallow incline to the estuary, Alison turned to look at him.

'Don't you like it?' she said, before she could stop herself. 'Not good enough for Morgan?'

'It's beautiful,' he said, and she could see that he meant it, the great silvered expanse of estuary reflected in his face as he drove. 'That's what I meant. Don't you think so?'

And now they were coming fast down between high hedges, the sinking sun behind them. At intervals Alison registered a cottage – a long wall, a big shabby barn alone in a field, a row of poplars – and knew them instantly, one after the other, without even turning her head to look. Every feature of the landscape crowded in as the little car descended towards the first village houses, jostling for her attention. The apprehension she'd been holding at bay since they left London bloomed until it was all around her, there was nothing she could look at that would not hurtle her back thirteen years except the sealed interior of the car. She closed her eyes. She surrendered.

'You all right?' She blinked her eyes open. Paul had turned to look at her just as they came into a bend, too fast, a low building loomed and filled Alison's line of vision and she saw dusty windows and a lopsided gate. He wrenched at the wheel and they were round.

But too late: she was back, she was here.

49

'Sorry,' said Paul, shaken. He changed gear, slowed the car right down, breathed out. 'Nasty bend.'

'Country roads,' she said. 'Give me London any day.' And Paul made a sound of assent but he was concentrating on the road now. Alison looked back again surreptitiously, trying to remember. She'd spent so long trying not to, it was a rusty mechanism; how did you do it? Detail. One dark stormy evening, a November night, a friend of Joe's, hit by a car on an unlit road. He'd died.

Things jostled in the luminous twilight. There was more to remember, a whole forgotten childhood unfolded in colours, showed her how grey her life had been since. There had been days on the water, borrowing someone's boat, dreaming, walking out on the marsh. Watching, spying, giggling with Gina, their heads so close she could smell Gina's gum, her perfume from the chemist's discount basket. Alison turned back to look at the road.

'It's somewhere around here, isn't it?' she said, and as Paul flicked his head to examine her she made herself smile back. His car didn't have satellite navigation, he didn't even have a smartphone. 'I mean,' she said, 'I looked at the website. I think we're nearly there.' They approached a junction. 'Left,' she said. 'I'm pretty sure it's left.' He paused, turned. Left.

'You were right,' he said, his indicator ticking, and there loomed the two cypresses, sooty-dark in the evening light, and behind them the red-brick and painted gables of the Edwardian roadhouse. There was the big bay window that used to be crowded with hoarded rubbish, the cluttered drive now cleared. The car crunched in on the gravel and a light blinked on in the hotel's porch.

Stock-still in the car, Alison suddenly remembered a hairless child climbing out of an ambulance, sickness and the first blunt shock; cancer and the incontrovertible fact of death. What had come to the crooked house wasn't the first horror to be visited on the village, after all. The car felt stifling then, sweat on Alison's upper lip as if she was on the edge of fever. There was worse, crowding into her head. Her father whistling in his workshop; the twins' fifth birthday, opening presents in the garden among daffodils; Joe's arm around her on the beach as his friends teased her.

She climbed out of the car, and smelled the sea. Esme.

Chapter Eight

With her eyes shut Alison would have known where she was, if she'd been blindfolded and walked into the Old Ship on Paul's arm rather than blinking on the threshold. She shouldn't have come.

'We could do room service,' she'd suggested back at the hotel as they dropped their bags and surveyed the room, and he'd looked at her sideways.

'Can you imagine what room service is going to be like here?' he said. The decor was chintzy and suffocating.

'Some sandwiches and a bottle of wine?' she pleaded. 'Aren't you tired?'

Paul had stepped up to her and put his arms around her, locked them behind her back so she couldn't move, his face very close. His grey eyes danced, he seemed delighted with something. Being there, being with her? She didn't know.

'They're not here yet,' he said gently. 'Morgan and what's his name. If that's what's on your mind.'

Alison shook her head, marvelling. 'No,' she said dully. 'I'm just tired.' Tuesday evening. The wedding on Saturday. The week yawned ahead of her, frightening.

'Ah, come on,' he said, and his lips brushed hers. 'Don't you think this place is rather – extraordinary? Geographically, I mean; the estuary, the feeling of being on the edge of nowhere? Rather interesting.' He pulled his head back, examining her. 'Besides, we need to get some air, after all that driving.' And leaving her no room to respond, he released her abruptly.

The twilight had intensified outside and it was warm. A soft wind rustled in the darkening countryside and Alison pictured reed beds down along the sea wall inland. She had listened to directions from the hotel owner in silence, although she could have walked down there in her sleep.

'It's very . . . authentic,' the woman had said, making a face when Paul asked about the pub. 'Basic is another way of putting it.' She'd told them to call her Jan – she was in her fifties, a groomed, stiff-haired blonde, and had come from another part of the country entirely: the far side of London, a place of clear streams and paddocks and expensive cars. 'The prices were so good here,' she confided. Her voice was nasal, carefully enunciated and to Alison's ears it defined her as an outsider straight away. 'A place like this, all these original features? I'd never have been able to afford it.'

'We'll give it a try, anyway,' said Paul of the pub, to their hostess. Kindly, because Alison had known instantly the hotel wasn't the kind of place he liked, even though she'd never been away with him before.

Paul had looked at her, amused, when she stuck her arm tight through his and hung on – she wasn't a toucher, not in public – but he said nothing. They walked first along the empty unlit road, then past the village sign, a shabby petrol station, a barn, a terrace of houses, a farmhouse, all familiar – she also noted as they passed a small new development here, a conversion there. The estuary was no longer visible, but Alison could smell it and as they got closer she could hear it too, the trickle and gurgle, the slap of halyards ringing on the boats as the wind got up and the tide lifted. They passed the row of tall sail-lofts, silent and unlit, the boatyard, the waterfront with the sea lapping below it. She pointed nothing out, walked past. The yellow glow of the pub windows appeared.

She blinked on the threshold, as if it might transport her somewhere else. The pub smelled the same, or almost. Beer-soaked bar towels, stale steam from the dishwasher: all pubs probably smelled like this but Alison had avoided them, since. At thirteen she'd just begun a job collecting glasses here on Sunday afternoons. It had used to smell of ashtrays too – one of her jobs had been wiping them out, the smell of slops and fag ash had made her gag. Now the smokers were outside among the wooden tables, murmuring by the water, the ends of their cigarettes flaring in the blue dusk.

Mum had only allowed her to do Sunday afternoons: there was homework to be done, had been her excuse, there was her room to tidy. But thirteen-year-old Esme had known it was that her mother wanted to minimise the chances she'd see her dad in there, because he didn't go in until the evening on a Sunday.

Behind the cramped bar stood the bad-tempered landlord Ron, fatter, jowlier, redder. He gave her a glance as she came in, perhaps he paused a fraction but no more. An old man with a grey beard mumbling to himself on a bar stool, a youngish woman with untidy hair and cracked heels in high sandals as far from him as she could get, running her finger around a tumbler containing dregs. Vodka and tonic. A table of underage drinkers in a corner huddled over pints, would-be surfers with dirty dreadlocks and smelling of dope. The nearest surf would be a hundred miles away, up to Norfolk somewhere. There was a tacked up poster for a barge match on the wall beside the bar; abstractedly Alison registered that the race – between the

54

big old Thames coastal barges whose home the estuary would have been a hundred years earlier – would take place on Friday, the day before the wedding. The matches had been a feature of their years here, a couple every summer, an endless awards ceremony in the pub, heckling and singing and someone ending up in the water. Little boats loaded with drunken men heading back out to their barges moored in the estuary.

The floor was still dusty boards, the tables topped with chipped red melamine, the greasy glass cabinet on the bar holding cheese rolls in clingfilm still advertised a cheap fizzy drink. Funny thing was, in London it might all have been some kind of ironic reference but Alison couldn't smile. She felt sick.

'Gin and tonic?' said Paul. 'It's probably safe enough.'

'Vodka,' said Alison. She hesitated, located an empty table and sat, her back against the wall. She watched Paul go to the bar, inserting himself between a bar stool and the old man with the beard. Watched him wait for Ron to finish some pointless restacking of crisp boxes, a gesture Alison recognised from out of the past, designed to show them all that the landlord was nobody's servant.

The old man leaned down on his bar stool, reaching towards Paul as he stood patiently and said something Alison couldn't hear. Even from the reckless lean of his body she could tell how drunk he was, and how ancient, but Paul turned politely towards him and answered. And then instantly she knew the old man, of course, something about the shabby coat he wore, a heavy tweed stiff with age and dirt, something about the point to his beard and the walnut gleam of his old bald head and there it was, even his name. Stephen Bray, the tilt of his boat on its side out in the marsh, the reek of home brew and unwashed clothes.

Still here? Alison was astonished, but then it occurred to her that those you thought were ancient, at thirteen, perhaps had only been middle-aged. She saw Paul answer politely, saw him nod just faintly in her direction in response and the old man looked over. She pushed her glasses up on her nose and frowned down into the contents of her bag, pretending not to notice them looking her way. Out of the corner of her eye she saw Paul get Ron's attention at last but Stephen Bray's hand was on his arm, detaining him.

His boat had always been out on the marsh, out along the shingle path from the waterfront that was buttressed with timbers sunk decades ago into the mud and now rotting. In theory you could make your way from there to the crooked house but it was a maze of creeks and dead ends. A memory came to her, of her father getting in more than once with mud up to his knees, saying he'd been to see Stephen, and had struck out across the marsh afterwards.

The drinks were on the bar now, Ron's hand not as steady as it had been. Stephen Bray was still talking, up into Paul's frowning face; now he was trying to pay for the drinks and Paul's hand was out and up, refusing.

Her father had taken her along to see him on his boat once or twice, when she'd been smaller, when they'd been happier. Their family on an even keel: that was a funny phrase in this place. She remembered clambering down the narrow gangway into the crowded space – it had once been a rich man's yacht, her father had told her, sixty years before. And still there'd been something fairy-tale about it, even frowsty and cluttered, with the long sweeping curve of the hull inside, the tarnished rails and the narrow shelves stacked with cans and pots, the bunk covered in an ancient army blanket and all of it tilted at forty-five degrees. Her father whispering before they got there, 'He's all right,' and holding her hand tight. 'He's just a lonely old man.'

There'd been a bottle he'd fished out from a cupboard that smelled of diesel, a liquid, straw-coloured and viscous, that had made her eyes water just to sniff it. He called it parsnip wine and never at nine or ten having even tasted wine Esme had known no better. He'd got out tiny dusty glasses etched with grapes, one for each of them, and they'd laughed kindly when she spluttered and retched at the single sip she took.

Lonely. Maybe. Paul looked over at her but not in desperation, not yet. He seemed actually interested in what the old man was saying and she felt a tightening in her gut at his kindness, his patience.

Something wrong with Stephen Bray: her mother had thought that. Eccentric, her father had countered, and what was wrong with that – *Kate*, dismay in his voice chiding her for her cold heart – but she had given him a warning look. Esme could tell that her mother imagined the two of them huddled over illicit booze, outcasts on the mud, her husband turning into the old hobgoblin's apprentice, talking to himself and holding his trousers up with string. If only.

What had they talked about? When she'd been there Bray had shown little interest in Esme, mostly talked to her father about the boat, listing races and classes and owners, the wood used in the hull and the decking, oak and spruce, maple from the Balkans. Charts and lists and numbers, he was happy as a kid reciting them. He'd been married once, long ago; she'd heard her father tell her mother that too and Alison could remember even now the sceptical sound her mother had made in reply.

Had she been right? Her mother hadn't always been cold-hearted, perhaps wasn't even then, perhaps she had just had to toughen up. When she'd come home from hospital with the twins she'd been a mess but overflowing with joy, in a grubby dressing gown all day, crying one minute, grabbing Esme the next, wrapping her arms around her. A sweet smell on her, milk and sleeplessness and sweat, nappies and bloodstained pads all over the place. Joe disgusted and laughing, too much mess, too much chaos, too much joy. It had to end.

There was a clatter of laughter from the surfer-boys' table that turned the old man's head and she saw Paul finally, almost regretfully, slide from the stool where he'd settled, and lift the drinks from the bar. The dishevelled woman was waggling her empty glass at Ron but at the same time turned to follow Paul's progress, and on instinct Alison shifted, out of her line of sight. Paul lowered the glasses.

That night, she thought, a small shock. That cool June night when her world ended. The last person who saw him, who saw my dad off at the back door of the pub, was that old man. Stephen Bray.

'Well,' Paul said. 'Talk about the Ancient Mariner.'

She laughed shortly. 'You were nice to him.' To her relief Paul lowered himself into the seat opposite her, shielding her from the room. 'Local colour?'

'He hadn't heard about the wedding,' said Paul, sipping his murky pint with a grimace. 'I wondered, you know. It might have been the social event of the decade, I thought.' Pushed the pint away a little. 'I should have got something to eat.'

'I'm not hungry,' said Alison, and lifted her own glass. The ice, if there had been any, had melted, the warmish liquid thin and watery.

'Oh, yes,' said Paul, quizzical at the memory. 'All that lunch.'

'Just a bit tired,' she said, lifting her hand to her mouth, making herself yawn. 'What was he talking about?' She took her hand away. 'The ancient mariner.'

'He said you were a pretty girl,' said Paul, lifting the glass to his lips and giving her a quick sideways glance.

'And?' She frowned.

Paul sighed, setting the glass down. 'God,' he said. 'You forget. I suppose living here it's impossible to get away from it.' He shrugged, and his face was grim.

'From what?' She knew what.

'In a bigger place maybe it would be different.' He frowned down at the scratched table then raised his head to look at her, sheepish. 'There was a murder here. A . . . multiple murder.'

58

He tilted his head. 'In cities I suppose these things have less impact, they must happen all the time,' he mused, distant. He came back into focus. 'You'd be too young to remember it.'

She just shook her head, not trusting herself to speak.

'He hasn't forgotten,' he said, half turning to nod in the direction of the bar. 'I suppose it leaves its mark on a community.' A pause. 'Some guy,' he said then. 'The old salt knew him, as a matter of fact, or so he was saying. Killed his whole family, out in some isolated farmhouse, then tried to kill himself.'

Not a farmhouse, she said, inside her head. Not the whole family.

'Maybe,' she said vaguely. 'I don't know, was that here?' What else had he said? She took another gulp and to her surprise the glass was already empty. Paul's pint hardly touched. 'I suppose when you're as old as him it doesn't seem so long ago,' she said.

'I hadn't thought of that,' said Paul, frowning. 'Thirteen years? A third of my life. Something like that. Half yours.' He glanced across at the bar. 'Maybe it seems like last week to him.'

At the bar Stephen Bray was mumbling to himself and the landlord was looking at him with distaste. The sound was malevolent, suddenly, he wasn't an innocent any longer, not a harmless eccentric, these were the mutterings of a madman, reflected in Ron's stiff red face. It was the sound that had filled her ears as she crouched beside her father's body, the sound of the invisible mob pressing against the walls. Had the sound been in her head, in the hall with them, or had there been someone out there, all that time?

The last one to see him.

'There seems to be one a week, these days, men killing their kids.' She heard her voice, sad, lost.

'He did say you were pretty, though,' said Paul, trying for light-hearted. He took her hand. 'Maybe there's hope for him.'

'Can we go?' Alison said stiffly. Letting go of her hand Paul looked at his drink in surprise. She pushed back her chair and the woman dangling her sandals at the bar looked over at the sound. Paul stood and half-drained his glass, and it seemed to Alison as though the bar stilled to watch them leave.

She walked fast in the dark, a buzzing in her ears, Paul at her side keeping up in silence. At the village sign she slowed fractionally and he put a warning arm on her elbow. 'What's got into you?' he asked, and she stopped. She was out of breath.

'I just . . . just . . . it's been a long day,' she said. 'That place wasn't exactly welcoming.'

'There's something else,' he said, his hand on her elbow.

She placed herself in front of him, hip to hip, blocking him. 'Let's get to bed, shall we?' she said boldly, and in the dark she lifted her face to his.

He said not a word, but once in the room he averted his face from hers as he undressed. The kiss he'd given her on the edge of the village had been cool, as light and dry as a shed snakeskin. She took the slip from her suitcase and laid it on the chair, but he didn't look or comment.

'You're right,' he said, turning on his side as she climbed into bed naked. The heaped pillows were on the floor and his shoulder was towards her; he reached a hand back and squeezed hers gently, then let it go. 'Let's just get some sleep.'

She lay in the dark, her body electric all down its length, sounding its alarm. The old man, Paul, the wedding, this place. This place.

Chapter Nine

They came in the night, thick and fast: images, pictures, names, places all returning, stepping up to her out of the darkness. The bad things that had happened here before the one great catastrophic thing, her big bang, had wiped them from her conscious mind. Beyond the window in the night, among the houses and lanes and hedges, the poplars and the reed beds, all the way down to the estuary the village stirred and whispered, reminding her. It seemed to Alison that she didn't sleep for a minute, the curtains at the big arched window weren't lined and she saw the leaded pattern of the glass through them, she listed the horrors.

A baby died. It had got on to the front page of the local newspaper. *Newborn dead in blaze.* Eyes closed she knew the house, down to the colour of the front door and the littered front garden. The child's father howling abuse on his doorstep before collapsing. Mum in tears over the newspaper on the kitchen table, looking up at Dad.

An uncertain summer's day, hot but cloud thickening on the horizon, a sticky Sunday afternoon and trippers watching the big boat glide up the brown river, a windsurfer dipping and swerving in its path. The big boat silent under sail, unable to slow or stop, a woman lifting her hand to her mouth as the windsurfer tipped and flattened and was under. A horrified laugh soon stifled as they all watch and wait for the bright triangle to reappear, the big boat's master stepping leisurely out from behind his wheel to look. They wait, and wait.

A boy's body in a ditch.

A young girl walking in the street hairless from chemotherapy, alone as if she'd escaped a bomb blast.

Not statistically unusual. Cells mutate; accidents happen. Every place had those tragedies, London must have a hundred million of them, people die wherever you go, for reasons just like this. No such thing as a cursed place.

She didn't sleep, and then she did. As the sky lightened she sank like a stone drifting soundless into deep water and she was blessed by unconsciousness for a bare half-hour. And then it was over and she was jackknifing back to the surface, gasping for breath. Steadying herself she reached for her glasses, careful to lift them off the side table without a clatter. Beside her on the bed Paul didn't stir, his face pale and still in the early light. This man. How could she think it would work? A man who could sit and work through historical matter for hours at a time, patient and unmoving, a man who never raised his voice. And her? He thought she was the same, with her glasses and her quiet facility with numbers and her refusal to need him – he thought her cool and in control.

But there was the gun, buried away in its stained cloth. Alison watched, remembering the thing's cold weight in her hand, and his eyelids fluttered as something played out behind them. Did he dream of chaos, of battle scenes? She thought of him stroking her, stroking until she was calmed. She imagined the gun as some historical artefact to him, a totem, a touchstone. Perhaps he brought order to chaos in his sleep and the gun served as a warning from a violent past.

Six o'clock. She slid out of bed.

Outside there was a wind. Alison put her face between the curtains and saw the heavy cypresses being buffeted but the sky was a clear bright blue, a couple of clouds scudding fast and high. She opened her suitcase silently and extracted her trainers, the old shorts, the sports bra she hadn't worn in months; Paul wasn't to know she'd run barely a handful of times in the previous year. Pausing in her scruffy disguise she went back to the suitcase and took her mother's scarf, twisting it into a bandana around her head. She hadn't known how exposed the cropped hair would make her feel.

Six ten as she closed the door carefully behind her. She calculated she had an hour, maybe two, before it started looking weird. She'd left a scribbled note, *Back soon!!* The exclamation marks would give it away, she realised, even as she started downstairs – not her style, or Paul's. Too late.

Downstairs there was some life, she heard kitchen sounds and a voice raised but mercifully the reception desk itself was empty. She could imagine Jan looking at her curiously, storing the information for later, for Paul. *She's an early bird.* The hotel's door was on the latch and she slid it open and was out, tiptoeing over the gravel and on to the road, alone.

The wind was warm and blustery, the sound of it in the trees exhilarated her as she headed down towards the sea, a cleansing rush inside her skull. It had been high summer when they'd come here first, the start of the holidays spent unloading the van in a green twilight and she and Joe skipping and running and getting in the way and the next morning a rinsed blue morning just like this. A new start.

She began to run: making herself go slow, and breathe, down the blustery lane between hedges. The village appeared ahead of her, bleached and empty in the morning sun and she thought of the dingy little pub down on the waterfront shuttered up against the light.

It was silent – or almost. She had passed no more than a handful of houses when she heard it, a sound you never heard in London. The whine and clink of a milk float. It appeared now, swaying in the turning to a little close as she crossed the road, jerking to a halt to let her past and she turned her head to examine the milkman. He yawned, a stranger, twenty or so, but he still wore the old-fashioned white coat with the dairy's insignia.

The boy who'd died in a hit-and-run had been found beside the road by another milkman coming in to the village at dawn, pulling his float to a halt on the verge. The man had gone himself to tell the boy's mother, taking off his cap at her back door, the float still loaded with undelivered milk. Not the first time the boy had stayed out all night, only this time not drunk in a hedge but dead. His brother had told Esme about the milkman, days later when he reappeared at school, black rings under his eyes and his breath sour with sleeplessness. A friend of Joe's. The name was there in some recess of her memory along with those of his brothers, but Alison didn't pursue them, not now. Her boys had been all the woman had, she remembered that: three sons, her husband had drowned in a storm just after the youngest's birth.

Leaving him behind her, Alison heard the sound of the milk float recede. As she headed down, the village street narrowing to the occasional glimpse of marshland, her breath burned in her chest. She'd never been much of a runner: bad at pacing, reluctant to take instruction. She had a tendency to speed up, and to let her heart beat too fast. She'd bought the trainers to get herself through a bad patch a year or so earlier, the time the boy wouldn't stop calling. Exercise resets the body, the counsellor had said. Even if it's just to fill the time, just to get out of the house. Just to stop yourself thinking.

She bounced, slowing herself down. The shoes were perished with underuse and she could feel the tarmac through them. She dodged to the left and down between tall brick villas put up by the same Victorian developer as had built the crooked house out on the edge of the marsh, back when Saltleigh must have looked like a prospect, the wind off the estuary healthful and full of ozone, and not a muddy backwater. Names like Avonlea and Camelot and Burnside on weathered stone lintels and built in pairs, propping each other up where Creek House had been left to slip and tilt alone. Some were double-glazed, with rows of china birds and artificial flowers in the windows and polished cars out front, but there were others still tatty as she remembered, with overgrown front gardens and bicycles rusting in the salt air.

She felt the road surface grow uneven as the houses thinned and the village petered out. At the end of the road there should be fields with a path between them that ended on the sea wall, but instead she saw new brick, link fencing, some kind of development. Alison felt her breathing turn erratic. She kept on, all the same. It was all right, she saw as she got closer, there were no more than a handful of houses, and unfinished at that, with churned mud between the buildings. She slowed to negotiate the fence. She didn't stop altogether: some superstitious ticking in her head set up when she had started to run told her, Not till you get there. Don't stop till you're there.

And there it was, at the last minute, a lopsided arthritic tree she recognised, and a gap in the undergrowth she knew of old. Still there. She darted down it. The foliage closed around her. The air trapped between the hedges smelled of dusty dogshit, and Alison felt the sweat prickle between her shoulder blades, her eyes stung and she squeezed them shut.

This had been their route up into the village, she and Joe on errands to the post office or the cluttered village mini-market or the baker's with its cottage window half full of plain

65

loaves and iced buns that was now, she'd seen in passing, net-curtained and silent. The girls had just started going, the two of them on Saturday morning begging to be allowed. Dad was always bad news on a Saturday morning by then, cursing as he filled the kettle and swallowed painkillers, so Mum had let them go reluctantly, frowning as they raced each other along the top of the sea wall. The twins, skipping silhouetted against the endless sky, bright and wicked and loving – and strange.

They'd turned more so, towards the end, hiding in cupboards together, writing in secret notebooks; there'd been a reason. Alison faltered, almost stopped. She remembered Mum pale and depleted, unloading the two of them from the car after a hospital visit, when had that been? When had that started? Mum distant. There had been other trips to the doctor's, blood tests, the girls tired and scrappy and bickering afterwards. How could Alison have forgotten? Mum had made light of it, routine, she said, but Joe had said one evening, *She's worried*. And whispering back to him Alison remembered observing then that Mum still thought of her and Joe as extensions of herself, she didn't understand that they saw things. Understood things. Such as, not everything grown-ups said was true.

Another hundred yards downhill, fifty, with the stones loose and treacherous under her feet, and then the hedges parted and there it was. The horizon: the power station, the church, the grey tufted marsh and the sparkling distance where the flat water met the sky. At an angle to her path the wide bumpy track led out from the back of the village and where they intersected it still stood. The crooked house, its brick dark and its angles wrong, a blotch on the pale lovely morning. She had to make herself breathe.

As she ran that last stretch, its tilted shape jumped and shifted until she was dizzy so Alison just stared at the path and then she was in its long, cool shadow. The tide was low but not fully out yet. She looked up.

66

The house was boarded and derelict, weathered plywood splintered and graffitied at each window and the purple spikes of some plant sprouting above the lintel over the front door. The little enclosed yard behind where they had hidden and whispered and left secret messages. Thirteen years.

Approaching in the lee of the seawall, hidden from the village view, she skirted the house. She put a hand to its brick flank and found it already warm from the sun. The brick was crumbling and pitted with neglect and salt erosion; looking up she saw that the roofline sagged, a piece of guttering fallen away.

Her heart would not slow down, in fact she felt as if it would rise and swell into her throat and choke her. What had she expected? That the house had been sold, renovated, extended, a family living there? The truth was she had expected nothing: in her brain she had forced the house into the setting of a horrible story, of a bad, bad dream, branching into cellars and cluttered attics and corridors that had never existed except in her imagination and she would come here to find nothing at all. A windswept marsh, a bumpy track that led to nowhere but another empty berth. That hope blew away on the wind. Because here it stood.

The graffiti on the boarded bay window to what had been the sitting room was layered and faded, scratched messages and crude diagrams. One word isolated itself, *Joe*, written in pale marker almost gone and if there'd been anything else attached to his name it had been written over or obliterated. *Joe*. Other names, some she recognised, some were strangers.

And then her brother was there in her head after everything she'd done to hold him at bay all this time. Watchful, quiet Joe, helping unload the car right here the day they arrived. And later, years later, fierce tongue-tied Joe, out on the beach below the power station, smoking dope with the other boys, getting angry about something. Those boys. Joe surly and refusing to come home. One night on the beach with Joe, Esme the only girl tagging on the fringes. Late summer and Esme just thirteen. The year before her family died.

She pressed her cheek to the plywood, she closed her eyes. Behind the boarded window the sitting room sat dark and silent, she felt it waiting for her on the other side. She would not go in, she didn't need to know what was or was not still there, who might have been in there since, leaving cans and dirty blankets. She moved on, pressed close to the wall as if she'd climbed out of a high window and might fall. She came around the window bay to the porch and then stepped back.

The board over the front door had a word scrawled huge in white spray paint. If it had been on council property someone would have come along and removed it, scrubbed it clean or replaced the board, because it couldn't have been allowed to stay there. It was an offence. Her scalp prickled.

BITCH.

Backing off, Alison stumbled, corrected herself. *Who?* She turned to look inland. The village could barely be seen from here, not much more than the pointed line of the sail-lofts' roofs, the tilted shapes of boats beached behind the yard, the tops of grey-green trees buffeted in the wind. The pub was invisible from where she stood; even thinking of the place the smell was in her nostrils, the smell of beer slops and fag-ends.

BITCH.

It could mean anyone, it could be any kid raging because he'd caught his girlfriend out. And for a moment the house looked like a crooked ugly lightning rod out on the marsh, hatred narrowing and finding its way like electricity to the battered boarded front door. She lurched away from the porch, her legs jelly – after the run – round to the other side of the house and the tongue and groove door she knew she'd find in the wall. The door that led into the yard: paint peeling, it hung skewed from a broken hinge.

She closed it behind her and the wind died, her ears buzzed in the respite. It smelled of old rotted things, low-level stink: ancient dustbins, stale air, blocked sewage. With her back to the rough flaking door she surveyed the yard.

It was here he'd kissed her. Her first real kiss. The windsurfer, his chin rough with golden stubble, his crinkled smile, his smell of sweat and cigarettes. She had seen him on the water, had seen him on a ladder in overalls, painting someone's house, and then one night outside the pub he'd talked to her, standing close, asked her where she lived. Older than her: Esme still with her centre parting, her starter bra. And her best friend Gina wanting to know all about it, rough and jeering.

The yard was smaller than she remembered. To her right was the shed for bins and junk, a piece of wall, the back door, and the hidden place. Their place. A niche created between the crude flat-roofed kitchen extension, the original rear of the house and the yard wall, a space big enough to accommodate a child, or two if squeezed together and giggling in a game of hide and seek. And more tempting still, the single brick, low down, the first in a row above the stone base, that had been loose from the start and that within weeks Joe had begun to dig at with a kitchen knife. A space behind not big enough for more than a note or a penny or possibly a pocket knife, a shard of something. She squatted now: the brick was in its place.

Alison thought of the police here, searching. She didn't know where they'd looked, what they'd been looking for – perhaps it had all been clear-cut to them from the beginning. Had it been to her? She remembered the emergency services operator's voice even now, asking her, *Is he still there?* The killer, the man who might kill her too. And she'd known then, that's Dad. The long gun between his hands.

Her adult fingers weren't so much bigger than Esme's aged ten: she worked them either side of the loose brick and it shifted with a scrape and was out.

69

Alison felt in the space with her hand, and had to bend lower to see, pushing her glasses back up on the bridge of her nose. There was nothing there.

What had she expected? She squatted on her heels, leaned her back a moment against the wall and something crunched under her feet, snagging her attention. She peered down between her trainers.

A curved wire, a single tiny teardrop-shaped piece of transparent plastic attached to it, where she'd have expected two. She frowned, and put her hand to the dust and rubble, sifting it with her forefinger. After thirteen years? *No.*

Shifting position, Alison was on her bare knees now, heedless of broken glass. She passed her hand across the rubble, searching intently. Knowing what she was after. Not his, not necessarily his. She felt a sob in her throat at the thought that, after all this time she would know it when she saw it. If she saw it. There.

The metal was bent, snapped off, but the tiny logo was intact. The arm of a pair of glasses, long ground in the dust. She stood, it fell from her hand. In the rehabilitation unit his eyes had leaked tears, sightless. No one had thought to help him see. No one had thought to look for them.

Her father's glasses.

She saw his face, pressed sideways into the dark-soaked hall rug. She blundered, blinded, back through the rickety yard door and gasped for air.

Out on the marsh the wind flattened the samphire and as she gazed back towards the peaked line of sail-lofts something caught her eye, halfway to the foreground. Upright as a totem in the early sun someone stood on the mud, turned her way.

She was being watched.

Chapter Ten

When the middle-aged couple appeared in the doorway of the sun room Alison's first feeling was of relief. Theirs had been the only table laid for breakfast, near the French windows that opened on to the rickety veranda and a stretch of rough grass. As she watched, a man in white decorator's overalls with a rough mop of hair walked past outside carrying a bucket of tools.

With only one table to serve the waitress had hovered incessantly, urging foods on them: bacon, kippers. 'From the next village, nearly,' the girl had urged them in accented English. 'Artisan smokehouse.' Alison wondered if it had been this girl Jan had been shouting at in the kitchen this morning – perhaps they had a fridge full of food and no guests. She and Paul must be the only ones to have turned up so early for the wedding, and she wondered now why she'd agreed to it, why he had wanted it.

Paul accepted the kippers, and toast, and coffee, good-humoured although she knew by now that he wouldn't like the coffee, he was particular. Queasy, Alison asked for toast and tea.

'Really?' he said, as the waitress finally left. 'I'd have thought you'd be starving.'

'I only went a couple of miles,' she said, forcing herself to smile, deprecatingly. 'Terrible. I'm not fit at all.'

It was his first overt reference to Alison's expedition since she'd got back. It had been almost eight when, breathless, she'd slipped back into the dim room. The bed was empty and the shower drumming loudly the other side of the bathroom door. She'd stripped everything off in a panic and gone in there with him quickly, reaching for him in the steam, under the fierce jets of the hotel shower. He let her take hold of him: she had the feeling he was playing along, amused, that he knew she was trying to distract them both from something, and that he grew hard as part of a game of his own. Only at the end did he move, raising his own hands to her upper arms and holding her in his grip, and only then did she feel herself rise to the bait, instantly impatient.

She couldn't find her own glasses for some time after they came out, but was grateful for the blurred world, as if it made her less visible as she groped and searched through the bedcovers. Paul had found them in the end, straightening to pick them off the floor. 'You were in a hurry,' he observed mildly, and she tilted her head back to smile up at him, afraid.

At first she had thought, looking at the fragment of metal and plastic, that there would be an explanation. Carried out to the yard on a policeman's boot. Caught in her own clothing as she stepped around her father's body. Her reflexes buzzed a warning, but her brain tried to rationalise. Only this wasn't normal, there was nothing rational about holding a weapon to a child's head, seeing your own child torn open, blood and guts and splintered bone.

His glasses. Always by her father's bed, as hers had been since she'd turned sixteen. It occurred to her only now that that little tic of mortality, or dread, that sounded every morning

72

as she turned to reach for her glasses was not just the fear of helplessness without them, it was because the action set some obscure clockwork of memory going, unacknowledged. It made her think of him, her father picking his latest pair off the side table and setting them on his nose, his face rumpled from sleep, his thinning hair tufted, owlish.

Had he had a spare pair? One or two, old pairs stashed in drawers. A pair in the workshop, hanging from a red string. She also remembered him out for a run with his glasses on – never contact lenses because like hers his eyes couldn't tolerate them. It must have been early on, he had long since stopped anything so worthy at the end, when work had dried up and he'd have had the time to run but drank instead. A branch had knocked his glasses off and he hadn't been able to find them, he'd got home in a blur and almost weeping with help-lessness. They had gone out on their bikes, she and Joe retracing his steps, and found them for him. He'd hugged them with a teary fierceness that worried even Joe, disentangling himself.

But the question was . . . Her thoughts fractured. His face side-on in blood on the rug. She willed herself to concentrate. Had his glasses been there, or near, smashed or fallen or kicked aside, had they been there, anywhere? Had the force of the gunshot sent them to a corner of the hall, twisted and shat-tered?

But she didn't know. She couldn't remember.

The police would know. Alison felt a slow burn of anxiety, somewhere at the centre of her chest. But would they? Had anyone even said, *He wears glasses*? She bent over her plate and, head down, she saw Paul's long fingers delicate on the knife and fork, meticulously lifting the bones out of the coppery fish.

Facing the doorway, Alison saw the couple first. A tall man, broad-shouldered in a pale-coloured jacket, freckled and tanned, a good head of sandy hair mostly turned to grey. The woman beside him wore a flowered silk dress, delicate, pretty, girlish but no longer a girl. His wife, not his daughter. Her hair curled up on her shoulders and her eyes, even from where Alison sat, were big and dark blue, with spidery lashes. She looked nervy.

Quickly Alison understood they weren't guests – something about the way they stood, they had a purpose. Then the man raised a hand in greeting. 'Paul,' he said heartily, and Paul laid down his knife and fork.

'Dr Carter.' He stood, putting a hand out to Alison. 'This is my . . . my . . . my girlfriend. Alison, this is Dr Carter.' The man clapped him on his shoulder and Paul cleared his throat. 'Morgan's father.'

'Father of the bride,' said Carter, with a theatrical grimace. 'For my sins.'

'Darling,' the woman admonished, nervously. He looked at her in irritation then turned to Alison. 'Roger,' he said with a stiff little bow. 'And this is my wife, Lucy,' and he put his hand back on Paul's shoulder, proprietorial.

Morgan took after her father, then, thought Alison. Not just their sandy blond vigour, either, it was a sort of steamroller quality, a greedy energy. The word was probably arrogance.

'You look lovely, Lucy,' said Paul with conscious gallantry and Lucy Carter pinked, her eyelashes turned starrier as she gazed at him. 'When do they arrive?' he said gently. 'Morgan and ah . . . ah . . .'

'You'd better remember his name, at least,' said Carter, bluff, 'if you're to be best man. He'll be staying here until the wedding, too. He's called Christian.'

Paul began to remonstrate but Carter stopped him. 'Oh, I'm sure you've done your homework, Paul, I'm only joking. And you were the natural choice.' Alison must have been looking confused because he turned to her then. 'Christian's South African, the old friend he'd marked out couldn't make it over, and Paul – well, Paul stepped in.'

So Paul barely even knew the groom. Alison didn't know what to make of that fact but it made her uneasy, it seemed like a deception. She found herself dreading the speeches. Carter had turned back to Paul. 'Of course if it had been up to me to find her a husband . . . well.' He darted a glance at Paul from under sandy eyebrows. 'Water under the bridge, I suppose.'

'They're arriving tonight?' said Paul.

'Yes. The happy couple,' said Roger Carter, looking around the room. 'Come for a drink, we're having drinks, aren't we?' Lucy Carter brightened.

'Yes, do come, Paul,' she said. 'Sixish? I mean, it won't be anything glamorous.' Her husband snorted.

Alison sat back down carefully and Roger Carter glanced down at her, put out. 'Darling,' whispered his wife.

'What?' said Carter, frowning at the kipper congealing on the table. 'Oh. Well, I suppose you must get on with your breakfasts. I only came to tell you the rehearsal's at four tomorrow. Of course there'll be another run-through, last minute, next day, bloody endless. Anyway, St Peter's on the Wall, you remember how to get there?' He had Paul's hands between his, now, as he glanced at Alison. 'You too, ah . . .'

'Alison,' said his wife.

'You're very welcome, too, Alison,' said Roger Carter, and bowed again. She saw that his hair, which had looked so thick, was thinning on top. 'So glad you could come at all, short notice I know. Although the rehearsal will be a chore, don't feel . . . anyway . . .' He dropped Paul's hands, at last, pulled out his chair for him. 'Eat up,' he said. 'Six o'clock, remember.'

And they were gone, leaving dust motes and Lucy Carter's scent drifting in their wake and the waitress bobbing futilely in the doorway.

'Well,' said Paul, prodding his cold kipper.

'Well,' said Alison, knowing she shouldn't. 'Why didn't you tell me?'

75

Chapter Eleven

The gears grated as Alison put the little car into reverse, but when she looked up at him Paul wasn't even wincing. He leaned down and smiled through the window. 'Have fun,' he said. 'See you later. Whenever.'

As she turned to check there was nothing behind her he put a hand to her cheek. 'It'll be fine,' he said. He meant Morgan. His hand stayed. 'I've waited a long time for you, you know,' he said softly. She searched his face and he smiled wearily. 'I do want to make you happy, you see. It'll be fine.'

Perhaps their row had softened him up. Not that it had been a row, by most people's standards – the waitress certainly hadn't seemed to notice but perhaps she'd been too anxious about the abandoned kippers. 'So sorry,' she'd said. 'I bring you something else? Is all included, breakfast. There is no charge?'

It felt like a row to Alison because they'd never had one before: it consisted mostly of silence but it was like being at a crossroads, and the wrong path would lead to catastrophe. She had to think really very hard before saying the next thing.

Paul had laid down his knife and fork and set his hands flat on the table either side of his plate. He hadn't drunk his coffee, as she had predicted.

'Come *on*,' he said. 'Really?'

She made herself smile. 'You know what I'm talking about, though, don't you?' she said. Beyond Paul the sunlight dazzled through the big windows; she saw the decorator lighting a cigarette on the veranda, cupping his hand around the flame. The gesture stirred something in her memory.

'Morgan? You knew,' he said. She looked at him then. 'You always knew. Come on.' He leaned his arm back over the chair and examined her thoughtfully. 'Didn't you?'

Had she always known? She was pretty sure they'd never had a conversation about Morgan Carter and what she meant – or had meant – to Paul, even if on the one occasion she'd met her, turning her back and tumbling blond hair on Alison to talk to Paul, there'd been something palpable between them. But he seemed quite unruffled at the breakfast table, no trace of guilt.

'And now I'm just looking for a fight?' she said.

Paul shrugged, smiled. 'Well, I surrender,' he said. 'We went out for quite a long time, quite a long time ago. I met her parents. We broke up. End of story.'

'Perhaps I did know,' Alison said slowly, as something surfaced uneasily. She just wanted to get away from it now, she had no interest in being the girlfriend jealous of his exes. Except it occurred to her that looking upset might buy her some more time to herself. 'I just didn't think . . . Oh, never mind.' There were so many other questions she might ask: *Did you live together? Why did it end? Did you love her?* She discarded them all. 'So you know this place already?'

'Over three, four years – I came up here a lot,' said Paul, readily. But he was watching her closely. Don't lose it, Alison told herself. 'Weekends. Once upon a time,' he continued. 'I was part of the family, you know how that goes.' She almost shook her head. No, I don't. 'Christmases, even,' he said, and his face softened. 'It's quite different in the winter.'

It shook her and she felt herself stiffen, working to hold her composure. She thought of her father kneeling to light the fire on dank November evenings when it grew dark on the marsh long before tea, the sun setting as they walked from the bus stop after school. The hit-and-run that killed Joe's friend had been in November, she recalled then, a hushed announcement before the Remembrance Day assembly, a warning about taking care walking home in the dark.

Paul went on. 'I remember a Christmas Eve service. The church was freezing.'

Alison's family hadn't been attenders of religious services. She imagined the little party from The Laurels, the Carters like royalty setting out for the tiny church. Village royalty — although she couldn't remember or visualise the house, The Laurels itself. Perhaps it was a big new-build somewhere on the other side, the Carters looked like the type. The waitress was back, taking away their plates, making small sounds of apology and disappointment over what they'd left. Alison waited, trying to think of how to put it to him. *I want to be alone.*

But Paul headed her off, on his feet before the waitress had even turned away from the table. Alison followed him up the wide carpeted staircase, along the little panelled corridor that smelled of wax polish. She sat on the bed, that had been made, saw the fresh towels on the rail through the bathroom door. She tried to imagine a life where the two of them got up and went to bed every day together, where sex wasn't much more than a ripple in the day, and failed. Paul was at the small writing table in the corner, clicking open the briefcase he'd brought with him. In her pocket her mobile rang and she got it out.

'Work,' she said to Paul, as he turned to her with a look of mild inquiry. It was Rosa, immediately launching into some halting questions about the terms of an author's contract, the disbursement of funds from a foreign deal, something Alison barely had anything to do with but she answered as best she could. Then Rosa blurted, 'How's the weather? They say it's set to be nice over there. You could do with a holiday. I hope you're OK.' All in a rush.

'It's lovely,' Alison replied slowly. 'Thank you.' She had the feeling that this hasty stumbling question was the real purpose of the call; at the same time she was aware of Paul watching her. 'Back on Sunday.' She hung up, puzzled, turned to him but couldn't ask the question. How did Rosa know where she was? She'd only told Kay. Kay wasn't the type to dish out information unsolicited – but you never knew.

'Darling,' said Paul, behind her now, his hand on her shoulder. He sounded hesitant, weary. 'Look I should have said but . . . I've got some work to get done today. Could we . . . would you . . .' Alison twisted to look up at him, wrong-footed. Had he known what she was thinking? Was he giving her space?

This is where Morgan grew up, was what Paul had said, as they crested the hill and looked down. So the Carters would have been here, they'd have known about that night, it would be part of their lives. The killings. It occurred to Alison that everyone in the village probably knew more about the killings than she did.

'I might get out and explore, then,' she said quickly, making her face sunny. 'Would that be OK?'

She didn't even have to ask for the car. He was back at the briefcase, fishing out the keys. 'As long as you're back for the drinks at six,' he said, dangling them. The light poured in through the window behind him, his face in shadow, but as she reached for the keys he took her hand and held it. 'Give yourself time.'

Now as she reversed across the gravel he had already turned to go back into the hotel, walking quickly. He didn't look back to watch her go.

She drove out of the village, leaving the estuary down behind her, heading inland. She knew where she was going.

The big ugly police station on the dwindling edge of the town where they'd used to go for the Saturday morning supermarket shop, a ten-mile drive. Remembering no more than a wall of grimy barred windows and a blue lantern, Alison knew she would find it. She would find the female detective with her straight brown hair and her big nose and her gentle voice, and as the face swam up to meet her she remembered. The last time.

The last time she had seen the policewoman was when they were loading Polly's car with Esme's things.

A suitcase full of clothes that she would have grown out of within the year, some books, a carrier bag of threadbare soft toys she should already have grown out of. She had left the letters that spelled her name on the shelf, not because it was no longer her name, that occurred to her only later. But because her father had made them. Because that relationship was gone.

Beside the car the policewoman had put her arms around her, so hastily that Esme wondered afterwards if she'd been mistaken, the detective immediately straightening back up and tugging at her jacket. Perhaps it was against the rules. Almost certainly. Esme had looked up into her face then and had seen her, for what seemed like the first time. A woman of thirty years old or so with a straight fringe and hair tied back, a worried-looking woman. Esme had wondered if she had children. *Keep me.*

'Good luck,' the policewoman said, her mouth set in a line. 'I won't see you again.'

80

Why had they come here, her little family, why had they come here, to be entangled, to be destroyed?

We need more space.

Alison had never consciously thought about it but she'd always known, deep down, that there'd been more to their move here, twenty years ago now, than that. The old house had been in a town a bit more than an hour away, inland, one in a terrace of houses, they'd had neighbours, a garden with apple trees.

When they lived in the old house Mum had always had a job: dinner lady, doctor's receptionist, then full time at the artists' supplies shop. Sometimes Dad would take her to pick Mum up at the end of the day and Esme would play among the shelves, squeezing the packs of clay and grabbing whole handfuls of new pencils. Mum had been trained in fine arts at the college where she and Dad had met: there had been a portfolio of sketches in a drawer that Esme and Joe used to sneak a look at, marvelling at the things their mother could do. Had once been able to do. Dad had once told them she'd stopped drawing when they were born and then looked as if he regretted it, seeing their puzzled faces fall.

There'd been no job for Kate Grace in Saltleigh, nor in the nearest town. She'd looked, once the twins were in nursery, but there'd been nothing. Dad had held on to some of his old contacts, building firms, private clients, but one after the other they evaporated, settling for someone closer, more available. More sober.

Because his drinking was why they'd come away, that much had always been clear, if unspoken. In the year before they moved she remembered him odd, distant, morose, remembered giving up waiting for the bedtime kiss. There'd been a night she'd been woken by a terrible clatter and Mum gasping, then she'd appeared in the bedroom door telling Esme it was all right, to go back to sleep. But it wasn't all right: he'd fallen down the stairs drunk. He'd come to breakfast with a black eye. They'd moved no more than a few months after, and for a time the drinking receded, became an uncomfortable memory. A blip.

So it seemed to have worked, and if the house wasn't noticeably bigger than the old one there were other reasons to be here, better reasons, if you asked Joe and Esme. There was the grey sea, Power Station Beach and the paths through the marsh and the big empty sky; they were more space, all right.

But then it stopped working.

Behind the wheel of the strange car Alison slowed. Here was where it went wrong – and she stared, as if the front gardens, the net curtains and empty pavements might have an answer. A small row of council houses appeared, she recognised them. They must have been built in the 1970s, dull beige brick boxes with double glazing. They looked as though, against the odds, they were still council houses, each front door painted the same red. On impulse Alison pulled up and parked.

This was where she'd lived, the local girl who'd had cancer. Alison groped for the name but it was evading her. She remembered seeing the girl climbing out of a taxi with her mother. The hood of her coat was up but that didn't disguise the hairless forehead, the face smooth as an egg, no eyebrows or lashes.

A name bobbed up out of the dark waters. *Kyra Price*.

The house she identified as the sick girl's had net curtains that looked like they hadn't been moved in some time, and windows filmed with dust. Suddenly it seemed important to Alison to know if Kyra Price had lived. She'd had leukaemia, which could be survived – at least children could survive it, if you believed the magazines and their feel-good stories, their campaigns. The dirty windows offered nothing in the way of hope. Could she get out, ring the bell, ask, did your child live? No.

Leaning a little to turn the key in the ignition, in a sudden hurry to leave, in the wing mirror she saw a figure approaching along the pavement. It was a woman pushing a buggy. Still crouched over the ignition, Alison watched her approach. Hair pulled back, broad-shouldered, she shoved the buggy along with one hand, careless, a cigarette in the other. The dishevelled woman from the pub last night, thought Alison with sudden certainty. But there was more, there was something about her, the heavy breasts, the way she brushed the hair back from her face with the flat of her cigarette hand. Alison sat up in the driver's seat, waiting for her to draw nearer, to be sure. The child was asleep, slumped a little in the flimsy stroller. Eight or so, too big for a buggy.

They disappeared from the mirror, in the car's blindspot, then suddenly the woman was there at the window, leaning in with aggressive curiosity. Their eyes met, something about the movement must have roused the child because there was a wail and the woman straightened, the woman she knew. Her heart pounding, Alison fumbled for the ignition, turned to reverse, pulled away.

Gina. Her friend Gina. Gina had a kid, Gina still here, disconsolate on a bar stool, big handsome fearless angry Gina. Alison accelerated towards the edge of the village, before she could look round, before she could turn back and get out of the car and grab Gina and hold on to her, arms around her, Gina. Gina, it's me.

And suddenly she was on the edge of the village, at a junction with what they'd always known as the fast road, the road the buses rocked along on the way to and from the town, the supermarket, the school. A sign on her left, half buried in the hedge said *Dyke End*, and she turned to see a lane that led to trees. A car loomed in her rear-view mirror, a horn tooted. Panicked, Alison made as if to pull away but out of nowhere, across her path, came a truck loaded with turnips, swaying,

83

scattering grass and dust in its wake. The car behind her pulled out and past, a man glowering sideways at her. Alison leaned her head on the steering wheel and sobbed.

Gina had a kid. She must have still been a kid herself when she got pregnant. Gina was unhappy: that much Alison knew, from how she'd sat on the bar stool last night and how she'd glared through the car window, just now. Their eyes had met, and in that moment the years evaporated, Gina might have been jeering from her bedroom door as Esme hurried down the stairs. 'We're supposed to be friends, remember?' Gina had shouted after her. 'Remember? Well, don't come to me when you start freaking out.' Had they got it out of her, had the nice policewoman been so nice when she talked to Gina, asked her why Esme hadn't stayed after all, for the sleepover? Had it been boys? Had you been drinking? *What about drugs, you girls into drugs?*

Gina wouldn't have cracked: Gina wouldn't have said a thing to the police, not a thing.

Gina. *It's me.*

Chapter Twelve

Alison sat in the car opposite the police station watching a man on the far kerb smoking. She saw him look up and down the street before going inside, head down, hands in his pockets. She could hardly go in and say, *She had a fringe, she had a big nose*: thirteen years on, who knew what she'd look like.

By the time they'd come for her down the track, in their emergency vehicles, Esme had no longer been able to move or speak, she had sealed herself over. Because if she didn't the thing behind her in the house, the black horror in that house that lay over the bodies and fed, would gather and swell and come shrieking out through the door, the windows, the cracks. It would batten on her and she would be gone, the police would find only buttons and bones.

Sitting in the car now, looking at a head moving in one of the windows on the police station's second floor but only seeing the grey line of that dawn horizon, Alison knew it was still there. It was out on the marsh, and it was waiting for her. She leaned down and rested her head on the steering wheel.

It had been the woman who'd talked at her through the

succeeding days who'd saved her, even if she had only been doing her job. The policewoman, turning to shush the younger male officer, lowering her voice when it needed to be lowered, carrying on talking, asking, not letting it go. Alison needed her name.

Hold on. She thought of Aunt Polly's little cottage in Cornwall, and of official letters on the small table in her dark hall. Telephone calls, Polly's hand over the mouthpiece waiting for Alison to run upstairs to her room and out of earshot. Alison got out her mobile, scrolled with her thumb through the names. She dialled.

'Hello?' The voice was rusty. Old.

'Polly?' There was a silence. 'It's me, Aunt Polly.'

'Alison.' She cleared her throat. 'How lovely. To hear your voice.' Heartbroken was how she sounded: for a moment Alison lost the thread.

'Are you all right?' she managed eventually. 'Polly?'

'Do you need something, Alison?' And the old angry Polly was back.

'I need a name.' There was no point hedging. She didn't say, *I know you went on talking to the police. I know there must have been things you kept from me. I know.* It was how Alison had wanted it, after all. Someone had to do it, to take Alison to the inquest, to hold her gaze in the cleared coroner's courtroom while she recounted her evidence. Someone had had to shield her as she climbed into the black car afterwards and someone had to go on shielding her until she could walk away from it all on her own. Polly might not have had all the right skills but she had done her best. And she'd been all there was.

'She was called Sarah Rutherford.' The answer was immediate: Polly didn't even need to think. But her voice was stiff and strange. 'Detective Sergeant Sarah Rutherford. Why do you want to know? Now, I mean. After all this time?' Panicky.

'It's all right, Polly,' said Alison. 'I'm not going to do anything stupid.'

Polly had always known when Alison was lying, and she probably knew now.

'Where are you?' she said, swift and afraid.

'Don't worry,' said Alison. Then, 'I'm at home.' And it almost wasn't a lie.

They put Alison in a room with no windows bar an internal one, high up. She had sat in the reception for a bit but then the desk officer had gone off and she'd heard a door bang and some voices and he'd reappeared and taken her further inside the police station.

Detective Sergeant Sarah Rutherford was at an incident but she was expected back in the station within the hour.

'You want a coffee?' The man who'd led Alison in there was no more than five years older than her, wearing a shirt and tie but the tie was loosened. She didn't know what it meant about rank, if they didn't wear uniforms: the uniformed officer at the front desk had mumbled some introduction but she hadn't registered any of it.

Alison shook her head, imagining the plastic cup, and thought of Paul, working quietly in the hotel, turning up his nose at their coffee. The policeman hesitated a moment, then he was gone.

The room's chairs were battered and the table scarred. An interview room. She hoped they hadn't brought Gina somewhere like this, after. Her dread grew, like darkness. Detective Sergeant Sarah Rutherford knew things she didn't. And knew things about her no one else did.

The door banged open: the tall woman in the doorway was looking back over her shoulder. 'Not yet, Jennings,' she said, and Alison glimpsed the young officer with his loosened tie, peering past her from the corridor. When he saw her he stepped back, out of sight. 'I'll give you a buzz if I need you.' And the door closed and she was there. Alison's heart was suddenly in her mouth, it was like seeing someone you'd thought was dead.

Sarah Rutherford wasn't wearing uniform, but close to it: trousers and a jacket shiny at the elbows. Older. Broader in the beam. Her skin was duller, but Alison's heart still leapt to see her. Found her wide-set blue eyes the same, the fringe unchanged, the strong nose. Sad. Was that beauty? To Esme it had been. She sat down at the desk, then stood up again, her hands – bare of rings, Alison noticed, but perhaps that was just because she was at work – on the table. She came around it and sat next to Alison: she smelled of hospitals, some kind of antiseptic.

'I'd have recognised you,' she said, and frowned. 'Even with that hair.' She put a hand to her own, and Alison saw the grey in it. 'I'm sorry I wasn't here.'

'Where were you?' said Alison, thinking even as she said it that Sarah Rutherford probably wouldn't be able to tell her.

But she did. She sighed. 'Pile-up,' she said, and Alison had a picture in her head of debris spread, bodies covered up on a roadside verge and this woman kneeling to look at them carefully, respectfully. She probably had to wash her hands in that hospital spirit after. 'Kids chucking breeze blocks off the motorway bridge.' And without missing a beat. 'What are you doing here?'

Alison took a deep breath. 'There's things I need to know,' she said.

Chapter Thirteen

Alison didn't go straight back to the hotel. Instead, she drove out down the single-track road along the spit and parked.

Close to, the church seemed somehow even smaller in its modest churchyard, a single yew at the gate, tiny against all the wide silver-grey of the sea as the land fell away to either side. The roof was low almost to the long grass of the grave-yard. Far out in the estuary she saw the distinctive shape of a big barge moving stealthily across the horizon under sail, a peaked dark-red quadrilateral with chalked letters on it. They would be gathering for the race.

She'd dreamed once of funerals in this church, of all the bodies in their coffins here, side by side in the nave. It was so narrow they'd been pressed together like sardines. The twins' coffins had been white and tiny and heaped with flowers. It hadn't been like that in real life.

The police had released the bodies more than a year after, in October. In real life Polly had pared the funeral down almost to nothing. There was no money, apart from anything else, no money for handwoven willow or flowers. Fifteen-year-old

Alison had stared and stared and stared at the shiny yellow wooden boxes as the crematorium's minister read some psalm or other. Inside there. Inside there was something that had been deep-chilled for more than a year, cut and folded back then sewn together again, blood and brains and organs. Matter.

She had no idea what had happened to the ashes. They were gone.

A woman emerged from the church, an old woman, hunched over an armful of vegetation, trailing stuff and spikes of browning flowers that shed petals as she walked painfully slowly towards a smouldering heap up against the church wall. Her hair was chopped thick grey and despite the warmth she wore a man's sweater, down almost to her skirted knees.

Alison took her mother's scarf from her pocket and held it up to her face, to stifle the catch in her throat. She breathed, eyes closed, she searched it for her mother's smell, but there was only her own soap, her own hair.

Look, Sarah Rutherford had said, sitting, looking earnestly into her face, a hand creeping towards Alison's across the table but stopping short. *I don't want you to think . . . to have any sort of false hope. He did it. I'm afraid there's no doubt that he did it.*

Alison stared back at her, mulish as a teenager, saying nothing. She pulled her hands off the table and stayed stubbornly silent as to what she knew. That the dark predatory something she'd hidden from that cold midsummer night was still there. And that they were. *The glasses*. She might tell. But not now.

Sarah Rutherford tried again. 'I want to help you.' She glanced around, her eyes flickered up at the window glass above them. When she spoke again her voice was uneasy, defensive. 'I can help you, up to a point,' she said, clearing her throat. 'That is, I can give you access to those files that relate directly to you. But I have the right to refuse you access to those if I believe they might prejudice any future investigation.'

Alert, Alison sat up straighter. 'I see,' she said slowly. The purpose she'd so long suspected, those days in the immediate aftermath, this woman asking her quiet questions in the foster family's sitting room, grew solid. 'So you did investigate me?'

Rutherford's face was a weary blank now, a policewoman's face that gave nothing away. 'Esme,' she began, but Alison jerked forward on the chair, she suddenly wanted to throw up.

'No,' she said, choked. 'I'm called Alison now.'

She sat in the car in the lee of the church's wall and thought of Sarah Rutherford with longing. She had passed a field with the gate open where gravel had been laid down and registered that the Carters were making arrangements for their guests' cars with their farming neighbour.

'Him he got the gun off,' she'd said to Sarah Rutherford. 'The farmer.' Not caring about her grammar: she sounded like the child she'd been, back then. 'My dad showed him the rats.'

The policewoman had shaken her head, looking at Alison from under her fringe, unblinking blue eyes. 'He cried,' she said. 'The farmer. Old Jackson. He said, he should never have given your dad the gun, he knew there was something wrong about it. Only he felt sorry for him. He said, you know when someone just wants to end it. He said he thought he was helping him.'

'He gave my dad the gun to kill himself with? He knew?' She couldn't even picture the man, and he'd cried for her dad.

'He said, it never occurred to him your father could do what he did.' The policewoman looked into Alison's face. 'It's a human instinct, not to believe a man could kill his own children. But it happens.' She leaned in, the hair swinging. 'It's difficult to kill yourself with a shotgun,' she said gently. 'It requires determination. He had to get both hands on the trigger to hold the barrel in place.' She put her own hands out to Alison across the table, and Alison pulled hers back again.

'Does anyone know you're here?' There'd been a warning in Sarah Rutherford's voice then. Alison had stared her out.

'No,' she said. 'No one knows. I haven't . . . no one knows me any more.' Closing her eyes a moment before making to stand up and push past the policewoman. But Rutherford had put out a hand to stay her.

'I wouldn't count on it,' she said, and she made sure Alison looked back. 'You need to be careful.'

If you're so sure, she wanted to hold her fast and say, if you're so sure it was my father, why do I need to be careful?

'Alison.' Sarah Rutherford softened. 'I'm sorry. Look. I'll do what I can – I mean it. But it's thirteen years. D'you think we'd have let it go, if we thought there was any doubt?' She waited: Alison said nothing. 'And you've sprung it on me. Come back tomorrow, all right? I'd like to help. I mean it.'

'I want the pictures,' blurted Alison then, and as Detective Sergeant Sarah Rutherford opened her mouth to protest she added, 'I don't care if it's protocol, or whatever. I don't care if it's allowed. I want to see the pictures. The crime scene.'

Because I can't remember, because I need to remember.

Because they'll tell me if there's something still out there.

BOOM.

Behind her glasses Alison formed a smile at the old woman, who stood there weathered and impassive, her arm still thrown up against the sun. Then she turned to walk back inside the church. Relieved of her burden of stalks and branches, she wasn't as old as Alison had first thought. And – though Alison couldn't have said if it was the shape of her man's sweater or the eyes, slanted like a Laplander's, screwed up against the glare of the horizon – there was something about her that was familiar too.

She climbed back into the car and directed herself towards the hotel.

★　　★　　★

92

Stuart Jennings had come in behind her but Sarah Rutherford hadn't turned. She'd stood at the second-floor window, a finger to the dusty glass tracing the girl's route, out through the car park, across to the gates. She had watched as Esme Grace crossed the road without looking and climbed into the driver's seat of a small silver car. She had grown a foot taller, she'd learned to drive, she'd cut her hair.

Sarah Rutherford imagined her own daughter playing oblivious in the back garden, growing, growing. A plant growing towards the light, shedding whatever hurt her, moving on.

Briefly she closed her eyes to shut down the feeling that started up whenever, over the preceding thirteen years, she'd had cause to remember Esme Grace. Playing with a puzzle cube in the foster family's front room, head bent over it, tangled long hair that the foster mother confided she wouldn't let her touch. There was so much hidden inside Esme Grace, and they had never got to any of it.

When Sarah Rutherford had opened her eyes again the little silver car had gone. She had turned to Stuart Jennings.

'Not good,' she said. 'This is not good.'

'You don't have to wear it,' said Paul, pushing the package into her hands. 'But I thought . . . I just thought . . .'

Alison took it. It was soft and heavy: another present and she hadn't even worn the first one. He looked nervous and she made herself smile.

She'd got back to find Paul tidying his papers away, and his relief when he turned and saw her seemed disproportionate.

'I thought you might have done a bunk,' he said, putting his cheek against hers. 'I don't much fancy it myself, now.' She blinked at him. 'The drinks at The Laurels,' he clarified. She registered that there was a bottle of champagne in an ice bucket on the side table, a card dangling from its neck.

She set the package aside carefully. 'I'm fine with it,' she said. 'Morgan's marrying someone else, after all, isn't she?' He was frowning at the package and obediently she picked it up again.

'You got champagne,' she said as she pulled at the tissue. He turned and lifted the bottle dripping from the ice and with careful fingers peeled back the foil. 'Morgan sent it,' he said, then corrected himself. 'Morgan and Christian.'

Even before she held it up she could tell the dress was old: it was clean and pressed but the faint scent of years in drawers still lingered in its folds. The weight of it wasn't modern, rough crêpe under her fingertips, the shape of the shoulders. She held it up. An old-fashioned colour, cornflower blue, a line of buttons down the back.

'It's got the utility mark,' he said and when she looked puzzled, 'Made under wartime rationing.' He smiled, distant. 'Sorry,' he said. 'My specialist area. But it's pretty, isn't it?'

The cork popped.

'Yes,' she said, uneasy. 'It's lovely.' She heard him exhale.

'You see,' he said, frowning, uneasy. 'Morgan could never wear anything like that.' His hand ran delicately down the little buttons.

She looked at the dress. He was right: she imagined Morgan bursting out of it, all broad shoulders and hair, too strong, too tall, too modern, too healthy. She felt herself contract to fit it, old-fashioned and fragile.

'I was going to give it to you for the wedding,' Paul said. 'But then I thought maybe you'd want it for this evening.' He was looking at her with a kind of stern exasperation, and with a prickle at the back of her neck Alison suddenly wanted to be out from under his gaze.

'I'll just,' she said, 'I'll . . .' and she almost dodged past him into the bathroom and closed the door.

Inside she laid the dress carefully over the rail of fresh towels and looked at herself in the bright mirror: pale as a ghost, cropped hair. She looked like she might get blown away in a wind, or lost on the marsh among the tall silvery grasses. Wandering out there with the other ghosts. Alison looked at the glass of champagne in her hand and drank it, in one: she set it down and rubbed at her cheeks. She stripped off her practical clothes, jeans, T-shirt, socks, trainers, and her body emerged in the mirror. Perhaps it was the sudden lightness in her head but it seemed like someone else's. She saw how thin her arms had got. How?

And then for some reason the therapist came into her head, the woman she hadn't seen in six, seven years, with her anxious, flushed drinker's face. This was what the woman had wanted to protect her from, this moment under the bright light with the dead and the lost whispering at the door and demanding to get in. Ghosts.

Breathe. She tried to remember a single piece of the therapist's advice, a single strategy. She turned on the shower and climbed inside, letting the drumming of the water fill her head, willing the feel of it on her skin to block the prickle of panic. She stood under there a long time.

It was as she dried herself off that it came to Alison who the old woman bent over the compost heap at the church had been. Not old, not ancient after all, she must be more or less the same age as Alison's parents, in her fifties. As old as her mother would have been, had she lived. Her sons were at school with Alison and Joe, her three sons, Joe's friends. She had been the woman, already widowed, who'd opened the door to the milkman and been told that her youngest child was dead by the side of the road. His name had been Joshua, a beautiful boy, a boy you would stare at hoping not to be caught looking. Oh. A sound, a breath escaped her lips.

Cathy Watts. The name repeated itself, drifting like a floater before her eyes. She had never looked like this, old and bent;

95

she'd been a big woman, a matriarch, big forearms, unsmiling except at the corners of the deep-set blue eyes. Now she was hiding here among the gravestones, bent and shrunken, a servant of the church in one of her sons' sweaters.

Chapter Fourteen

There was a gust of laughter that brought the sweat out on the back of Alison's neck, and Roger Carter at the centre of it, his sandy head thrown back. 'I swear,' she heard. 'The constitution of an ox. The Watts woman keeps an eye out for him, God knows why. Last year they had to fish him out of the mud before the prizes. I don't know what he puts in that home brew but it hasn't killed him yet.'

They were talking about the barge match, the race still two days away. Wednesday now – Wednesday night, one day gone. Alison looked with longing towards release. Thursday to get through; Friday the race; Saturday the wedding; Sunday, they'd be back in London.

The party had been in full swing when they arrived, the house not a new-build after all, Alison registered, but only thirty or so years old, a big ugly solid building in unfaded brick, with an over-imposing porch and heavy lintels. Lucy Carter met them at the door with a glitter of excitement about her and a glass in her hand. The fragile, tentative woman they'd seen at the hotel had gone: elegant in high-heeled shoes she had paused dramatically to take Alison in, her sandals, the strong, old-fashioned colour, the scarf twisted in her cropped hair. Paul stepped back slightly, showing her.

'What a lovely—' Lucy Carter put her hand towards Alison's head. 'Lovely, is it a scarf?' Her smile glazing slightly.

Feeling suddenly self-conscious, Alison reached up and pulled it off. She must look mad. 'Thank you,' she said, and before she could stop herself, 'It was my mother's.' That was stupid. Dangerous. She didn't know why she had this urge to give herself away.

But Lucy Carter was holding out her arms for their coats, the glass in one hand tipping precariously. 'You go on, darling,' she said to Paul, 'you know where it is, don't you?' *Darling.*

There wasn't much doubt where the guests were gathered: a din of party noise came through a door beside the wide baronial stairway. A woman's loudly delighted laughter. Alison knew it would be Morgan and as she came through the door there she was, glowing and excitable at the centre of it all, looking over the heads at them. At Paul. Alison had a moment to take in the room, the big windows, antiques, flowers, a poorly executed amateur oil painting of Lucy Carter above the fireplace, hands in her lap, big-eyed. Roger Carter gesturing up at it with pride. Paul leaned down and whispered in her ear, 'Quite the Renaissance man, our Roger,' and she realised the doctor must have painted the hideous thing himself.

And then Morgan was raising her arms in greeting and pushing towards them. Alison's eye was caught by a man watching her passage through the big room: a pale, watchful face, light hair brushed back, in a city suit and tie. The husband-to-be, Christian: the man she'd seen with Morgan in the pub. Alison was diverted by Lucy Carter at her elbow, steering her into the room.

'You must meet, let me think . . .' and again she was absorbed by Alison's dress, putting out her hand to touch the fabric. 'Is it old?' Alison mumbled something, still uneasy. The dress made her feel like a doll dressed up, the colour attracting too much attention, the crêpe clinging. They had stopped beside a big bay with window seats and Lucy Carter sank on to a cushion. Awkwardly, Alison sat beside her. Through the window on a big lawn a marquee was being erected, three white walls up already, and a floor, and a stack of gold chairs. The garden was surrounded by dark trees and the grass was deep green in the midsummer twilight. Looking back into the room Alison saw that Morgan was talking to Paul beside another fireplace, leaning to look up into his face.

'You mustn't mind,' said Lucy Carter quickly. 'They're old friends.'

Alison just smiled. 'It's a lovely house,' she said politely, thinking actually how horrible it was. Lucy Carter didn't seem to hear. She lifted her glass to her lips, looked puzzled to see it already empty.

She waved across the room and a sullen-looking girl in a white apron began to make her way towards them with a tray. Lucy took two glasses and thrust one at Alison.

'How long have you lived here?' Alison asked, and it was at that moment that Roger Carter laughed, not far from where they sat, and his head turned to take them in. Lucy Carter carefully set her glass down.

'More than twenty years,' she said. 'Isn't that funny. Morgan was a little girl.' She gazed across at her daughter without noticeable affection. Alison saw Paul glance across at them, and he held up a finger to Morgan and leaned to say something.

Alison looked away, feeling something perverse stir inside her. 'It's one of those places, isn't it,' she said. 'In the pub last night someone was talking to Paul about . . . well, it was ages ago now, I suppose.' Lucy Carter's head turned slowly and her big luminous eyes rested on Alison, suddenly anxious. 'The killings,' said Alison.

99

'Oh, that,' Lucy Carter said, and her hands fidgeted in her lap. She reached for her glass again. 'The killings. It was a terrible time, awful, the reverberations in the village, it seemed to go on for ever. That poor family. Those children.' Her eyes brimmed. 'But really it's all forgotten now. So long ago, as you say.'

'What can you two be talking about?' Alison started at the voice at her shoulder. It was Paul, his grey-green eyes meeting hers, thoughtful, intent, moving from her face to her breasts in the dress and back up again. Lucy Carter gazed at him and he smiled.

'We were talking about the . . . the village's history,' said Alison. She felt the alcohol in her system making her reckless. 'About how terrible the murders were. How hard for a place to be known for . . . something like that.' She glanced to see Lucy Carter looking faintly confused, as if wondering that that had indeed been what she'd said.

Paul nodded. 'Well, certainly it doesn't seem to have gone away, to judge from the pub last night.'

Lucy Carter's face fell abruptly. 'Oh, dear,' she said. 'It's the last thing . . .' She became agitated. 'It's hardly what I want the wedding guests to be talking about. I really thought . . . who's bringing it up after all this time?'

Paul sat between them on the window seat. 'Lucy, don't worry,' he said gently. His face was concerned, his voice solicitous. 'It was only some old drunk, I don't know if I've ever seen him before.'

'Old drunk?'

And now it was Roger Carter, looming over them, affable. 'Darling,' he said. 'There's something going on in the kitchen.' And Lucy Carter fled.

On his feet, eye to eye with the doctor, Paul grimaced.

'Sorry, Roger,' he said. 'Said the wrong thing. Poor Lucy.'

Carter rolled his eyes, then smiled down at Alison without

seeing her. 'Never have daughters,' he said. 'Weddings are a bloody pain in the arse.' He looked back at Paul, who had held his hand out to her. She stood. Morgan was approaching.

'I suppose it's that old story rearing its ugly head again, is it? Well, no doubt it's all terribly interesting if you're into history.' With a dismissive look at Paul. 'But it's hardly breaking news, is it? Happens every day.' Morgan came up and threaded her arm inside her father's elbow proprietorially.

'It does seem to,' said Alison and both men looked at her. 'Women never seem to do it, do they?'

'Well, there was a suggestion in this case . . .' Carter tailed off. 'But no, you're right. A certain kind of man, anyway. Sadly, it is rather a familiar story.' He was pompous. Alison kept her face still.

'How d'you mean?' she said. She felt Paul close to her. Perhaps after all he knew her well enough by now to hear the danger in her voice.

'It was pretty much a classic case,' said Carter. 'The man's a failure, financially. He's a drunk. And she's . . . she's not interested in him any more.'

'Unfaithful,' said Morgan, looking at Paul over her glass.

Carter shrugged. 'Some people simply don't have the . . . what would you call it? The mental resources to deal with it.'

Unfaithful. Alison felt hatred surge and balloon inside her. 'Oh, unfaithful,' she said. 'Well, I suppose.' Carter looked down at her, patronising. She imagined him as a GP, this must simply be his bedside manner.

'Did you know the family?' she said, and felt Paul's hand tighten on her arm. 'Or are you just guessing?'

At last the doctor looked uncomfortable. 'Oh, well, I suppose, you're quite right. I didn't really know them, and one shouldn't, God knows.' He turned his head. 'Look,' he said, already moving off, 'I think I'm supposed to be making some sort of announcement.'

Mum, unfaithful. *BOOM*, went the flash in Alison's head. Dead on the floor in her best skirt. Two glasses on the draining board.

Roger Carter was already at his mantelpiece, holding up a glass and chiming it. Morgan stood tall and triumphant at his side, scanning her audience. Alison felt it move then, uncoiling inside her, the murderous flash of white rage. She knew she should never have come back.

Paul got her out in the end.

He stood at her side with his head raised, attentive to Roger Carter's hearty self-satisfaction and she thought, if he looked down at her, if he so much as shifted position it would be over, he would know, she would lose it. But he didn't move.

In the hotel room before they'd come Paul had asked her where she'd gone in the car, waiting till she had finished the first glass, and she'd felt her insides contract.

'Nowhere much,' she said, impossibly calm as adrenalin counteracted the alcohol. But suddenly so scared she couldn't stop herself holding out the glass for another. How weird was she being? It seemed to her as though it was written all over her face, but she had no way of telling. He watched. She drank.

But now in the Carter's sitting room Paul didn't look down. Slowly, slowly she felt herself subside, and when at last Morgan's gratitude and anecdotes and gay laughter stopped he leaned down and said, in a whisper, 'Thank Christ that's over. Let's get out of here.'

'I'll get the coats,' Alison had said, 'if you say goodbye.' But Lucy Carter had disappeared from the crowded room, and she didn't know where to find the coats without her. She retreated into the hall.

It was empty, but standing at the foot of the wide staircase with its mahogany banister Alison heard their hostess's voice, raised. She followed it to a kitchen and there she was, Lucy

Carter, her cheeks red under the room's bright lights. The girl in her apron was standing over a broken glass looking sulky. 'They're upstairs,' said Lucy, in response to her query, trying to convert her annoyance into a smile. 'On the bed. My bed.' Alison backed out again.

The upper floor of the house was warm and stuffy, carpeted and wallpapered with a gallery of doors but to Alison's relief the first room she looked into was the right one. A vast flounced bed, silver-framed photographs on a dressing table; this was what a happy marriage looked like. Alison couldn't wait to get out of there. Their coats weren't far from the top of the pile, she grabbed them, flying around the gallery and down the stairs. Paul was waiting for her at the bottom, with the tall pale man Morgan would be marrying.

'I said we'd give Christian a lift,' he said.

It had seemed like an eternity stuck in the baronial sitting room but when Alison got in the back and looked at her watch it wasn't even nine. As they drove back the high green hedges were just turning darker either side of them and in the front seat the men were talking, but she couldn't have said what about. She could see the back of Christian's head: she tried to remember his surname, something Germanic. His head was squareish, and he sat very upright. He and Morgan were getting married: the thought was suddenly awful to Alison. They'd met over a conference table, he'd said when Alison had asked when she'd found herself awkwardly, briefly alone with him in the Carter's sitting room, and he'd given her that underpowered smile. *Morgan refers to it as a merger. Do you see?* She'd had to turn away, at the awful metaphor. How could you ever know enough about another person? To shut yourself up with them. And then Paul turned his head a little to say something, she saw the line beside his mouth that had become familiar, the half smile and she thought, he's different, though.

As they came into the hotel behind the reception desk Jan

looked up from under the blond helmet of hair, alert with curiosity, with some piece of news, and on instinct Alison moved to block her.

With Paul at her back she crossed to the desk, looking in her bag. It had begun as a distraction but something was missing, something was wrong. 'I'll just go upstairs a minute,' she said over her shoulder to him. 'Will you get me a brandy?' Smiling to forestall any word from Jan until he was gone, out of earshot. Turning back she heard the swish of the bar door behind him. The manageress had a scrap of paper in her hand, holding it out, her expression turning slightly bewildered.

Nodding as if the message was exactly what she'd expected, thank you, taking the number Jan handed her, thrusting it casually into her pocket as if it could wait. But as she turned the corner of the big staircase and was out of sight of all of them, she ran.

Sitting in the hotel room with her hot cheek pressed against the big window and her bag in her lap Alison dialled the number, looking down into the lit circle of gravel where the cars were parked. She stared down at the contents – purse, bits of paper, old tampons – but it wasn't there, her scarf wasn't there, but she couldn't think for the phone's tinny ring in her ear. It'd be in the car.

The voice answered, the voice from long-ago, lower than before, rougher, but that old jeering familiarity. 'I knew it was you,' she said, then softly, '*Ez.*'

Coming back down later Alison had made herself yawn as she came into the bar and they'd both looked across at her. Christian had got to his feet, incorrigibly polite in a European sort of way, nodding. He had the very faintest accent. He was South African by birth but had lived everywhere: Switzerland since university, he had told her that in the car, apologetically.

She didn't sit down. 'I don't think I could eat anything after all those canapés,' she said, looking at the sandwiches that had just been set down on their table, and it seemed to her that Christian averted his eyes from her thin arms when she said it. She yawned again to stop the blush. 'I might just head up.'

Paul was up there before she'd removed the dress. He set both hands on her shoulders to keep her in place and then, once she was there, obediently still, he began meticulously to undo the tiny buttons, one by one. She could hear his breathing.

'It's from 1943,' was all he said, his breath on her neck. 'It has the clothing mark, clothes produced under rationing.' Carefully he hung it in the wardrobe. Turning, she saw what he wanted next. And then he turned off the light.

He had hurt her.

In the dark Alison explored the new sensations. The inner part of her thighs, her neck where he had tugged her head back, on the soft insides of her upper arms. She had been pulled apart. She had offered quiet determined resistance and he had exerted silent force. He had made her still, holding her down while he entered her with a blunt repetitiveness until he had pulled out and come on her, making a sound in his throat as he did. Only when he was off her and lying at her side did he touch her kindly: she'd let him stroke her. Patiently, he restored her. She didn't know if she'd wanted it; her body hummed and whispered to itself in the aftermath, still excited. Did you always know?

She didn't know how she would get away in the morning, but she would. She had to. A children's playground out along the spit, carved out of the marsh, she didn't remember it but she'd find it. 'Not too early,' she'd whispered into the phone. 'I'll need to . . . give me time to think of something.' She felt her body stiff with panic, her strategies and evasions deserting her, her lies looking ever balder, more obvious.

105

'Did you think I wouldn't recognise you?' The rough, sad, mocking voice. 'I'd know you anywhere.' She felt joy bubble up, even knowing it was wrong, that old perverse longing, trailing fear. My friend.

Gina.

She slept.

Chapter Fifteen

It was cool and grey in the early light and Sarah Rutherford, called from her bed at six, leaned across the steering wheel of the patrol car.

Thursday morning, and she thanked Christ for small mercies it wasn't race day yet, with all the idle gawpers that pulled in. Beyond them the ambulance was leaning alarmingly in the soft ground, but in the end it didn't look like them getting stuck in the mud would make a difference to the outcome. She gazed at the men in fluorescent jackets struggling knee-deep in mud to retrieve something past saving.

They'd got almost right to the scene, thanks to the shingle track Jennings of all people knew about. He spent his weekends walking here, he'd told her gloomily on the way, as Sarah drove too fast between the hedgerows in the thin dawn light. If she turned her head just a little she'd be able to see the skewed black roofline of the Grace house, a way back along the sea wall, but she didn't turn, she didn't need to. Creek House came to her in nightmares, it wasn't going anywhere. She could hear Jennings, outside the car and leaning on the roof muttering something into his walkie-talkie about timing, trying to chivvy a forensics team as he watched the paramedics grappling in the mud. Too late.

The body was hardly distinguishable from its churned element, a coated thing hauled from the slime, slipping in their arms, streaking and spattering them while they struggled to get a purchase. The mud was black underneath, and stank. Arms, legs, trousers all in a slick of grey, hair matted, a shoe clogged, an ankle exposed blue-white against the sludge as at last between them they got him on to a stretcher.

Out in the estuary two barges duelled on the horizon, while others gathered further off, smudges beyond the power station, jockeying already, a day ahead of the start of the race. The tide crept in.

The man in decorator's overalls Alison had glimpsed the day before was leaning over the desk in reception, his mop of hair dusty and stiff from behind and a paint-spattered bucket on the floor beside him.

'Eight hours, I heard, give or take. Plod pulled him out the mud out past Mulville's Hard. There's a police car out there now. They say the race'll go ahead tomorrow though.'

He spoke in a hoarse whisper to Jan behind the reception desk. She smiled stiffly over his shoulder at them and, nodding, Alison turned away, not wanting to be seen listening. And there was Paul, smiling down at her while the words echoed in her head. Police car? And as his smile persisted the question evaded her and the things Paul had done to her came back with a secret, fearful jolt, that hum setting up again like electricity in power lines. Her body loosened and aching at the joints, tenderised.

'I'm going for a walk,' she heard herself say. 'I thought out along the sea wall.'

His smile hovered. 'There's some good walking, I seem to

108

remember,' he said, and as if anticipating what she might feel thinking of him here with Morgan, his hand brushed hers, the touch of his forefinger on her wrist. 'I expect she's got some maps.' A nod towards Jan. 'Don't get lost, will you?'

'I'll ask her,' said Alison, placating him so he wouldn't see inside her head and know that she could have traced those paths blindfold.

Turning at the sound of her voice the decorator leaned and picked up his bucket of tools. She saw his eyebrows white with dust, his stubble, his shock of hair and then he was past her and walking out through the front door, a skinny, stooped figure, old before his time.

I know you.

Jan did have a map, a photocopy of a hand-drawn thing that Alison just accepted, hardly focusing. *I know you.* She turned away and Paul was still there, waiting, his hands in his pockets.

'Sure you'll be all right on your own?' he said lightly. She stood in front of him, awkward, her face tilted up, and he leaned and brushed her dry lips with his.

'I won't be long,' she said.

'And then there's the rehearsal. You don't need to come to that,' he said, and shifted, uneasy. She thanked Roger Carter in her head for his rudeness. 'Honestly.'

She nodded, hiding her relief. 'Whatever.'

The decorator's van was out there on the gravel and his name still on it: *Simon Chatwin.* Faded, the same lettering as he'd had thirteen years before. When he'd been brown from windsurfing, something otherworldly about him, something strange and beautiful about him. Simon. He'd tried to persuade Alison into the back of the van, once, after the kiss in the yard she'd glimpsed inside it, sacking laid down. She'd said no, but she'd lain awake wondering, for nights after. Lain awake thinking of the rough skin on his hands. She walked

109

on past and out into the road, the map she didn't need in her pocket.

The playground had been there all the time, snug behind the dyke on the power station side, instantly familiar. It had just been hiding from her, and when she pushed through the low gate she knew why. The twins: this had been their place, until the accident. The heavy wood and iron swingboats, ready to crack a child's skull, had gone. The girls had used to stand up on them, hanging crosswise as if in rigging, wild and hollering as they flew higher, but as Alison heard the creak of the playground gate something else came back to her. Here: something had begun here.

The lopsided roundabout had also gone, but she could still see it in her head. Letty on her side half under it, an awful sound catching in her throat. Mum had come running, fetched by Joe, Letty white with pain and not letting anyone touch her but the blood soaking her shirt where some broken-off cast-iron shaft under the thing had gouged her. Esme begging, Mads stiff and pale perched up on the roundabout, her eyes gone dark. The ambulance had arrived within minutes that had seemed hours with Mum's two hands like a vice round Letty's arm the whole time to stop the blood. That had been the start of a new phase, of hospital visits and doors closed on Esme and Joe.

There was a bright painted climbing frame, all curves, instead. The old slide was still there and on the bottom of it, knees together, feet apart, sat Gina hunched in a parka.

The wonky pushchair sat empty beside her. Her child – her daughter – was tangled in the climbing frame, hair hanging down. Thursday morning but Alison didn't need to wonder why she was there. Gina might even have had a child just to keep her off school, just to show them.

'You're back.' She was the same old Gina, just roughened

110

round the edges. Her lips looked bruised, high cheekbones under reddened skin, dark under the eyes. Heavier but careless of it; everything about the way she sat and her black gypsy stare said that she didn't give a fuck. She fished in the parka's pockets and pulled out a packet of cigarettes. She stuck one in her mouth then shook another out for Alison, lit them both without asking and Alison didn't say no. It had been thirteen years since she'd smoked and she felt it hit the back of her throat. The child was perched right way up in the climbing frame now and still, watching them.

'I had to,' said Alison, suddenly helpless to explain it. 'The wedding.'

The cigarette hung in mid-air halfway to Gina's mouth. 'The wedding?' Scornful. 'Not her? Not that Morgan Carter bitch? You didn't come to *my* wedding.' And laughed suddenly, a machine-gun rattle. She took a drag and with her eyes screwed up against the smoke said, 'You never even knew her.'

'*Did* you get married?'

Gina shook her head, blew out a plume, eyes flicking over to the girl. 'What do you think?' she said. 'Not the marrying kind, am I?'

'It wasn't me she invited,' said Alison, pleading. 'They don't know. It was him. My . . . my boyfriend. Paul. No one knows I'm here.'

'Oh, no,' said Gina, her voice rich with scorn, 'sure they don't.' Tilted her head to look round the smoke. 'Boyfriend?'

'What do you mean?' Alison said, trying to catch her breath, sidestepping the idea of Paul. 'You didn't tell anyone? How did you find out where we were staying?'

Gina looked at her, expressionless. 'Only one place to stay,' she said, 'in this poxy little dump.' Alison gazed, waiting. 'I don't tell,' Gina went on, with grudging pity. 'I tell no one, I don't say nothing. You know that. You know me.' On the climbing frame the girl was threading her way down, hair swinging. Her mother's long legs.

'The police,' said Alison. 'After. After.' She searched her brain for words but she was dumb. Gina leaned in, their faces very close, smoke on her breath, the sore-looking cheeks Alison suddenly wanted to touch, to kiss.

'I don't tell,' Gina repeated, and she jerked back, flicked the cigarette away. Her eyes were flat now. 'You stupid or something? Me, tell that one?' She meant Detective Sergeant Sarah Rutherford.

'She's all right,' said Alison. Gina didn't seem to hear. 'Tell her what, anyway?' she said. 'That we was doing mushrooms, that night? And where would that have landed me?'

Alison stared, thirteen years of trying not to wonder, and in a blink the panic rushed back in, the hairs on her neck stood up. 'We . . . I didn't know,' she said, her lips numb. 'I was up in my room and I was feeling so . . . so . . . messed up. My head was all over the place. I . . .' That sensation, of being out of control, sitting up there and listening to sounds that didn't make sense and having no idea what would happen if she stepped out of her room, flooded back in an instant. The chunk and clatter of a gun being re-loaded.

Gina stared back, eyes narrowed, realisation dawning. 'Christ,' she said, disgusted. 'It's not like you took anything. You didn't swallow enough to get a cat going.' Shook her head wonderingly. 'You never,' she said. 'You never thought you was high?'

'We didn't know, did we?' said Alison, feeling a sob in her throat. 'Not then. Not even you knew how much you needed, to get out of it. I didn't know.' Gina's arm went out and was round her shoulders and suddenly, roughly, she tugged Alison to her, Alison's face burying in the parka hood.

'Fuck,' said Gina, reverently, somewhere above her. 'You were up there, though. All the time he was doing it. That true?'

112

Alison nodded into the soft acrylic fur that smelled of her hair. 'I don't know, though,' she said.

'Don't know what?' She felt Gina go still, waiting.

'I don't know if he did do it,' Alison said, muffled.

And then abruptly she was pushed away, back into the air. 'You what?' Gina's face was suddenly changed, alert. 'You *are* joking?'

'Joking?' She repeated the word in wonder. Gina grimaced impatiently. 'I didn't see him do it,' said Alison, and it was an effort not to close her eyes to blot out what she did see. 'I heard . . . I don't know what I heard. His glasses. I found them in the yard. There was . . .' She felt herself begin to tremble: subdued it. 'My mum.' *Unfaithful.*

She started again. 'I don't know how to explain it. She was in the kitchen wearing her best skirt. I think . . . I think . . .' Gina had both hands on her shoulders now, her face rough.

'What?' said Gina. 'You better be sure. Because if it wasn't him . . . fuck. Why did you come back?' Her voice was strained with fear. 'Why?'

And finally it was out, like something that had been choking her. Alison said, 'I think there was someone else there.' She stood abruptly, looking out over the marsh. She saw the white and fluorescent shape of a car over to the north beyond the crooked house. Mulville's Hard, the name came back to her from long ago – and then again, from this morning. Simon Chatwin had been talking about the police at Mulville's Hard. Eight hours, give or take, he'd said, and understanding began to tick down. Something had been there eight hours, waiting for the police to find it.

But Gina was turning away, looking away, and the child stood in front of them, solemn, brushing the hair from her face.

Narrow little face, something strange and beautiful, something different, the barest hint of Gina in the set of her mouth, otherwise she was all her father's.

113

'She's . . .' Alison looked from the girl to Gina and back. 'She's his.' The girl whirled and was gone. 'She's Simon's.'

For a moment her face seemed to close against Alison, boarded like the house, swept blank as the marsh. *Get out*, it said. *Stay out.*

'She's *mine*,' said Gina.

The night, that last night of her old life had started so well: midsummer and the bright day lingered on and on, a day that would never end. A cool grey-blue evening, the tide still high and bringing with it the glitter of the open sea; it was lapping under the sea wall as she left the house, a sound like a whisper, like a kiss. Esme rode at breakneck speed up the bumpy path to Gina's house, her mouth smiling wide with joy and a secret bubble of it in her chest.

She had no lights for the bike, but it was midsummer and here on the edge of the world it never got dark. She rode through the village in triumph. *She had been kissed.* Behind her, home dwindled. Dad at the pub, Mum in the kitchen, only shrugging, nothing new. Esme stood up on the pedals, her hair blowing back, and she flew.

It wasn't that it was Simon she wanted. She tried to say that to Gina, but it seemed to make it worse. She looked for him as she flew: a man stood on a street corner, not him, but his head turned to watch her go.

The high street was quiet, the long twilight subdued every-thing to shadows and murmured voices in back gardens, but as Esme came round the bus shelter she saw them there, inside. The brothers. Sobered, she sat back down in the saddle, freewheeling past, turning her head. Danny and Martin Watts. The younger boy, Danny, tough and golden and beautiful, was standing stiff and upright with an arm around his taller

114

brother. Martin the older one, his face roughened already with misery and weather, head bent and shaking from side to side. Danny stared back at her as she passed, over his brother's shoulder.

It had been more than six months since their little brother Joshua died. Martin was the oldest by three years but it had been him that had lost it at the funeral, standing up jerky and ranting in the pew in the middle of the first reading. Yelling about murder. Joe had been there, as the friend of Joshua and Danny both, but he'd said nothing when he got home red-eyed, only pounded upstairs and banged his bedroom door. Mum looking stricken in the kitchen all day. Esme had wanted to go to the funeral but Mum had said no. *They don't want a mob there*, and Dad for once had backed her up. Esme had overheard an old woman talking about it in the shop as she lurked by the biscuits, weeks later: *They say Cathy Watts's older one's on sleeping pills and all sorts.*

And there was something in the sag of his shoulders as she went by, something in Danny's warning look that said Martin wasn't right, he might never be right. Danny had a place at university already sorted, he could go, he could fly. *It's OK*, she wanted to say as she freewheeled past, *you can fly, like me*, only there was his brother's head on his shoulder.

Gina's house was silent and dark but she was there all right, smoking in the back garden among the weeds, sat up against the broken fence flicking ash into a shard of flowerpot. There was an alley that led to the back gardens and a field beyond it that sloped down to the estuary, because everywhere did in Saltleigh: all roads led to the water. The village was on a muddy peninsula that narrowed to the church on its spit, the sea wall snaking off to either side, advancing and retreating according to mysterious laws, around the ruins of farmsteads, the fossilised stumps of Saxon villages. Gina looked up at the sound of the gate, her face smooth and abstracted and peaceful

115

for once and Esme sniffed the heavy-scented smoke, as telltale as Gina's expression. Gina held up the joint and Esme took it from her.

They headed upstairs to her bedroom, Esme shouldering her little backpack that held pyjamas and make-up bag and hair straighteners. Because she didn't forget the straighteners, she could never have. Gina with her thick stiff crazy hair had an obsession with them, along with a boy she wouldn't name to Esme. She would only scowl when Esme tried to worm it out of her.

Light-headed from the smoke Esme dropped her bag and subsided on to Gina's unmade bed. It smelled of him, she realised, or he smelled of it, Simon's hair, his neck where he'd held her against him. Dope. She should have thought then, perhaps, that it might be from him that Gina got the stuff. And the mushrooms she held out reverently once she'd parked herself at Esme's side on the bed, folded in a Kleenex, grey and dusty and dull-looking.

'I've made them into tea,' said Gina, reaching for a flask and unscrewing it: an odd smell was released, of dead leaves and earth. 'Show us, then. You bring them straighteners? You did, didn't you?'

And Esme had shaken her head in a sudden access of mischief she'd never have dared without the dope scorching her insides. 'Maybe I forgot,' she said. 'You guess something first. You guess.'

'Guess what?' Gina angrily pushing the hair back from her face, a warning sign.

'Guess who.'

And that was when it began to go wrong.

Esme never told, she never knew what Detective Sergeant Sarah Rutherford had said to Gina or learned from her. She'd stuck to it being the straighteners because anything else would have tied her into knots, trying not to mention the dope, the slopping tea Gina had pushed into her hand with a fierce jeer,

116

the way her friend had finally flared up, her face burning, *No you never, you stupid, you stupid little . . .*

So it must have been Simon Gina was after, all those years ago. Simon had been her secret.

And what difference, anyway, did it make? Because what Sarah Rutherford really wanted to know was not why she'd come home but who knew. Who knew she was supposed to be at Gina's that night, and who knew she had come back home? Did she see anyone, did she tell anyone, would anyone have heard them argue, or seen her fly out again, rattling down the cool blue high street on her bicycle with her backpack hanging from the handlebars, in too much of a blind hurry even to put her arms through the straps?

Martin Watts had gone to bed early that night, he'd taken sleeping tablets. Danny had said so when he'd given evidence at the coroner's inquest, called because he'd gone to the police with his mother to say he'd heard shots across the marsh. Their house was behind the boatyard and sound carried across the water in odd echoes and eddies – sometimes you could hear laughter from as far as Power Station Beach. Danny hadn't looked at Esme from the wooden witness box as he told them, but she'd looked at him. It was Power Station Beach she thought of, her and Joe and the Wattses the summer before and Esme hiding in the marram grass, realising as they wrangled that something had changed, she was too big, too grown to be one of the boys any more. And Joe was made uncomfortable by her being along. In the courtroom she'd seen that Danny had always looked a lot like his little brother, she just hadn't seen it before.

Who knew she'd come home? She'd just shaken her head to Sarah Rutherford, no one. Danny and Martin had seen her head up the high street to Gina's but they hadn't been there when she'd flown back down it, burning, shame burning her from the inside, her hair on end.

117

Later, that ride came back to her at odd moments, in waking dreams and nightmares, the downward ride through the village with its shadows and whispering, out along the path towards the crooked house. Plunging into darkness, her last ride home.

Chapter Sixteen

There was a smell of pub lunch when she walked back into the hotel after midday. In their room Paul rose quickly from the little writing table where he'd been working: he seemed surprised to see her back, as if he'd forgotten he wasn't on his own. He could live without her. But then he stretched and held out his arms and she entered them, grateful he couldn't see her expression.

Had she imagined that look on Gina's face? It had gone almost as soon as it appeared. She had only shrugged, while Alison calculated. The child was eight, nine; Gina must have had her at seventeen.

'It never lasted with Simon,' she said. Then added, 'Thank Christ. I don't know what I thought I was up to.' The girl had run off again. 'She's called May. Month she was born, I couldn't think of anything else but it stuck. May.' She stared away, the child dancing against the sky reflected in her eyes.

'So we fell out over nothing,' Alison said, 'if you never wanted him that badly.'

Gina looked at her, thoughtful. 'You could say that,' she said.

'If it hadn't all gone tits up that night we'd probably have been all right. You mightn't ever have got out of here. Think of that. Out of this dump.'

'You still at your dad's?' asked Alison then, and Gina stared at her a moment before shaking her head.

'Council give us a place on Western Avenue,' she said. 'Two beds, new kitchen an' all.' Contemptuous of anyone for being such a soft touch as to house a wildcat and her kid. Same old Gina.

'That's where the baby died,' said Alison, automatically.

Gina's head swivelled. 'You remember that?' she said warily. 'The fire?'

Alison nodded. 'It was in the paper,' she said. 'It made Mum cry.' Her memory stirred, like dust rising. It had made her father cry too, she remembered now, big gulping sobs at the kitchen table. Drunk crying didn't count. 'What happened to them?'

'The father topped himself,' Gina said shortly, fumbling in her pocket for the fag packet again. 'You don't remember that? Week before your dad . . . before. Frank Marshall. He'd done the rewiring himself to save money – they weren't council, see. It was electrical.' She squinted around the cigarette. 'She's still around, somewhere.'

Gina didn't hug her when she went, the arms round her shoulders had been a one-off. She'd never been one for soft-ness, not like that, she'd always been more of a puncher and a shover for showing affection. When Alison turned at the playground gate she saw Gina standing beside her child, looking down into her face. She couldn't see Gina's expression but May was rapt, searching.

Walking back she'd looked in her bag for the scarf again, but it really wasn't there. It nagged at her, knocking her off course. It would turn up. She wished she felt safe without it, but she didn't.

120

She looked up into Paul's face now. 'Lunch?' he said, wary. 'Or are you running off again?'

On the stairs she asked him, but he hadn't seen her scarf. They sat in the hotel bar and ate something deep-fried beside a window that looked into the garden, and talked about Paul's morning. A breakthrough in his research, apparently. He ate quickly as he described it to her, fired up. He'd uncovered a witness statement to a massacre in Northern France in 1944 that no one had seen before. Once or twice, watching his face lit up, last night came back to her, the distinct memory that he had wanted to hurt her and that she had colluded, but he showed no sign. Was that how it worked? Their secret violent life, under the civilised meals and books and quiet conversation. It sat inside her, mysterious, wrong, fascinating. She allowed a knot of resistance to form against it. No.

Alison worked her way through the food; it took about half a plateful before she remembered the fried clusters were fish. She made herself taste the stuff, made herself enjoy it. Salty, greasy, delicious. She kept an eye on the grass through the window in case Simon Chatwin walked past again, but he didn't appear. The thought of him turned her stomach, she didn't know why, but at least she could be fairly sure he hadn't recognised her.

'Does he see her?' she'd asked Gina. 'Does Simon see his daughter?'

A quick shake of the head and Gina had looked away. 'Not him. He's on a lot of medication.' Hunched on the slide. 'Prozac, that sort of shit.' A quick glance at Alison. 'He went off the rails. Too much dope. Or something.'

She would need the car again, she realised, as she forked the scampi into her mouth, calculating how she might put that to Paul.

'You wolfed that,' he said, amused, pushing his plate away. A pause. 'Not pregnant?' Smiling.

'What?' Mouth full, Alison laid her fork down, swallowed. 'What kind of a question is that? Of course I'm not pregnant.' They had never had a contraception conversation: she took care of it and she assumed he had worked that out. She felt an odd shiver as she saw she should have wondered why he'd never felt the need to make sure.

Paul shrugged, unruffled. 'Something's different, though,' he said. 'Since we got here.'

Alison coloured. 'I'm fine,' she said. 'Sea air.'

He looked at her a moment then turned to signal to the girl behind the bar. 'So,' he said, turning back to Alison, 'you want the car this afternoon? While I'm at the rehearsal.' He grimaced. 'You can drop me at the church, if you like.' And then he smiled properly, the modest, determined smile that by now was familiar, the line appearing at the side of his mouth. He leaned in and kissed her, as the waitress appeared.

Chapter Seventeen

Alison felt like she was in the car with something dangerous, a bottle of poison or a snake. She held the big buff envelope in both hands, it smelled of offices, of institutions, nothing more sinister, but that was sinister enough. Her family, in a drawer in that place for thirteen years.

There had seemed to be a lot more going on today when she arrived at the police station. Two patrol cars were parked at the front and as she sat there wondering what to do next she became aware of the buzz and crackle of urgent communication. A series of uniformed officers went in and came out with purpose, like drones at a hive. She remembered the police car out on the marsh and it coiled in her gut. Just leave it, forget it. Go to the wedding, go back to London, forget it.

But instead she opened the door and got out, came round the police cars. As she approached the tinted reinforced glass of the station's door Detective Sergeant Sarah Rutherford was coming out, her face clouded.

'No,' she said, when she saw Alison's face. 'No, I—' and she stopped. The policeman Jennings stood beside her. His tie was straighter today but he looked older, weary and pouchy-eyed, and as his eyes met Alison's Rutherford turned between them, deflecting him.

'Ma'am . . .' he said, resisting, but Sarah Rutherford stood firm.

'You go on, get in,' she said to him, gesturing to the car. 'There's something I've forgotten. Five minutes.' And then she was shepherding Alison ahead of her, back inside.

Rutherford hesitated as they passed down a corridor. 'Wait here,' she said and disappeared through a door. When she came back she had the brown envelope in her hand, then they were back inside the room with the high window, and it was just the two of them, the door closed. They didn't sit.

'This isn't how it should work,' said Rutherford, her back against the door. 'You know that, don't you? You should have put in an official request. Perhaps you should have talked to a lawyer while you were at it.' A hand to her head. 'Perhaps I should.' Alison stood in front of her, dumb, staring at the envelope. 'I'm only doing it—' Rutherford broke off. 'Christ knows why I'm doing it. Because I remember you.' Roughly she thrust the envelope at Alison. 'You don't have to look at them, just because you've got them. Do you have someone – someone who can be with you?'

Alison nodded slowly, thinking, *No. Not in a million years.* 'Yes,' she managed, her voice rusty.

'Because there's something else you need to know,' Rutherford said.

Alison looked down at the envelope in her hands. 'My father,' she began, 'was he—'

But the woman interrupted her. 'Not him,' she said. 'Not about him. About the twins.'

Alison hugged the envelope to her chest. 'What,' she said. Not really asking, not wanting to know, suddenly. 'What.'

Now she sat there, in the car, watching the door to the police station. Rutherford had climbed into a waiting patrol car, not turning to acknowledge her but as the car moved away Alison saw Jennings' upturned face, curious, in the passenger seat. They were going back down to the village, to Mulville's Hard, where the body had been found.

'Do they know I'm here?' she'd asked Rutherford as they left the room with its high window. Under her breath. 'Who knows?'

In the empty corridor Rutherford had shot her a glance. 'I've told no one,' she said. 'But that doesn't mean no one knows.'

Now Alison laid the envelope against the steering wheel of Paul's neat little car, and put her hand inside.

It was nothing she hadn't seen before, that's what she'd said to Rutherford, but when the policewoman just shook her head they both knew, this could be worse. She was like a suicide bomber about to pull a cord, and the clean little space would turn to blood. She pulled out the first photograph, just halfway.

A fold of bloodstained nylon. A mouth half open, the gleam of baby teeth. An arm flung out, torn. Mads. There was a little sound in the car, a small soft catch, a groan: it came from her, it choked her.

The activity outside the police station had ceased. She looked from the photograph back to the dusty windows behind which Sarah Rutherford had told her what it was she needed to know. Rage rose in her. It roared.

They weren't his, you see. The twins weren't his.

And now she remembered, now what Rutherford had told her lined up with what she already knew, even though she hadn't known she knew it. They had come back from taking Letty to the hospital, white with exhaustion after the accident at the playground. Something to do with blood groups, nothing

125

to worry about, though you wouldn't have known it to look at their stricken faces. Genes were odd things – and twins were mutants, that was what Joe was always telling them, grinning cheerfully.

The girls had flopped on the sofa over each other like dogs, Letty's nose buried in Mads's armpit. Esme had chucked the sleeping bag over them and gone to stand in the hall, listening. She could see Dad's profile through the kitchen door, she could see him frowning as he made sense of it. Tried to. That had been early autumn, leaves turning. Letty bandaged up.

It was pretty straightforward, Rutherford said. Letty had needed a transfusion after the accident, they were short of blood in the hospital, tested everyone to see who would be a match. Letty's blood group was AO positive, which meant she couldn't be her father's daughter. There was the record then of an appointment, Mum and Dad together, and DNA testing. November.

Months before the shootings, Alison protested, but her brain galloped ahead. November. Why not then? Why wait eight, nine months?

Rutherford had only looked at her, sorrowful. 'Sometimes it's how it works,' she said. 'Your father was an educated man. He may have tried very hard to resist what he was feeling. Sometimes feelings accumulate.' Alison had stared, unable to deny it.

'You knew, then,' she said. All this time, strangers had known. Mads and Letty not her sisters. Half-sisters.

'We have the right to access medical records when someone is dead,' the policewoman had said, gently. 'Why would we tell you? It would only have hurt you.'

Hurt her.

Had Sarah Rutherford felt it, or seen it? Had her training taught her, or had her experience, to detect that thing that rose up inside Alison as she heard that her sisters had not been her sisters, not really? That one thing had tipped the next, on and on. That her mother had been fucking someone not her father. It was a force, an energy that was not containable, there was no place to put it, it would have to burst loose and lay waste to the room, the building. But it stayed inside, a *boom* that pushed at the walls of her body and turned back inwards.

Alison stood on the waterfront against the flaking weatherboarding of the chandlery, its window filled with coils of rope and weatherproof jackets. She'd parked the car at the other end of the quay; the envelope was beneath the passenger seat.

Across the marsh beyond the house now she could make out white tape that flickered in the wind as three, four figures in white boiler suits bent and straightened, came together and moved apart. There was a police van parked near the house. It was Stephen Bray who had died in the mud off Mulville's Hard last night. Sometime just before midnight.

Had Rutherford even meant to tell her? The policewoman had waited till the last moment they were alone together, the corridor in which they stood briefly empty. And then she'd said quickly, 'Do you remember a man called Stephen Bray?'

Why now? She'd seen that question in Rutherford's eyes, gleaming in the police station's striplighting. *You come back, and he dies.*

'I saw him,' Alison had said. 'I saw him in the pub the night we arrived. He didn't recognise me.' But she didn't know if that was true or not.

A movement distracted her: two men were hauling a dinghy down across the muddy shingle at the end of the road. She could hear the scrape. Out in the estuary two barges had come to anchor, the big black hulls jostling against each other, the dark sails gathered up on the forked masts.

'It wasn't the first time he'd been hauled out of the mud,' Rutherford had said, preoccupied – one eye on the envelope of photographs as if regretting handing them over already, another on the swing doors at the end of the corridor. 'Only this time he wasn't just drunk, he was dead.'

'Was it an accident?' Alison had thought of the old man's hand on Paul's arm in the bar. Of the crowded, magical interior of his boat. But the policewoman had only shaken her head.

'We don't know yet,' she said. 'He was an alcoholic. He was only still alive because people looked out for him. He had . . . difficulties. We don't know yet.'

The two men were almost at the water with their dinghy. They might be headed down the creek to see the barges gathering for tomorrow's race, but she found herself wondering, how far round, by boat, to where the body was found? As she watched, the smaller of the two gave it one last shove and followed it, vaulting around on one hand in one agile, practised move, the boat bobbing and settling. The bigger man waded stolidly into the water and the stern dipped as he climbed over the transom. She saw a heavy profile, puffy. The other sat back in the boat from stepping the mast, tangled hair falling away from his smooth brown face turned up to the sky, and she knew him, too. The last time she'd seen him had been thirteen years before, in a witness box. Danny Watts.

The other one, the one with the weathered, puffy face was his brother, Martin. It was Danny she couldn't take her eyes off.

A little peaked square sail flew up with a distant rattle and with magical swiftness the dinghy began to move, gliding across the tide towards the estuary and abruptly half hidden behind a spur of mud.

The little church sat there beyond the boat on the horizon:

it was six and the rehearsal would be finishing. She should go, she should talk to Paul and smile and be sociable. But the pictures lay under the passenger seat in the car. She had seen half of one photograph and no more. She was afraid. Alison turned away from the water and began to walk back towards the car. As she walked she took out her phone and dialled Polly.

'You knew,' she said, straight away, hardly able to breathe for getting the words out. 'You knew, didn't you? The twins.'

And Polly answered as if she'd been expecting the question for a long time. 'I've always known,' she said. 'Why do you think we stopped talking, your mother and I?' She sounded weary to the point of despair.

'Who was it?' said Alison, staring sightless through the window.

A sigh. 'I never knew his name,' said Polly. 'She wanted to move to get away from the whole business. I think he'd dropped her.' There was an intake of breath and when she spoke again there was a sharpness to her voice. 'You're not at home, are you? You're there.' Silence. 'Are you in Saltleigh?'

'This is home,' said Alison.

'It's not,' said Polly, hard as nails. 'It never was. You can't stay there. Get out of there.'

Alison ignored her. 'So Dad – Dad knew. About the twins.' She thought now of their light eyes and hair, their otherness. 'How could he not know?'

'He didn't know,' said Polly flatly. 'About the other man, about the twins. I told her she had to tell him but she wouldn't.' Her voice was savage. Alison realised that all this time, all these years, she'd thought it was her father Polly had fallen out with. 'Your mother was selfish.' Her voice was congested. 'There was a lot he just put up with.' A pause. 'Please,' she continued. 'Please. Go home. Go back to London, come back here. I'll . . . I'll tell you what I know.'

129

She sounded desperate. 'Is there any more?' Alison said, hearing how cold she sounded, feeling the temptation to soften and say, it's all right, it's all right. Would there be time for that? Not now. 'What else did he put up with?'

A silence. 'She'd stopped telling me anything.' A sigh. 'But the police said.' Polly stopped.

'Said what?'

'There were rumours. Another affair. In the village. A local man.'

The best skirt. Two glasses. Voices below in the yard.

'Alison?' She said nothing. 'Alison? Come home, please.'

Her mother's top drawer, with rolled underwear and things she hadn't wanted the children to find. Even as she'd headed unerringly for the same drawer in Paul's flat, she realised, Alison had had her mother's in mind. A tin with locks of their hair. A pack of pills whose purpose Esme had pondered, a circle with days marked on them. The scarf had been in there. Had Polly gone to the drawer and opened it or had the police already turned it out?

Alison stopped. She had arrived back at the car, it sat where she'd left it, under a low-hanging tree beside a patch of grass and the village hall. Only as she got closer she saw that parked behind it, nudged up too tight, was Simon Chatwin's van.

'Alison?' She hung up. Polly's voice echoed plaintive in her ears and she thought of Cornwall with a painful tug, the dripping hedgerows, the low-ceilinged, clean-swept cottage that had never felt like home but now, she saw, had been a safe place. Polly always there on guard. She circled the cars. The village hall was dark and its double doors padlocked, the grass glowed in the twilight. There was no one there. She got in and turned the key in the ignition. In the split second before the engine responded she already knew, the hair on the back of her neck told her.

The sound was wrong, the dying cough of a lost

connection. She turned the key again, but this time it was no more than a wheeze.

She heard a voice, muffled. She thought it said 'dead'. She turned and his face was in her window, his paint-spattered finger raised to tap.

It was Simon Chatwin.

Chapter Eighteen

'Your battery. It's dead.'

She was fairly sure Simon didn't recognise her: he showed no sign of it. His face was inches from hers as she rolled her window down but he seemed to have trouble with eye contact, blinking, turning his head from side to side. She remembered what Gina had said about medication.

'In town for the barge match?'

'A wedding,' she said, and Chatwin's blinking increased.

'I'll jump-start you,' he said. Abruptly his head was withdrawn.

She climbed out and he stepped back from her hurriedly, indicating the van. 'This is me,' he said, 'I've got leads.' He opened the rear doors and was inside before she could answer. She climbed back into Paul's car slowly, released the bonnet and stayed in the driver's seat in silence as he brought his van round to the front and took his time connecting the leads.

How could he not know her? It seemed impossible. But there was the medication. And he might have been the first man she'd kissed, but – and oddly she hadn't thought this before she came back – she would probably have been one of many to him. She felt nauseous.

His head emerged from around the bonnet, pale. 'I'll start up,' he called, staying back. 'Give it a minute then you try.'

It occurred to her as she looked at the rusted bonnet of his van that his would be the vehicle you'd expect to break down, not Paul's. Why would Paul's battery be flat? She turned the key, and to her disproportionate relief the engine fired.

Chatwin reappeared at the window, still standing back, as if it was he who didn't want to be recognised. 'Don't use it much?' he said. 'The car? Can happen.'

She nodded, feeling the comforting throb of the engine, readying herself to thank him, preparing for questions, introductions. But he was gone, the bonnet down, the door slammed and the van already in reverse.

The wedding rehearsal seemed to be winding down: voices echoed cheerfully off the little church's steeply pitched wood and plaster ceiling. Roger Carter was laughing again at the centre of the little knot of them at the font and Morgan, wearing a pale shining dress and taller than all the rest in her high heels, had a hand resting on her father's shoulder. Alison stood in the doorway.

The flowers were done. The tall blue spikes of delphiniums along the pews, electric in the dim plain church. Cathy Watts would have done them, that diminished figure all swathed in her son's sweater. There had been no sign of her when Alison pulled up at the church.

She had driven slowly back through the village, wanting to give the engine time to recharge the battery. She came past the row of houses where she'd seen Gina and slowed further. The row where Kyra Price had lived. Her mother had been called Susan: the name came to Alison as she lifted her foot

133

from the accelerator to give herself time to look. She willed the girl to have lived.

A small white car was parked outside the house. Peering, slowed almost to a stop, Alison saw boxes on the car's back seat and then the house's door opened. A woman in a nurse's tunic, black tights in the heat, was coming through the door. She carried a bag, strapped in dayglo nylon – but Alison had to get her eyes back on the road.

Safely beyond the parked cars she had glanced in the rear-view mirror and seen the district nurse straightening from depositing her bag and standing, looking in her direction. Alison had driven on.

She stood in the church doorway now, looking in, and wondered if Kyra Price could have been ill all this time. She had always thought with leukaemia – children anyway – either you died quickly or you survived. Kyra Price had had big dark eyes, she remembered that much about her, without hair and eyebrows they had seemed huge, that time Esme had seen her, climbing out of the taxi. She would have been eleven or twelve. Old enough to know what dying was.

She must have let in a draught because by the font Morgan in pale silk, mid-laugh, turned her head a little towards the door, and then they had all turned to look at her.

Paul started towards her straight away. His face bent to her neck he said softly, against her skin, 'We're going back to their place for dinner. I hope that's all right.'

There wasn't really an answer she could give. *No.* He raised his head, and she just smiled.

The Laurels' broad drive held three cars – a sleek, dark, over-powered one, a convertible and a jaunty yellow Italian number; of course they'd need one each, the Carters, she thought, and no trouble with their batteries – and two trucks, one belonging to a catering company, the other the marquee people. At the church Paul's car had started without a problem and she hadn't said anything to him about what had happened before, only holding her breath as he turned the key.

The Carters all seemed in a state of high excitement in the wake of the rehearsal, and the doctor was flushed with particular triumph, in spite of how much it was all supposed to be costing him. Alison noticed that in any situation he and Morgan gravitated towards each other, conspirators. Of all of them Christian was the calm one, remaining pale and faintly amused. To her surprise Alison found herself fascinated by him, the way his eyes rested cool and thoughtful on Morgan. There was a dining room and Lucy Carter led them to a big table with a high shine on it, laid very formally.

The dinner had obviously been part of the deal with the catering company because a waitress appeared and Lucy Carter sat down with them straight away, next to Paul. Morgan was on his other side. Alison was seated between Roger Carter and Christian. She couldn't imagine what she would say to them. She closed her eyes for an involuntary second as she sat, behind her eyelids seeing the tide coming in and the big boats gathering out in the estuary, the crooked house in the dark. When this was over she would never come back. She would never see any of it again.

Even before the first course – something mounded under cream sauce – was set down Roger Carter was talking about Stephen Bray, loudly, as if addressing all of them at once.

'Of course, he was an alcoholic, and he probably had un-diagnosed Asperger's. The Watts woman looked after him, but she didn't get any thanks for it.' He prodded his food. Alison looked down at the white thing on her plate: it was hard, under blue cheese sauce. She lifted her knife and fork but hesitated, without appetite.

'There seem to be plenty of alcoholics around here,' said Paul, and Morgan laughed, lifting her glass to her lips and

135

looking at him over it. Alison put a slice of the thing on her plate in her mouth. It was pear, hard and tasteless under the sauce: she wished she could spit it out.

'Was he your patient?' Christian's voice was mild and uninflected, but Carter looked up from his plate frowning.

'Not mine,' he said. 'You know the surgery's fifteen miles away, Christian. I wouldn't want this lot on my books.'

Lucy Carter was on her feet. 'There's something – I must just . . .' but she didn't finish her sentence. Creating a diversion, was Alison's impression. She disappeared towards the kitchen.

'Where was he found, exactly?' said Christian. He had pushed his plate away. Alison laid her fork down.

'Quite odd, that, actually,' said Carter, putting a big piece of pear into his mouth, chewing. 'Mulville's Hard's not on the way anywhere. Out past . . . well . . . out that way.' He gestured with his knife. He meant past the crooked house.

'How would he have got there?' Paul asked the question. He was eating with a fixed expression of distaste.

'He'd have walked, of course. Across the marsh, most probably.' Carter's plate was clean. 'From that old wreck he lives on. Lived on.'

'There's a footpath, too,' said Morgan, her eyes merry. 'From the village, the other way. Past the new houses.' Where Alison had run. 'Or along the sea wall. I mean, if we're talking murder.' They all looked at her and then the waitress was back, circling the table for the plates, disapproving. Lucy Carter came in behind her and sat back down.

'Murder?' she said, brightly.

'The old drunk,' said Morgan, rolling her eyes.

'He spoke to me in the pub,' said Paul thoughtfully. 'The night we got here.'

'You said,' said Carter. 'I don't suppose you got into a fight with him, did you?' And laughed, leaning back in his chair, looking for the next course. 'No, seriously. It's happened a dozen times before, Stephen Bray face down in the mud. No one's even slightly surprised.'

'What was he talking to you about?' said Morgan, leaning into Paul. Her nails were long and silvery on her glass, she glittered.

'Oh, guess,' said Paul, and he drained his glass. 'Ancient history. The murders, what else. It's a pity nothing else has happened since, couldn't you have given them a new scandal, Morgan?'

Alison watched Morgan. She leaned back in her chair, hard and beautiful in her shining silk. Christian was watching her, too. 'The murders didn't really surprise you either, did they, Daddy?' she said, and her father blinked, a little bleary suddenly, Alison saw.

'Well,' he said. 'What's the expression? A car crash. An accident waiting to happen. It didn't come out of the blue.'

And Alison thought of the kids throwing breeze blocks from the motorway bridge, of Sarah Rutherford clearing up the mess, and from there to the photographs still in their envelope under the car's passenger seat.

'I saw him getting into a fight outside the pub, though.' Morgan was almost gleeful. 'The man. John Grace.'

The waitress was back, with some chicken and pale potatoes. She began to move around the table.

Carter shifted in his chair, uneasy, but then Alison saw he couldn't resist. She hated him. 'Well that was a sad story,' he began, steepling his fingers, pompous. 'Young man, whose child died in a fire. They'd had some dealings, I believe. Grace had done some work on his house before the accident and the young man – Frank Marshall – decided he might have had something to do with the fire. They ended up rolling around in the mud one evening, both drunk, Marshall wanting to kill him, or vice versa, God knows.' Morgan had an expression of sleepy satisfaction as her father spoke.

137

'The young man had a criminal record,' added Carter, dismissively. 'Ended up killing himself, I believe.' He peered at his plate. 'Anyway, what's this?'

'Chicken Véronique,' said his wife, pale as the plate.

Alison thought of something. She needed to change the subject. 'That power station,' she said, and all at once everyone was looking at her. 'Does it still run? Is there a cancer risk?' Although Kyra Price was the only one she had ever known, she imagined others, hidden behind their front doors, in bed. Attended by the district nurse. 'Leukaemia?'

'They decommissioned it,' said Lucy Carter. 'Didn't they, darling?'

'They did do some kind of, ah, risk assessment,' said Carter, frowning at his wife. 'But they found no evidence of any effect at all, as a matter of fact. Did all sorts of tests. Analysed the oyster beds, even.' And laughed heartily. 'Heresy!'

'You didn't notice any . . . greater incidence? Among your patients?' Alison's voice was steady and quiet: they were all still looking at her, taking her for some green zealot, perhaps. She took a drink, to cover an inappropriate desire to laugh, or shout.

'I have cancer patients, of course,' he said, dismissive. 'In the usual proportions.'

'He's about to retire,' said Lucy Carter, bright-eyed.

Roger Carter chewed. 'This is good,' he said, unconvincingly. Alison watched him, saw him grow uneasy again under her gaze, but didn't drop it.

'I don't know what you're getting at, ah, Alison,' he said, irritable at last. 'But this is a perfectly normal village. A happy place.'

Clearing his throat, Christian raised his glass. 'A happy place,' he said, and one after the other they followed suit, sheepish, until it came to Morgan. She sounded jubilant.

'A happy place,' she said, and drank.

Chapter Nineteen

That night an ancient alarm sounded, an iron clapper mounted high somewhere and hammering so hard it rattled her teeth as she lay in bed.

Blindly she sat up in the dark, felt her head swim. Paul lay on the bed, just beginning to stir.

Lights went on outside and she groped for her glasses. What was she wearing? The dark-red silk thing. Beside her Paul flung out an arm and she started up.

When they had come up to bed the gun had been sitting there, wrapped in its dirty old serge on top of a shirt in his suitcase quite openly. More than openly, it was as if she was being shown it, because the suitcase was open on the bed.

'What's that?' she said, pointing, although she recognised it straight away. Her head was thick from the wine, and from the Carters' dining room.

Paul picked it up, weighing it, the cross-hatched grip sitting comfortably in his palm. 'This?' he asked.

She nodded, dumb.

He sighed. 'Oh, superstition,' he said, looking down. 'Lucky charm, or something. It was given to me by old Saunders.' It sat there, dangerous. She didn't like the idea of Paul being Saunders' friend, it ranged him against her, somehow, the world of men whose job is being clever. 'Second World War, used by the Germans in France.' He held it out. 'You want to hold it?' She'd stepped back so hurriedly she had to steady herself, and he set it down. He put a hand in the small of her back, pulling her to him, her hips squared below his.

'That dinner was an ordeal,' he said lightly. She felt him press against her. 'Christ. Poor woman.'

He meant Lucy.

Had any of them been sober by the time they were herded back into the Carters' big sitting room, with its baronial fireplace? Roger Carter had stood at the mantelpiece while Lucy pressed brandy on them.

Paul hadn't seemed drunk at all, even though she had tasted the alcohol on his mouth, later.

'Of course, women like that,' Lucy Carter had said, handing a glass to Christian, careless, the liquid slopping inside it. 'What do they expect? Basically just animals. Men, I mean. If you deceive men.' She was flushed, unable or unwilling to compose a full sentence. 'How do you think a man will behave? It's . . .' She stumbled over the word. 'Programming. Evolutionary.' Christian's expression was stony.

'Really, darling,' said Roger Carter, feebly. 'That's rather an old-fashioned view.'

The uncomfortable silence barely lasted a second, and then from her perch on the arm of a sofa, long legs extended in front of her, Morgan spoke.

'Alison.' Her voice was warm, golden. Alison held her breath. Morgan tilted her head and her hair swung. 'So. Where are you from, exactly?' Poised.

Alison felt Paul shift closer. Terror moved inside her. 'Alison's from Cornwall,' Paul said, before she could answer.

140

'Parents?' said Morgan, looking up at Alison. Her intentions seemed purely malicious and Alison felt panic spin, out of her grasp.

'My dad's dead,' she said, meeting Morgan's eye, trying to be methodical. Morgan tilted her head, waiting for elaboration. She's distracting them, her mother's pissed, she's embarrassed. She's being a lawyer, creating a diversion. 'Heart attack at the wheel,' Alison said. 'Car crash.'

Morgan didn't look embarrassed. Her smile was light, she was all glossy-haired composure. Alison made herself speak again.

'My mother's still down there.' Polly, nothing like a mother. *Sorry*, she said in her head. 'In Cornwall. I talked to her on the phone today.' She felt Paul stiffen, but he didn't turn to question her. Her brain scrambled its emergency responses, *what if, what if*.

What if it goes further? Paul will want to meet her.

'I swear I heard them, you know,' said Lucy Carter, unstoppable, holding a glass out to her. 'The shots, so loud.' Mechanically, Alison took the glass and Lucy threw up her hands, miming. 'Boom.'

There was an intake of breath from someone. Lucy looked around at her audience glassily. 'We were out on the patio, weren't we? Brandy on the terrace. It was such a cold night.' Vague, her eyes settled on Morgan, who looked up at the ceiling as though counting in her head. 'You remember, darling?' Her gaze shifted. 'Paul?'

'You were here when it happened?' said Alison quickly. Halfway through the sentence she heard her voice rise, trying to sound merely interested.

At her side Paul nodded, absently, watching Lucy. 'I don't remember hearing the shots,' he said, thoughtful.

Lucy looked back at Morgan. 'Not Daddy, of course.' At the word on his wife's lips, *Daddy*, Alison had to turn away. 'There was a baby somewhere with a cold or something, and the mother called in the middle of the night. I tried to put her off but Roger had to do his duty. Freezing. A freezing night for June. I went out on to the patio and I heard it.'

Alison thought, I'm going to have to do something. There was no route out of this that she could see. If they asked her one more question . . . In the darkness beyond the wide expanse of glass she saw the patio, the ghost-white shape of the half-erected marquee beyond it, and she imagined Lucy Carter standing there with her glass in her hand, listening.

Carter shook his head gently. 'It was Mrs Jonas,' he said. 'Actually the child had pneumonia, it turned out. So just as well.'

Morgan shifted. Now, thought Alison. Before she looks at me.

'Did they never suspect anyone else?' she said, and Morgan stilled. 'I mean, apart from the father?' Christian was looking at her too, his face weary at last. 'It seems to happen all the time.' In spite of herself, she pursued it. 'Fathers killing their children. It seems too easy. For the police, I mean.' Her lips felt numb. 'You hope they do their job properly.' And then she took a drink from the glass Lucy Carter had given her. 'That's all.'

Fire.

Did she smell smoke?

In the dark bedroom now, from below them in the hotel Alison heard thumping, voices. Already half out of bed, blindly she put out a hand to Paul. Someone rapped on their door and abruptly he was upright.

'It's the fire alarm,' she said, in the middle of the room.

'Christ,' he said, and was out of bed reaching for his clothes.

The corridor was bright, no smoke, but there was a whiff of something acrid on the air. Alison's feet were bare, she felt half naked in the slip, she should have stopped to put

142

something, anything, over the top but it was too late to go back now. Paul was ahead of her on the stairs. Below them she saw Jan in the hall, her stiff hair disordered from sleep, in a dressing gown and slippers. Holding open the door she turned to look up at them, her face crumpled with tiredness and temper. Feet stood on the gravel beyond her.

Behind her on the stairs someone cleared his throat. It was Christian, in dark pyjamas. She turned and saw him look down the dark silk that slid against her skin. He smiled, wearily knowing.

They'd given him a lift to the hotel when finally, just before midnight, their conversation had drawn to a close. She knew she should never have asked the question, not even to create a diversion. But once it was out there, she had wanted to know. To know the other side of Sarah Rutherford's carefully guarded responses.

Roger Carter had sighed. 'Well,' he said. 'It's a long time, now. They seemed to be talking to an awful lot of people.' Morgan moved to his side, setting her drink on the mantelpiece. She could be his young wife, a big handsome blond pair.

'Ghastly,' said Lucy Carter, sitting forward on the big plush sofa, her hands thin on her glass.

'The boy,' said Morgan, ignoring her.

'Boy?' Her father looked at her, bemused.

'Well, young man, maybe,' Morgan amplified. 'Bit older than me? The one who was found on the marsh almost frozen to death the next morning.'

Alison's heart thumped, fast and loud. What boy? she thought, and those two in their boat came to mind, heading out into the estuary. Brown-skinned Danny and his sad brother Martin.

'Oh, yes.' Carter looked thoughtful. 'Hypothermia, he did nearly die, yes, but it was nowhere near the Grace house. Accident-prone. Simon Chatwin.' He shook his head, glanced

143

back at Alison. 'The police spoke to him, I believe. They spoke to all sorts of people.'

It hit her like a thump between the shoulder blades. Accident-prone. Simon Chatwin's windsurfer drifting abandoned past the barge's bulk. Alison turned her face just slightly so Carter's look fell past her. She stared at the wall, at decanters on the sideboard, anywhere so as not to meet a human eye. She and Simon Chatwin had both been out on the cold marsh after the gunshots, separated by what distance? Chatwin lying unconscious. How? Why?

She said nothing: someone else would have to speak, she didn't trust herself even to look.

'It could have been him, though, couldn't it, Morgan?' Lucy Carter sat up, excitable. Her daughter regarded her levelly.

'Do you even know who we're talking about, Mother?' she said. 'As far as I remember Simon Chatwin barely has the energy to roll a cigarette. And what about your theories about husbands being animals?' Her mother subsided.

At the door, saying goodbye, Morgan had pressed her cheek against Alison's too long. 'Let's get together tomorrow,' she said. Alison had pulled back, dumbly. Paul's eyes on her.

'Sure,' she said. 'Lovely.'

'Just us girls,' said Morgan. 'I'll show you the dress.'

In the car Alison had held her breath, waiting for the ignition to fire. Paul was looking at her as he turned the key, he didn't know, of course, and Alison felt the questions start up again. Why had the battery been dead?

She didn't know enough about cars. Chatwin had an explanation, something about it having been sitting idle, but he'd been uncertain too, hadn't he? She thought of his dull eyes, the sandy stubble with grey in it, already. How old could he be? Once he'd been golden, once he'd leaned down to kiss her smelling of cigarettes, the sun shining in his eyes, his hands warm. Pity for him softened her.

144

The ignition fired, she breathed, and Paul reached for his seat belt. 'Morgan's lovely,' he said. 'Go tomorrow. Give her a chance.' Behind them Christian had looked out of the window.

'Of course,' she had said.

Fire.

As they came through the hotel's front door to join the others on the gravel, Alison groped to find Paul's hand. He looked down at her, amused. 'I *can* smell smoke,' she said.

'Cigarette smoke, maybe,' he said, but he squeezed her hand briefly. Alison raised her head to locate the smell. Something – a bonfire, someone's barbecue – but not a real fire. The hotel stood behind them, solid and empty and safe. In the small group of guests and staff Alison felt a movement, a head turning to watch her, and she looked away. Paul's little car was visible across the gravel in the dark.

They'd all fallen silent by the time they pulled in from the Carters' that evening and she'd let Paul and Christian climb out while she stayed sitting there, alone inside the car.

Not quite alone. The photographs had been there all along, beneath the passenger seat. Not for one moment since she had pulled that top print out and thrust it away again had she forgotten them; they lay like a stain, a shadow. Alison had leaned, fingers creeping between the footwell carpet and the seat, feeling for the envelope. There: the flap of paper.

'Darling?' Paul was back, his head inside. Turning to smile awkwardly over her shoulder she felt something else, a slippery fabric thing, pulled at it.

'My scarf,' she said, straightening. Frowning. There all the time, as if it had worked its way under the seat to wait until she needed it, the cover story for her hand reaching for the envelope. Gratefully, she held it to her cheek for a quick embarrassed second.

'Told you it'd turn up,' he said, and held out his hand.

They had said goodnight to Christian on the stairs and Alison had felt it start up then, the flutter of anticipation, or fear. But he had been gentle, this time. He had seemed tired, at first, folding the gun back up in its serge: she had waited. Before Paul had she been so acquiescent? She didn't think so. She had been the one impatient, the one to experiment, to insist. She had never wanted to submit, to surrender. He lulled her, he quieted her. She wanted to be quieted.

He'd laid her back on the bed, gently, and set to work, crouched over her. She remembered thinking, while she still had control, What do you want? – and then thinking, It doesn't matter. He'd gone on, stroking her, soothing her, until she forgot the gun wrapped in its dirty cloth, forgot Morgan, his mouth on her softest places until she came and then slid away from him, into the blissful deep, and slept. She didn't know what he did then, if he stayed awake, if he watched her.

A fire engine had arrived, blocking the drive with its bulk and three, four, five men climbed out and stood about. Cautiously Alison looked at their faces, and knew none of them. The first one took off his helmet, and Jan went over to them. Alison tiptoed, trying to hear. Jan pointed back towards the building and Alison heard 'Kitchen'. Jan and the lead fireman, his helmet still on, went inside.

It was five, ten long minutes later that they re-emerged. 'False alarm,' said Jan, to a ripple of tired assent from the staff. At the sound Alison quickly examined them. A thickset man she thought was the chef; the foreign waitress; a bony, pimpled boy, barely out of teenage years; a woman approaching middle-age. Their faces blank with sleeplessness. She slowed, looked closer – but Paul's hand was on her elbow. 'Back to bed,' he said. The older woman's tired face followed her, imprinted on her retina, a look she couldn't dodge.

On the stairs she detected something in him, impatience or

146

short temper, his head down as he climbed beside her. She should have slept, slept long, not waking until nine or ten, missing breakfast, she should have woken to find him smiling down at her. That was what should have happened, only now they were awake, examining each other in the weird early hours, under artificial light. Their sleep had been disrupted, that was all. She was safe. Safe with Paul.

Back in bed at last Alison dreamed of fire.

The ashes burn where they're buried, on Power Station Beach, and Esme hunkers down in the sharp sea grass in the lee of the dyke. The boys are talking at the water's edge, the tide is high and the wide expanse of mud is covered, the broken bottles and chunks of brick and rotted posts hidden under the surface. Behind her the power station hums.

The boys are there, Danny and Joshua and Joe, the brothers burned biscuit-brown and gold, their eyelashes white from days and days drifting out on some borrowed boat or other, following races or rowing up creeks, to lie on their backs on the bottom boards, under the sun. Joe is paler, Joe is skinny and awkward, Joe has passions he keeps secret: music and sunrises and who knows what else.

A disturbance, and Esme burrows further down, feeling the cool damp firm sand below the silky shifting stuff. Hide. Something is happening, more than just messing about, she can hear it, she can hear Joe's voice going up. She hears him shout words, angry words, and before she rolls away, to blot out what she hears, she sees Joe's fist, Danny grabbing him from behind after he makes contact. Joshua's cheek is bleeding, the trickle is black in the glow from the ashes.

Fire.

Someone else is there, in the dunes, a head rising behind the grass, gazing at Joe.

Why do they fight? In her dream Alison knows that Joshua will die and Joe won't be able to stop crying, but he'll never tell her.

Come back.

Chapter Twenty

Beyond the car's window the hotel rose grey and calm in the misty dawn, no sign of the disturbances of the night before. Only in Alison's body the panic still turned, the terror, her insides like iron.

She'd woken from the dream knowing with a sickening certainty that it was real; or worse, that it told her something but she didn't yet know what. Knowing that it had risen out of what had passed for conversation around the Carters' dinner table, the annihilation of her family picked over for entertainment. How could she have thought she could move through four, five days here unharmed? She'd started something and she had to go on with it.

She sat in the driver's seat with the envelope in her lap.

Had he really been asleep? It had been dawn, before five, when she'd sat up, a sour taste in her mouth. Paul lay on his side, turned away, his shoulder rising and falling evenly.

There had been someone, among that small crowd assembled for the fire drill. She knew that middle-aged woman with her battered, weary face, and that woman knew her.

The hotel had been silent in the dawn, deserted, all the doors closed as she passed along the corridor, down the wide staircase. Leaves unswept on the hall mat. They were all sleeping soundly after the alarm, and Paul among them. Why would he pretend?

Pausing a moment after coming around the bed she had scanned his face, seen his cheek pressed immobile against a hand, before picking the car key from the table, noiselessly. Bare feet on the carpet, the door eased closed.

In the driver's seat Alison pushed her glasses up her nose. The windows were filmed with moisture, she could escape attention in here for a second or two, if anyone came out. Was she hiding? Not exactly. But she had to bide her time before she climbed out of the car.

The woman had known her last night out on the gravel, but here people who recognised her could be everywhere. Someone in the pub, someone at the church, someone standing on the marsh early that first morning, someone who couldn't sleep, like her. Someone who'd watched her pressed with her back against the crooked house as though she was up a high building and might fall. *Take care*, Sarah Rutherford had said. In her lap the envelope of photographs. With a quick movement she pulled them all out, they spilled and slithered and she grabbed for them before they fell.

She stared.

Driving across the country thirteen years ago beside Aunt Polly, dozing on faceless motorways, waking from the blanket on the back seat to watch Stonehenge pass in the twilight, they had brought no pictures. There were no other photographs of Esme's family. She had never asked Polly if she had any: they had been hidden away, if they ever existed. These, then, were her family photographs. Longing and horror ballooned inside her, compressing her lungs. *Look.*

It's not possible. It's not bearable. She looked.

Mads's missing tooth. A small hand uncurled, the back of a head, hair sticky with blood. Letty. Alison felt her face move: I'm sorry. She didn't know if she said it out loud or not. She had held Letty, not looked at her, had held her hidden in the soaked fabric of the sleeping bag. And here was her face framed in a fold. Her sweet face, unmarked, eyes shut, heart-shaped, dead.

Joe on the sofa, leaning slightly, eyes open, the lower part of his face not recognisable as human but the headphones in position. They had cost a lot of money. He had saved for them himself from his job on a record stall at the market; they were very effective at blocking out noise. He must have known nothing. If he'd known, if he'd seen . . . In her head Alison saw him look up, she saw him start up from the sofa, she saw him struggle, she saw him kneel, she saw him weep. But there he still sat, only startled. She had to breathe. She squared the photographs and laid them on the seat beside her carefully. *There.*

Her mother lay face down on the kitchen floor in her flowered skirt, a broad spreading stain across her back and beneath her on the vinyl floor. Kate Grace, beautiful Kate Grace. Mum. Alison blinked, and breathed. She looked, tracing the photograph with her fingers. Things she had forgotten: the mug tree. The cupboards Dad had built, the stainless steel draining board. Two wineglasses, overturned, on their sides. They'd been drinking together? After he got back from the pub?

Esme lies on her bed and hears voices at the front door, this chill midsummer night. The door bangs again, a car starts up. There is a whispering in the yard. A crunch and scuffle.

There were the blue and white vinyl floor tiles Dad hated, yellowed and turning up at the edges. They couldn't afford to put a new floor down. And there was a shoe.

151

Alison lifted the photograph closer to her face. She had forgotten that. Her mother wearing those shoes, her only pair of heels, suede with scalloped edges across the instep. Mum kept them in their box in the back of the wardrobe and had got furious when she caught Mads clopping around in them one evening. One heeled shoe was on her foot, the other on its side on the floor, half under a cupboard where it must have slid. When she went down. Bare legs.

The sole of the shoe was dirty, marked. She had been in the yard. Had those hissed whispers Alison had heard through her bedroom window been a row? It wouldn't be the first time a row had been taken outside so the kids wouldn't see, only on this occasion it had come roaring back into the house like a forest fire.

Slowly Alison laid the photograph face up on the passenger seat, beside Joe and the twins, and looked down at the next one. Her father. But he was absent: there was an odd arrangement of red string and chalk marks on the hall carpet, there was the rug, stained and rucked. A bloody mark in the doorway to the living room.

Of course, he had not been dead. They didn't have the leisure to photograph him, they had to keep him alive until he was taken away in an ambulance. Was that it? Had someone worked on him, had they pumped his heart, resuscitated him, while Esme crouched in the mud, unable to move? She didn't know – they'd kept her away, in the passenger seat of a police car.

In the picture there was no broken glass on the hall carpet, no twisted metal. Might the police have taken the glasses away?

Joe had been the last to die, her mother had been the first, the inquest had found. Her father had been the last to be shot, and all while Esme lay on her bed with her hands over her ears. *BOOM*. Alison squeezed her eyes shut. In her head she saw a leg outstretched, mud and dust on his shoe, his shirt pulled out, blood . . . but nothing told her definitively what she wanted to know, the impression was of chaos. She tried to remember, until her head hurt.

Someone had wrapped her in a blanket and taken her away. Later, Sarah Rutherford had asked her where she had gone, which rooms she had entered, had asked her over and over and then she couldn't think. Now, she knew, she hadn't gone into the living room. She put her hand to the photograph, the bloody imprint in the doorway; she thought of the policemen moving between the rooms. Blood on their shoes?

There had been a raw mark on her father's neck. Had they seen that? They must have seen that.

She couldn't remember if he had glasses on. Did it make a difference? She closed her eyes and tried, she set herself back against the wall in her hall, she saw the hands reaching down the gun's stock, she saw his callused thumb. The blood. She saw no glasses, she saw no broken glass. She upended the envelope and a card slid out. DS Sarah Rutherford. A mobile number.

She took out her phone. Startled, she saw she'd missed a call, Kay had called, just after one in the morning. Her friend Kay who inhabited the other universe that was London, had phoned when Alison had been dead to the world.

Something began, it ticked down, something from last night. Paul putting her to sleep. A face in the dark that had made her think of that other fire, and her mother crying over the newspaper at the kitchen table.

It was six thirty, the phone said. Too early to call but she had no choice. How long till Paul woke? This car was the only private place she had.

That other universe was too distant and Alison dialled not Kay's but Gina's number, and waited. Beyond the misted car window a white shape drove in through the gate, the gravel crunched. Alison stayed very still, the phone ringing at her ear.

153

Hang up, hang up. Too late. She wedged the phone under her ear and in a panic stuffed the photographs back in the envelope, leaned down to put it back where she'd hidden it. She couldn't go back inside carrying it. What if— There was a click as someone picked up.

'What the *fuck*.' Gina sounded drugged.

'I'm sorry,' Alison muttered. The decorator's van had pulled up, on the far side of the drive, close to the hotel. He couldn't see her from the driver's seat, because she couldn't see him. No one got out.

Gina coughed painfully. 'What do you want?'

'The couple whose baby died in the fire,' said Alison, dogged. 'Did he have a fight with my dad?' There was a silence, that grew longer. 'The baby's father? What did his wife say to the police? After the . . . after the shootings. Did she talk to them?'

'Christ, how should I know?' said Gina. 'He was dead by then. The baby was dead. Why would it have anything to do with . . . with that? Just leave it.' There was a warning note in her voice.

'There's no one else to ask,' said Alison. With a finger she rubbed a window in the misted glass. The door of the decorator's van was still closed. 'Does he help you?' she said. 'Simon? Does he give you money?'

'I don't want his money,' said Gina flatly. 'He's a creep.'

Mads and Letty had had a biological father. From what Polly said, he knew they existed, at least. Mightn't he have come looking for them? There was a silence from Gina.

'Can I phone you later?' said Alison, pleading.

'Whatever,' said Gina, and she was gone. In the ringing silence Alison felt abruptly alone. Only she wasn't – there was the decorator's van.

Joe had hated her kissing Simon Chatwin. It had been Joshua that had told him. That was why the dream had seemed real – there *had* been a fight on the beach. They'd gone down

154

there for one of those barbecues to mark the tail end of the summer – she and Joe and Joshua and Danny, Martin too grown-up to come, who else? – only this time she should have stayed away, she wasn't a kid sister any more, she was something trickier. A fight between Joe and Joshua, and Danny had been trying to break it up, and she had burrowed down in the sand dunes so as not to hear, only she did hear. Joshua saying, in that voice, jeering, *Your sister.* Angry. *Your sister with her tongue down his throat.* The way they'd looked her over when she laid down her bike in the grass had been down to that.

Joshua must have been out on the marsh watching, out in his boat or messing about in the mud. He must have seen the decorator arrive, seen him lean down, his hand on the back of Esme's neck, seen her look up at him.

Shut up, shut up, Joe had said, his voice thick. *Don't say that.*

And for a moment Alison thought, was that him, then, watching me when I went back to the house, was it only yesterday? But of course it hadn't been Joshua yesterday, because he was dead. He'd been dead before Joe, before all of it. Dead by the side of the road on a November night, while Esme sat in front of the fire with the twins and Dad kept disappearing into the kitchen. Drinking standing up at the counter, down in one.

In the car's front seat she blinked through the glass, jolted back to the present as Simon Chatwin climbed out of his van and walked around to the back of the hotel. Hold on, she thought as she watched the set of his shoulders, saw his stiff hair that had been gold now streaked grey. Hold on. Her mother had worn those heels before.

Simon Chatwin had been in the yard more than once. The time he'd kissed her, what had he been doing there? She'd thought he'd come for her, she thought he must have seen her gaze at him as he sat on the shingle running a rag over

155

his windsurfer, he must have registered her hanging about outside the pub on warm Saturday evenings. Months before, though, before Esme had grown fascinated by him, when he'd been just some bloke, he'd been there. Hanging about in the yard as she came back from school, she'd pushed past him into the kitchen and there her mother had stood, tall and awkward in the high heels at the counter. Lipstick. Waiting for someone.

He was back, opening the rear of the van. He mustn't see her. The doors clanged shut again and he was walking with a ladder, slowly. He disappeared again around the hotel's veranda to the back. Taking her chance, Alison was out of the car and running across the gravel, swinging through the heavy door and past Jan looking up in surprise from the reception desk.

Upstairs, Paul was still asleep. As she set her mobile down quietly Alison saw that clutched with it in her hand was Detective Sergeant Sarah Rutherford's card.

Chapter Twenty-one

It hadn't exactly been a tactic, asking him to come for a walk with her. Coming back into the hotel room after breakfast that morning – Christian silent on another table over a sheaf of newspapers and a laptop, barely raising his head to acknowledge them – Paul had gone straight over to the little desk as if to get back down to work again himself. She saw him frown down at the words on top of the file. Alison wondered what he was thinking.

Didn't he even wonder what she got up to? Where she went, in his little car, to another world of police stations and ring roads, a world clogged and dirty as mud? When she made excuses, disappeared – this morning heading back upstairs from the dining room before they'd even sat down returning only as the full English arrived – what did he think? Perhaps he knew. She dismissed the idea, only not completely.

He hadn't touched her either, at seven or whenever it was she had crept back into the room. She had sat quickly on the bed beside him and he'd looked up. Suddenly she'd been aware of the scent of outside in the folds of the sweater, of the dawn cool on her skin, and she'd jumped up and into the shower. Was he angry?

It had been, in part, by way of testing him for a reaction that she'd suggested it, sitting on the bed and watching as he lifted his briefcase to the desk. 'Come for a walk with me?' Holding her mother's scarf in her lap.

'Sure,' he said, barely even looking up.

She knew where she was going – but she couldn't show it. Out there somewhere, between the quay and the crooked house – if it was still there. Simon Chatwin's boat.

There was a big old barge halfway out along the marsh she hadn't seen before, its mast gone, nudged in low-lying and indistinguishable from its element. It had been decommissioned and turned into some kind of activity centre, up against a patch of shingle that served as beach. A gang of kids in life-jackets were being loaded into a fleet of little dinghies, they shoved and jostled in a queue. Further out a boat bobbed at anchor, its sails stowed; it swung a little and she saw the name painted on its transom. *Bluebell*. It was the dinghy she'd seen Danny and Martin Watts sail out in the night before. How far around could you get? Where had the tide been when Bray was killed? They might have seen what happened, out there in the dusk. Their mother looked after him, who had said that? *The Watts woman*. Roger Carter had said it.

Paul was watching the children, frowning. Leading him all the way out here, she might have betrayed herself twenty times simply by knowing exactly where she was going, but Paul hadn't seemed to notice anything.

It was windy but warm. As she tied the scarf Paul put his fingers to her cropped hairline under the fold of silk, tucking something away. On the far headland, just short of the shining square bulk of the power station, the tiny figures of a family group were walking out to sea and she fixed on them, too

158

aware of his hand at the soft part of her neck. The church on the closer spur of land, from here it sat inside the power station's silvered silhouette.

Somewhere far off a horn sounded the start. 'They'll be out there all day,' Alison said, surprising herself by still remembering, regretting it almost immediately as panic flared in her. How had he not guessed?

But Paul was looking out to sea. 'Can we get any further?' he asked. Anxiety ticking she shrugged, not very convincingly. *How would I know?*

'Why don't we try along here,' she said, following a narrow slatted boardwalk that meandered ahead of them through the clumped sea lavender.

Stephen Bray's boat lay, tilted as she always appeared to Alison in dreams, a long, smooth-bellied elegant curve undiminished by the muddy berth, the long-gone spars and ropes. She was a certain famous class of yacht. On his chart table in the tilted cabin Bray and her father had pored over old photographs of her racing at regattas. Paul stopped, admiring.

Her decks were muddy as if the tide had come up over her, there were bootprints stamped all over the teak and the neat varnished cabin doors had hardboard crudely nailed over them. Because the police would have been here. Because he was dead. She raised her head and looked past the boat to the sea wall. What had he been doing on Mulville's Hard? It wasn't on the way to his boat. It was past the crooked house. She thought of him staggering in the dark, falling to his knees in the cold mud. The sound of the tide, creeping and lapping, in his ears.

Back on the shingle the little dinghies were setting off one by one now, bobbing in the water, the small passengers sitting trussed stiff and obedient in their lifejackets. She thought of Mads and Letty; she thought of Simon Chatwin.

Paul followed her gaze. She saw him frown again.

'You don't want children, do you?' she said.

'Don't I?' he said, looking down into her face. In the sharp clean light she saw the fine lines around his eyes, the gleam of silver in his hair, his half smile, her insides churned. *Have me.*

His hand came up and rested warm on her cheek, turning her face to him.

'I don't know anything about you,' Alison said, feeling the ground shift under her. So dangerous. 'Your family, your home, where you went to school, university. Your work.' Even as she said it, as he looked down at her, smiling, it all sounded so trivial, so safe, so dull. Who needs to know? And anyway, you could make it all up. She knew that better than anyone.

'My *work*?' Now he was mocking her. 'My family? I haven't bored you with my idyllic childhood?' He smiled, but his eyes were narrowed against the sharp light.

'All right,' she said, roused. 'Why you haven't . . . why you're still single.' He brought his hand away and suddenly she felt cold. She'd gone too far.

'You're the first one that meant anything,' Paul said, looking away from her, out to sea. 'Do you believe that?'

'If we got married . . .' she said, and he raised an eyebrow, but she persisted. 'If we got married, who would come to the wedding?'

'Now that,' he said, and took her wrist, 'that is an interesting question. I'd like to know that too.' His hand gripped her tight. He raised the wrist and put his mouth to the inside, where the blue veins sat close to the surface. 'Will you marry me?' His hand warm and tight. For a moment the memory of the time before, the night he'd held her down, made her close her eyes for wanting that violence back. She thought of them bound close together, just the two of them, for ever, and she didn't know what she should say. She saw with sudden certainty that she needed to be tied close to something and it opened

160

like a sinkhole inside her, a terrible lost feeling, as she saw what would happen if she let this go, let him go. She opened her eyes again quickly. He looked at her a long moment then he laughed and released her.

There's something I need to tell you. The line was in her head, but she said nothing.

'Children,' he said, turning to watch the dinghies gathering speed as they headed towards the estuary and the bigger boats on the horizon. The sky was pale, some high wisps of cloud. 'I don't think we're the sort, do you?'

What sort are we? wondered Alison. The defective sort. In evolutionary terms. Damaged.

There was a sudden gust and the tiny boats heeled in unison. Alison watched, feeling her heart pound with panic at what she might have said. What if he hadn't meant it, if it had been some kind of a joke, and because she believed it, because she wanted what she thought he'd been offering so badly, his mother's engagement ring and his white-painted bedroom above a bustling London road for ever – she'd told him everything?

What if he asked her again?

She turned away from the horizon and there was Stephen Bray's boat tilted in the mud, still there, turning derelict before her eyes. It would soon disintegrate: did anyone own it? The home-made landing stage, the slimy planks of the step. Her father used to hold her arm tight, handing her across to the slippery deck. *Try to remember*, Sarah Rutherford had said all that time ago, when Esme's memory had been like a scrapyard in the dark, full of sharp things you could trip over and she hadn't wanted to try. *Anything at all.*

She remembered her father with his head suddenly in his hands over Stephen Bray's chart table. 'I don't know what she wants,' he'd said. 'I'd do anything for her.' The older man pushing his glasses up his nose and reaching around for the bottle of home brew, moving between Esme and her father.

161

Something shifted in Alison's head at the memory of her father's voice. He had taken her there, his girl, his favourite, she hadn't really understood that before, how much he had loved her. She'd thought he loved all of them. And now he was sitting in that chair at the end of that corridor where the linoleum gleamed and the CCTV camera watched him, and he was alone.

If she had told Sarah Rutherford that her father's voice hadn't been angry when he talked to Stephen Bray about her mother, would it have made any difference? That when he said he would have done anything for her, it had been true? He had sounded lonely, he had sounded helpless.

Paul's arms were around her. 'Come on,' he said, his breath on the nape of her neck.

They walked on, their backs to the power station, the crooked house on the skyline, black against the early sun, every step taking them closer.

Further along the sea wall was Mulville's Hard, where Bray's body had been found.

Earlier, as they had come into the dining room for breakfast, Alison had stopped on the threshold. 'Damn,' she'd said. 'Forgot my phone.'

'You don't need it,' he'd said, his expression clouding, and she'd made a face. 'Kay tried to call me last night,' she'd said. 'I'd better make sure it's not urgent.'

'Kay.' So he *didn't* like her.

'I'll be quick,' she'd said. 'Get me the full works. Eggs, all that.' Which might buy her some time.

But it wasn't to phone Kay back that she'd gone upstairs. The reminder sat there blinking, missed call, but Kay belonged to another world, a world where they gossiped and drank and dreamed, where Esme had become Alison, where everything was possible and none of this had ever happened. She might never go back there.

162

Sitting on the unmade bed, she'd phoned DCI Sarah Rutherford.

When the policewoman answered she sounded breathless. In the background Alison heard a tap running, a chink of plates. Washing up. 'Do you know a man called Simon Chatwin?'

There was a sigh. 'Esme,' Rutherford said, resigned, and then Alison heard a muffled voice. Hand over the receiver. The background sounds were gone. A door closed.

She stood from the bed. 'Alison,' she said. 'It's Alison now.' But at the sound of her real name something had stirred in her gut, fear, derailing her. 'Does anyone know what happened to me, afterwards? Where I went?' She walked to the big bay window and looked down. The woman from last night stood at the centre of the gravel. Alison saw a hand come up holding a cigarette. Stocky, middle-aged, her arms folded across her body, her hair under a kind of white cotton cap, she didn't move. She was looking at Paul's car.

'There was a court ruling,' said Sarah Rutherford. 'Didn't your aunt tell you?' Alison made no answer, and she went on. 'The media were banned from reporting anything that might identify you or your whereabouts.' She cleared her throat. 'Of course, it wouldn't have stopped someone trying to find you. They just couldn't make it public. But if you didn't want anyone to find you, why are you back?'

The woman turned on the gravel below and hurriedly Alison stepped away from the glass.

'I'm not back,' she said, stubborn, illogical. 'In a day, two days, I'll be gone.'

'I hope you will,' said Sarah Rutherford.

'Why are you even worried about me?' said Alison, turning away from the window. 'If you're so sure my dad did it?'

Paul's things were piled neatly on the desk, and she took a step towards them. On the top was a clear folder, and she could see the typed title on the top sheet below it. *Retribution in Occupied France*. It was more than a centimetre thick; she put a finger down to the plastic. Other folders were stacked beneath it, cuttings, the edges of photographs, some books with the university's library stamp on their spines. With a finger she pushed at the pile and there was a wartime crowd scene, a woman at the centre of it, shaven-headed She pushed it back in.

A silence. 'People can be . . . this kind of incident . . . people don't always react rationally.' Sarah Rutherford sounded tense, wary. 'You're your father's daughter. You could get hurt.' There was a pause. A sigh. 'As for your question. We know who Simon Chatwin is, yes. We know who he is and where he is now.'

'You do?' Sarah Rutherford didn't answer, and Alison took a breath. 'Did you know my father wore glasses?' she said. 'Like me. It's genetic, runs in families. Short-sightedness.' And she heard something, or rather nothing, the sound of Sarah Rutherford holding her breath. Then the policewoman spoke.

'Your father was short-sighted.' A question pretending not to be.

'Yes,' said Alison, letting the fact settle between them. 'And he wasn't wearing his glasses when you found him, was he? Did anyone even know? Did anyone ask?'

'I – I'd have to—'

'I found a piece of his glasses in the yard,' said Alison, not waiting for her to finish. 'If it wasn't him, who was it? Simon Chatwin came to our house at least once. Was it him my mother was having an affair with? Was he . . .' And she grappled with the timing, how old Simon was when they were born, how, where he and her mother might have met, the artists' supplies shop, the distance to the town. 'Was he their father? Was Chatwin my sisters' father? Did you check that DNA, while you were about it?'

164

'Alison,' said Sarah Rutherford, and Alison heard alarm sound in her voice. 'Are you sure? The glasses. How bad was your father's eyesight?'

And it was Alison's turn to hesitate. 'I don't know,' she said. She took off her own glasses. She held out her hand in front of her. How close did you have to be, to shoot someone? Could she do it, if someone had left her glasses smashed in the street? She thought of her father at the kitchen table, taking off his glasses to read. Rubbing his eyes. 'I don't know.'

On the stairs she had heard voices then: Jan, talking to someone. A low female voice answering, sullen, submissive: the woman she'd just seen outside, somehow she was sure of it. She crossed to the door and stood with her back to it; she needed to get back downstairs. 'Simon Chatwin,' she said again.

'We ruled him out,' said Sarah Rutherford. A pause. 'He wasn't their father. We tested him, he gave his permission. I can't . . . I can't talk to you about him, Alison. But you need to believe me, we ruled him out. When we found him out there, the morning after . . . there's no way . . .' There was noise again in the background, the door banged louder and Alison heard a child's voice. She brought a hand to her mouth – she had a kid. 'Can you come over?' the policewoman said. 'Come in to the station?'

'I – I have to go now,' said Alison. 'I have to go.'

It *was* still there. Simon Chatwin's boat.

The look Paul gave it was very different from the one he'd given Stephen Bray's. The cabin looked like it had been made of chipboard by a child. It looked as though you could open the lopsided doors with a kick.

If the police had ruled Chatwin out, why were they still watching him? In her pocket the phone rang, and Paul's head turned, looking for the sound. Reluctantly she took it out. *Gina*, said the screen, and with her heart thumping, Paul's eyes on her she put it to her ear. Smiled at him.

'Hi!' she said brightly.

Chapter Twenty-two

The Watts brothers were in their boatyard, planing a boat on blocks.

'You're good at this,' Paul had said, when Alison led them back towards the quay by a different route on instinct, picking her way between jetties, not even knowing how she knew which path to take back, realising only as they got there that they would end up coming alongside the boatbuilders' shed.

'Fluke,' she'd said, watching the men bent over the upturned boat. Martin had always been the quiet one, the peacemaker between Joshua and Joe, Danny more heedless, doing his own thing. But they seemed in unison now, heads down. Maybe it was how you got through stuff. 'You can have a go next time,' she said to Paul. 'You know this place, I don't.' He shrugged.

The Watts's house was a low cottage behind a patch of shorn grass at the back of the boatyard, a splash of green startling in the grey that stretched to the horizon behind it. That was where the milkman had come that morning, to tell their mother, his float abandoned in the yard. Alison no longer knew where she'd been told the story, if she'd overheard it whispered in the kitchen, between her parents. Had it been Joe who told her? November. Her and Dad and the twins in front of the fire, the night it happened.

Joshua Watts must have been very clearly dead when the milkman found him, because otherwise you'd stay with him, wouldn't you? You'd wait for an ambulance. Esme hadn't stayed with her father. She'd stepped over him and gone into the dark.

'It is an amazing place, isn't it?' said Paul, watching the Watts's rhythmic movements along the curved length of the upturned boat. 'The land that time forgot.' He turned to her. 'So who was it?'

In her pocket Alison's hand tightened around the mobile. 'Who?'

His arm came around her and she held very still, small in his embrace. 'On the phone,' he said, smiling down, patient.

'Gina?' The name came easily. A lie has to contain elements of truth. 'An old friend.' Something came to her. 'Bloody Facebook, can you believe it? There's no hiding place these days.' She thrust her hands down in her pockets. 'Not even in the land that time forgot.'

'Really,' said Paul, his lips on her cheek. 'I didn't know you did Facebook.'

'You don't have to,' she answered, smooth, 'if everyone else does. Your so-called friends will dish out your mobile number.'

Paul nodded, raising his head to look back at the boatyard, making no objection. Did he have reason to? She didn't know how much he'd heard of their conversation.

Gina had launched straight in. 'They know you're here,' she'd said, urgently. Alison had to concentrate so hard, to keep smiling with Paul's eyes on her. She'd taken a step away from him, then another, holding a hand over the speaker and making an apologetic face before turning. 'Who?' she said to Gina. Now her back was to Paul. 'Who knows?'

'All of them,' said Gina. 'You know this place. Someone must have seen you. Recognised you.' Then when Alison said nothing, she went on, hissing, 'It wasn't me, you know. I said nothing. Nothing.'

They knew? Alison stood still and cold despite the sunshine, gripping the mobile tight. Who knew? She thought of Rosa in that grim London basement pub and her questions, her inexplicable phone call. *Take care.* Did she know? And all these years she had thought herself invisible, below the radar.

'Tell me names.' On the quay she saw Simon Chatwin's van pull up outside the pub. Identifiable by his overalls, some kind of bandana over his shock of hair, he got out. Ron the land-lord was only just opening up, and he had to wait on the doorstep. He didn't look in their direction.

But Gina exhaled impatiently. 'You think I've gone door to door asking? We knew it was Cornwall you'd gone to, you know that, don't you? We left you alone, didn't we? Safe out there, we thought.'

Across the marsh Chatwin disappeared inside the pub. The place was full of drunks, Paul had said, and it looked like Simon Chatwin was one. Esme had only worked at the place three Sundays, before that midsummer night that ended her childhood, and already she'd hated it, the bleary sozzled sticky afternoons, daytrippers and locals, laughter breaking out at tables. She didn't think the landlord had given Esme a second glance, not then, nor Alison the night she and Paul had gone into the pub, either.

'How do you know that was what I wanted?' Alison said, keeping her voice low. 'To be left alone?' She'd thought of Gina so often. She'd wondered. 'And who's we? The Wattses?' She paused. 'Simon?' She glanced back over her shoulder. Paul had moved away a little and was watching the horizon, his hands behind his back.

'Ron knows,' said Gina. 'You went to the pub, right? If he

knows, everyone's going to know, sooner or later. Why did you have to come back?'

'I told you why,' said Alison. 'It's a wedding.' And something occurred to her, the knot tightening in her chest. 'You don't think they know? The Carters?' She searched her memory. They'd given no sign. Could Roger Carter be so good an actor?

Gina made a sound of contempt. 'I don't mean them,' she said. 'They're not us, are they? See them down the pub ever?' A quick intake of breath. 'There's something I've got to tell you,' she went on quickly.

Alison heard Paul's feet shifting on the gravel five, ten feet away and she turned.

'I think I know,' she said, raising her hand to shade her eyes, looking at him. Smiling. He stood, hands in pockets. Alison turned back.

'I can't talk,' she said quickly. If he heard her mentioning the Carters' name . . . 'I'll call you when I can?' Gina had hung up without waiting a beat, leaving Alison turning back to Paul, all too aware of her heart thudding in her chest.

And now, as they watched, Danny Watts straightened from the boat and Martin with him, and the two men looked straight back at them. They were a hundred yards away, maybe less. Poised beside their boat, each with the heavy implement in his hand, they watched. Alison pulled the scarf close around her ears, hands in her pocket.

'I'm cold,' she said. 'Let's go.'

It was close to midday but upstairs at The Laurels the curtains were drawn. From the driver's seat Paul looked up at Alison as she hesitated between the stucco pillars of the Carters' porch.

His expression was the same one he'd had in the hotel room as she changed: he looked entertained by her discomfort. Alison had gone to put on lipstick in the gleaming bathroom, reflected

170

back at herself in half a dozen shining surfaces every time she moved.

'You don't have to go, you know,' he said, though his amusement made it impossible to stay. If she stayed it would end in the row about Morgan that had hovered since Alison had first read the invitation parked on Paul's mantelpiece – or maybe that would just be where it began. 'Morgan won't mind.'

'She's winding me up,' said Alison. 'You know she is.'

'Then call her bluff,' said Paul, good-humoured from the desk. He'd said he'd drop her then come back and work till she reappeared. Then with a lifted eyebrow, 'You look nice.'

She'd put on more lipstick than she intended: her lips were a hard red in the bathroom mirror. He stepped inside the room and taking hold of her elbows he kissed her. Alison tried to pull back, knowing the red would come off on him, but he held her, his mouth pressing hers almost until their teeth met and then he let her go. He wiped his mouth with the back of his hand.

'Don't want to go overboard,' he said, looking at her in the mirror. The lips were softer, blurred. He ran a finger under her mouth where there was a smudge. 'You don't need to impress Morgan, you know.'

She saw herself colour in the mirror, and said nothing. 'And if you give Morgan an inch . . .' he added, turning back into the bedroom.

There had been a reminder from Morgan waiting at the front desk when they walked back in. *Longing to see Alison. Sometime this morning?* Hand-delivered – so someone at least in The Laurels had been up early. Alison noticed in passing that the writing was the same as it had been on Paul's invitation. There'd been no misunderstanding, then, no farming out of the guest list. She felt the murmur of secrets between Paul and Morgan. A wind-up.

From the porch she watched him drive away. She'd told him she'd walk back.

If she hadn't got back by two, he said, he'd be out with Christian, doing some stag activity. A round of golf. 'Isn't there supposed to be a whole gang for a stag party?' Alison had said, her turn to stir.

Paul had just laughed. 'The Carters like their incomers to be unattached,' he said. 'It makes them more manageable. It's why I got on so well with them.'

The door was answered by Lucy Carter in a dressing gown, her face taut with hangover, two sharp lines between her eyebrows. 'Oh, hello, dear,' she said without enthusiasm. There was no trace of curiosity in her look or her voice. She couldn't know who Alison was. Esme. She stayed in the doorway and turned to call up the stairs, 'Morgan?' Wincing. 'Little Alison's here.' Only then did she step back, pulling the thick dressing gown tighter around her.

'Thanks so much for last night, Mrs Carter,' said Alison, and then she did catch a sharp look from under the drawn brows but Lucy Carter didn't reply. Morgan was on the wide staircase, soft-footed, a light silk thing flying out behind her that she tugged at as she stopped, halfway down.

'You came!' she said, delighted by some prospect Alison couldn't determine. She leaned down over the banister. Alison saw cleavage carelessly revealed, two pale curves soft under the silk. 'Up here.' And was already halfway round the galleried landing when Alison started up the stairs behind her.

The room was huge, cream and pink, with a big bay window, a deep carpet and a four-poster bed that dominated the space. A doll's house stood on a table by the wall, the front open, the tiny furniture laid out, not a single chair overturned, not a trace of dust. For a second Alison imagined Lucy Carter up here on her knees, cleaning the minuscule kitchen implements. It was a princess's bedroom, the room of a child who always got what she asked for, and more.

On the deep window sill there was a tray with an ice bucket

172

and glasses, and Morgan was standing beside it fiddling with the foil on a champagne bottle. Expensive champagne. Morgan would always have money, one way or the other, that seemed obvious. Alison realised she didn't know if Paul was rich or poor – he owned his flat, she knew that much. He was comfortable. Would that have been enough for Morgan? She'd have made something different out of him, maybe, or would have tried. Not for the first time, she wondered why they'd broken up.

The cork popped, the bottle foamed and Morgan handed her a glass. It was so full Alison had to put her lips straight to the brim to stop it spilling, and looking over it she saw Morgan's smile. She straightened, the champagne dry and good on her tongue: it was not even midday. Swallowing, she thought of her father, slipping to the pub from his workshop at lunchtime; Simon Chatwin, on Ron's doorstep; and she felt the warm hit of alcohol softening the outlines of things, like mist.

Morgan lifted her own glass, no more than half full. 'Cheers,' she said, bringing it away before it touched Alison's. 'So sweet of you to come.' Alison looked around for a level surface and set her glass down carefully on Morgan's bedside table.

'What a room,' she said, putting a hand to the curtains around the four-poster, some kind of stiff heavy silk. The bed was king-sized, where Esme's had been a narrow single under the window, posters stuck over it. A girl's bedroom, the place she ran to, burying her face in the pillows to cry over some boy, her parents oblivious downstairs.

The image of the room at the top of the crooked house hovered at the back of Alison's mind, but she didn't step into it, she didn't allow it into focus. The shapes sat in soft darkness, the letters of her name on the shelf, the alarm clock, the door, ajar. The line of light from the stairs, and voices.

You drink too much.

You've got a problem.

You're a fine one to talk.

Had Morgan ever done that? Lain up here, and listened, lain and sobbed. It was hard to imagine. Had Paul slept in this bed with her? In her stomach the sip of alcohol warmed, burned, provoked her. Next thing, they'd be scrapping, she and Morgan in a catfight and Morgan just holding her at arm's length. Perhaps that was the plan. She smiled, instead.

'How does it feel?' she said, feeling nothing herself but a kind of dread. 'Tomorrow you'll be a married woman.' Paul had said *Marry me*, it came back to her with a jolt. She looked over at the glass she'd set down, wanting just another sip.

'How did Christian propose?' she said on impulse and Morgan made a small, distinct sound in her throat, quickly suppressed. She didn't like the question: it was why Alison had asked it. Because it raised the possibility that Paul might ask Alison, might already have asked? And because from what Alison already knew it was quite possible that Christian hadn't actually proposed at all, that all this was some kind of an arranged marriage, contracts signed between professionals.

But like the lawyer she was, after that first intake of breath Morgan just blindsided her opponent, standing there looking without answering, champagne glass in hand, the dressing gown pulled tighter. Everything about this set-up seemed designed to remind Alison that she was the lesser woman, the upstart, the child with no breasts and a single bed. I'm not the one playing princess, she said, in her head.

'Lovely bed,' Alison tried again, thinking, Horrible. 'Most girls would dream of one of these.'

Morgan wrinkled her nose. 'I must have loved it once,' she said, wafting an indifferent hand. 'Cost a fortune.' She set down her glass, untouched; her dressing gown slipped from her shoulders, a collarbone gleamed, the velvet hollow of an armpit was exposed before she pulled the material together again. In her head Alison saw Paul's hands on her and she had to blink to clear the image.

'D'you want to see the dress?' said Morgan, picking up the glass Alison had left beside the bed and handing it back to her. 'I don't believe in bad luck.'

'Yes, please,' said Alison obediently.

'Drink up,' said Morgan. 'Plenty more where that came from.' And she disappeared through a door without waiting for an answer. Alison glimpsed shoes ranked up to the ceiling beyond her, coloured leather, tall heels, the edge of a hanging rail. Sod it, she thought, and drank.

The dress was a column of raw, white, heavy fabric. Morgan hung it from the four-poster and it dominated the flounced room straight away, not floating or ghostly but statuesque, as if it already had a body inside it. It was discreetly laced down the back but otherwise quite plain. Alison touched it, then coming closer she saw tiny stitches, made by hand; she felt the weight of it, she imagined Morgan's strong shoulders rising up out of the column.

'It's beautiful,' she said, and she supposed it was, though for a moment it seemed like a kind of expensive straitjacket, with the lacing and the rough dull silk.

'Twenty grand,' said Morgan carelessly, taking Alison's glass and turning to refill it.

'No,' said Alison, too quickly, before softening it. 'No thanks.'

Morgan stopped pouring but she gave the glass back to Alison, half full. 'I always get what I want, you see,' she said, smiling, leaning back against the wall beside her doll's house. 'Christian insisted. Has to be the best.' And then without drawing breath, tilting her head. 'He'd come back in a heartbeat, you know.'

Paul.

The glass trembled in Alison's hand, what she'd already drunk pushing her to be reckless. She stayed silent.

Morgan examined her. 'I suppose he has some idea of . . . I don't know. Moulding you? That might be fun for him. For a bit. Curiosity value, a little tiny challenge.'

175

Hostilities were laid out, unmistakable. My enemy. Alison found herself holding her breath at the nakedness of the attack, looking around for witnesses. Lucy Carter, in her dressing gown? She'd just smile and pretend she hadn't heard.

'A challenge,' Alison repeated, feeling the stiffness of her smile but keeping it there. Pretend it's a joke. 'Maybe.'

You're the first one that's meant anything. She said nothing.

'He always liked one to put up resistance,' said Morgan. 'Have you found that?' She shifted her hip and the doll's house quivered. In its kitchen a figure fell, bringing a tiny clatter of miniature implements with it.

'What about Christian?' said Alison, finding some small space for manoeuvre with the sound. 'They're off on some stag thing this afternoon, Paul said. They seem to get along so well.'

The ghost of annoyance passed over Morgan's face. 'Christian does what he's told,' she said shortly.

As if on cue there was the sound of a heavy door closing downstairs, followed by voices raised in hearty conversation, getting louder. Men's voices, in the big baronial hall below them.

'Is that Paul?' said Alison, starting up from the bed. Morgan shook her head, too quickly.

'This has been nice,' she said, not even pretending to sound sincere. 'But I think I'd better get dressed.'

Alison set her glass down. 'I'll get going,' she said, but Morgan had already turned away, fabric floating behind her.

Christian was in the hall as she came down the stairs, and he looked up at her, his hands in his pockets. He was wearing a T-shirt, trainers; he looked different, not bland at all.

'Are you all right?' he said, frowning, as she reached the bottom, and she was startled by his concern.

'I'm fine,' she said. Christian set a hand on the banister, drawing closer. He hadn't shaved – Alison hadn't noticed that in the hotel's dining room this morning, but then she'd been distracted.

176

'She likes to wind people up, you know,' he said, and she heard his odd accent come out stronger. 'Only happy when she's making trouble. Pay no attention.'

Alison laughed awkwardly. 'I don't think you're allowed up there,' she said. 'You don't want to catch sight of the wedding dress.'

He smiled, his grey eyes cool on her. 'I wouldn't dream of dropping that kind of money on something I hadn't seen,' he said.

So he'd paid for the dress. And neither of them believed in bad luck.

As she came out through the front door Roger Carter was standing on the drive, chest puffed, hectoring a man with the marquee company's logo on his overalls. She was pulling her scarf back over her ears as he turned to eye her, in mid-rant. She raised a hand and smiled but kept walking, and he watched her go. She felt his eyes still on her back as she turned out into the lane and smelled the hedgerows in the sun, saw the cow parsley dancing along the verge. What had she seen in his face?

She came around a bend in the lane and saw the sea, the wide channel snaking olive-green out to the horizon and the big dark sails, gliding across each other's paths as they made their slow way across it.

Roger Carter might have had trouble with her name at first, but there was something about her he recognised. She wondered how long it would take him.

Chapter Twenty-three

Gina's daughter danced between the mooring ropes on the quay. She looked down, intent on her own small clever feet, hair tangled down her back.

From the pub's backyard Alison heard the girl's breathing as she skipped, heard her count her steps. May was nine. Not far off the twins' age when they died, not far off Esme's when she saw the crooked house for the first time. When they unloaded all their belongings and smelled the mud and the strangeness of their new home, hoping to start again.

Joe had been the older by so little, but already he'd known so much more. His face had been pale and watchful climbing out of the car. He'd looked from Mum to Dad, checking for something, as they stood and looked at their new home. Following suit, Esme had seen only tiredness. When the last bag was set down inside the hall and Dad put his arm around their mother's shoulders, narrow over the big belly, Joe had turned away.

They'd found their rooms, Joe slinging his bag down in the gloom, the two of them alone together. He'd put his arms around his sister. Joe had known.

Even as she had the thought Alison saw May's head fly up, saw her look around, monitoring her surroundings, seeking her mother, eyes skating over the empty tables. The younger one is protected, but May had no older sibling to hide the truth from her, to allow her to think she was safe. She had Gina, though.

Gina came out of the pub's back door with two pints of lager in her hands and an unlit cigarette in her mouth. Straight away Alison had said, I'll get them, but Gina had given her that look. Alison had known she was at the pub when she called from the lane, something unmistakeable about the too-loud voices in the background. She wondered if Chatwin was still there.

Two o'clock: Paul would be on his way to the golf course with Christian. Alison eyed the lager, grimaced. Lighting her cigarette, Gina laughed. 'You've been away too long,' she said.

'You've changed your tune,' said Alison. Gina looked away, her eyes narrowed. In the lee of the building, the tables were still damp from last night's dew. The backyard was filling up: a couple in anoraks were on the next table, watching the boats through binoculars.

'Stephen Bray was the last one to see my dad,' Alison said. 'That night.'

Gina tilted her head, looking at her through the smoke. 'Was he?'

'As far as they know,' she said. 'And now he's dead. You knew that, right?'

Gina threw her head back, blew smoke straight up, brought her chin down again. 'I knew he was dead,' she said carelessly, stubbing out the fag and taking a long drink from the tall glass. 'He was old. He was a pisshead.' She shrugged, but her free hand on the table jittered a moment, and Alison shifted her ground.

'You said there was something you hadn't told me,' Alison said. 'On the phone.'

179

Gina stared her down, mulish. 'You said you already knew,' she countered. She leaned forward and Alison smelled smoke on her. 'You said you couldn't talk,' she went on. 'That boyfriend of yours. He doesn't know, does he? He doesn't know who you are.'

She pushed the big glass over towards Alison, moisture beaded down its sides. The champagne had gone from her system, leaving the nagging beginnings of a headache, and a small, horrible emptiness. A hundred yards away at the water's edge May had stopped and she stood watching them. Alison lifted the glass to her lips, and something inside her came loose.

'My mother had an affair,' she said. 'They moved here to get away from it. But Mum did it again.' *Bitch.* 'Another man, someone here.' Gina was sitting back against the wall, relaxed, her hand out on the table and her green-brown eyes shining gold in the reflection off the water, lager eyes. 'My dad had just found out the twins weren't his.'

Joe knew. She suddenly felt sure of it. Joe had known something about Mum, and he'd been angry that Simon Chatwin had kissed Esme, but as she held those two certainties in suspension they seemed to move together, they bumped softly. A connection.

Gina sat up a little. 'Never,' she said, but her disbelief was detached, almost dreamy, and she lifted her glass. Alison put out a hand to stop her.

'Was it Simon?' she said. Gina frowned. She tugged her hand with the glass in it out of Alison's and the liquid slopped.

'You what?' Her voice was sharp.

'Simon. Having an affair with my mother. I came home and he was in our backyard. More than once. The time he kissed me, I thought he was waiting for me . . .' That distance that had opened up between Esme and her mother had a shape now.

Gina was scrabbling for her cigarette pack on the table. May was standing on the edge of the pub's yard now, scuffing a foot, not coming any closer. The anoraked couple were watching her, disapproving. Behind them the back door to the pub opened and someone stood there.

'Simon wasn't interested in your mum,' said Gina, contemptuous, squinting round a cigarette. She lit up.

'She was in the kitchen in heels then. And later. The night she died, heels and her best skirt.' She frowned, remembering the glasses on the draining board. 'She . . . she might have been drinking with someone. I told you.'

Gina blew the smoke out. 'She might have been interested in him, all right.' She gave Alison a hard look. 'He can lay it on when he wants to, or back then he could, anyway.'

'Are you jealous?' said Alison. 'After all this time?'

But Gina didn't rise to it, she just laid her hand on the table, the smoke drifting up in the blue air.

'She wasn't his type,' she said flatly, and as Alison watched she gave a little nod in May's direction. Not needing more encouragement the girl skipped towards them between the tables. Gina raised the arm with the cigarette and May was under it.

'Morgan Carter says she saw my dad fighting with the man whose baby died,' she said. 'Do you remember that?'

'Your dad was an arsehole, welcome to the club,' said Gina. Under her arm May squirmed, looking up at whoever was standing in the pub's back door.

Alison turned to see.

'Hello, Esme,' said Danny Watts.

The night Joshua Watts dies. November.

They're sitting by the fire when the telephone rings. Dad's been fidgety all evening after the second hospital visit, looking

181

up from his paper to the bottles on the sideboard every five minutes, and Esme knows he's making the same calculation each time, the half-inch of cooking brandy, the old vermouth, the Campari there was nothing to mix with. In and out of the kitchen, cups of tea he leaves to go cold. The twins are on the rug playing Monopoly as the fire smoulders, the logs are wet as usual and Dad just pokes it distractedly; it collapses white into ash.

In the hall the phone rings and the girls jump up from Monopoly and run to answer it, squabbling. Letty gets there first, frowning into the receiver, her face falling, holding it up through the doorway to someone else, to Dad, to Esme, back to Dad.

'It's Joe,' she says. 'He sounds funny.'

Dad takes it from her, his face set. 'All right,' he says into the receiver, Letty skirting round him back into the room. 'How much have you had? All right. All right. Where are you then? Mum'll come for you.'

That's when Esme knows Dad's got a stash somewhere else. He won't get in the car if he's had a drink. In and out of the kitchen; it must be in there, in the back of a cupboard, under the sink, somewhere Mum won't find it. He's been in the yard.

Dad comes back into the room, talking to himself. Esme is on her knees with the girls tidying the Monopoly. They don't look up.

Chapter Twenty-four

She stood on the edge of the water with them. *Esme*. It was on the tip of her tongue to say to him, *It's Alison now*, but she just looked up into his face and nodded.

'Hello, Danny.' They stood shoulder to shoulder on the pub's back step looking down on her, not boys any more, close-up. Men. Nearly thirty: life was taking them. 'Hello, Martin.'

Gina had jumped up and drained her pint at one go, May still nestled in her armpit. She nodded warily to the brothers, all three, it seemed to Alison, careful not to start anything – and she was gone, tugging the girl after her.

The two men stared at Alison; she couldn't see if they were friendly or hostile. She tolerated it. She felt something circle the three of them, binding. They had violence in common, they had the dead, who refused to go away. She pulled off her scarf.

'You cut your hair,' said Danny. She shrugged, standing up. They walked to the water's edge, Alison in the lead, wanting to get away from the anoraked couple.

They flanked her in silence. Then Martin spoke, and it took

her a moment to realise he was answering the question she'd asked Gina. 'Frank Marshall had a go at your dad because he'd done some work in the house before the fire,' he said. 'Was that what you wanted to know? He thought he'd put a nail through some wiring. But Frank must have known it was his own fault all along. He topped himself, after all.' His voice was rough – she didn't know if he was trying to comfort her.

Danny made a sound, raising his shoulders, shoving his hands down in his pockets. 'Why did you come back?' he said.

'I had to,' Alison said, because the wedding seemed meaningless now, the resistance she'd put up. How could she have ever thought she could stay away? Live out a whole life without coming back? Whatever happened, she'd had to come.

'How's your dad?' It was Danny, looking at her from under dark brows. The question almost felled her.

'He's a vegetable,' she said, unable to use a kinder word. 'I've only seen him once. Since . . . since.' Martin nodded; Danny looked away. Of course, she thought, they knew, that picture in the paper. Alison sensed that they felt sorry for her, and the feeling brought something up, dangerously close to the surface. She could break down, after all this time, in front of these boys who knew her whole story, she could ask for help. Forgiveness.

'How's your mother?' she said, polite. 'I saw her in the church.' She hesitated. 'She knew Stephen Bray, didn't she? The old man that died.'

'She never got over it,' said Martin bluntly, and she knew he wasn't talking about the old man. 'Looking after the old bastard was a distraction. She got obsessed, fussing over him. She never got over Joshua.' And they hadn't got over it either. Were they married, attached, had they even left the village, since? She had only seen them together.

'Did they ever find it?' said Alison, and they both turned to look at her, a pincer movement. She blundered on. 'Find

184

the car? The driver, the hit-and-run?' A quick shake of Martin's head that meant, shut up. Danny turned to look back out to sea.

'No,' he said.

And then they were all looking out towards the horizon because all at once it looked as though the big dark sails were on top of each other off the spit beyond the power station and somewhere out there a horn blared. A smaller motor boat bobbed in the mouth of the estuary, a tiny figure holding up a flag off the bow.

'Warning,' said Danny, and the brothers exchanged a look across her.

'You know who that'll be,' said Martin. 'Likes cutting it close.'

'Who?' said Alison. They stood either side of her like guards.

'It's the *Lady Maud*,' said Martin, and with the name that day came back, the heavy skies, the hot humid air and the brown water. The small crowd on the quay, the letters etched blue along the big boat's bow as it came on, the sunburned figure on his board tipping and going under. Down under the brown water.

'Isn't that . . .' she said. 'Isn't that the one . . .' They turned, waiting for her. 'The one that ran Simon Chatwin down?'

'Bob Argent,' said Martin grimly. 'The *Lady Maud*'s master is Bob Argent. God, remember that? Chatwin must have needed his head examining.' Alison stared from Martin's face out to sea where the sails had disentangled, the big shapes moving slowly apart, regrouping like pack animals.

'It wasn't an accident?' she said.

Danny laughed shortly. 'Bob Argent does nothing by mistake,' he said. 'He wanted to teach the bloke a lesson. Chatwin went after the wrong girl that time.'

The last of the magic ebbed from that kiss in the backyard. 'What d'you mean?' she said, but it was obvious.

185

'He'd been after Bob's daughter,' said Danny, and his voice was cold.

'And if he'd died?' She remembered Bob Argent's face now, unruffled at the commotion on the quay, people rushing to the edge to look down. A tall lean man, the polished gleam of a high forehead, his hand resting on the wheel.

Martin Watts shrugged. 'Who'd have cried over Simon Chatwin?' he said, dismissive. 'I suppose Bob'd have had to answer some questions. But the police are so fucking dumb round here.'

He turned away so she couldn't see his face but there was a ragged edge to his voice. She pictured Sarah Rutherford sitting at a table with these two, getting nowhere. Stonewalled.

'Are you staying?' said Danny, his eyes on his brother's back. Martin's hands were in his pockets and he was looking at the pub.

'Me?' said Alison. His gaze shifted to her and for a second something like a smile was there – then it was gone.

'You,' he said. 'Staying for the prizes, in the pub. Tonight.'

Alison nodded yes, uncertain, but in that moment only wanting to comply, and watched as he felt in his pockets. He brought out a pen. He took her hand, turned it, and before she could be surprised he wrote a number on her palm. She felt calluses on his fingers, hard skin. He raised his eyes to check on Martin's back again.

'They'll all be in,' he said, straightening. 'Even Bob Argent comes to the prizes. If you're interested.' He let her hand go. 'His daughter's training to be a doctor, I heard.' Alison searched his face for the smile, wanting to see it again, but he was impassive. She thought of him pinning Joshua's arms back as he went for Joe and she had lain in the dunes in the warm dark and covered her ears. She held her palm up to her face, adjusted her glasses to look at the number. 'If you need anything,' he said, and stepped across her to go.

She touched him quickly as he went and he turned immediately. She pulled her hand back. 'I'm not Esme any more,'
she said, her voice almost a whisper. 'You can't call me that.'
His eyes met hers and then he was gone, but she'd seen it, a
sad smile that said, perhaps this is where you belong, after all.

There was nowhere to hide out on the marsh. Every human
figure on the flat grey landscape stood out. There might, Alison
supposed, watching another family group further out, walking
along the dyke towards the crooked house, be safety in numbers,
but she was on her own.

The scarf, it occurred to her too late, served in this situation
as the opposite of a disguise. By now to everyone in the village
she must be the girl in the scarf, but then there'd always been
more to it than hiding. She put both hands up to the silk, she
pulled a corner across to search it for that smell, she breathed in.
There was nothing left of her mother in it, it smelled of a stranger.

She had arrived back at Simon Chatwin's boat, only this
time she was alone.

The afternoon was wearing on: it was almost four o'clock
now. The sun was halfway to the horizon, the low yellow light
was warm but the wind kept up steadily, the big boats getting
closer in. The buoy that marked the last leg bobbed in the
glitter of waves, waiting for them.

Simon Chatwin had picked the wrong girl. Her mother
hadn't been his type – but there she'd been, waiting for him
in heels, not once but twice. Did Dad catch them?

Alison looked at the boat's filthy sides and cluttered deck.
She focused on the flimsy chipboard that served to secure the
cabin and, wondering briefly what had happened to the original doors, she looked from left to right before stepping across,
from the soft treacherous mud to the slimed shambles of a
deck. She crouched, edged crabwise. He would be working at
the hotel, she told herself.

She jumped as in her pocket her phone rang. On her hand as she took it out she saw the number Danny had written.

It was Paul. 'Where have you got to this time?' His voice was even, reasonable, but he was angry. Something in his tone made it hard for her to catch her breath.

'You're back already?' she said, shifting so she was propped against Simon Chatwin's cabin top. She drew her knees up to her chin, hoping to make herself invisible. 'How was the golf?'

'Morgan said you left hours ago,' he said levelly.

'Don't you think sometimes Morgan's not very nice?' Alison said, before she could stop herself. She heard an intake of breath and went on quickly, 'I'm trying to clear my head.'

'Where are you?' he said, and as she held her breath, not answering she heard his patience slip. A click: he'd gone.

Hurry. She looked across the marsh back inland. She saw the family on the sea wall, couples hand in hand on the hard, a man with binoculars standing on the end of the quay looking out to sea.

She edged around to the rear of the cabin, set her shoulder to the chipboard and suddenly, before she was ready, she was down there, in the dark. Inside.

The only other boat she'd been below in had been Stephen Bray's, and more than once its smell had come back to her, paraffin and wood and raw alcohol, an oily clash with the sweet bad-egg whiff of the mud. This was different. She raised a forearm to her face, breathing through the cloth of her shirt. A stale, crusted combination of stagnant water, soiled clothes. Unwashed sheets. Something else. Something worse.

How had Esme imagined this boat, in the days, weeks after Simon Chatwin had kissed her? Standing in the pub's backyard and looking across the mud, wondering what excuse she might make to walk out here, to step on to the deck, to knock at the cabin top. Rehearsing. *Hello.* A knot formed in her gut, Esme at thirteen, stepping down into the dark. Into this.

Alison took the arm away from her face, looking around for light. Something swung beside the hatch and she took hold of it: an electric lantern. She felt around its base, found a switch and it brightened slowly, to a dull glare. She looked around. A wide bunk with tangled sheets, grey and sheeny in the flat light. A crusted sink opposite, mugs with mould puffed inside them, a grillpan tilted on a filthy hob, full of grease.

A stack of magazines sat beside the bed – at the sight of them she moved abruptly. She waded through clutter on the floor, kicked something and a gust of rubbish smell rose up. She felt the creeping horror of this man kissing her. She had to stop, her heart pounded, it did not slow. Dirty magazines. She leaned across the bed, her bare knee in the greasy sheets, she smelled but did not see a chemical toilet.

The magazines were old, dog-eared. Alison had no experience beyond a glance up at a petrol station's top shelf but she knew there were worse things than this, worse than tits and spread legs. The torn pages, the curled-up corners, the signs of use were what tightened the knot inside her, but somewhere in there too, alongside the distaste, there was a spark of relief. Could have been worse, a small voice repeated in her head, only then something stopped it, stopped her too, where she knelt on his filthy bed, magazine in hand. She listened.

All around her, something was happening. Small creaks, a distinct shifting, something familiar about the sensation from long ago. She held very still with the stink in her nostrils. The creaks escalated, the boat groaned and bobbed and suddenly Alison was weightless, light-headed. She shoved the magazine back where it had lain, reverse-crawled off the bed into whatever was on the cabin floor, wading back to the busted chipboard and – no longer caring who she might find on the deck waiting for her – through it, gasping, into the air.

Around her the tide was right up, lapping across the path. The boat had come afloat, that was all, the physical memory of it happening in Bray's boat was what she'd felt below in the dark and now came the visual, that swelled in her throat and burned behind her eyes. Esme bracing her feet in panic as Stephen Bray's liqueur glasses chinked and trembled, and her father laughing and taking hold of her hand to steady her.

That other night. Dad might have been as frightened as me that night, the thought came to her, astounding. She had lain crouched behind the door waiting for the next boom, until it never came. Downstairs her father had struggled with someone, with something. Her father had seen what she'd seen. Joe with his face half gone. The bloodied, weighted sleeping bag that held another man's exterminated young. And Mum, face down, the mole on her calf, the high-heeled shoe skittered from her hand. *I'd do anything for her.* Had he stared, as she had stared? She raised her head and looked across the marsh.

Out along the winding path the figure of a man was coming her way, hunched into the wind, not looking up. Alison scrabbled around the deck out of his line of sight and splashed heedless into the water, her heart pounding. It was warm. Her sandals slid under her in the mud and as she crouched to take them off she knew he was coming, he was coming for her. Still bent, she shuffled as far as she could get from the boat before straightening – she knew already that she would have to pass him. She risked a glance up, searching for the white shape of a van parked along the quay, outside the pub, but could see nothing. The man moved slowly, hands in pockets, she ducked her head.

Danny Watts had been trying to tell her something about Simon Chatwin. Head down, watching her own bare feet pick their way through the rising water, she told herself, Trust no one. If Danny wants you to think a certain way, ask yourself why. She reached the main path. Her head still lowered, she turned towards the mainland and she could feel him, up ahead.

Ask yourself why. Danny and Martin. If she closed her eyes and thought of the brothers they were blacker than the dark in her head, more void, they were weighed down with something terrible. Still grieving their brother, after fourteen years?

In her ears the wind blustered, under her feet the path led her back and she knew there was something she had to do. Think, sort, rearrange: had there been a moment when things changed, when they turned? That late summer afternoon when Simon Chatwin tipped on his board in front of them all, and the big boat slid quietly over him. What must it have been like down there, sucked under the great hull in the dark? One thing for certain, when he came up he wasn't golden any more, he was jittery, he was afraid. Or was it in the days after the house fire, when the smell of smoke hung in pockets across the village and fights broke out in the pub's backyard? Mum crying over the paper. The father had killed himself, but Gina said the dead child's mother was still here.

Or when Alison stood waiting for the school bus the wet winter morning after Joshua Watts had been found, the small group of them standing there stunned into silence, the warm promise of evenings on Power Station Beach suddenly gone for ever. They'd never found the driver who killed Joshua Watts and not for the first time that fact caught her, stopped her. A filament grew, between two nights joined by violence. Was the connection real, or was it in her head?

Sarah Rutherford thought it was when Dad found out the twins weren't his, when he started asking if anyone had a gun, and when he'd got hold of one, killed them all. Did she still believe that? For one fervent moment she wanted Sarah Rutherford there at her side to face Simon Chatwin coming towards them across the marsh. The police monitored

191

his whereabouts, she'd said, so they must still suspect him of something. Now he was in front of her, she felt his shadow.

Adrenalin tracked through her system, telling her to run. She stopped.

She looked up. The man was Paul.

Chapter Twenty-five

The pub was quiet inside, dust motes drifting in the low yellow light that shone through the back door. Everyone was at the finish, out along the spit, Ron had said, handing Paul his pint. Not looking at Alison.

'Really?' she'd said, trying not to show her reluctance when Paul suggested they go. He'd taken her arm.

'You want to go back to the hotel?' His expression was cool. She'd shaken her head.

'The police were there when we got back,' he said, sipping his pint, setting it down. 'Christian and me. We came back early. Our hearts weren't really in it, to be honest. Morgan's idea.'

'Uh-huh,' said Alison, taking a bigger gulp of hers than she'd intended. Something in her system was stopping her feeling drunk but she didn't feel normal, there was a low-grade buzz that blurred things. 'What did the police want?'

'I think it was something to do with the fire alarms going off,' he said. 'They were talking to some woman.'

'Some woman?' Casually.

Paul shrugged. 'Some woman in an overall. Smelled like an

ashtray, so maybe it was smoking-related.' *Her*, thought Alison. The woman on the gravel with the cigarette in her hand, looking at Paul's car. 'Jan told me there was no fire, it was just routine. So maybe it was a prank.'

'I did smell smoke,' said Alison.

He nodded. 'Yes,' he said, giving her a sideways glance.

That woman. Who was she?

A shadow passed across the open door, paused, moved away. Not everyone's watching you, Alison told herself. She took a sip: she'd trained herself for so long to keep quiet, not to give herself away, waiting for him to speak first came easily.

Paul frowned. 'Look, I'm sorry,' he said.

'That's OK,' she said. Then when his frown didn't go, 'What are you sorry for?'

'Hanging up on you,' he said, staring fixedly at his drink. It wasn't really an apology. He raised his head. 'It's just . . .' And as Paul hesitated she thought, Here it comes, this is it. It's over.

'What did Morgan say to you?' She heard the hostility in her voice, but she couldn't stop herself.

'It's just this . . . . paranoia,' he said, and she could feel his unease. 'Insecurity. It's immature. I don't know if . . .'

He paused again, looking at her. She thought of what would happen if she told him what Morgan had said, and kept quiet. Paul made an explosive sound. 'You're suspicious of everything. Everyone.'

Which of course was true. Alison held the big glass casually in her hand, feeling him watch her. She lifted it to her lips and drank.

'Not everyone,' she said, feeling the small hit settle her. She smiled. 'Not you.'

Paul made an impatient sound. 'You know who I mean,' he said. 'Morgan. Morgan's family. You've got to get over it.' There it was again, the warning in his voice. She realised he was

194

right, though. She did suspect Morgan's family. Blustering thoughtless Dr Carter and his sweet little Lucy. They wanted her out of the picture just like Morgan did.

I'm not going, thought Alison. But what she said was, 'I know.' And made herself sigh, admitting it. 'I'm sorry.' He looked away and quickly she drank again. Over the glass she caught Ron looking at her across the room. She didn't know if he was shunning her or protecting her, by keeping quiet. It came to her he'd been fond of her, looked after her a bit, when she'd worked collecting his glasses.

He'd shifted his gaze and was looking at Paul now, calculating. Paul rubbed his eyes.

'You're tired,' she said in wonder. She realised she'd never thought of him as susceptible to any kind of weakness, and seeing him weary, something expanded inside her, something softer, more tentative. More loving.

Paul laughed, but it was strained. 'A bit,' he said. 'The alarm last night, I suppose.' He sighed. 'Work. I've got to get something finished and all this wedding stuff, rehearsals, stag business. Keeps getting in the way.'

'And I'm not helping,' said Alison.

He glanced at her. 'Well,' he said, clearing his throat.

Might she lose him? She held still, feeling a little pinball game of panic set up, not so much in her head as between the cells of her body, escalating.

But then he smiled, took her glass just as he had that first time, and set it down. 'Let's say you're a distraction,' he said, thoughtfully, shifting. His knee was between hers suddenly, behind the table. His hand was under her skirt, but above the pub's table he kept his distance, just looking at her, quite relaxed. Across the room Ron wasn't moving, a cloth and glass in his hands, half polished.

'Do you really like this place?' she said, in an effort to keep control, her throat constricted at what he was doing.

195

He nodded a little. 'I could see us here, somehow,' he said, leaning back. Her skirt fell back and his hand stopped, warm and heavy. If anyone came around the table they'd see it. He sighed a little. 'Only if it was what you wanted.'

He spoke reasonably, lightly, but under his hand volition slipped from her, she felt as though she might agree to anything. Come back here and be Esme again: the dream unfurled in her head with the buzz of what she'd drunk.

Only then he cleared his throat and took his hand back, talking about something else. Alison saw that Ron had come round the bar and was wiping down the tables.

'And no one could say it was dull here, could they?' She focused; Paul smiled. 'Fire engines. Murders. Police. She talked to the decorator, too, I saw them. I suppose that stuff is flammable. Thinners, white spirit. Whatever.'

Hold on.

'She?' said Alison.

'The policewoman.' Paul was on his feet, his hand held out to her. 'Let's go back, shall we?' Sarah Rutherford was here. In the village.

Her head swam as she stood up; around her the world contracted, the voices whispered in her ears, all of it getting closer, pulling tighter, with her inside. Paul folded her hand in his.

He wanted her to make a noise, and he wanted them to hear it.

The windows were open in the hotel room but the curtains were still drawn, shifting in the warm air. He didn't turn on the light, he made her kneel in the gloom and from behind her he leaned down and whispered in her ear. *Louder.*

They'd passed people outside, in the reception area, on the stairs, but Alison had looked down, seeing shoes, a skirt, letting the faces blur if she had to raise her head. She'd heard Jan's

196

voice calling after them but Paul had answered, she hadn't heard what he said.

Kneeling on the bed she felt the repetitive, mechanical force of him, felt the breath shoved out of her. *Louder.* Were they all gathered out there as they'd been for the fire alarm, were they listening? She heard sounds in her throat, they sounded like pleasure. On his desk she could see his work in disorder, and her thoughts seemed like the scattered papers and photographs, all sliding from each other.

A police car had been parked in the lane outside the hotel, the vehicle empty as they came around it. Alison's heart had leapt but turning into the forecourt there'd been no sign of them, no uniforms, no serious face under its chopped fringe turning to look at her. And Paul's hand had been around her waist, propelling her, so her head had gone down, it seemed better not to look. Sarah Rutherford might appear round a corner or through a door. Alison's mind scrambled at the thought of what she might say, in front of Paul. The hotel bedroom door had closed behind them and in the dim light he had moved her into the position he wanted and she'd gasped. He'd made a grunt of pleasure that had shocked her. She'd liked it. *Louder.*

His mobile had rung on the way up through the village and looking down at it Paul had detached himself from her hand and moved away from her, an arm held out to keep her at a distance. She'd hesitated but – smiling – he'd gestured to her to keep going and she had, up to where a hedge fell away and a terrace of houses appeared. *Yes,* she heard him say behind her. Impatient. *What is it now?* She was coming level, she realised, with Kyra Price's house. No lights were on inside, the windows shut tight. She half turned and saw him talking intently into the mobile but even as she turned away again, not wanting to look nosy, he jerked his head up and snapped the phone shut.

197

When he caught up with her Alison didn't ask who he'd been talking to. Of course. Although when Gina had called he, she remembered even as she took the hand he offered her in silence, had asked her.

In the half-light of the room he had one hand on each of her shoulders, pulling her back and then something stabbed, something sharp inside her, and her back arched, a noise came out of her louder than she could control. And suddenly Paul's hands were gone, she was released.

He had finished without waiting for her. He was out and gone from behind her, and falling back in shock on her heels she felt jarred, panicked. He was moving in the dim room, saying nothing though she could hear his breathing as it slowed, heavy and ragged then muffled as he pulled his shirt over his head. He threw his clothes down on the bed and then the bathroom door closed behind him.

Alison could hear voices below the window but she couldn't move to see, she felt as though her legs might not hold her up. And if she went and looked down, they'd see her face. They would probably be looking back up at her to see who'd made that noise. Her skirt was still at her waist and tugging at it she felt heat under her shirt, spreading up her neck, behind her ears. Her glasses had fallen from her face, on to the bedcover, and she put them back on. Paul's trousers lay on the bed in front of her, his phone half out of the pocket. She picked it up.

It wasn't a flashy phone, it was such an old model, it even folded – and it didn't seem to have a lock function. Either that, or Paul had nothing to hide. She clicked on the dial button to see his recent calls, although she already knew. Of course. Morgan. Alison held the unfolded phone to her, screen down between her breasts, stopping herself looking at anything else. And listened. Behind the bathroom door the shower was still running. Sliding her legs out from beneath her to sit on the edge of the bed she did look again. Messages. A list: Morgan, Morgan, Morgan. Scrolling down, she could see, even trying not to, the first word of each message. *Darling. Hello. Please. Longing.*

How recent? When had they last slept together?

The sound of the water stopped, just as another name appeared at the foot of the scrolling list, she didn't have time to register whose. Hastily she folded the phone, shoved it back inside the trousers and went to the window. She stood behind the curtains, looking down. Sarah Rutherford stood there, her centre parting gleaming white from above, her hands in her pockets, talking to the stocky woman in her overalls. The woman was smoking another cigarette, the free hand across her body holding the other arm at the elbow. The policewoman looked up, and stepping back too late Alison heard her own sharp small intake of breath. As she moved she saw the number still written across her palm, already fading. Had Paul seen it?

Then he was behind her, still damp, kissing her neck. She dropped the hand away from her. From below the window she heard steps on the gravel, and the slam of a car door. He smelled so clean, Alison became aware suddenly of her own body, of the sex and sweat and panic rising off her. She turned her head away from him slightly and her glance fell on his desk.

'I'm sorry,' he murmured into her neck, and for a second he did sound it, almost heartbroken. 'I couldn't stop myself.'

She heard his words and saw the scattered papers on his desk in the same moment. The corners of some photographs emerging from a folder, a book with its spine cracked, face down. A stapled sheaf with the close print of an academic paper. 'Massacre and Survivor Guilt', she read. Below it some dates. 1942–43. Paul's hands rested on her upper arms, his head heavy against hers. He was quiet.

''S all right,' she heard herself say mechanically, and she felt

199

him step away, humming something to himself. The wedding march.

'That was Morgan,' he said, and she turned to see him pulling on his trousers. He had his back to her.

'Morgan?' she said.

'On the phone, before.' Something uncoiled inside her, briefly murderous. Before what? She said nothing. 'There's some last minute bit of the service she wants to go over.'

I bet. 'You want a lift?' she said casually. 'Shall I come too?'

He had crossed to the desk and was beginning to shuffle the papers together, stacking them. Unhurried, pausing to look at the written pages.

'What?' he said, after a moment, looking up. 'Oh. No, I'll walk.' If he even said, come if you want, now, she'd have to. But he didn't, he just looked at her, worried. He picked up his jacket.

At the door she stopped him. 'Shall we go to the prize-giving thing, though?' she said. 'I could meet you back at the pub later? The barge race.' Looking down, he examined her, as if waiting to be entertained. 'It'll be lively at least,' she said. 'Music and stuff.' She hesitated. 'Get away from the Carters for once?' Defiant. Paul looked as though he was deciding whether to be impatient with her or not. She smiled.

'Why not,' he said, but he was already turning away and she couldn't see his expression. She felt the panic response set up again, imagining his thoughts: immature; hysterical; insecure. They just needed to get away from this place, and they'd be fine, it was a test, that was all. Marry Paul and move back? The last thing she needed was to be Esme again. She made herself close the door.

Watching from the window Alison already had her phone in her hand. Paul sauntered across the gravel, leaning to peer around the side of the hotel as he went. He walked out into the lane and she saw that the police car was no longer visible through the hedge. She lifted her palm to read the number Danny Watts had given her, and dialled, feeling her heart gather speed as she listened. Waited, until that insistent question made itself heard: *Why would you think you can trust him?*

She hung up and dialled Gina.

Chapter Twenty-six

This close to, the boats were huge. Alison saw tiny figures bracing themselves, a man running forward at a crouch under the shadow of the sail.

Gina had her back to the sea, smoking at the edge of the water. She was alone. Alison had wondered where she'd left May, if she was with someone or playing alone in the back garden, but she didn't ask.

'Christ, I'll be glad when you've gone,' said Gina and Alison almost laughed but then she saw there was something different. Gina turned her cheek away into the wind and blew the smoke defiantly but she was quiet. Fearful: staring into the dunes.

'There was a barbecue,' said Alison, waiting. 'We all came here.' Silence. 'You remember, don't you?'

But Gina didn't seem to have heard. 'I know what they'd have said about Simon.' Her jaw was set. 'Those Watts boys. I know what they think of him. But the police talked to him, they did tests and that shit, I don't know what. But they let him go.' Resting her chin on her knees she drew her lower lip into her mouth and when she spoke again it was swollen as if she'd bitten down on it. 'He's the father of my kid.'

'But he doesn't see her.' Ducked back behind her raised knees Gina froze, her eyes gleaming slits. 'He doesn't even have her for an afternoon? Where is she now?'

'No,' said Gina, muffled. 'She's with a mate.' She cleared her throat, and then she turned and looked. 'I remember,' she said. 'There was a barbecue, yes.'

And then it was all there, that evening, before it got dark. Gina has been there all along. She's the first to arrive, in the low September light, she's standing with her arms wrapped around herself as they stumble down through the sand off the sea wall and she is staring, staring, as if she could eat him.

'It was Joe you fancied,' said Alison. 'It wasn't Simon. Why did you settle for Simon,' she said, 'if it was Joe you wanted?' But even as she said it she thought, would Joe have had her? Messed-up Gina.

Above her knees Gina's eyes glittered. Her voice was low, strangely muddied, Alison strained to hear. 'He was dead, wasn't he,' said Gina, and to her astonishment Alison realised she was crying. 'Joe was dead by then.'

So Gina hadn't turned on her at the sleepover because she was jealous of Simon's kiss, because at the time she'd wanted Joe, not Simon. So why did she flare up, telling Esme she was stupid? *Stupid girl.* All she could think was, Joe had been still alive when they'd rowed, when Esme had banged out of Gina's back door and pedalled furiously back down the high street on her bicycle. For another two, three hours, her brother would live. Alison's head spun as she resisted the longing to howl, *Take me back, let me start again. Let me stop it, this time.*

'Do you remember the night Joshua Watts died?' she said, and slowly Gina's head turned, she nodded. 'Joe was out that night,' Alison went on. 'He was in a state when he got home.' It couldn't be unsaid. 'Mum had to go and get him, nearly midnight.'

A scrape on his cheek, hair wild. Eyes bloodshot with something, drink or dope. Mum white-faced, in a stand-off with Dad in the hall and Esme at the top of the stairs shivering. Listening. *And where were you when he needed you?*

'Did they catch him?' she said. 'The hit-and-run driver? Did they ever catch him? Because he'd have had to be someone local, wouldn't he? All the way out here in the middle of nowhere? Some drunk on his way back from the pub?' She heard her voice rising; she saw Gina staring. Dad too drunk to drive. *Bitch.*

'Don't,' said Gina, stiff. 'You don't know what you're talking about.'

But she couldn't stop. 'Are they even sure it was a car? Not a . . . a fight or something? Couldn't he . . . couldn't they—'

'Joe was with me,' said Gina. Alison turned and stared, but Gina didn't look at her. 'That night. They got into something, I don't know what, if it was about you or who it was about.' She ducked her head. 'Joe came to me. He rang you from my place.' Silence. 'He talked to . . . one of the little ones first, all right? Was it Letty answered? I heard him telling her to get someone.' Gina's face was stone.

Horns blared, one after the other, and both at once they looked up, across the grey water. Two boats were racing, neck and neck, so aggressively, sinisterly close it must, thought Alison, be dangerous. She braced herself for a grinding crash, a horrible tilt and dive but they were still moving. A tall man stood quite calm at the wheel of the vessel closest to the shore, not even looking at the other boat whose wake frothed over his gunwales. The barge's name was etched in yellow on bright blue at her bow. *Lady Maud.*

'Are you going to the prize-giving?' she asked, and hearing her own plaintive voice it occurred to her that soon she would be gone. She would never see Gina again.

'You're kidding, aren't you?' said Gina, her eyes fixed on the man at the *Lady Maud*'s helm. 'All those bearded weirdos? Not a fucking chance.' And she turned her head to stare straight into Alison's eyes. 'Not if you're coming along with that boyfriend of yours,' she said, and immediately Alison felt winded, as if she'd been slapped.

'When have you even seen him?' she said, although even as she spoke she worked it out. It must have been the first night in the pub, Gina with her cracked heels on the bar stool and Paul getting the drinks in.

'Oh, I've seen him,' said Gina. 'Good-looking bloke.' Her voice was flat. 'He went out with her, didn't he?' And she jerked her head back towards the clustered houses of the village, across the inlet and the marsh. 'Morgan Carter the bitch. He dump her? Or is it one of those things, you know. A quick shag now and again and no one the wiser. For old times' sake.'

And Alison was on her feet, heels slipping in the sand. 'Why . . . why . . .' But she didn't say it. *Why do you want to hurt me?* And she realised what hurt her was partly just the thought of the lost years here, Gina at the pub, Gina growing up without Esme.

And then Gina was up too, the rage and poison gone out of her face, and only misery left. 'I miss him,' she said. 'I miss Joe.' Her voice, high and sad and lost, blew away from them on the wind.

The police car gleamed white and striped below the crumbling churchyard wall and at the sight of it Alison braked the little car in panic, looked around for somewhere to turn, to escape. There were no other cars there and the chapel was unlit: whatever Paul had come over here to help with had been sorted. Hold on, she told herself. Hold on. What can they do to you? You're not the suspect.

She parked under a tree further back down the lane and sat. Not Joe. How long had she been afraid it had been, without allowing herself to admit it? Thank Christ for that, not Joe, her brother hadn't killed Joshua Watts throwing a punch in some new drunken argument – or the same one they'd had on the beach in September, boiling over again that November night. She didn't know why it would be such a relief, except that she knew if he'd hurt someone, if he'd killed someone, even accidentally, he would have been in agony, he would have been destroyed. Why had she believed it, why had she wondered, even for a second? Because losing a child might have driven someone to come out to the crooked house and take revenge. Driven someone to savagery.

Joe's life was gone, all the same.

Two people were sitting in the police car. Alison got out and stood in the road, looking through its back window. She waited, one eye on the car, one on the little chapel's double doors.

The police car's passenger door opened and Sarah Rutherford stood there, looking back at Alison. The policewoman leaned down and said something into the car and then she was walking towards her unhurriedly, strong-shouldered, wide-hipped, the gleam on her shabby trousers visible in the evening light. Alison turned quickly and walked away from the chapel, listening for Sarah Rutherford's footsteps behind her. She kept going until she was out of sight of the churchyard and an open gate appeared, a tufted field. She felt the policewoman come after her. The gate banged behind them.

The grass was clumped and boggy underfoot as if the field was reverting to marsh. The hedges were tangled and hugely overgrown, tumbling with blown hawthorn, and Alison set herself with her back to it, facing Rutherford.

'It wasn't him,' said Alison. 'I can't do this on my own. It's your job to do this. Isn't that why you're here? You know it wasn't my dad.'

She saw pity flicker in Sarah Rutherford's wide grey eyes, and her heart sank.

'It was him,' said Rutherford. Alison took a breath but the policewoman held up a hand to stop her then stood there, feet planted square in the long grass.

'You're fooling yourself,' she said. 'There was ample evidence, biological, circumstantial, that he did it, no evidence that anyone else did. To start with, another perpetrator would have killed your father first, would have made sure he was dead.'

Alison took a step back, she could give in, she thought, but then something clicked in her head. Think. All right. 'How do you know he wasn't shot first,' she countered, 'and the killer believed him to be dead? He wasn't going to get up and fight, was he?'

Her voice sounded brutal in her ears and she heard Rutherford's intake of breath. 'We have ample evidence,' the policewoman repeated, and took her by the upper arms, gently, holding her in place. 'And who do you think would have wanted to kill your family? Your whole family? To shoot a woman, a boy, two eight-year-olds?'

'They were shot through the sleeping bag,' says Alison, remembering then. Fibres in the blood, the brown and orange fabric, holes in the nylon. 'Whoever did it couldn't bear to look at them.' Faltering.

There was silence, and she filled it. She might not have another chance. 'A mother lost her child in a fire,' she said. Somewhere far off she heard the organ rising, she tried to blot it out. 'And then the child's father died.' Still silence: Rutherford dropped her arms, looked away, looked back. Was she even listening? 'Two boys lost their brother in a hit-and-run, and they had to watch their mother destroyed by it.'

Sarah Rutherford was frowning now, a deep vertical line between her eyebrows. Alison felt cold, suddenly, in the deep shade of the big hedge, the ground beneath her feet had soaked her shoes.

'Do you think we didn't talk to people?' said Rutherford,

roused from weariness to anger. 'Do you think we're stupid?' She leaned closer, her face was in Alison's but she spoke gently. 'Your father did it.'

'You never caught anyone for the hit-and-run,' said Alison, not looking away. 'Two boys lost their brother. She's destroyed by it, their mother is, did you know that? And for the house fire. You never had to catch anyone for any of those deaths. Where is she now? The woman whose baby died, whose husband topped himself? She works at the hotel, doesn't she?'

'Karen Marshall,' said Sarah Rutherford.

Alison registered the name, found a place to store it. 'My father wasn't wearing his glasses when he shot himself,' she said, holding Sarah Rutherford's steady blue gaze. 'How could you not have known he wore glasses?' The policewoman's eyes darkened, and at last Alison saw what she'd been waiting for. She saw doubt.

'What are you doing here?' she said. 'If it's all over?'

'There are other crimes,' said Rutherford wearily. 'Believe it or not. This is my job.'

A sound came from inside her jacket somewhere, and she turned her lapel to her mouth and spoke into it, shielding herself from Alison as she did it. Alison saw her back tense, saw a hand come up to rub at the place between her shoulder blades, saw it stop.

'No,' she heard Rutherford say, almost with a groan. Then, 'All right, all right.' The policewoman's head turned just slightly, to gauge where Alison stood, then back again. 'A hundred yards, I'll be at the gate.' She turned back, letting the lapel fall back and with it the tiny microphone.

'Talking of which,' she said, 'duty calls.'

'What?' said Alison. 'What is it?'

Rutherford frowned a little, shaking her head. 'Kids,' she said. 'It'll be nothing.' But she chewed the inside of her cheek. 'Are you going to be all right?'

'If my dad didn't do it, who did?' said Alison, standing her ground.

Rutherford put out her hand. 'Don't,' she said, a warning note in her voice. The lapel crackled again – 'Wait' – then she put a hand over the mike and spoke to Alison.

'Please,' she said. She was pale. 'Go to your wedding. Listen to the speeches. Then go and get on with your life somewhere as far away from here as you can.'

Alison stepped back, as if Rutherford had shoved her, but the policewoman's hand reached after her and took hold of her arm.

'Leave it,' said Rutherford, gripping her. 'Please.' And then she let go and she was striding away, uneven in the clumped grass. Alison saw the white shape of the car beyond the gate, Rutherford's long straight hair swinging as she ducked to climb in and then it was moving off, neon stripes flickering past the hedge.

As she came around the bend and the chapel was back in view Alison saw that where the police car had been parked a woman stood in a shabby coat. As if she'd been waiting. The moment she saw Alison she began walking towards her. She came slowly, with a kind of rolling walk, as if her joints gave her pain but she kept coming, her slanted Eskimo eyes slits in the low sun. She stopped squarely in front of Alison.

It was Cathy Watts. Her face had deep creases and a gleam like soft leather. 'Why did you come back?' she said, unmerciful, and without warning, somewhere inside Alison anger turned and sparked and caught.

'Why not?' she said, ragged with rage. They all wanted her to disappear. They wanted her to have died along with the rest. Cathy Watts folded her arms, but she stood her ground, she didn't turn and walk away.

'I couldn't stay away for ever,' Alison said, the anger ebbing. 'My father's still alive,' she said. 'Did you know that?' A small

209

movement of the head, yes, but Danny's mother's arms were still folded. 'Do you know what it's like to be me? To have people say, people tell you someone you . . . someone you loved all your life could do that? Wouldn't you want to be sure?' She ran out of breath.

Cathy Watts looked at her, unmoving, a long moment before she spoke. 'We all know,' she said, and her voice was hoarse. 'We know he did it.' She sounded grim, but still she didn't turn and leave.

'How do you know?' said Alison. And then, gaining courage, 'Was it Stephen Bray? He saw my dad that night, didn't he? Maybe he was the last person to see him. Did he tell you something? Did you tell the police?' Cathy Watts watched her, silent. 'You looked after him,' said Alison. 'Mr Bray.'

'Someone had to,' Watts said, unfolding her arms at last. Alison saw her hands were knobbed and curled with arthritis as she let them hang by her sides. She looked at Alison strangely: accusingly. 'He took it very hard,' she said. 'Your dad killing those girls.'

'What did he say to you?' Alison stepped towards Cathy Watts. 'What did he know? Why did he die now, why now? I saw him the night I came back, did he know it was me? Was he going to tell me something?' The older woman's face was cold but Alison only became more desperate. 'He died out near our house, didn't he? What was he doing over there? It's not on the way back to his boat from the pub, is it?'

Cathy Watts was shaking her head now, she was shifting on her arthritic hips, turning to set herself in motion. 'Don't you start that,' she said, holding herself steady. 'Not with me, you don't. Why are you asking me when you know the answer? You know what he was doing out there. The boys saw you.'

'What do you mean?' Her hand was on Watts's arm, anything to keep her, and the older woman stared down at it with her black eyes as if an animal had got hold of her. Alison let go at once.

'You shouldn't have come back,' said Watts, and then she was walking away, lopsided with silent pain.

It hung in the air behind her: a warning, the same one they'd all issued her with. *Go. You are his child*, it said. She had brought him back, brought it back, the bad thing that had lain there all the time in the marsh, that had sat dormant in the boarded house like disease, and when she drove over that hill and looked down to the estuary, under her gaze it had broken the mud's surface and was exposed.

You will never be clean, the warning said, *you will never be good, you will never be free.* They are drawn to her, they stare at her. The one who'd walked out of the rubble, the survivor.

They must have suspected her. Any investigations relating to you will be restricted, Rutherford had said. Of course they had investigated her, they had to. Perhaps they'd all wondered, whispering up and down the village's high street as Esme sat in the foster family's kitchen and talked to Sarah Rutherford, as she sat motionless in the strange bedroom among the battered toys. Children had been known to kill, even if it had always happened in America, where there were guns everywhere, guns and drugs and computer-game-addicted teens. The Wattses, the pub landlord, Stephen Bray — even Gina, even Kyra Price and her mother. Had it crossed all their minds, and did it still hang over her, even now, that under the influence of childish, murderous rage, not understanding she couldn't take it back, she had found the rusty old shotgun and pulled the trigger again and again until they were all dead?

At least as likely as her dad doing it, her gentle hopeless dad, who'd never once even slapped a child.

In the lane Cathy Watts had turned the corner now and was gone.

Sometimes, sometimes, in the intervening years Alison had

wondered too, lying in the cold bedroom in Polly's cold house or starting awake in a college room hundreds of miles away. At bad moments, she let the idea grow in the way clouds grow out of nothing until they turn the sky black that all she had heard as she lay on her bed were the sounds of a violent argument. That in fact it had been Esme who had come down, high on whatever had been in the cup Gina had goaded her to swallow, stirred up with their argument and ready for a fight, and that something had boiled up inside her when she came downstairs and saw them. Saw her mother in heels and lipstick ranting at her father from the kitchen doorway and him swaying drunken and blank and useless, saw the twins, entwined in their sleeping bag, turned silent and alien against her, and Joe, maddeningly oblivious, nodding under his headphones. And it flew out of her black and shrieking. *Wake up. BOOM.*

So no wonder.

Alison stared down the empty lane, seeing the cow parsley gleam like silver in the shadows, listening to the birds beginning to sing in the hedges as the twilight crept up. Listening.

She put her hands to her eyes so that there was only sound, she was Esme perched high up in her bedroom. Voices. She listened. Yes.

Voices in the yard, where she found the twisted piece of metal from her father's glasses.

Someone screaming. Shrieking words.

Voices. Her mother's voice, lowered. A man answering. Was she talking to Simon?

A car far off.

Out here in the crooked house you learn to listen for that, you know, when the sound detaches itself from the village, when it bumps and revs on the track coming closer, that someone is coming out here, because there is nowhere else, nothing else, only mud, concrete remains, rotted timber. Just us.

It was all thrown in the air, she couldn't get the order right, what came first, what was the last, the very last thing she heard?

Alison took her hands from her eyes. The night he died Stephen Bray must have been coming to meet someone in the crooked house, because there was nothing else to come for. Just their house, the Grace house, and her thoughts flew off, scattering; he was coming out to see ghosts, to see the dead. For a moment she couldn't breathe, thinking of what that house might contain, behind the boarded windows. She put her hands back to her eyes, shutting herself in. Esme. Inside her own head.

The car is stopping, the voices in the yard are raised. Panic. It begins.

Chapter Twenty-seven

Kay's voice. In the car on the way back to the hotel with the phone pressed to her ear, Alison almost sobbed to hear it. She pulled up at random: she was on the high street.

It was just a message. Her mobile's screen had been telling her about it for days, only she never registered that stuff, it had been just that she got the phone out to catch Rutherford and bring her back, before she got to whatever had called her away, to tell her she'd remembered something, and the icon had caught her eye at last.

'Jesus, are you dead, or what?' Kay's voice, urgent. 'I . . . there's something . . . it's too complicated to talk about on the phone.' There was a pause. 'Are you locked up in the bloody honeymoon suite? Can you stop shagging him for five minutes and call me at least?'

And her voice was gone. There'd been the noise of a bar in the message's background, there'd been a moment when the voice faded then returned, when Kay must have turned from the phone to nod or get out of someone's way or take a drink, and it came to Alison in that pause that she could just . . . leave. Climb out of Paul's car, walk to the hotel, call a taxi. She could buy a ticket and get on a train until it pulled in where there would be strangers, a thousand people heading across each other to their destinations under a big vaulted echoing station roof: just another Friday evening. London.

Alison pressed to return the call. It rang, and rang: it was close to six o'clock. Just another Friday evening. Kay would have left work. Maybe she was back in the same bar. Who would she be with? 'Hello,' Alison said awkwardly, to Kay's answerphone message that said breathily, jokily seductive *Sorry, I can't get to the phone, tell me everything.*

'It's me,' she said, and stopped. What was that? A sound? Was there someone coming? She looked in the wing mirror, but the pavement was empty.

'What's too complicated to leave a message about, then?' She tried to sound upbeat but her voice was reedy and anxious. She remembered something. 'Rosa phoned,' she said. 'Is it to do with that?' Then something overwhelmed her. *I just want to talk to you.* And before she could take it back, it was out. 'Rosa knows, doesn't she? About me. Do you all know?' She heard her own intake of breath, horrified, trying to climb down. 'Call me back, anyway. Please.'

When she got back to the hotel Paul was leaning on the reception desk, chatting to a pinkly pleased Jan.

'You walked back,' Alison said.

'I said I would,' he said, smiling easily, pushing himself off the polished counter, apparently unaware of Jan gazing at him.

'Jan,' said Alison. 'Did you say you had some books about the area?'

Paul stretched. 'I'll get back to work,' he said, eyeing the two of them with amusement.

'I'll be up in a minute,' said Alison. She waited until he'd turned the bend in the wide staircase, then waited some more before turning back to Jan, catching that adoring look on her face again.

'Does someone called Karen Marshall work here?' she asked.

'I . . . she . . . I . . . yes,' Jan said, ruffled.

'I'd like to talk to her,' said Alison, the same smile on her face as she'd given Paul, brooking no opposition.

Jan summoned up authority. 'She's on our kitchen staff,' she said. 'She's not on duty for half an hour.'

'In that case,' said Alison, 'could we have some tea sent up?' She smiled. 'In a little while?'

When she came into the room Paul was lying on top of the bed, and he seemed to be asleep. Alison sat down at the desk, where his papers lay undisturbed, and looking down at them she wondered. In her head she mapped connections, down university corridors, at conferences, in emails. Paul's life, who he knew, what he knew, where he'd been. Paul knew Saunders. Did Rosa know him too? They all exchanged information, they knew each other's interests. Rosa knew. Holding still, Alison waited for the pieces to align, to give her an explanation: the machine in her head ticked and whirred, but it needed more time.

There was a soft knock at the door. On the bed Paul didn't show any sign of having heard and Alison went to answer it.

At the door holding a tray of tea things, Karen Marshall smelled of cigarette smoke. She was the woman who'd stared at Paul's car, smoke drifting up from the cigarette in her hand. She looked at Alison, sullenly suspicious, and Alison stepped out into the corridor, letting the door half close behind her. She took the tray from the woman.

'You know who I am, don't you?' she said. Marshall clenched her empty hands and Alison saw that the skin on them was rough and red, the nails bitten to the quick.

'Yes,' said Marshall. 'I know.' Waiting. 'Here for the wedding?' A note of disbelief in her voice.

216

'I don't think my dad did it,' said Alison, finding herself without any strategy, with the woman's hard, wary eyes on her. 'I don't think he could have.'

Marshall said nothing.

'Do you think it was his fault your baby died?' Alison couldn't waste time.

Something flared in the woman's face, a blotch on each cheek and Alison thought of the smoke that hung in the village's lanes. 'Why are you still here?' she asked, and at last Karen Marshall spoke.

'I tried to go,' she said, hoarse. 'I ended up living rough for a bit.' She wiped a raw hand across her nose. 'She's buried in the churchyard. It's a live-in job, here.'

From somewhere distant a police siren sounded and they both turned to listen to it. 'They talked to me after the alarms went off,' said Karen Marshall, looking down at her bitten nails. 'You see them? Seems to me I'm still the first one they think of when there's a fire.' Her face was grey, as if the blood had stopped flowing inside her.

But then she raised her head and looked at Alison with the smallest gleam of a response. 'They talked to us back then too, you know that, right? Because of Frank, only he was dead by the time your dad . . . well. Maybe they thought *I* could have killed someone else's kids, I was off my head, anyway. Everyone knew I was.' She spoke flatly.

'And could you have?' As she looked at Karen Marshall Alison felt another presence shift in the back of her mind, shadowed and waiting. The tray felt heavy in her hands; she listened for movement behind the door to their room. Marshall's arm came across her body in a defensive motion and Alison saw a tattoo on her wrist, crudely done, blurred blue. The child's name, that she hadn't spoken, Mia.

The tattoo said, she hadn't done it. The tattoo, the trembling hands. She couldn't say why she was so sure, only she was.

217

'I was working that night,' said Karen Marshall, and her eyes flickered to the door behind Alison. 'Thought I had to keep going. Waitressing at the Plough.' The same pub she and Paul had stopped at on the way to Saltleigh. Small world, thought Alison, dully unsurprised.

'They was busy that night.' Marshall was staring at the door.

'What?' said Alison, but the woman refocused, shook her head.

'It wasn't never your dad's fault,' she said roughly. 'Not even Frank thought it, in the end. That night, when he had a go at your dad in the pub, he'd just gone mental.' She said it as if it was routine. Her arms still across her body she turned, looking along the corridor and back, checking exits. Then unwillingly she looked back at Alison. 'He put in the units for us,' she said. 'Kitchen units. They said the fire started in the upstairs hall, nowhere near.' She looked away. 'Ever so sweet with her, he was. The way he'd look at her.'

With the baby. A picture came into Alison's head, of Dad joggling one of the twins against his shoulder to soothe her, the little head weaving, wobbly. Must have been not long after they moved, the twins just born.

Karen Marshall was frowning. 'He was drinking, though.' Alison nodded. 'I weren't sure about letting him hold her.' She looked sideways at Alison, who was concentrating on not seeing something, staring down at the tray in her hands. Marshall went on. 'We should have gone, left, after the fire, only we couldn't think straight. Sometimes it . . . it just gets you under and you can't even get up of a morning.'

'He's not buried here?' Marshall stared and Alison blundered on. 'With . . . with the baby? Your . . . Frank.'

'They won't let them in the churchyard,' she said. 'He took pills. They won't bury suicides in . . . whatever. Holy ground.'

She drew a breath, staring at nothing. 'I begged 'em.'

Standing on her own at the crematorium. The tray in Alison's hands sat between them, but Karen Marshall had no hope or expectation of comfort, anyway, Alison could see that. The thought of putting her arms round her was only stupid. 'I'm sorry,' she said.

The woman barely nodded in acknowledgement. 'Just leave it outside the door,' was all she said, but something had moved across between them, not understanding exactly, but a fragment of it, a token. Alison pushed back into the room, the tray ahead of her.

Paul was sitting up in the bed, and he was holding her phone in his hand. Alison hoped that the great clumsy lurch her heart executed inside her didn't show on her face.

'Your friend,' he said.

She set down the tray carefully, trying to stop herself grabbing for the phone. 'I was only outside the door,' she said. He shrugged, smiling, letting her take it. 'She doesn't like me much, does she?'

Alison swallowed. 'Who?' she said.

'The Facebook one,' he said. 'Gina? The one you were talking to earlier.' Her face felt stiff. 'That's who it said it was on the screen, only when I answered she just hung up.' Alison looked down at the phone, moved her finger on the screen. Recent calls. Gina.

'Call her back,' he said and she let out a quick laugh, throwing the phone down on the bed, the chemical rush of panic in her veins.

'She can wait,' she said. She felt drained, shivery, as grey as Karen Marshall. She sat down abruptly beside him on the bed. 'I'm worn out. Isn't that funny?' He reached his arms around her, his body warm.

'It was a busy night,' he whispered in her ear. 'Fire alarm and everything.' She let her head fall on his shoulder, and gently he took off her glasses, he set her down on the pillow. 'You sleep,' he said.

The tea,' she murmured and she heard the tray chink as he lifted it, then she was under.

In the half dark she dreamed, sounds and voices entering and leaving the room that opened in her head. There were footsteps on gravel outside her window.

In her sleep she kisses a boy who looks like Danny Watts, his eyebrows bleached white, she closes her eyes and hears the wind rustle in the stiff grass under the sea wall, and the power station hums. Then it is Simon she is kissing, and he tastes of mud and diesel, she flies, she flies, she lifts off and flies, and she looks down.

Moving slow across brown water is the long lozenge of the big boat and there he comes, swooping, a thin brown man with a shock of hair, riding on a sliver of plastic board. He tilts as he comes across the broad snub bow, he tilts and falls and he is down. He is under.

Below her they run like ants up and down the big boat's rusted decks, looking down her sides. They wait, they stare and stare down into the lapping brown waves. He's down too long, he's under too long. Then something's there, long hair trailing up through the water, the pale planes of a face stare back and as he comes up into the air he is a merman, he is a corpse, all that's left of him is bones and slime and weed and a gleam of pearly eyeball. His jaw is blown away.

The phone rang and Alison started up.

The room was quite dark. Someone had drawn the curtains. The phone went on ringing: she could see a screen somewhere down at her feet on the bed pulsing blue but she didn't know where her glasses were. Fear surged as she felt for them on the side table and heard them fall. 'Paul?' There was no answer. She slowed herself, she leaned, and found her glasses, she put them on.

220

The phone was at the foot of the bed in the blankets and Alison picked it up, still ringing, and put it to her ear. *Don't hang up, Gina.* 'Hello?'

Paul wasn't in the room. Paul was gone.

An explosion of breath. 'At last, Jesus Christ,' came the voice. Kay.

Chapter Twenty-eight

The pub was packed, she could see that from the road. Light and noise and people spilling over into the dark yard and along the quay where the big boats that had come all the way upriver after the race were moored three deep. Inside, someone was playing an accordion and a song eddied. She stopped.

She'd found a note from Paul on the bedside table. For a while she hadn't been able to focus on it, Kay's voice still in her head, and the buzz in her veins.

See you at the pub. Walking down there. No kiss, no love. No exclamation marks.

From inside the pub came the sharp rapping sound of someone banging on a table and a shout, calling for order. A jeering set up in response then another ragged chorus.

Up in the village the police were talking to Gina.

From the opposite side of the road Alison had seen them as she walked past the bus stop with the little square beyond it where the buses turned, or had always used to. The bus shelter was so vandalised and tumbledown it occurred to her, before she saw Gina, that perhaps the buses had stopped coming here. They'd been antiques back then, with coarse velveteen seats and roll-down windows and a driver seated high above a big steering wheel. Perhaps it wasn't worth anyone's while to come here any more, even if tonight, for one night of the year, Saltleigh was busy.

That was what she remembered, listening to the noise from the pub, when she'd been eight, nine, ten: barge-match day had been carnival and sports day and speeches all rolled into one, cars coming down through the village and the light and smell of beer spilling out of the pub.

From the far pavement she'd seen the car first, then Sarah Rutherford and a male officer, standing with a smaller figure between them. Then the figure banged a fist down on the car's roof and she'd recognised it as Gina immediately. There was a murmur from Sarah Rutherford, a soft, pained sound and Alison had hurried on past, just glancing back to look for confirmation that it was who she thought it was, looking for the pushchair or the child. Seeing nothing but Gina's head turning, alerted by her movement, she had kept on going.

Leaning against the shed Alison got out her phone. No one was looking at her. With half an eye she monitored the wandering crowd, listening for Roger Carter's booming voice, looking for Morgan's shiny hair. Looking for Paul.

If Alison closed her eyes now he would be there. His eyes that were somewhere between green and grey, the vertical line beside his mouth. She'd never had that before: before if she'd been asked to remember a face, the face even of someone she'd kissed and touched and wanted, she couldn't have done it. She remembered trying once or twice, in wonderment, and drawing a blank – the therapist would probably have had a theory for why that was. A decade of shying away from remembering a smile. Joe, his face gone.

They must be inside.

Saw you by the bus stop, she tapped in the message on the

phone, to Gina. *What was that about? What did they ask you?* Even before she'd sent it, it seemed, the phone shivered in her hand, a reply coming in. Only it wasn't from Gina, it was from Kay.

I meant it, read the message. *You just have to say and I can get there, borrow a car, get on a train.* Inside Alison it pulsed hot, the last resort. If only it was that easy, just to reach out to Kay and say, save me. *You can't do it on your own.* She put the phone back in her pocket and walked through the crowd.

The din hit her at the door, the heat, and the smell, sweat, beer, diesel. More sweat. Men. The lights were bright but it was so crowded she didn't feel exposed: the man right in front of her in the doorway just shifted to let her in, not even breaking in his conversation, pint glass rising to his lips, talking about tides. 'Better shift yer car,' he said, elbowing the man beside him. 'Highest one of the year tomorrow.' Alison remembered it all. A big-bellied man with a beard in a spattered blue smock standing at the bar beside a tarnished silver trophy was some way through a rambling account of something that happened long ago, safely distant, the Dunkirk evacuations. People were talking through it steadily and she couldn't tell if the trophy was his, and he'd won.

She remembered the heat of the packed bodies, the same faces coming back from other estuaries and inlets, a bit older, more battered, like gypsies. She pulled her scarf around her face and stepped to one side of the door.

Kay would come, if she asked, and then what?

'So why haven't you been answering my calls?' she had said, blunt, as Alison sat up in bed in the darkened room. 'Has he brainwashed you or something?'

'You mean Paul?' She felt slightly sick, something in Kay's voice warned her.

'I've spoken to that Rosa,' Kay said then. 'She told me all about him. Your Paul. He doesn't like me much, does he?'

224

And now in the pub at the memory Alison suddenly felt hot, stifled; she tugged at the scarf. She heard people talking off to one side of her, men's unfamiliar voices and a broad back blocking her view. They were talking about Stephen Bray. Her head buzzing with other things she tried to connect, to make sense of. The room was a blur of faces. Where was Paul?

'If it was booze, maybe. But they say he hit his head on something.' The voice was disbelieving. 'On what? Nothing out there but mud. Nothing to brain yourself on between here and the power station.' A murmur. 'Oh yeah. And that. That place. And what was he doing there, anyway?'

Hit his head. Her stomach clenched against the smell of beer and diesel, the heat and the droning voice made her queasy.

'Paul knows who you are.' The words in her ear in the dark hotel room had set her head spinning: she'd braced herself against the pillows.

'And you,' Alison said, only then she found she couldn't say any more. *You know who I am.*

Kay's voice was gentler then. 'Not exactly,' she said. 'A while back, someone said something, there was a rumour. People make things up, they get things wrong. First it was a plane crash, then a pile-up, a break-in gone wrong. A fire.'

'Did people know or not?' Alison spoke stubbornly, but she felt choked.

'You mean at the office?' Kay said, uneasy. 'It's an old story, details get lost. Some were interested, some weren't. Mostly people had stopped thinking about it.' There was a pause, and Alison imagined going back to the office, walking in, pulling off her scarf, sitting down at her desk. It looked impossible, a world seen down the wrong end of a telescope.

Kay went on. 'I only knew the outline. But it wasn't any of my business. I didn't know . . .' And she took a breath. 'I didn't know it happened . . . there.'

225

'But Paul knew.' Alison stated it patiently, not a question. 'Paul knew it all.'

She moved against the wall of the saloon bar, so that the big beergut outline of the man who'd talked about Bray half-hid her from the rest of the room. The speech-maker was building to a climax, talking about the winner in a voice half resentful, half admiring. Something about taking risks, nerves of steel. A tall spare weathered man with hair springing up from a high forehead stood beside him, so still, so camouflaged in battered clothes faded to the same shades of tan as his skin that he was almost invisible. Bob Argent, who'd run the other boats down.

'Apparently' – Kay's voice was level, cool – 'apparently it was a preoccupation of his. Knowing Morgan, and all. According to *Rosa*,' and Alison registered the dislike in her voice, 'according to Rosa it was what got him started on massacres. And survivors, of course. He wasn't at that launch by accident, when he met you. *Rosa* kept dropping hints and . . . I'd just had enough. I cornered her yesterday and made her tell me.'

'Rosa.' It was the way she'd said it. 'He . . . did he and Rosa . . .' Rosa was three, four years younger than she was. That long dark hair, streaked with gold. What did Morgan think of Rosa?

Kay sighed. 'I don't think it lasted very long,' she said, reluctantly. 'Jeez. I didn't want to have that conversation with her. He was . . . he didn't actually teach her but she met him through . . . well.' Another sigh. 'Roy Saunders was her supervisor, that's how they met. I bet she thought she was being all grown up, you know. Those things don't last long.'

Alison thought of Rosa's slyness at the party, slipping away as Alison turned to look up at Paul, that first time. *I thought you wanted to be alone.* And now she's wondering if she did the right thing. *Take care.* Her stomach turned.

'Are you all right?' said Kay, into the silence. 'You don't

226

sound all right.' Her voice was tense. 'What a mindfuck, though.' Awe, turning to fear, crept into her voice. 'Being back there.'

'So Rosa knew Saunders, too?' said Alison. 'Their little gang.' She took a breath. 'You remember that gun I told you about? Paul takes it everywhere with him. He brought it here and showed it to me. He told me it was Saunders who gave it to him.'

Kay made a disbelieving noise. 'That's weird,' she said. 'Christ. Men and guns. I always wondered about Saunders, all that military history shit. Maybe he's – maybe it's a homoerotic thing.'

She laughed, but her heart wasn't in it and Alison said nothing. Even down the hissing line Kay seemed to know. 'Something's up, isn't it? Is there anyone there you can talk to? Who knows . . . what happened?'

'I'm all right,' said Alison. She didn't feel all right. In the darkened room she felt like a madwoman; it was in the air she breathed here; it was in every face she saw; it was outside the window. She didn't want to tell Kay about Gina: something told her Gina wouldn't put Kay's mind at rest. 'There's a policewoman from back then. Sarah Rutherford.' She said the name for comfort. 'I made contact.'

'Uh-huh.' She heard Kay process that. 'And him? Paul? Are you going to tell him, now?'

'I don't know what I'll do,' she said, grim. 'Shit. I don't want to be anyone's case study.'

'I expect it helped,' said Kay drily, 'that you don't exactly look like Shrek.' A pause. 'I'm sorry,' she went on, and she did sound it. 'What I mean is, I expect he . . . it's also possible he . . . he's really into you,' she said, grudgingly. 'I mean you're . . . you're . . .'

I'm what? thought Alison. What am I? Sexy? Beautiful? Interesting? I'm Alison from accounts, I keep my head down.

Kay let out an angry sigh. 'What a fuck-up,' she said. 'If he loved you, how could he take you back there?'

227

In the pub now Alison stood with her back to the wall as though on the edge of a cliff. In the bedroom she'd leaned against the headboard and willed the world to stop spinning. How? How? The question wouldn't go away. 'Perhaps he . . . perhaps he wants to . . .' She stopped.

'Perhaps he wants to make you better?' said Kay, gruffly.

'Is that what you think?' Alison couldn't bear how forlorn her voice sounded.

There was a long, long pause and when Kay spoke she sounded tired. 'I hardly know him,' she said with finality. 'It's what you think that matters.'

And now in front of her in the crowded gaseous air of the public bar the groupings shifted and a woman turned, a woman Alison knew. Not knew, really; a woman she'd seen before, and recently. Beside her more people were crowding in through the door, the woman met her eye and then someone else was between them but something had already clicked into place. She was the district nurse Alison had seen coming out of Susan Price's house, boxes of medicine on the back seat of her car.

'Oh God.'

She heard the words whispered with distaste almost in her ear, and recognising the voice Alison shrank back. She could see Roger's hand on his wife's shoulder, pale reddish hairs on the knuckles. It was Lucy Carter she'd heard speak: now she was looking down at the handbag she clutched. They were less than a metre from her. Alison waited, but Morgan wasn't behind them. She peered.

'And the winner is Bob Argent!' came the announcement and she saw the tarnished little trophy raised over the heads at the bar, saw the weathered face of the tall bargeman still immobile, unsurprised. 'Mr Argent. And the *Lady Maud*.' And under cover of the ragged applause, cheers mixed with some barracking sounds, she ducked behind the Carters and was back out of the door.

228

Her phone blipped in her pocket as she sidestepped, out of the light, and she looked at it. Two messages, from Gina. She opened the first: all it said was *Ma*. She looked up again, puzzling, focusing only gradually on what was out there. Two figures stood at the river's edge with their arms around each other, both tall. The door swung and the beam of light broadened, she saw the gleam of blond but by then she'd have known Morgan. The man was only an inch or so taller. Paul.

The phone sat heavy in her hand but Alison didn't look back down, she was watching Morgan raise her hands to take Paul's face between them. Watching her kiss him.

Alison turned and stumbled. Someone's hand was at her waist to stop her going over but she didn't look, she pulled away and was back in the pub. She stepped to one side of the door, and inside her it expanded, under the lights, in the din, her head hammered with what she'd seen. No. Why. *No.* If she had a gun she would shoot them.

The hand was on her waist still. 'You all right?' It was Danny Watts.

Say nothing. Give nothing away. But when she opened her mouth she gasped like a fish. Stopped herself. 'Fine,' she said. His face was close, his eyes were very bright blue in the dark skin, she could see his soft face beginning to weather, to seam. Water gypsy. Her thoughts were scrambled.

Danny stood between her and the door, looking at her, his jaw set – something about her seemed to be making him angry, but the hand was still there. Behind him the door banged and she saw the gleam of a blond head: Morgan strode past them into the crowded bar not looking right or left. Her face was like thunder. As if she felt the glare Lucy Carter turned from where she stood behind her husband at the bar, and saw her daughter.

Ma, said the message. *Ma?*

She looked at the phone, not caring what Danny thought of her, and there was another message. *May's run off.*

The thing inside her sprang back down, it shrank to a hard pebble. She looked up again into Danny's face and behind them in the bar someone began to sing, rusty but strong. She knew without looking that it was the day's winner, Bob Argent, but other voices were already joining in, and it was turning raucous.

May's run off again.

Danny was leaning down and whispering in her ear and she could feel stubble against her neck. His hair was stiff with salt, it smelled of the marsh. She heard him say, 'Joshua and Joe weren't fighting about you that time, you know.' His bright eyes fixed her and all she heard was, *This isn't about you.* She blinked. 'Gina let you think that.' Was it contempt that made his voice like that? He raised his head and looked across the room towards the bar. 'It was your mum they fought over. Not just on the beach. The night Joshua died, too.' His eyes dulled, he looked back at her. 'Her and Chatwin. Joshua never knew when to leave it.'

She stepped back. 'No,' she said. 'What did he say? What did Joshua say about my mum?' Her lips felt numb. She turned to look at the bar to see whose eye he'd caught but saw only Bob Argent raising a glass to his lips, looking back at them.

And then as her head swivelled back to him instead of Danny she saw Paul, a head taller, coming into the room. He looked down into Alison's face expectantly but she couldn't smile, she couldn't pretend that she hadn't seen what she'd seen. They blocked her exit between them, Danny frowning, turning, Paul's mouth opening. *I can explain.* Was that what he was going to say?

Alison couldn't run. She turned the other way instead and pushed deeper into the room.

There were the Carters, in a tight uncomfortable knot,

230

Roger Carter with his elbows raised up against his body in the scrum, Morgan shaking her head. Lucy turned to look at her. Alison skirted them, not looking back, and stopped only when she reached the bar. She held on to the counter – out of the corner of her eye she saw Paul moving through the room but she turned her back. Ron was there, hands on the bar, waiting for her. Just one, she thought. *Run off again.* Wasn't that serious? She was like Gina's kid. For a woman stuck here all her life she'd been permanently running.

'Miss Grace,' he said. She thrust a crumpled fiver at him. 'Vodka and tonic,' she said and he said nothing, only reached up to the bottle with a wineglass but she knew what he was thinking. Her dad's drink.

Ron set the glass down and turned away from the fiver, leaving it in her hand.

'Miss Grace, then, is it?' His voice was amused, with the deadpan see-saw sound of those who never left the villages out here, on the muddy edge.

It was Bob Argent.

'You look just like your mother,' he said.

Chapter Twenty-nine

The letters had been sprayed across the cabin top. PEDO.
Alison stood in the dark, looking back at the lights on the
shore.

Gina's number had taken her to answerphone. 'Let me know
what's going on,' she'd whispered into it, hearing her own
hoarse breath as she ran, feeling the mud slide under her sandals
thinking, You could fall.

You could fall. Careful. You could hit your head, like Stephen
Bray. What had Dad said to him, that night before their lives
had ended?

Who was she running from? All of them. Her chest still
burned from the great tearing panic of her escape.

Taller than most of the crowd, Morgan had turned to watch
her push her way through the public bar and like a sheep
Lucy Carter's head had followed her daughter's, her face blotched
and anxious. Roger Carter had called out after her, jovial,
brutish, *Alice*. The Carters were probably the only ones there
who didn't know her real name, and he even managed to get
her fake one wrong.

The word had appeared on the cabin top since she was last here. Alison took a step on to the rickety landing stage and crouched there: the tide was going out. She could hear it trickle and creep, she could hear the boat settle. She listened for something else.

She squeezed her eyes shut and saw the girl, May, dancing in and out of the coiled ropes on the quay, looking down at her own clever feet. Long legs hooked over the climbing frame, sun-streaked hair hanging down. She felt cold.

Paul's hand had reached out to her from between bodies as she made for the door and he'd got hold of her wrist. She hadn't looked back at him but she knew he was watching and she was almost there, but he got her. Lowest common denominator, basest need. *You're mine.*

But she shook his hand off, and then she was out of the door.

He hadn't followed. Outside, Danny Watts was nowhere to be seen.

Bob Argent's face, unsmiling, was all she held in her head as she began to run. Ahead of her the sail-lofts loomed, their roofs dark points against the night sky.

Bob Argent had looked down impassively, his eyes ranging across her face, seeking out her mother, and for a moment he and Paul might have been the same man, she a child raging while they stood cold above her keeping back what she wanted.

She took a gulp of her drink and the glass sloshed. 'What did my mum have to do with you?' she blurted, reckless. The vodka was warm and slimy, she felt it burn as it hit her stomach, then wiped her mouth. 'You ran him down, didn't you? Simon Chatwin. Were you after my mum too?' Something came into his weathered, expressionless face, his eyes creased. Was he laughing?

'Your mother.' Bob Argent's accent was slow and halting, from deep in the marshland. He held his full pint in front of him and contemplated it. 'Simon Chatwin after your mother?'

233

It seemed Alison had entertained him. He set the drink down untouched.

'Danny said you never do anything by accident,' said Alison, and her own glass felt sticky in her hands.

'You got any ideas,' he said, ruminatively, 'about what Simon Chatwin goes for? Sex, like.' An upward lilt.

Me, Gina, Mum. Alison felt her throat close, but she managed to get it out. 'So tell me why you tried to kill him,' she said. Then, something dawning. 'Danny said it was your daughter he wanted.'

'Tried to kill him?' he said, and there was something danger-ously warm in his voice. 'Police never said anything about that to me.' She stood dumb, waiting. He eyed his glass on the bar but didn't touch it. 'They know, we do things our way,' he said. 'Police do. I run him down, but like Watts told you, nothing by accident. If I'd've wanted him dead, he'd be dead. It wasn't your mum he was interested in.'

'So it was me?' she said, faltering. And for a second she saw pity, only then he lifted his head to look away, across the room.

'You had sisters, didn't you?' he said, not meeting her eye. 'Them little girls. It was Chatwin your dad should've killed, not them.'

'My sisters.' She didn't understand, and then she did. Perhaps she always had.

'My girl,' said Bob Argent distinctly, turning to study her with narrowed eyes, chips of grey. Alison thought of the girl. Studying at university now, Martin Watts had said, looking hard at her.

'My daughter,' Argent said, and the words grated, like iron on iron. 'He asked her if he could put his hand in her knickers.'

Something sparked and floated in Alison's vision: she saw Simon Chatwin's face up close, his mouth moving towards hers in the backyard. The words came as if from a distance. 'She was eleven.'

★   ★   ★

PEDO.

Alison stepped on to the cluttered deck and heard something scrabble below her feet. She crouched to listen. She heard a sound, a low sound that might have been a dog chained in the dark. Frightened. 'May,' she said, her face close to the chipboard cabin doors, putting her fingers to the crack between them. 'May. Is that you?' Something fell and smashed inside and it was Simon's voice she heard.

'Please,' he begged. Alison thought of her sisters, and a wave rolled and gathered inside her, compressing her chest.

'Where's your daughter?' she hissed. 'What have you done with her? Is she down there?'

'Nonononono.' It gibbered, keening. 'They came. She's not here. They came.' She could visualise the dark space behind the doors, the pit filled with junk and unwashed dishes. The grey sheets and the magazines. To take the girl there even once would be too often. It had gone very still below; she put her ear to the crack and listened. She heard breathing, quick and uneven.

'You don't know who I am,' said Alison, and for a second she felt power surge unmanageable through her veins; she was a black angel spreading her wings in the dark. Silence. 'My family . . .' The breathing behind the doors stopped, caught, there was a stifled, choking sound and satisfied he knew now, she went on. 'Were you after my sisters?' There was something intimate and horrible about it, her mouth to the gap whispering precious things to him in the dark. 'Is that why you came round to our yard? Did you try it on my mum too? Is it why you kissed me?'

It was in her throat then, she thought she might vomit and to stop it she raised her fist and brought it down on the chipboard, hard. The pain jolted her, the sound reverberated across the water and her knuckles were raw and bleeding but she couldn't stop, it was like a hunger. 'I've come back for you,'

235

she said, and then she did stop, before something terrible happened, she stopped with her cheek pressed against the rough surface.

The chipboard trembled in front of her, she saw broken fingernails in the gap. Then one side was pulled inwards and Simon Chatwin's eyes were there in front of her; she saw patchy stubble and something dried at the corner of his mouth. His eyes were roaming uncontrollably, looking anywhere but at her. Your father should have killed him, Argent had said. We do things our way, he'd said. Was that right? Alison felt the toxic residue of it in her system, her willingness to go along with that. PEDO.

She pushed herself back on the deck and crouched, ready to run. 'I take my medication,' Simon said. 'I go to my therapy.' His mouth was slack between words, but his eyes had stopped moving, they had settled on her. 'May runs off sometimes,' he said. 'They'll find her. I don't see her. I don't go near her.' His eyes were black, bottomless.

'My family,' she made herself say, although her certainty had come loose, it drifted out of her reach. Simon's head moved from side to side but his eyes stayed on her. 'I wasn't there,' he said. 'He tell you that too? Argent. He knows I wasn't there.' And trembling he lifted a hand, blunt-fingered, to the side of his head. He lifted a flap of stiff hair behind his ear and she saw a line, a long vertical seam of white in the scalp. A scar.

The odour inside the cabin drifted out past him and Alison was on her feet. She groped behind her for the rail, and stepped away from him: she ran. Turning as she reached the gravel path she saw he was still there standing between his cabin doors, watching her go.

She slowed as she came up to the sail-lofts, looking for the narrow place where she could pass through, then she saw it and stepped in between the high weatherboarded sides. As she entered the dark space she first registered that the sound had dropped, the soft wind in the marsh grass and the clink of the boats bobbing cut out by the tall wooden walls, and then that she wasn't alone. She smelled beer and sweat and a hand seized her upper arm, a hand as strong and thoughtless as a vice. It hurt her.

'So now you know.' He spoke and for a second her heart leapt foolishly, treacherously, and then he slammed her back against the boarding.

Chapter Thirty

So now you know. At first she'd thought the voice had been Danny's, and her heart had risen with her face turned up towards him in the dark between the sail-lofts, even if he sounded angry. And drunk. But it had been his brother. Martin. The one who'd gone to pieces at the funeral, the one 'who'd never recovered.

Why did they hate her? She hadn't asked him that as he ranted in the dark. It wasn't just her Martin Watts hated. He swayed over her in the dark, not touching her – after he'd heard the thud of her head hitting the boarding he'd pulled back, letting her go. But she stayed where she was.

'So now you know what that creep was up to,' he said, and she smelled beer. 'Chatwin. That what you came back for? Worth it, was it? He liked them even younger than you, we all knew that.'

'He killed my family,' she said, feeling the breath leave her, and the certainty along with it. The words sounded wrong, but she had to go on. 'Maybe my dad was going to go to the police. Maybe Simon needed to shut him up, shut all of us up. And . . .

and . . . he thought I wasn't there because Gina would've told him I was at hers.' Making it up as she went along. 'None of you thought Simon had the balls, maybe, I don't know, you'd rather think my dad was a murderer. *My* dad.'

Watts made an incredulous noise, a pitying noise. 'Your dad . . .' he began, unsteady.

'Yes,' she said, before he could say another thing. 'He wasn't like you. He'd never . . . he's not a fucking savage. He was, is, he's a . . . a . . . civilised man.'

'He was a pisshead,' said Martin Watts, slurred but succinct, stepping back with a slight stagger. 'Ah, don't give me any of this,' he said. 'I saw you out there. I saw you out there hiding your face. It was you he was going to meet.'

Leaning against the high flank of the sail-loft he tipped his head back and she could see the pale sheen of his face, blank. Somewhere there was a moon but she couldn't see it. The words settled, stubbornly incomprehensible.

'What do you mean?' she said. 'Meet who?'

Martin smiled up at the dark sky, saying nothing, and she grabbed hold of him by the sleeve, feeling the worn ragged fabric, the skin and bone underneath it, there was nothing to him. He looked down. Pushing himself off the boarding care-lessly he took her by the wrist and detached her.

He had turned away from her then, not towards the road and the village but into the unlit marsh, where the tide trickled and the wind blew. 'Meet who?' she'd shouted after him, swaying away from her into the dark. 'I'm not hiding from anyone. Meet who?' But he hadn't answered.

There was a car stopped on the dark verge a little way ahead.

The pub had been quiet by the time she came out on to the road, and most of the crowd dispersed. Alison's legs had been unsteady and she'd had to concentrate hard to keep going in a straight line as she turned up into the village.

239

She might have called someone – Paul? Gina? – to come and get her but she didn't want it. Her thoughts were overloaded, they jumped and fired at random, and she needed to be on her own. Distantly the thought of May floated: *She runs off*, he'd said. *I don't go near her.* The phone hadn't rung: would Gina tell her though, either way? Stupid to think they were still friends. She kept walking as the little car waited for her. She came up on the inside and saw that the driver's window had been wound down. She hesitated.

The hand on the passenger window of the little car was a woman's. Tentatively the indistinct oval of a face peered out, turned towards her. 'Is everything all right?' the woman said. Coming alongside Alison saw boxes on the back seat and then she knew who it was. 'Let me give you a lift,' the nurse said, and as she came closer Alison saw anxiety in her face, and kindness.

'Yes,' she said, defeated. 'Thank you.'

Inside the little car it was as though her ears were blocked, her head buzzed. She had to ask the woman to say it again, as they set off. 'Where are you staying?' The nurse's voice was soft, her glance sidelong.

'Oh.' Take me anywhere, she thought. Take me away. Take me home. Who would be at the hotel? Paul. Christian. Would the Carters be there, camped out in the bar, avid for gossip, where had she been, why had she run off? 'The Queen's Head,' she said.

'It's not safe,' said the woman at the wheel. Eyes shone white in the headlights low down in a hedgerow, something crouching. 'These unlit roads, I mean.'

'A boy got killed, didn't he?' said Alison and the nurse's glance flickered towards her, then back. Alison thought she would be about fifty.

'That was a long time ago,' she said carefully, eyes on the road.

'They never caught him,' said Alison. It didn't matter any more, after all. She was in plain sight now.

'Him?' They were at the junction and the nurse was leaning cautiously over her steering wheel, looking left and right.

'The hit-and-run driver,' said Alison. Engaging gear the woman made a sound in her throat, not so much contemptuous as despairing.

'They're useless,' she said. 'The police.' The lane narrowed, the unkempt hedges feathering the car's sides. They slowed to a crawl.

'Must be difficult for them,' said Alison. 'In a place like this.'

The nurse just frowned. Alison went on. 'Everyone knows everyone else,' she said. 'And none of you seems to trust the police.'

Silence. The car accelerated jerkily, a bend, another bend. Something flew low beside the passenger window, a big soft wingspan and then its dark shape lifted off over the roof and the lit gables of the hotel appeared. The nurse pulled up in the road and turned off the engine. She turned to Alison.

'She wants to see you,' she said, and Alison felt herself freeze in fear, without knowing why. A ghost, she thought: *Mum*, she thought.

'Who?' she said.

'Susie,' said the nurse. 'Susie Price. Susan Price.' Alison let out her breath.

'Mrs Price,' she said. A ghost. 'What happened to Kyra?' She thought of the child walking hairless on the high street, survivor of a blast. 'I remember Kyra.'

'We lost her,' said the nurse sadly, and Alison felt it like a thump to her chest.

'She died?' The privet hedge's leaves looked ghostly in the light cast out from the hotel, silver-blue and gleaming, like poison. Privet *was* poison, she thought, errant. 'When?'

The nurse turned to her, her hands in her lap. 'She hung

241

on for eight years,' she said. 'Advancing and remitting. She could take a lot of treatments, she was strong. But in the end it got her.' Her face was pouchy and sad in the blue light. 'Now it's killing Susie.'

Run, Alison told herself, run now, get out of here. She felt for a moment that if she opened the door and set her foot on the ground it would get her too, the poison would enter her body. She stayed where she was. 'What's killing her?'

'A different cancer, but it's all part of the same thing. That's not a medical diagnosis, of course, but it's still true.'

Alison turned to look through the hedge at the hotel: she could see heads moving through the big front door. She saw the gleam of car roofs. 'She wants to see me?'

The nurse set her veined hands on the wheel. 'When I told her . . . you'd been seen in the village.' Alison drew breath, but didn't ask, how. Who. 'It was the first time she'd opened her eyes properly in months. She sat up.' The woman stared straight ahead into the dark. 'She's on medication,' she said wearily. 'She's had these . . . dreams. But when she said it, she wasn't under, I was about to top her up, she was in pain, she was lucid.'

'Said what?'

And then the nurse turned to look at her. 'She said, bring her to me, I've got to tell her something.' She put out a hand and touched Alison, lightly, on the wrist. 'She said, I've got to tell her something about her mother.'

The police car was parked at the far side of the hotel, and Alison only saw it when she was at the door. It wasn't Rutherford she saw first, it was the other one. The man.

'He's gone up,' Jan had said to her brightly from behind reception and for a moment Alison didn't know who she meant. 'Your husband.'

'Right,' she said, but the word made her stomach clench. It

was gone eleven on the clock over the door – it had been two, three hours since she had shaken Paul's hand off her in the public bar.

Jan frowned. 'Are you all right?' She peered over the desk, and Alison looked down at herself. There was a scratch on one of her bare calves, her feet in the sandals were edged with mud.

'I think I'll just have a quick one before I go up,' she said. 'In the bar. It's got cold, don't you think?' Jan made a non-committal murmur, looking carefully away.

In the toilet mirrors Alison saw her lips were pale, her temples blue-veined. The hair suddenly looked much too short, like something that would be done to you in prison. She took off her glasses and rubbed her eyes.

There was a solitary middle-aged couple in the bar, holding hands across their table, and the foreign girl who'd served them breakfast was wiping things down behind it: she looked resigned when Alison asked for a glass of brandy. Alison sat down where she could see the door into reception, and through it Jan, weary under her neat helmet of hair and careful make-up, talking to the young policeman. Jan hadn't signed up for this, thought Alison. She must have wanted a quiet little country hotel with the clink of glasses and the murmur of conversation. She had come round the reception desk as if to head the policeman off. Jennings.

The policeman hadn't come here to see her, was Alison's thought. If they had, Jan would have said something. But he looked at her. Then he was gone.

She waited. Through the bar's long windows the garden was dark, but something gleamed in the distance, mud snaking away silver under the moon. Across the room the middle-aged man had his hand to the woman's cheek. And then Sarah Rutherford came through the door, half turned back towards the man to say something, her hand gesturing to him to wait. The door swung closed.

243

Rutherford sat next to her, a solid presence. 'We got her,' she said, and the thing inside Alison that had just begun to settle leapt up again in panic. 'It's OK,' said the policewoman. 'I thought you'd be worried.' Alison stared. 'Your friend's kid . . . she went missing.'

Alison subsided, allowing relief in. 'Where was she?' she said.

Rutherford's eyes flicked up to the ceiling and back. 'May?' she said. 'It's not the first time she's run off.' So Chatwin had been telling the truth. 'She was hiding, out on the beach, in the grass. Some guy saw her there, we came here to thank him, as a matter of fact – he saw her and it was getting dark, and . . .' She cleared her throat. 'Fortunately for us he wouldn't leave her till she told him where her mum was.' Rutherford smiled, dead tired. 'She gave him all sorts of grief,' he said.' She looked around, restless, and her eye settled on the middle-aged couple. She looked away quickly, leaning forward with her elbows on her knees.

'Why are you here?' Alison asked, wondering who'd put Rutherford's own child to bed. She must have a husband. 'You didn't come here to tell me that?'

Rutherford's wide-spaced dark blue eyes examined her. 'The man who found May—' she began, but Alison interrupted her.

'I went to see Simon Chatwin,' she said, 'but May wasn't with him.' The policewoman shook her head, frowning.

And then the question rattled out of her, before the policeman watching through the door to reception could come in and stop her. 'Chatwin was after my sisters, did you know that?'

Rutherford raised herself wearily. 'Simon Chatwin is on the Sex Offenders Register following a conviction for indecent exposure to a minor eight years ago,' she said. 'He takes his medication. He's never missed a therapy session.' Her voice was low but tough. 'I shouldn't tell you any of this. We couldn't trace your sisters' father but we know it wasn't Simon Chatwin: apart from anything else he'd have been seventeen when they were conceived. We also know he didn't kill your family.'

'How do you know?'

Rutherford looked up steadily from under her heavy fringe. 'When paedophiles kill,' she said, 'they kill the defenceless. They kill their victims: they kill children and almost always on impulse. They don't go into houses where there are men with guns who can fight back. It's statistics. It's profiling. It's science.'

'Is that all?' Alison found herself saying, Alison who'd studied maths and physics and chemistry, only girl in the class half the time. Alison who knew science doesn't explain everything.

Rutherford tilted her head and shook it and the ponytail swung. 'We had a body of evidence. This isn't a matter of glaring facts, not always. It takes us months. Just believe me, Chatwin couldn't have done it.' She studied Alison, grave. We also know your father's myopia had been improving, as yours will, as it does with age. Even without his glasses his eyesight wouldn't have prevented him from killing your mother, your brother, your sisters. The shots were fired at close range.' She paused, earnest: Alison saw how she'd recovered from panic, reassessed. 'This isn't good for you.'

Alison held herself very still. 'I can decide what's good for me,' she said. 'It's my life. It's my life.'

Rutherford said nothing and, goaded, Alison felt something slip from her control. 'It's not like you're worried about me, are you?' she said, suddenly angry. 'After all this time? I mean, you've got it covered, haven't you? My dad did it, so it's not like there's a murderer out there.'

But Rutherford's head moved, slightly, and following it Alison saw that Jennings had appeared in the door to the bar and was looking at his boss, questioning. Rutherford had shifted forward on the seat, about to leave.

'As a matter of fact,' she said, looking straight at Alison, a look that cooled her skin, immobilised her. 'There is.'

'What?' said Alison, and everything hung, the honeymooners,

245

the girl behind the bar, the gleam of the estuary through the window.

'Stephen Bray's death wasn't an accident,' said Rutherford.

She spoke deliberately, levelly, and Alison saw that this was what she'd come for, after all. This woman who had appeared in Alison's dreams, whom she had always, down the years, thought of as having been on her side, was watching her for a reaction, like a suspect. And for a terrible suffocating moment Alison understood that it was connected to her, because it had to be. She was bound to the dead weight of Bray's body in the cold mud.

If they wired Alison up, if they monitored her responses, what would it tell them? Her heart was racing, her mouth was dry, even her skin felt weird and clammy. She thought she had learned to hide what she was feeling, but with Sarah Rutherford watching her, guilt rose inside her like sickness.

'Who do you think killed him?' she said, her tongue like rubber in her mouth.

'Stephen Bray didn't drown, he didn't fall and hit his head, there was nothing he could have hit it on out there.' Sarah Rutherford leaned close to her across the bar table. 'But he sustained a massive depression fracture to the skull and consequent brain injury that killed him almost immediately.' The policewoman sat back. 'He managed to stagger a couple of steps into the mud but by the time he hit the ground, he was dead.' She passed a hand over her forehead, rubbing: her skin looked dry at the temples, her hair coming out of its ponytail now. 'There was still whisky in his stomach, but everyone knew he couldn't afford whisky, and the last witness we have, someone who saw him after the pub had closed, said he wasn't drunk.'

If she closed her eyes Alison could smell the home brew and paraffin and tar, she could see the old man poring over maps and photographs, his head next to her father's. She managed to say, 'Who was the last person to see him? He knew something. Maybe that's why. My dad must have told him something.'

But Sarah Rutherford looked at her strangely, and Alison knew something was different. 'Cathy Watts saw him,' Rutherford said, watching her. 'She said, he was excited about something. He said he was going to meet someone, someone he hadn't seen for a long time.' And then she stood as if she was about to leave, but still she didn't go.

The lights were off in the hotel bedroom when Alison opened the door but Paul wasn't asleep. He was waiting for her: she could see the gleam of his eyes as he watched her move about the room in the dark. He lifted the covers to let her in and she lay against him. He didn't speak and although since Kay's phone call, since the pub car park, the conversation she needed to have with him had changed shape twenty times, nor did she.

By now it all seemed like something that had happened a thousand miles away and years ago. Did it even matter, him and Morgan, whatever that was? A woman about to get married gets drunk and kisses her ex-boyfriend, big news. Kyra Price had died after eight years fighting to stay alive, getting sicker and sicker. An old man had been beaten to death out on the lonely marsh, a hundred yards from where her family had died. And she was a suspect.

Paul knew who she was. Did he think she might have done it, too, was that what he wanted her for, he wanted to play detective? Perhaps he wouldn't even be surprised when the police came back for her. His body was warm, his heartbeat at her ear steady, she closed her eyes and the thought took shape, seductive as smoke. He knows me.

Sarah Rutherford had stood there fiddling with something in her hands, turning to look at the policeman waiting for her in the doorway, and then she said, her voice low, 'Someone says they saw you out there, Alison. Out there by the house.'

Yes, thought Alison, hypnotised by the way Rutherford was looking at her. She'd seen someone watching her herself, she almost said it, agreeing, *yes*. Standing by the crooked house in the wind in her trainers that first morning, someone had stood out on the marsh and watched her, yes. But Rutherford seemed to mean something different: Alison struggled to understand what she was saying.

'When?' she said stupidly. 'Someone saw me when?'

'You went to meet Bray.' Alison couldn't even shake her head: Rutherford was avoiding her eye as she went on. 'Cathy Watts said. Stephen told her it was you he was going to meet. Did you give him whisky? What did you want from him?' And then she'd straightened her shoulders, cleared her throat. 'I won't make you come now,' she said, remote now, 'but we'll need to talk to you tomorrow, Alison. You know that, don't you?'

Sitting there frozen in her seat Alison had not remonstrated, she hadn't stood and shouted because it had seemed impossible. Don't make a fuss, was all she could think. And all she could manage was to say, 'The wedding's at midday.' Her voice had sounded distant, mechanical. She had no idea how she should sound, how to convince Rutherford of anything. 'There'll be a reception afterwards. You'll know where to find me.'

She had an alibi, of course. Didn't she? She hadn't asked when Stephen Bray had died, and she realised that Sarah Rutherford had not told her. All she knew was, it had happened after the pub had closed, twenty-four hours after they'd seen him there. She'd have been in bed with Paul.

Paul.

His arm around her had slackened: he was asleep.

Chapter Thirty-one

Was he avoiding her?

Alison had fallen asleep properly not long before dawn and by the time she woke, it was half past eight. She saw his suit for the wedding hanging on the outside of the wardrobe, fine dark grey wool, she saw the five-button cuffs and the polished old-fashioned shoes, but Paul wasn't there.

Raising herself in the bed, she stared at the suit. She hadn't seen it before and it set something ticking. What kind of man was she in love with? She'd never seen her father in a suit: everything about this one, like everything Paul owned, was carefully chosen. Was it expensive? She thought it probably was, like the flat and all the things in it. Not much of it but all of it good and all of it sending the same message. Order, tradition? Strength. Power. She got out of bed, crossed to the wardrobe and put her face against the cloth. He knew who she was. It wasn't the same revelation as it had been yesterday, when Kay made it: then it had been a shock. It had been horrible. Now she walked around it tentatively, wondering what it meant. An aspect of it was almost . . . exciting. It was new. It might even have worked, the next phase. Only there was Morgan, too.

There was a note on the desk: *Gone for a run*. No exclamation marks, no extraneous information. His work had been cleared away. She looked around for it and saw his briefcase leaning against the chair. It was heavy when she picked it up: she could look inside if she wanted to. She set it down.

Simon Chatwin hadn't done it. Rutherford said so. But something crawled still inside her at the thought of him, of him creeping around her car, of his wooden attempts to ingratiate himself. He'd tampered with her car, she was sure of it. She shivered.

Her dress hung behind the suit, the blue dress with tiny buttons down the back that Paul had bought her. The gold sandals were on the floor. He must have put them there for her but it tugged at her. You can't have him. This was a test and you've failed it. He's gone. She closed her eyes and thought of him running through the lanes, across fields, to Morgan. Morgan would have him: for all the marquee and the flowers in church and the twenty grand dress she'd take Paul in exchange, she'd take him into her four-poster and her mother could coo over him and bring him breakfast. Alison couldn't offer him any of that.

Naked, she crossed to the window, looking for a draught, feeling where it found its way around the heavy old window frame. She put a hand to the cold glass. Outside the blue had gone from the sky, it was leaden and low, but the wind was still buffeting the cypresses.

She thought of Simon Chatwin cowering in his battened cabin, and of what Rutherford had said. It's science, statistics. But if not him, then who? She sat back on the bed, her mobile in her hand, she groped for what she knew, who she could trust. She could trust Gina. She closed her eyes: something Gina had told her was lodged there in the red dark – she looked for it. Was it Simon? Gina would know.

250

May had been found, she was home safe with Gina: something good had happened. It would be OK to call. Alison picked up the phone and dialled. But as she waited, she heard him. Paul was in the corridor, calling back to someone, to Jan, or maybe Christian. In a flurry of panic and relief she fumbled with the phone and hung up before Gina answered.

He was at the door, the handle turned and Alison abruptly became aware of her nakedness. She grabbed for the slip and was inside it and on her feet, facing him as he came through the door.

She'd never seen Paul running: she'd had no idea he went. He was wearing shorts, trainers, a grey T-shirt, not new, he must have gone out and bought them once, he must have packed them. He looked different, more ordinary, ruddier. It could happen, thought Alison with wonder, we could live together, we could get married, have a life. Children.

He was sweating. He picked a towel off the armchair and wiped it across his forehead, looking at her.

'My turn to clear my head,' he said, dropping the towel but still looking at her.

And before she could answer, as she stood there, feeling the heat rise on her own body under the slippery silk as she looked at him, he said, 'I know who you really are.' And he raised an arm to wipe at his face again.

'Who am I?' asked Alison, and she felt cold.

'You're Esme Grace, and your father killed your family. Here in this village.' His voice was steady, resigned. 'I've known it since I first met you.'

Alison stood as still as she could manage but she felt breathless, winded.

'I wanted to know if you'd tell me,' he said. Hold on, she protested silently, grasping for the unfairness of the statement, but all she could focus on was that it *had* been a test, after all. She had failed.

'I would have,' she said, although it was too late.

Paul stripped off his T-shirt, patched with sweat, dropped it on a chair and he stepped towards her. He put his hands on her arms, but didn't come any nearer.

'I should have told you,' he said, frowning. She stared, trying to process what he was saying. Was it too late, or not?

'I know,' he went on, staring down. 'I'm not good at . . .' He made an impatient sound. 'I didn't really understand how cruel I was being. Until . . . until we got here.' He lifted a hand off her and rubbed the back of his neck to ease something. 'Believe it or not, I thought it might help. It was a mistake.' He let her go and sat down, his face in his hands, his muffled voice resigned. 'Morgan will tell you, no doubt. Someone'll tell you. Some might call it reserved, private. Or alternatively classic academic, unable to empathise.' He raised his head. 'I thought you and I were alike. In that way.'

'Morgan thinks only she understands you,' said Alison, and she folded her arms across herself, letting the cold take hold of her, she couldn't let herself soften, say *Yes, we are alike.* 'Maybe that's true.' He kept looking, she saw his grey eyes cloud. 'Was that why you were kissing her?'

'Is that what you think you saw?' Paul said, very quietly. 'Well, in that case, who am I to argue?' And reaching for the towel, he got up.

When he was at the bathroom door she said, 'They want to talk to me about Stephen Bray's death.' He stopped, frowning. 'Someone said he was going out there to meet me. Someone says they saw me.'

'What?' He let out an incredulous sound, that was almost a laugh. 'No.' But his face was alive, interested: he couldn't help himself. 'You mean, the other night? When the old man died?'

'This isn't a joke,' she said, and it was all hopeless, she could see that. 'This isn't a game.' Paul frowned. 'I'm connected, all the bad shit that happens here. This is why I should never have come back.' Her throat felt choked with the effort to explain: he looked only bewildered.

'I just know the police want to talk to me today,' she said, faltering. 'I don't know when.' His head tilted, waiting. 'About Bray,' she said, then before she could stop herself, 'It wasn't my dad. I know he didn't kill them.' And rushing on, 'I found . . . I found . . . What if they still think it was me?' And disbelieving, she repeated. 'The police want to talk to me.'

Gently he steered her on to the bed and sat beside her, his arm around her. She let herself be held. 'I'll be here,' he said. 'Whenever it is.'

She looked up at him in alarm. 'They won't let you be with me, though,' she said.

'It's all right,' Paul said. 'I mean, I'm not going away. I'm going to help.'

His arms around her felt like a luxury, something that had to be rationed: she made herself open her eyes, she made herself think. 'What did he say to you? The old man, Stephen Bray. We saw him the first night and he said something to you at the bar.'

Paul frowned. 'Yes,' he said. 'Do you think that's got something to do with it?'

'I saw him look at me,' said Alison. She was oddly calm: she didn't have to think before she spoke any more, she didn't have to calculate. It felt strange. 'Did he recognise me?'

Uncomfortably, Paul shifted his arm around her shoulders. 'I think he might have done,' he said. 'He said something about when you were small you had long hair.' Alison held still. 'I pretended I didn't know what he meant,' he added, but he looked worried. 'Did you? Have long hair?' She nodded, and he put his hand up to it now, smoothing the furry shortness of it behind her ears. 'I told him we were here for the wedding,' he went on slowly, frowning. Taking his hand away. 'I thought it was just . . . you know. Small talk. He was rambling a bit, like old men do.'

'What's the matter?' said Alison. 'There's something the matter.' Paul just shook his head. 'What did he say to you?' she said.

'Do you think they'll want to talk to me too?' he said. She looked at him. Something was making him uncomfortable.

'I suppose,' she said. 'I mean . . . do you want me not to mention it? You talking to him?'

'What?' he said, frowning. 'No, of course not. No. It's just . . .'

'What did he say to you?' she said again.

'Well – it might have meant nothing,' said Paul. 'I'm not even sure I heard it right, I wasn't paying much attention. I need it straight in my head before I go talking to the police.' He grimaced, rubbing his forehead. 'It's – well – it's frightening, isn't it? I can see that. They might not necessarily believe you. And if the police don't believe you . . . there are consequences.'

'Can't you tell me? What he said?' He looked uneasy. 'Sorry,' she said. 'OK.' She put her face against his chest then pulled back, trying to smile.

'You can't go to church smelling like that,' she said. 'Go on. Wash.'

He'd been in there five minutes when the phone began to ring. Not hers, his. She could hear it, not see it. Still in her slip Alison stood at the centre of the room trying to trace the sound and then she saw the lit throb of the tiny screen, somewhere through the thin fabric of his T-shirt on the chair: he'd taken it with him running. The shower had stopped. Alison picked the phone up: *Morgan*, said the screen.

Paul came through the door in a towel and she held the mobile out to him. It was still ringing. His face was set as he looked down at it and she quailed.

He put it to his ear. 'Yes.' He sounded exasperated. He glanced at Alison, frowning, distracted, then away. She heard the urgent rattle of Morgan's voice, some kind of diatribe that barely paused for breath. Then a command, then another.

'Yes,' he said. 'Hold on, all right, all right.' Silence. 'You're sure?' A murmur. 'All right.' He raised his head and looked at Alison. 'I'm coming,' he said into the phone, still looking at her. He hung up.

'She needs you,' she said, flatly. 'It's OK.'

'They think there's been someone in the grounds,' said Paul. 'She's panicking. A prowler. With the marquee, all the comings and goings.' He was pulling on trousers.

'What about her father?' she said, stubborn. 'What about her husband-to-be?'

He was buttoning his shirt. 'Roger . . .' His impatient tone, she knew now, disguised anxiety. 'He's . . . she doesn't want him to get worked up. She's worried about him, he's not as young as he thinks he is.' He tucked the shirt in, glanced at her. 'And it's bad luck to see the husband-to-be on the wedding day, isn't it?' He sat on the chair and lifted a shoe.

'What about the police?' she said, without much hope.

'I think the police . . .' He looked up at her.

'They've got other priorities,' she supplied. Paul stood up and came close to her, clean-smelling now, dressed. Civilised. He put his mouth to her hair.

'There *is* someone out there,' she said, almost to herself. He took her face between his hands.

'You don't think it was your father?' he said, examining her. 'You're serious about that?'

'It wasn't him,' she said, and she felt what had been longing and instinct solidify: it became certainty. And this time someone believed her.

Paul nodded, frowned. 'I was here that night, remember,' he said slowly. 'The night your family was killed. I always wondered . . .' But then he broke off. 'We've got to talk about this,' he said. 'When I get back.'

★   ★   ★

The van smelled of sweat and rust. There were dead leaves in the footwell. Alison sat in the passenger seat with Simon Chatwin beside her. He looked terrified.

It had been parked on the forecourt as she came into the foyer, and then she'd seen him, shuffling like a much older man, coming round it to open the rear doors. Without pausing to think Alison had walked away from Jan in mid-conversation, hearing the chatter about wedding dresses stall behind her, and she was out on the gravel. Chatwin had stared at her: she'd walked past him and climbed inside the van. Waited.

The smell had hit her straight away, unchanged since he opened those back doors to her all those years before. Iron and oil and perspiration. The driver's door had opened and he peered inside. He had looked back over his shoulder, frightened, and then he'd got in beside her.

He looked much smaller than she remembered, as though his bones had thinned, his shoulders had lost muscle overnight. His hands were rough and dry in his lap, and his trousers were muddy.

'You didn't know me at first, did you?' Alison said. There were spots of colour at his cheeks, but he wouldn't look at her.

'You can't say anything,' he said. She tipped her head back, then straightened when she felt it touch the greasy seat-back. 'I'll lose the job,' he said, sullen.

'I don't care about your fucking job,' she said. She didn't recognise herself. She had no compassion. Rutherford had said it wasn't him. But she felt such sudden uncontrollable hatred, for the memory of his prying fingers, his dry mouth, of what he had been panting for in their backyard. If that wasn't motive, what was?

'It was you,' she said. 'He told me, Bob Argent told me. You were after my sisters, and so you killed them all. My mother, my brother, my sisters. Did Bray see you, did he know? Did

256

my dad catch you?' A sob rose. 'He'd never have hurt anyone. My dad never. You took the gun off him, you smashed his glasses. You were in the yard. I heard you, I . . .'

And then Alison ran out of words or breath, she felt it all drain abruptly out of her, she felt like lead, sitting there in the seat. Silence. She could only hear him breathing, heavily. He killed them, and she was sitting next to him in his van, he could start the car, drive away. He could drive somewhere where no one could see them and kill her too.

But Alison felt nothing. She felt no danger. If he'd wanted to do it, he could have killed her last night, out on the marsh. It came to her that the only fear in the enclosed space came from him. But still she wanted to punish him.

'My sisters were wrapped in their sleeping bag,' she said. 'Whoever killed them couldn't stand to look at them.' He was blinking. 'I found them,' she said. 'I was there.'

He made a noise then, like something broken, he began to rock minutely, his hands still in his lap. 'I want to get better,' he said. 'I do what they tell me. I never hurt anyone.' Alison thought of the porn mags, an ache in her jaw as if she was going to throw up.

'Is it part of your therapy, trying to chat up . . . adult women?' she said. 'You did something to my car.' His eyes darted her way.

'I didn't touch it,' he said, too quickly. Then, 'You wouldn't have talked to me otherwise.' There was a whiny note to his voice. She felt hollow, the adrenalin going from her as she understood, Rutherford had been right.

'Was it you in the yard that night?' she said dully. 'Did you come to the house?' At the change in her voice he stopped rocking, he looked at her.

'Your mum talked to me now and again,' he said. There was something dreamy in his voice. 'She probably didn't think too hard about why I was there.' He gazed through the windscreen

257

as if at something far away and Alison had an uncomfortable feeling, that she was encouraging something like nostalgia. 'Other things on her mind. She wasn't interested in me. She did it to make him jealous.' His eyes flickered towards Alison and away. She sensed he was groping towards something, his brain muddied. 'They weren't your dad's, were they? I heard. Not your sisters. Half. Half-sisters.' He looked towards her hopefully, as if of having said the right thing. She clenched her hands in her lap.

'Make who jealous?' she said. 'My dad?' His head turned quickly away from her, he faced front.

'I wasn't there,' he said. 'I don't know.'

'You were found out on the marsh that next morning,' she said, looking at Simon Chatwin's profile, and she suppressed pity. 'You *were* there.'

Chatwin's head dipped, he shook it slowly from side to side. 'I've got an alibi,' he said. 'He'll never admit it. She knows it's true, though. She knows. The policewoman.'

'Who's your alibi?' There was movement through the smeared window. Someone had come out on to the hotel's porch and was smoking. She could smell it.

Turning to her, Chatwin looked almost crafty. 'Argent took me out to the spit that night and beat the shit out of me and left me there. I was the other side of the estuary and they said I'd had the injuries six hours at least. It was minus two and I could have died.' His head held high, the fear briefly gone at the thought of his own extinction. 'Coldest June night ever. I could have died.'

And as she watched his face changed and she glimpsed it, still there, the thing that twisted inside him. From the other side of the medication, from long ago when he'd grabbed her in the yard, something that had been there before he'd gone under the barge in the grey water, a mute reaching for what he wanted, blind as a worm in soil, innocent and horrible.

258

And then he turned away, not answering, his face against the side window and she saw him stop. She looked where he was looking. It was Christian standing on the porch, smoking, in shirtsleeves.

Chatwin rubbed at the glass. 'They found her,' he said. 'Someone here found her. My kid.'

Christian didn't look like a man about to take a momentous step. He looked bored, impatient. Good, thought Alison, a little spiteful reflex she couldn't restrain, and all at once she knew she had to get out of the van, something toxic was leaching into her.

'Yes,' she said. 'May. Good.' She set her shoulder against the door and paused.

'I stay away from her,' said Chatwin, and the fear was back.

'You better,' she said. And she was out.

At the tinny chunk of the van's door closing Christian's head turned and she saw him take it in – her, the van, the motionless figure in the driving seat – but he betrayed nothing. His face didn't change.

In Alison's head things spun and settled; rows of fruit coming into line; a counter clicking down. She walked around the van and then Christian did smile at her, although it was distantly. 'Plenty of time, right?' he said lightly, looking at her jeans, flip-flops.

'Sure,' said Alison, although it wasn't true. No time. 'I won't be late,' she said, 'don't worry.' She felt his eyes on her back as she turned and walked away, out in to the road. She knew where she had to go next.

Chapter Thirty-two

In the cottage's dim sitting room, in among the bookshelves and armchairs there were things that didn't belong in anyone's home. An ugly, oversized chair loomed under the net-curtained window: it was a commode, Alison realised as her eyes adjusted to the gloom. An oxygen cylinder, battered and scratched, leaned against it. Boxes and plastic pouches of medicines sat on a wheeled trolley.

Alison had knocked, and heard something only vague and frightening, the sound of disintegrating speech. She'd pushed at the door and it had opened.

The real furniture was pressed back against the walls, into corners, the three piece suite redundant. There was a bed in here now, too high for the low ceilings, a drip on its gantry beside it, and attached to the drip was Susan Price. Susie, the nurse had called her, because after twenty years of sickness together they'd be old friends. On the pillow her face turned slowly in the grey light. She looked at Alison.

'Mrs Price?'

On the bed the woman's mouth opened, dark.

The village had seemed dead as she walked up through it; a Saturday morning but in the soft grey light it was deserted. Alison had been grateful for the silence, for her invisibility. She wanted absolution, even if she didn't know what for, except for being her mother's daughter, her mother the slag, her father the drunk, the madman: that was why she was coming here. Gina wasn't in the business of forgiving anybody.

'Mrs Price?' she said again. 'It's Esme Grace. You wanted to tell me something.'

The mouth was a black hole. What could she tell Alison? What could she know?

But there was something in the room with them, it lay soft and dark in the corners, it crept and settled under the crowded furniture, hiding in the dust. The thing that had come into the crooked house hadn't been ordinary – if you exposed it to the light it wouldn't look like her father, it wouldn't lie there broken and defenceless. It was a shape-changer, it was crafty and swift, it was ruthless. It was here.

'Oh.' And then Susan Price was struggling on the bed like a creature crushed, her thin arms pushing down, but as Alison reached her something had been gained. She was upright, her breathing shallow but triumphant. Alive.

'Esme.' It was a small gasp. Alison moved closer, drawn by the sound of her lost name. There was a tasselled stool by the bed and she sat on it, low, her face at the same height as Kyra's mother's. Susie. She saw there was a little dial on the drip.

'Why are you on your own?' she said. 'You can't be on your own.'

'They're coming to get me this morning,' said Susan Price, and she was almost smiling. 'The hospice.' Another gasp. 'It's all right.'

Is it? thought Alison. No. Her hand crept on to the blankets, and rested there: the dying woman's hand lifted a bit and then fell back, but they didn't touch. She was looking at Alison, still and calm, just concentrating on breathing. 'It's better on my own but' – and then she shrugged minutely, ran out of breath – 'I wanted to tell you.'

She seemed unclouded, but it was only that she was conserving her energy for sentences worth finishing. Was that what dying was like? At best.

Susan Price's eyes fluttered, closing. She opened them again and looked around the room, her gaze resting on the mantelpiece, a chair, a picture then back to Alison. 'I was in a hurry,' she said, quite clear and distinct. 'November. Kyra had a fever, I was driving her to the hospital.' Her head moved restlessly on the pillow at the memory. 'First I saw the boy.' A breath. 'He was sitting by the side of the road, I only saw him at the last moment, he wasn't on my side of the road or I'd have, I might have.' She blinked. 'The boy that died.'

'Joshua Watts.' Alison saw the chest rise and fall, rise and fall. 'Was he on his own?'

'He had his head in his hands,' said Susan Price. Another breath. 'He looked up when the car came and it looked like he'd been in a fight.' There was more. 'I saw her further out, she was coming the other way. All white. Her face all white.' Her lips together. 'Your mother. The night the boy died.'

And her eyes wandered, inquiring, gentle, to the morphine pump at her shoulder on the gantry. Perhaps she's out of it, thought Alison, grasping at straws, but somewhere Susan Price had found more of whatever her failing biology needed, oxygen or glucose, her system, now in motion, wanted to keep going. She was still talking.

'Came out of the lane,' and she licked dry lips, 'she did. Came out fast, just before the junction.'

'Would she have seen him?' Her mother had never said a thing about seeing Joshua Watts that night. Not a thing.

'She was going very fast.'

And it grew and hardened, somewhere under her ribs. 'You mean she . . .' And it was her breath gave out this time.

Susan Price laid her head back, her fingers moving on the blanket, feeling for something. On the pillow her head moved, up and down. Yes.

Joshua Watts had died between that lane and Gina's house, where the road was still narrow, where his body had lain till morning. The lane just before the junction with the main road, where Alison had watched the truck full of turnips sway past, where a man had come around her shaking his fist from the driver's seat. In the fallout from the huge terrible thing her mother had done she realised something else.

'You didn't tell the police.' On the bed Susie's mouth opened, closed, opened again.

'Oh,' she said, her voice falling off, her eyes distant now, seeking. 'Police?' she said. 'What good are they?' Alison felt a painful tug: poor Sarah Rutherford, shaking her fringe out of her eyes, just trying to keep at it.

'It was Kyra,' said Susie. 'I was in the hospital with her that week, I never left her more than twenty minutes because they said she might go.' She turned her head away. 'I didn't care about anyone else,' she said, and Alison heard a kind of greediness in her voice, a longing. 'They can all die, I thought, just let me keep her,' she said. 'Let them all die.'

The girl had lived another eight years, the nurse had said. Advancing and remitting. That had been the bargain.

All Alison could see was the line of Susan's jaw, where the flesh had fallen away. Susan's eyes were looking somewhere else now, they were looking off into a corner of the room, where the dark was.

Esme's pretty mother had killed a child, and had driven away without stopping. Had she even known what she'd done? And in the dim room Alison prayed, she prayed that Mum hadn't known she hit him, she couldn't have left another woman's child to die alone beside the road. That she had only known when it was too late and the milkman found him, the next morning, battered and dead. Even then, had she told herself, it might not have been her?

Who else knew? Because in a place like this, it couldn't stay hidden, knowledge like this ran underground like the roots of trees. Who else?

Sometimes you couldn't choose. Sometimes the bad thing came to get you.

At first sight, before she turned and saw who had walked into her garden, Cathy Watts had looked different: she had looked at peace, looking down at all the flowers in her arms. Then she turned.

Standing there with her arms full and her feet slopping in ancient men's slippers, she didn't look startled at Alison's appearance in the patch of luminous green behind the boatyard, her expression only hardened into grimness. Under the heavy sky the grass seemed to glow even brighter. The flowers were roses: big, heavy, ivory-yellow heads already on the turn, petals dropping. Leaves and branches were scattered under the great overgrown bush that covered the back of the shed where Cathy Watts must have been cutting. There were scratches all up her dry brown forearms and her hair was a wild halo.

There'd been no sign of her sons. Crossing the muddied forecourt to the yard looking out for them Alison had noticed that their little boat was gone. The big peeling doors to the shed were closed and a rusted padlock hung from the chain that secured them.

As Alison had walked down through the village towards the Watts's boatyard, the crooked house had sat in the corner of her vision, waiting, even though the tilted gable had been

264

concealed from her until she got to the waterfront. Sometimes you couldn't choose: sometimes it came for you.

'Are those for the church?' said Alison, although she could see straight away they would be rejected by Morgan, their big heads too messy, some petals browning. And it must be too late, by now. The sun was no more than a glare behind low blustery cloud, but it was high.

'They've had bought flowers,' said Cathy Watts, looking at her levelly, and she looked over her shoulder at the house. 'You're not coming in.'

'Am I not?' said Alison, standing her ground. Watts looked at her and something new was in her face, it stirred fear up in Alison's gut.

'You dare, do you?' said Cathy Watts softly, and turned towards her door.

The house had low windows and through each of them the grey line of the muddy horizon was visible. There was a smell of oil and mud, and it was untidy: a battered sofa held a coil of rope, there was a bucket of something in the middle of the floor but in amongst it all on one wall an old sideboard gleamed with polish. Glass doors with plates behind and some photographs in frames. Cathy Watts dropped her armful of roses on top of the coiled rope and leaned stiffly to turn on a lamp standing by the photographs: shadows moved in the room's corners, as though something was hiding.

Alison was meant to see the photographs so she held her ground and looked. A big-eyed baby, half his mother's face visible behind him as she held him up for the photograph, Cathy Watts, her eyes soft with adoration. She looked no more than a girl herself although she must have been in her thirties, she already had two children. He was her littlest, her last. An intent toddler in a sandpit, a tearaway standing up on a bicycle's pedals, a young man with a bleached shock of hair and his mother's Eskimo eyes in a brown face, staring

265

direct and serious at the camera. Joshua. Alison felt her throat close.

'I've just been to see Susie Price,' she said, her voice low. 'She wanted to tell me something.'

'Yes,' said Cathy Watts, looking without interest at blood on her fingers from the scratches. She frowned around the room as if it was unfamiliar and leaned to shove the rope with the roses on it along the sofa. Lowering herself painfully she sat beside it and pointed to a wooden chair. Alison obeyed.

'She'll have thought it was time,' said Cathy. 'She's not got more than a week or so. Maybe she was waiting for you.' Her tone was musing.

The comment snagged on Alison's thoughts. She stared: Cathy Watts wasn't a whimsical woman. There was no way Susie Price could have expected her to come back, no way any of them could have, it wasn't like she'd known the Carters before . . . and yet. And yet. The idea was outlandish but there was a germ of something in it. Was it the wedding, was it even the slightest disturbance in the surface? The district nurse sitting down beside Susie and saying, the Carter girl's getting married, her patient raising herself to listen. Something, anything, to be the catalyst. Thinking, *This might be the time.*

Cathy Watts was looking at her, waiting for something.

Alison spoke. 'Susie never told the police,' she said, watching the woman's face. 'She told you, though, didn't she?' She felt it lapping at the edges, she saw the dark, she felt the cold. Had it come from here, from this room heaped with flotsam, rope and buckets, this half-wild family that let the marsh inside with them? *We do things our way.* The wrong way.

'There was no need to tell the police, once she'd told me,' said Cathy Watts, grim.

'Because you took matters into your own hands?' said Alison. 'When did Susie tell you?' *Bitch.* Would a woman scrawl that? 'Was it you, or your boys?' One dead child for a whole family.

266

She imagined a blackness like ink, seeping. What did you call it? Grief; rage; madness.

'You don't know what you're talking about.' Cathy Watts's voice was low, it vibrated in the room. 'My boys?' A dangerous edge.

'I don't know what it's like,' said Alison, back at her, 'to lose a child. But my sisters' – and she could hear herself as if from a distance, her voice unnaturally level – 'my brother.' She held herself very still. 'I was nowhere near Stephen Bray the night he died and you know it. You sent your boys to the police with stories about me.' She watched Cathy Watts for a reaction. 'Was he the only one that knew; had he started talking?'

'What stories?' the older woman said, calm. 'They saw you.'

'You mean Danny saw me running out there my first day here,' said Alison.

Because it had been him. Standing there as if walking on water out in the creek, upright with an oar resting in his hand, letting the boat drift with the trickling tide and watching her. He'd known then, she wasn't a stranger. Had he turned and gone home and told his mother?

'I haven't been back out there since.' But as she said it she felt the tug, the dark inside the crooked house calling to her across the marsh, its fingers reaching between the banks of mud and samphire.

'Stephen told me that night, when he got out of the pub. He said someone left a message for him,' said Cathy Watts. 'He said he was going to meet you.' Alison felt a prickle at the back of her neck: Cathy Watts believed what she was saying.

'It wasn't me,' Alison said, her voice rising. 'I didn't leave him a note, I didn't talk to him, I didn't touch him.' Me? she thought. Me? Hit an old man over the head? She felt her breath run away with her, like a panting dog. 'Did you come out to our house that night? Did you see my mum in the kitchen? The boys knew I'd gone out. I saw them at the bus

267

stop on my way to Gina's. Is that why you didn't come after me?'

The old woman, squeezed into the corner of her sofa, made a brushing motion with her hand, impatient. Unafraid. 'You think I could kill a child?' She turned her head slightly, so that the photographs came into her line of sight and she looked at them, a long unwavering look. There was nothing soft in her face that Alison could see, only iron strength. 'Kill another woman's child?'

'I think you could,' said Alison. 'If you had to.'

'I could never kill a child,' Cathy Watts said, turning her head from the photographs to Alison. 'Not mine, not another woman's.'

And Alison remembered the peace in her face, before she'd turned. Could you ever be at peace? If you'd done that? She couldn't name it but she could feel it, the sleeping bag's weighted nylon, slipping through her hands. When she spoke it came out hoarse. 'And the boys?' Cathy Watts watched her, her face almost mild. Silent. 'Your sons?' Still nothing.

Alison leaned, a physical pain under her ribs as she thought of Danny, his hand on her waist in the pub, his fierce gaze. Could he? 'I've got to know, see,' she said, pleading. 'Could they have done it? Knowing what losing Joshua did to you. Martin was out of it, wasn't he?' In her head she pictured the two of them, running silent out to the house in the dark, along the gravel path, catching Dad by surprise, drunk and reeling after the pub. Pushing past him into the kitchen: Mum. Going from room to room, Danny putting a hand on Martin's arm, the two of them looking up the stairs to her room. Esme's room.

BOOM.

She's not there. Remember? Their heads turning as she stood in the pedals on her way past them at the bus stop to Gina's. Had it been the sight of her that had set them off: there she goes, not a care in the world? Had they been high on adrenalin? Had they known that he'd got his hands on a gun?

'I don't want . . . I won't go to the police,' Alison said. It sounded hollow. 'But my dad . . . it's my dad. It's for him.'

The car, though. There'd been a car.

And then at last Cathy Watts sat back on the sofa, hands in her lap, and spoke. 'They didn't know,' she said, but she didn't look at Alison. 'I never told them it was her killed him. Things was bad enough. I know what boys are like.' She laid her head sideways as if tired and some of the peace settled back in the lines of her face. 'I'd've lost them all three that way, wouldn't I?'

Beyond the windows there was the crunch and scrape of something being dragged across muddy gravel, and muttered voices. They'd come back.

'Could they have found out from someone else?' She spoke quickly.

'It was an accident.' Cathy Watts was speaking, not looking at her. 'It's paid for, anyway, in't it?' she said. 'One way or another. Wiped out.'

But there was nothing resembling forgiveness in her face. This was wrong, it had been the wrong place to come.

She could hear them inside the front door now, taking off their boots, talking to each other in low voices like conspirators. She could run out the back door. That midsummer night when the shots had echoed across the marsh. She had the wild feeling these people knew all her secrets. Her mother's. Why had they gone to the police and told them they'd seen her going to meet Stephen Bray? The ceiling seemed very low suddenly, the sky outside very dark, and stepping back from the sofa in a hurry Alison banged her knee painfully against something.

'Ma?' Martin's voice, panicked.

'She'll be all right.' Danny calming him. 'That you, Ma?'

269

Alison blundered through the gloom towards their voices. 'She's fine,' she said to no one, and her voice was high and frightened in the confined space.

Martin Watts stepped inside the door and even in the dim of the room his face was raw. She smelled booze on him, it made her sick. 'Get out!' he shouted. 'Leave her alone.'

She said she hadn't told them. They knew something, though.

'We were, we were . . .' She swung back to see Cathy Watts watching her from the sofa, almost amused. 'We were talking, we were just talking.'

And then the light was blocked a moment and Danny was inside too, big men's bodies in the small room. In silence they watched her, without a word they stood to either side of the door as she stumbled past them towards the light.

Alison had got away from the waterfront at last, from the yard and the pub and the heads that turned as she ran, head down into the blustering wind. There were trees, a patch of green, some kind of pavilion, the scout hut. She recognised the place where she'd parked the car that time under a tree. Simon Chatwin. That seemed a long time ago. She skirted the hut and sat down hard, her back against it. She wiped her glasses: she thought she'd turned her back on the sea but a hundred yards away there was the sea wall: it had doubled back on itself, as if it was following her.

But down here she was out of the wind. The roaring in her ears abated. That first night. Where it started, that night, a November night by the fire that ended a summer later.

She closed her eyes.

Monopoly. Sandwiches for tea. Dad lighting the fire. *Where's Joe?*

It had been a Friday, she remembered that much, because Friday night was Joe's night to go out. They'd been to see a band in town, and they'd be hitching back, the Watts's mum

270

didn't drive, Joe and she had long since given up on Dad for lifts, there was always some pretext or other, your mother's got the car, it's late. Never, I'm pissed, though they knew that was why.

A Friday and the girls were tired, but they hadn't been to school. That day, they'd been out all day at the doctor's, Mum and Dad with them, and all Joe and Esme had been told was it was routine, something to do with being twins. Their little faces had been weary when they came in, but he'd lit the fire, they'd had their sandwiches, egg and tomato, cheese and ham. They'd pinked up again at the prospect of Monopoly, that's when they'd started asking for Joe.

Joe. *He'd only wind you up*, she'd said but Joe took Monopoly seriously, they had to have him. He would taunt them with his wad of bills, he piled up hotels and calculated rents and crowed when he cleaned them all out, one by one. Her back against the pavilion, Alison had her hands over her face and in the warm dark Joe was there.

She'd played with them. Dad had sat in his chair brooding, watching the levels in the bottles as if they might rise on their own; on the floor they'd all turned their backs on him unconsciously. He hadn't moved when the phone began to ring, Letty had run to get it.

It had been that day they'd had it confirmed, the girls' blood groups were wrong. AO positive and they couldn't be his daughters. Dad had been the one insisted they go back to the hospital, she remembered that now. To be on the safe side, he'd said, loading them into the car that morning. Get to the bottom of this. He'd been sober then.

By the time they got home it had turned, soured, all of them climbing out of the car one by one in silence.

'It's Joe, he sounds funny,' said Letty, holding up the receiver, and Alison saw his face, turning at the word, slack. Getting out of the chair like an old man, and Letty's face falling.

'Your mother will come to get you,' he'd stated into the receiver, a little slow, a little over-precise, perhaps no one outside the family would have even known how much he'd drunk. His finger down on the phone, hanging up, redialling. They had looked up at him from the floor, Letty back between Esme and Mads, backs to the fire but cold. Cold.

Your mother. But Mum hadn't been in the house.

That was why they'd had sandwiches for their tea, why they'd been allowed Monopoly, why he'd lit the fire. They'd been home half an hour, furious hushed words in the bedroom upstairs and then he'd come down, his face blotched and red and Mum had flown down behind him, white and silent, past their watching faces and out through the door into the car. Long before Joe had called, from Gina's house, needing to be brought home. She'd taken the car.

Against the pavilion Alison opened her eyes and stood up. On her feet now she could see the long grass at the top of the dyke flattened by the wind. The sky was layers of charcoal.

Something hurt her: she looked down and saw she was gripping her phone so tight her knuckles were cramped and white. She unbent them.

They'd waited. Monopoly dissolved into bickering and tears, Esme had cleared it away and given them a bath. Each of the girls had a plaster and a dab of cotton wool at the inside of their elbow, their arms thin and white, their veins fine blue-green threads. Downstairs the front door had opened, letting in the November evening, bonfires and seafog and Mum and Joe. Joe had thundered up the stairs, lurching side to side hitting the wall, and he'd banged the door behind him. On the landing Esme had listened to him retch, then a gush as if a bucket had been emptied into the toilet bowl.

She'd never seen him like this. Why had he got so drunk? He'd known, hadn't he? He must have heard them. Fought with the Watts boys again. His mother a whore.

272

Mum had been downstairs. Esme heard her.

Christ knows, I sometimes need an intelligent human being to talk to.

Dad mumbling. Not intelligent. Not even intelligible. Mum goes on.

There were people there, they had guests, I couldn't—

And she'd gasped, as if something came to her. She'd stopped, a sob in her throat choked off, and run out. Esme, halfway down the stairs and pressed against the wall, had let her past.

She had moved on slowly, but by then she'd known something terrible must have happened. Mum's face. Dad with his back to her in the kitchen, leaning on the cabinets as if for support. Whatever had happened was still unfolding.

Alison looked down at the phone in her hand. It was ringing but for a moment she didn't recognise the sound, nor the object, she didn't know what to do with it. Back then there'd been no money for mobile phones: Mum had never had one. The fact stalled her.

Creeping past her parents into the sitting room Esme had looked into the collapsed remains in the grate. It had seemed such a marvellous fire when Dad had lit it and stood back but now it had crumbled to nothing, a handful of cold ash.

Stepping away from the shelter of the pavilion Alison lifted the phone to her ear. 'Hello,' she said.

It was Paul.

'Do you know what the time is?' The phone had told her but she hadn't registered. Almost eleven not much more than an hour before the wedding: her heart jumped in panic. She realised she'd been bracing herself for anger but his voice only sounded flat and dead and tired. 'I thought you might have gone.'

'No,' she said, with a sudden access of pity: it kindled, a tiny warmth. She thought of his face, looking down at her. His smile. 'I'm still here.' And then the folded puzzle of that

273

November evening opened in front of her as she stared at her own feet on the scrubby grass.

Dad's finger heavy on the phone cutting Joe off. Redialling.

If there'd been no mobiles, how had he known where to find Mum?

In a part of London not even Morgan and Christian could afford, Kay stood frowning outside a tall, white, pillared town-house in a wide stuccoed street. It was hot but the sky was a low grey lid over the city and the street was quiet.

The house had four storeys, it was forty feet wide and a glossy-painted black lantern hung in the porch. Kay didn't climb the steps, she didn't ring the bell, she just waited, leaning against the low, white-plastered balustrade. Around her the city hummed across its twenty-mile radius, a shifting, gleaming ant heap, and she thought of her friend out there in the sticks. *Jesus, Alison.*

She'd looked the case up, in the end. She hadn't wanted to before, because friends were friends and Kay had known from the off, with Alison in particular, that once privacy was breached there was no going back.

Now was different. Jesus, though. Rosa had affected to be totally cool about it – *one of those family murder things* – or perhaps she'd cut off, didn't want to think about it. The part she'd played in the afterlife of a victim. Kay looked up at the

275

posh house, she saw the money that had bought it and done it up with white curtains and pot plants and all that shit. Did money buy you protection from what Alison had had to see? She wanted to bang on the door and shout through the window box. *It's real. It really happened.* But instead she waited.

It had been Rosa that had come to her with it in the first place, though. Kay had seen her across the open-plan offices hanging up the phone with a clatter, in a hurry as if it might bite her, and she'd given Rosa a long hard look before turning away. *It's not my fault,* the girl had said with a pout, standing in the street after work, fiddling with her fingers. *I never thought it would get this complicated.* Her pretty face uncertain. Though once she'd unloaded it on to Kay she was all brightness and swinging hair again, like she could forget it now, hurrying away from her in the trainers she power-walked home in. Let her forget it? Not likely.

At the top of the wide steps the door opened. Seeing Kay Rosa tried to back inside again, but Kay was up the stairs, two at a time. 'No,' she said. 'I want another word.'

Chapter Thirty-three

Paul was panicking: she hadn't seen him like this before. Turning around and around in the hotel room, nervous as a cat. Looking for a sock, unable to get his tie right.

Alison had barely tied one before but she set her hands on his shoulders to still him and had a go. She felt him stop, obedient under her hands. He looked at her.

'There *had* been someone in the garden,' he said. He was pale and she could still smell the sweat on him. She stopped, her fingers in the knot of his tie.

'What's going on over there?' she said.

'The undergrowth was trampled right down by the back wall. Cigarette butts.' He wiped at his forehead. 'And a couple of the guy ropes on the marquee had been sliced through, it would have come down if we hadn't seen them.'

She smoothed the silk down under the collar, thinking, with the smallest distracted fraction of her mind, what a strange thing a tie is. Something round your neck like that. 'Kids?' she said. 'I wonder how people feel about them. The Carters. People in the village.' She knew how Gina felt.

He was calmer, though still white. Something had happened, she was sure of it. 'Listen,' he said, and he swayed in front of her.

'Sit down,' she said, manoeuvring him gently towards the bed.

'There's something I've got to tell you,' he said, but then he stopped, his eyes darting around. Through the big window the cypresses swayed wildly.

'Stop,' said Alison, sitting down next to him, and he turned and looked into her face.

'Do they know?' she said. Those conversations. Around the dinner table. 'Do the Carters know who I am too?'

'They didn't recognise you,' he said, his eyes dark. 'Not Lucy and Roger. It didn't occur to me that they would. You didn't know them then, after all. Did you?'

She shook her head. 'I don't remember them.' He looked at her, appealing to be forgiven. 'But Morgan recognised me,' she said. 'Didn't she?'

He moved his shoulders, uncomfortable. 'I didn't really understand what this place was like. People talk. It was what we were talking about when you saw us outside the pub, she'd just heard someone inside in the pub, talking about you. The girl with the scarf.' He sat very still, shoulders lowered. 'Morgan said she remembered you riding around the village on your bike. When you were a kid.'

'It fixes things in people's memory,' she said dully. 'The murders. "That was the girl" – you know.' He was looking into her face, hopeless. She wanted to forgive him, but it seemed impossible. 'On my bike,' she said, and it came back to her again, the heads that turned in the market square as she stood in her pedals and rode uphill to Gina's.

Outside there were voices: she thought one of them was Christian's. The wedding, an hour away. Less. The bloody wedding; its timetable ticked down, overriding everything. She watched Paul; she wanted out of it, the whole countdown. But he was talking almost to himself now. 'I thought it would

278

help you to be back. I thought . . . if we were going to have a future, it needed to be addressed. I thought this would be the way.' She could hear pain in his voice as it rose. 'I didn't know.'

'Morgan worked it out,' said Alison. She held the pity she felt for him at a distance. A future. A future that wasn't for her. 'And she told her parents.' He nodded mutely, watching her, his face set.

'Was that what you had to tell me,' she asked quietly. 'Or was there something else?'

He raised his head slowly, and looked at her. 'When I told you how my parents died,' he said, 'it wasn't true.' He looked down, examining his hands, clasped loose between his knees on the bed, then up again. 'It wasn't like that. While I was away at school they killed themselves. A pact. My mother had MS. My father had depression.' His voice was flat. 'He gave her an overdose of his tranquillisers then he shot himself.' He kept looking at her, unflinching now. 'I suppose a shrink would say it's why I ended up where I did. When this . . . this thing happened to you I thought . . . Christ. I don't know what I thought. I thought . . . there was this connection. Together we could make things normal.'

She stayed silent: she thought of the boy in the photograph in Paul's bedroom, standing on the clifftop with his arms folded, staring coolly at the camera. Alone. 'You know what that's like,' he went on, remote. 'There are no connections. You feel a freak, there's no one out there who knows what you know.' His gaze refocused. 'Who's seen what you've seen.'

And slowly, slowly, she nodded. 'Yes,' she said, her voice falling away, past her into emptiness. 'What do you remember,' she said, as though from a great distance, 'about that night?'

Paul let out a long, tired breath. 'We didn't even know, to start with. Not then. We were off early the next morning, a Sunday morning. Morgan heard it on the news, when we got

279

back to London. Maybe even the day after.' He was shaking his head, she saw something happening, a line appearing between his eyebrows. 'You assume it's all happened to someone else, you listen to the news report.' Frowning.

'What?' she said, and she couldn't stop herself, her hand was on him, shaking him. 'What is it? What is it now? You remember something? Did you see anyone that evening? Were you out in the village, you and Morgan?'

'We had been out,' Paul said slowly, and he took her hand in his warm one, his fingers laced between hers. She thought of him holding her down, making her shout out. All that urgency was gone: he seemed quite blank with exhaustion.

Then he came back to life. 'It could be nothing,' he said, hesitating. 'It was so long ago.' He pulled, a little, she was closer to him. He put his free hand to her cheek and as she watched something came back to life in his face. 'It's funny,' he said slowly, and his eyes settled on her. 'It must be like this for you, too. Isn't it? You remember things. That didn't make sense at the time.' His gaze was inward, he nodded to himself.

'Like what things?'

Paul drew away, put his hands through his hair.

'I thought . . .' she hesitated. 'I thought it might be the Watts boys,' she said and he stopped, looked at her.

'Who?' he said, blank.

'The Watts brothers. At the boatyard. Their brother died.' She stopped.

She couldn't say it out loud. *Mum killed him. My mother hit him with our car and killed him and drove off.*

'I don't know who you mean,' he said, not a flicker of recognition in his face. Beginning to shake his head. So whoever Paul suspected, it wasn't them. Something like relief bubbled up under her ribs but she told herself to distrust it. Too soon.

'What, then? Is it to do with what you heard? Did Lucy

really hear the shots? The baby with pneumonia – did Roger Carter see anything?'

Paul stood, turning away from her. The voices outside on the drive had fallen silent. 'If I'm right,' he said, distant, looking out at the thick grey sky, 'I don't know what Lucy thinks she remembers, but there's something . . . there's something not right about it.' He moved his head a little, trying to shake something loose.

'What?' she said. Paul turned back and again took one of her hands in his, gently.

'To start with,' he said hesitantly, 'if she did hear the shots from the patio—' He stopped, frowned. 'If she did hear them she was on her own, because we were miles away. We were having dinner, we were in some pub. I don't know if she thinks she's helping, or . . . if Roger . . .' He stopped, lost.

Lucy?

'It's all right,' she said.

I can't believe I've told you,' he said, wondering. 'It feels . . . God. It feels so good.'

'You haven't told me, though,' Alison said stubbornly.

'In the southern Alps,' he said, and he let her hand fall, 'there was a settlement in a high valley cut off, inbred since the middle ages, the same four or five families for a thousand years. In the war a German jeep went up there, five soldiers looking for entertainment, it was said, to find women, to make fun of the locals, only they never came out again, no trace of them was found. The command sent a squad up after them two days later, searched the place, interrogated everyone, down to a four-year-old child. They found some bolts from the vehicle but they couldn't get the locals to admit anything. Executed seventeen men, one by one, and no one said anything.' He turned back to her, and she saw how his students must love him. He seemed absolutely involved, intent, he shone. 'The community absorbs what it sees as evil, even if sometimes it's only foreign. It's like a . . . a primitive organism. Its strategies are few and inflexible.'

A long speech. It chilled her.

'Are you saying the people here know who killed my family?' She felt breathless.

'I think someone must know,' said Paul, stepping to the window and looking down. 'I think the community – the organism – tried to digest it. Maybe because your family were from outside, maybe because the murderer was one of theirs, maybe just because they didn't want outsiders, they didn't want police. But it's still there.'

His eyes looking back at her were bright. She faltered under their gaze. 'But do you know?'

In two steps Paul was back beside her. 'It was me brought you here,' he said gently. 'Got you back into this. You didn't ask to be part of my . . . experiment. Let me . . . just let me handle it on my own.'

'You're not going to do something stupid.' Her stomach griped and churned. Not him. Don't take him. 'Please,' she said, hopeless, forlorn, and his arms went around her, right around her.

He spoke into her hair. 'Let's just get this done, get the wedding done. I owe Morgan that, at least. Then I'm going to the police. Then we'll be free to do what we want.' His arms drew in closer and at the same time she felt the tension shift in his body, she felt something releasing.

'All right,' she said. 'Yes. We'll be free. It's all right.'

But she was Esme, her eyes closed tight.

Chapter Thirty-four

Morgan was late. Of course she was late.

The church was packed: hats, suits, money. The crowded space hummed to the rafters, all the pews filled, brims bobbing as people turned and whispered, noise rising the longer the delay went on. The air smelled of lilies and incense and clashing perfumes.

Some grooms would have been pacing the aisle or hovering in the porch but Christian sat stolid in the front row, he didn't even turn around. Paul was beside him. Assuming the space would be needed for more important guests Alison had detached herself, sitting one row back. She told herself they both knew where Morgan would want her, but Paul had been too distracted to protest anyway. He'd stood a good five minutes outside the church after they arrived, talking into his phone in the lee of a black yew. He'd put a hand up to hold her at a distance. She couldn't hear what he said or who he was talking to and he didn't make any explanation.

The groom's side of the church was sparse as they entered. Christian had no family present, but Morgan seemed to have enough for both of them, overflowing quickly to fill the vacuum, and for a moment Alison had the vision of the three of them – her, Paul and Christian – rootless and untethered among the crowd of businessmen and aunts and godfathers.

A big woman with a feathered hat and a smaller husband behind her were ushered into the space Alison might have occupied, and a harassed couple with a baby bundled up in lace were shunted into Alison's pew. She moved gratefully to the edge, the shelter of a pillar at her shoulder, as close to invisible as she could be. She got out her phone, clutching it. The church had been so different when it had been empty for the rehearsal, its wooden beams and soft plaster, its barn smell: now it felt suffocating. Closing her eyes for one mad moment Alison imagined the mob thronging the porch outside, setting a fire at the doors: it would go up in minutes, a blaze like a beacon out along the spit. She pressed a button on her phone, recent calls, and saw their names, Gina. Kay. Did they still exist? Was Gina lighting up in her back garden while May played in the dirt, was London still there? Her desk was there, her job, the patient, weary faces, the buses, they were all still there. She had only to leave.

What was to stop her running out? She could slip around the pillar and run for the door. Instead she looked down at her phone and typed in, *This is a nightmare.*

But at the back of the church something was happening, she could hear the quality of the chatter change: it rose, then hushed. Someone was hurrying down the aisle, Lucy Carter, her face odd under an unflattering hat. The organ wheezed into life and people were looking back towards the doors. Alison sensed Morgan without seeing her, in the heads turning, in the intake of breath. She moved her finger across the tiny keyboard. Beside her the mother, sweating in a tight suit, was wrestling with the lace-trussed baby – glancing at Alison she saw the mobile in her hands and glowered.

Got to talk to you. What happened that night? When Mum came and got Joe from you. What happened?

'Not in *here!*' the woman was hissing at her over her child's red upturned face and, recoiling, Alison fumbled to switch the thing off, stuffed it into her bag. Sat up straight and finally, after one last glare, the woman turned away, muttering something to her husband.

Who knew? Who else? The words still glowed, though the screen was gone. That wasn't it, though. She had the strongest sense of being in the wrong place again, in a high-walled dead end, looking in the wrong faces. Along the pew in front of her now Christian did turn, and in the movement of bodies she glimpsed his face as he looked back. In its smooth planes she saw nothing: no excitement, no nerves, no joy. She turned to look back up the aisle.

Processing towards them Morgan seemed a head taller than her father: shining and majestic in a stiff cloud of veil, she didn't look right or left and the heavy dress moved like armour with her. But it wasn't just that she towered, he seemed smaller, Roger Carter looked old. His head was held up but it looked like an effort, as if the whole performance was draining the life out of all of them, propelling them too fast towards an unknown end.

The vicar stood on the altar step with his hands clasped over a green surplice, and watched them come. Even he seemed nervous, shifting from foot to foot ahead of Morgan's advance. In the aisle in front of her Christian faced the altar again and she realised, looking again at the back of his odd square head, that it must have been him who'd brought May back. He'd found her out on Power Station Beach and stayed with her till she told him who she was. Was he a good Samaritan?

Morgan came to a halt at the head of the aisle, the vicar made a gesture and with a rumble they were all getting to their feet. Morgan's face turned to look at Christian and it

285

came to Alison that he was a strange sort of man: the sort of man who might often take himself off on long walks on his own. She wondered what May had said to him out on the sea wall, and he to her; she wondered if he often spoke to children he didn't know, if Morgan would ever have a conversation with him like the one he'd had with May? She saw him look back at his bride-to-be, still calm. The alliance had nothing to do with love, it was a bargain, and for a moment she had the strongest feeling that his real interests lay elsewhere, somewhere she'd never have to go. One step above them, the vicar began to pronounce.

Hushed and obedient, they sat, and stood, and sang, and sat again. The maid of honour – a thinner, plainer blonde than Morgan, in a pink dress – read from the Song of Solomon in a fey, uncertain voice and Alison stared at her lap, trying not to hear the words. *Thou hast ravished my heart with one of thine eyes, with one chain of thy neck.* She imagined Morgan choosing it and she kept her head down until she heard the big book close.

The maid of honour had just left the lectern when the noise came. She looked up from picking her way down from the altar in too-high heels, her face like a panicked hen's under her feathered hat, and then they were all twisting in their seats to see where the racket was coming from. Someone was battering on the doors and outside a voice was raised, wild.

It was a man's voice, though high-pitched, and uncontrolled, someone drunk or on drugs. In front of her Paul was half up on his feet, and she saw Lucy Carter in the opposite pew also rising, giving him a quick shake of the head: he hesitated. The two ushers, beefy in pearl grey tailcoats, were heading up one side of the pews, and reluctantly Paul lowered himself back down. She saw him lean to whisper in Christian's ear; she saw his hand on Christian's shoulder.

Behind them the doors opened and she heard a single word

286

expelled through the gap, high-pitched and horrible, before they banged shut behind the ushers. *Bitch.*

The word expanded to dirty the whitewashed space, it was reflected in the faces the wedding guests turned to each other. But there was no more banging: the shouting had been terminated as abruptly as if the man had been thrown off a cliff. Martin Watts? His was the face Alison saw in her head, bloated and flushed with drink, telling her to get out. *Bitch.*

After a moment the vicar raised his hands and gradually the congregation's murmurs subsided too. Above his emerald brocade his face was strained, his gaze glassy but he beckoned to the bride and groom and haltingly, the vows began.

When the ushers slipped back in ten minutes later, as flushed and cheerful as if they'd won a Saturday afternoon rugby match, Morgan and Christian were man and wife.

Love, honour and obey.

The Carters' house was under siege: a field was full of cars and more were in the lane outside, carelessly thrust against the hedges.

The line of parked vehicles stretched almost as far back as the main road by the time they got there, and they had to leave the car and walk. Paul held her hand in the lane, but he didn't say anything, he seemed intent only on something going on in his head.

The word had gone around under the hats in the church porch, *obey.* The whispers sounded mostly approving to Alison, stuck in the bottleneck while Morgan and Christian were posed with a succession of relatives, attendants and godparents.

Alison felt stifled, as if she could feel each one of the tiny buttons up the back of the blue crêpe dress pulling tighter. She wondered if she was going mad.

'Who was it?' She'd waited till they were in the car to ask, stiff with nerves and cold. 'At the church door?'

287

Paul had gone over to the ushers while she waited at the gate for him: the three men had talked for some moments while she watched. Paul looked spare and elegant beside them and she wondered if they'd actually been chosen for their brawn. Had Morgan anticipated needing bouncers?

Paul frowned back at the windscreen. 'Some local guy with a grudge,' he said. 'I don't know these people.'

'I might, though,' she said and he flicked a glance at her, distracted.

'Martin Watts? Was it Martin Watts?' He shook his head, but the gesture was impatient, as if he was flicking off a distraction. 'No?' she said.

'They got rid of him, anyway,' he said. 'I told them they should call the police.'

'The police? Did he do anything . . . criminal?'

The line of cars ahead of them was slowing, the lane narrowed and Paul indicated to turn.

Where had her mother been coming from when she'd struck Joshua Watts?

'I think it could be the same guy,' Paul said, leaning to look down the road.

'What guy?' said Alison.

'The intruder. The man who'd got into The Laurels and cut the guy ropes. I told the ushers to get on to the police, only discreetly.' He glanced at her.

The police. 'They're coming to find me,' she said slowly. 'The police are. I'd forgotten.'

Had she thought it would go away? Danny Watts had told the police he'd seen her, heading out to meet Bray. *Bitch.* Cathy Watts had backed him up. Could they really think Alison would have hurt him? It wouldn't take five minutes to disprove. Could you ever say that?

'You're my alibi,' Alison had said to Paul's profile at the wheel, and his hand had come off the wheel a second to rest

288

on hers. It had been warm; in the passenger seat Alison had felt frozen through, to her centre. What if Paul didn't believe her? Remembering something, she fumbled with the stupid little bag she'd had to bring because it was a party but had no strap, retrieved her phone and switched it back on. *Searching*, it said. He was looking at her and she put it away again.

'What made you so sure,' he said, 'that it wasn't your father?' He glanced at the road then back at her. 'Were you always sure?'

'It was coming back here,' she said. 'I found something at the house. I ran out there that first morning and found something. I thought it was a clue.' She gave a little laugh. 'Stupid. The arm of his glasses. I told the police, in the end. It might even have come from someone else's glasses. But it made me think.' She frowned down at her hands on the stupid little bag. 'I started to remember things.'

He hadn't answered: they were at the junction where Susie Price had seen her mother and he was leaning to look in his wing mirror. Alison found she didn't want to say any more.

As they walked into The Laurels' choked drive she was still cold. The stiff breeze off the sea that funnelled down the narrow lane had a steadily chill undercurrent and the sun was invisible, not even a glare behind the darkening blanket of cloud. The white-tented tunnel that led to the marquee billowed and cracked in the wind ahead of them. There was a receiving line: Alison saw Lucy Carter in her hat and her flowered chiffon at her end, turning to see her, staring. Even as she shook the hand of some man ridiculously dressed in a top hat, she was staring at Alison.

Shit.

His face strained, Paul looked from Lucy Carter to Alison, but a family had come up behind them, they were stuck in the pipeline and surrounded.

This place. Up ahead she saw someone else she recognised:

what were the odds? Karen Marshall, in a waitress's uniform, hair scraped behind her ears. Holding a tray.

Who'd be Sarah Rutherford? They could all know, they could all be in on it, but they'd never tell her. Simon Chatwin, Stephen Bray, the Wattses, Ron the landlord if it came down to it. Someone must have seen something. Seen someone stumbling along the sea wall, seen a car come bumping down the track. They hated us, she thought with dull certainty. We came here, my miserable useless parents with their fucked-up kids, we made a mess. They hated us so they waited till we imploded then they just let the wind blow and the tide come up and they wrote their verdict on the crooked house. No need for police.

She stopped still on the gravel, turning her head this way and that. She couldn't see the crooked house from here but it was there, it was waiting. Someone further back on the drive tutted and they moved on.

They had arrived at the line and Lucy Carter took her hands, gazing at Alison from under her stupid hat. The feathers on it bobbed and waved.

'I'm so sorry,' Lucy said in a low intense murmur, but if it was an attempt to be discreet it wasn't working. The woman ahead of Alison in the receiving line – and in front of Roger Carter – was craning her neck to look back over her shoulder.

'So brave of you,' Lucy Carter continued, bending stiffly towards her.

Something in Alison's face must have warned the woman shaking Roger Carter's hand because she looked away quickly and got moving. Now both the Carters were looking at her. Beyond them even Morgan was looking, through the heads. She glittered with triumph in the gloom of the tented tunnel, Christian at her side leaning down politely to an elderly woman.

'So brave,' repeated Lucy Carter. 'To come back.' She seemed to be almost in a daze: as she leaned in Alison smelled wine.

A waiter stood pressed up against the tunnel's white pvc wall with a tray of tantalising glasses, moisture-beaded. Cold champagne. Alison would have liked to take one and drain it then take another, then she caught the faint distaste on Roger Carter's face. He seemed to have recovered himself. Detached from his strapping daughter's arm he stood straighter, the arrogance restored.

'I'm fine,' she said, pulling her hand from Lucy's, nodding at the doctor without touching his, moving on past him not caring how hasty she looked. In her head a question was taking shape, forming out of mist. These people. They knew more than they were saying.

From behind, Paul's hand was on her hip, steadying her; she slowed. She registered that Roger Carter's expression was for his wife as she saw him lean and mutter something in her ear and her face turn sulky. When Carter glanced back at Alison he seemed only embarrassed. Something bubbled up inside her, a stupid elation. Soon it'll be over. One way or the other. She turned and Paul's hand fell away. 'I can't do this,' she said, and nodded to where the tunnel opened out into the marquee. 'I'll be in there.' She knew he wouldn't follow.

And she went. She sidestepped the queue and entered the marquee itself. She stood and gazed at all its tables, its floral arrangements, its swagged sides and gilt chairs.

Someone was at her shoulder and resigned she turned, expecting Paul, but the waiter had followed her. Perhaps he had seen the way she'd looked at his tray – perhaps they all had. But as Alison reached for a glass her phone plinked in the bag under her arm, the bag too small for anything else that was useful, for money or keys. She scrabbled as the man waited patiently: she turned away from him. It was a message from Gina. *Outside*, it said.

291

Chapter Thirty-five

Where they stood, unobserved under the trees at the far end of the Carters' property, the garden descended into gloom and tangled ivy. The marquee obscured the house and so far the other guests hadn't ventured beyond it: perhaps the sight of Alison marching Gina past them had intimidated them.

Her fag carelessly ground out on the gravel behind her and still reeking of smoke, pushing through the smart crowd in her jeans, a faded pink T-shirt with a cartoon character on it that strained across her breasts, Gina hadn't looked like a wedding guest, nor a member of the waiting staff, she'd looked like their worst enemy. Alison stayed close, their arms linked tight, let them see whose side she belonged on. She looked for Paul among the faces that turned on them but he wasn't there.

The marquee was filling up, guests milling between the tables, scouting for their names. Alison tugged Gina after her out through a side entrance where the catering company had set up their kitchen, and dodging a girl in an apron they were outside, the wind whipping their legs. It was cold: far off inland something that might be thunder rumbled. They skirted the marquee and made for the trees, where the wind stirred and rustled.

Gina was lighting up again already, frowning down as she did so at a place where the undergrowth had been trampled and there was a scattering of white among the dark ivy. Cigarette butts. 'Naughty,' she said.

Alison looked past the litter through the spindly tree trunks and saw a sagging chain-link fence, a hole pulled in it big enough to admit an adult. 'Paul said someone got in,' she said. 'An intruder.' So it had been true. Had she thought he was lying? Morgan would lie.

'*Paul*,' said Gina, jeering as if they were back in the school playground, and before she knew it Alison's hand was out and grasping her, tight by the wrist, smoke from the cigarette in her face. Gina looked down in astonishment. With a sharp tug she freed herself.

'All right,' she muttered. She took a drag, blowing the smoke out of her mouth, and folded her arms across herself defiantly. Alison smelled her, sweat and dirty hair and fags.

'Tell me, then,' said Alison. 'Or are you just here to wind me up?' Gina shook out a cigarette, stuck it in her mouth with the first one, lit it, her eyes screwed up. She handed it to Alison. They were under the trees ten feet from the back of the marquee. Shapes moved inside, hats and suited shoulders silhouetted against the heavy fabric wall.

'That night in November,' said Gina. 'I'd fancied Joe a year or more.' She eyed Alison, who waited. 'Every time I saw him I wanted to do things with him.' She held the cigarette up, elbow against her hip, gazed up through the smoke and the shifting canopy of trees. 'He knew all right. He kept away from me because he knew. He thought I was bad news, like everyone else did.'

Alison frowned. 'He wasn't like that,' she said.

'*You* weren't,' said Gina. She shifted her shoulders against the tree. 'Maybe that's why I thought I had a chance. Anyway. I opened the door and there he was. He was in a right state and all I could think was, *It's him. He's here.*' The cigarette had burned down to her fingers and she threw it away. 'Blood on his face. Bruise coming under it when I washed it.' Her mouth was a grim line. 'Pissed. He threw up straight off. Thank Christ Dad wasn't home. I held his head.' She laughed bitterly. 'Then he told me what had happened.'

'So you did know what it was about?'

'They'd been out. They'd been drinking, and then they started fighting again. Joe got hit, he said he'd landed one on Joshua too. As to who wound who up – Joshua Watts always was a little fucker, liked stirring it. *He* was bad news.'

'He was little when his dad died,' said Alison, trying to find a reason. Beautiful savage Joshua. 'Is that right?'

Gina shot her a disdainful glance. 'That an excuse? He said the twins didn't look much like your dad, and Joe tried to hit him. Got him down.' Alison felt sick: she let the cigarette fall from her fingers. Had she ever looked at her sisters and wondered? But others had. 'Joe was crying,' Gina said. 'I looked after him.'

Something blew through the trees horizontally, a flurry of rain and wind that sent dead leaves scattering around their ankles. 'Joshua was all right when Joe left him, then,' said Alison. Gina was looking past her. Alison turned and saw a bulge in the marquee wall, a tall two-headed silhouette pressed against the white nylon.

'Yes,' said Gina, faraway. 'Joe said mostly they just rolled around. He kept saying he didn't know how hard it was, fighting. Then he'd cry again. He let me hug him.' She looked at Alison. 'I wish I could have that night again,' she said. 'Your mum came very quick.'

Whoever the two inside the back of the marquee were, they were very close to each other. Fighting or kissing. At weddings

294

these things happened, thought Alison. 'She wasn't at home,' she said. 'My mum. She was out in the car, Dad phoned her.'

Where do you go after a day like that? A day when your husband finds out he's not the father of your kids?

'She must have been close by,' said Gina. 'He must have known where to find her straight off. Simon said—' She broke off. 'Have you seen him? He was in a right state this morning.'

'He was at the hotel,' said Alison warily. 'Early.' She didn't elaborate: guilt stirred obscurely at the memory of her and Simon in his van. 'Why?'

Gina was frowning. 'He said, he was the one always got the blame, like yesterday when May ran off. Like the police hauling him in after your dad . . . after the shootings. He wasn't the one came to your house that night, he didn't kill anyone. He said, he'd had enough and now it was time to break it all up. Today. The wedding, and that.'

'It wasn't him came to the house that night,' said Alison, staring blindly at the grey horizon, trying to make her brain work . 'But someone else did come. Did he see someone?' She blinked and saw Gina scowling at her from under her fringe, resistant. 'Don't you understand? He was out there on the marsh when it happened.'

'Sure he was,' said Gina, her mouth set stubborn. 'But Bob Argent was beating the shit out of him.' She tapped her skull. 'Brain damaged, mate.' With dull recognition Alison turned and looked into the gloomy space under the trees: she saw the cigarette butts in the ivy.

'It was Simon turned up at the church, then,' she said. 'Calling me a bitch.' Not Martin Watts. Gina hunched her shoulders tighter. 'We're all bitches, to some of them,' she said, and Alison nodded. 'Why take it out on them, though? On Morgan? The Carters?'

The hum of the wedding guests was in her ears, the clink of the glasses: Karen Marshall walked carefully from the kitchen tent into the main marquee with a tray of champagne glasses, head held steady as if balancing a book.

Gina's mouth was twisted, tough. 'Dunno,' she said, musing. 'The doc. No one likes him. Because they're rich? Because they've got a nice life? They're . . . happy?' She spoke the word as if it was in a foreign language.

Happy, thought Alison. Are they?

'What did Simon say about my mum?' she said, but Gina didn't answer. 'She was seen,' she went on slowly and the pieces moved into place, one car rushing in the dark, the other passing it going the other way, the verge, the junction, the boy with his head in his hands, raising his head too late. It had to be. 'Kyra Price's mum saw her. Heading for your house.'

'Twenty minutes,' said Gina. 'After he phoned. She was white as a sheet when she got here. She was shaken up. She didn't say a word to me, she just wanted him out, in a big hurry.'

Something was happening between the two inside the marquee, pressed hard against the fabric and making a bulge. White as a sheet. Perhaps she thought she'd hit an animal.

'What?' said Gina. 'You know why she looked like that, don't you? You know what freaked her out.'

Alison nodded, looking at the marquee wall: two men, she guessed, from the height of the bulge, the silhouetted shoulders. She took a couple of steps towards them and Gina followed, close at her shoulder. There was a hum and clatter of conversation filling the tent behind the heavy rubberised fabric – if they wanted to eavesdrop they'd have to get closer.

'I know,' Alison said. 'I think I know where she was coming from too. I just don't know why.' She turned to Gina. 'Where's May?' she said, feeling a small flutter of anxiety separate itself from the hard sour knot in her stomach.

Gina's arms were goose pimpled where they emerged from under the faded T-shirt, and she rubbed at them. 'Ron's keeping an eye,' she said. 'Down the pub. He helps me out now and again.'

'Ron?'

'He's a good bloke,' said Gina defensively. 'Gives her a bag of crisps. Nice down there.' She glanced up at the sky. 'When the sun's out. She hates me, she says.'

There was movement and they turned towards it. From behind the marquee wall a voice that had been low intensified a notch. A warning. Alison took a step, then another, then they were so close, she and Gina, that they might have touched the men through the canvas.

'I love her,' she heard, and she froze. It was Paul. She registered a look of stiff scorn on Gina's face.

Her.

'Listen, Roger,' Alison heard, and Paul's voice was low again, and agitated. 'You've got to tell someone. I mean, if you're sure. If you're positive.'

'I was asleep,' Carter insisted. 'I can say that, can't I? Just because there was mud on the carpet the next morning. Doesn't mean . . . I knew nothing about it. Nothing.'

'But you saw her putting something in my car? After the dinner.' Paul sounded agonised.

In the car? Alison could only think of the photographs, and then she was there in the little car, craning her neck, reaching for something while Paul watched her, frowning. The scarf. The girl in the scarf.

Paul's voice was low. 'Where was she,' he said, 'when you got back from seeing that baby, the baby with pneumonia? Was she even at home? I'll come with you, when Morgan and Christian have got off. You're confused, it's natural. We'll go to the police. They'll find out, you know, in the end. I should never have brought her back here, I had no idea.'

Roger Carter was muttering, the figures moved and they could see that Paul, several inches the taller, had his hands on the older man's shoulders. Gina's head turned towards Alison and she mouthed something. *Tell someone what?*

'But what if they . . .' said Roger Carter, and all the boom and authority was gone, he sounded shifty, evasive. 'My daughter's wedding, Paul. Look at it all. Gatecrashers. Drunks.' He sounded choked, he whined. 'It'll all come out. Kate Grace. It'll ruin me.'

Gatecrashers. Gina's head was tilted so close to the nylon wall they must see her; if they shifted they would bump. The face she turned to Alison was lit up.

'It's him, isn't it?' she said, gleeful, she couldn't stop herself. 'That's it. The old doc. Your mum was fucking the old doc, and your dad found out.'

'He knew all along,' said Alison, feeling the misery rise and wanting to put a hand to the wall's heavy fabric, to reach through it to the other side and pull back all the things she had never been told, the secrets she had had to guess. To take hold of Roger Carter and force an admission from him. Had he heard what Gina said? Let them all hear. 'Dad knew that night they came back from the hospital, he knew when he phoned The Laurels to tell her to fetch Joe. He knew where to find her. She was here.'

There was a sound, a light metallic rattle, and they turned. A man stood at the torn garden fence, his hands held up and laced through the wire, his body a silhouetted cross. Danny Watts pressed his face against the links and his hand came through, pointing. 'You,' he said to Alison.

The police car was parked up a lane off the high street, behind a high privet hedge. DS Sarah Rutherford was leaning against it and looking between cottages across a field that sloped away from them to the grey water. The grass was eddying, blown silver by the wind. She'd known this place all her life, but it still turned its back on her. She turned towards Jennings.

'You think she did it?' she said patiently. She knew he went to the pub with the lads and moaned about her but she didn't think there was malice in it. You had to give them a chance to learn.

Jennings, leaning against the car, made an effort to stand up straighter. 'Killed the old bloke?' he said. 'Didn't get much of a look at her last night.' He gave her a quick, furtive glance and she knew he was thinking, she was a good-looking girl. 'Not exactly built like a killer. But maybe you can't tell?' Looking at her for help. 'After something like that. Involvement in an incident like that, you know, the . . . the family murders.'

He was frowning furiously, trying to look like he was thinking. 'You don't think . . . was she ever a suspect, back then? Kids have been known . . .' He broke off. At least, thought Sarah Rutherford as she eyed him gloomily, he had some idea of his own limitations. She stepped away from the car and walked to the end of the row of cottages and the horizon opened up.

The line of the dyke meandered along, where the land dissolved into mud and the pale tufted grey of whatever plants grew in the salt and slime. A swamp, a place where bodies could get sucked down, who knew what was under there, remains moving through the sludge. Creek House still stood, against the odds, black as an old stump. It should have been bulldozed years back, it should have been condemned and razed to the ground, and all the crap shovelled into the sea, shards and rubble and bits of someone's old glasses and all.

The tide was already high, and still rising. Sarah could see where it lapped against the bumpy track that led down to the house. She scratched at her shoulder through the thin fabric of her jacket – the sight made her uneasy.

'Yes,' she said out loud. She turned to Jennings. 'She was a suspect. Esme. She had to be treated as a suspect. It wasn't nice. She was . . . what's the word? Pretty much unreachable.' She looked beyond the house to the far shore and the power station that squatted above the dunes and the fringe of grass.

It was due to be decommissioned, but they'd leave it standing, too dangerous, too expensive, to dismantle it. The cooling wall was dark offshore like a great rusting radiator in the lapping grey water.

'You were one of the first at the scene?'

She only nodded, focusing on the line of the horizon, her voice, when it came, sounded distant. 'Kids do go on killing sprees,' she said. 'We all know that. Kids kill their parents – rarely but they do. Mostly male children, but not exclusively, so we had to look at her. We had to ask her questions.'

'That's America, right?' said Jennings, uneasy. 'When Dad takes away the computer game?'

She looked at him flatly, and shrugged. 'Not always,' she said. She turned back and began to walk briskly to the car. 'Sometimes it's learned, it's abuse, it's deprivation.' She felt his dull regard. 'Sometimes there's not an explanation. Some kids just have poison in their systems, from birth. Some adults too.' She climbed into the driver's seat and started the engine.

They turned down the high street, heading for the water: the village was silent under the grey sky. They passed an ambulance outside a house in a row of net-curtained cottages as the front door opened and a stretcher edged out. A woman lay prone on it, an oxygen mask obscuring her face.

'Everything said it was the father,' said Sarah Rutherford, staring ahead, talking to herself. 'All the evidence. Statistically it's overwhelmingly probable. He had the gun in his hand, he'd just found out about the kids, his wife . . . his wife . . .'

It wouldn't do.

Jennings was quiet but she kept talking. 'The only contra-dictory evidence was the old guy but he changed his story every five minutes: he saw John Grace getting into a car with a man, then it was a woman, then he didn't see it at all. You'd have never got him into a witness box and if you had no one would have believed a word of it.' Still talking to herself. 'How

300

could I say it to her? To Esme? Alison. Give her hope? Hope of nothing. Hope a killer's still out there.'

From the driver's seat she shot him a glance, then looked back at the road. 'She didn't do it,' she said quietly. 'Unless I've never had a good instinct in my life, that night when someone killed her mother, her brother, her sisters, Esme Grace was hiding upstairs. She'd have been a victim too if the murderer had known she was there. So she didn't have anything to do with Bray's death either, and I don't care what the Watts boy thinks he saw.'

But Jennings's head was turning away, looking. 'The kid,' he said, subdued, and Sarah looked too, and as they drew level with the pub there she was.

'Nightmare,' she said. Gina Harling's kid. May. Chatwin's kid, too. Sitting in the wind at a pub bench, her sharp red nose in a bag of crisps, May looked up to watch the police car. She stood. Those skinny legs they have, thought Rutherford. Her own daughter was with her dad, Saturday morning at the shops. *I can't talk about bad mothers.*

They pulled up on the muddy gravel outside the boatyard, and climbed out.

'But if it wasn't him and it wasn't her,' said Jennings, but when she turned on him he faltered. The boatyard's big doors were locked, you could see a flash of green, bright in the flat light, to one side. 'What kind . . . what kind of person does that?'

'What I said about poison?' Sarah Rutherford examined her subordinate's face for a sign he understood, and saw nothing. 'Sometimes I think there's something wrong with this place, something in the soil, salt or something that stops things growing straight, it's land where it should be all sea, I don't know . . .' She broke off, feeling his eyes on her, his alarm. She took a breath. 'You saw those kids we brought in, they'd been chucking breeze blocks off the bridge, just for the hell of it. You might see them running about on a football field, or ten years on chatting some girl up in a bar – they'd give you a cheeky smile, charm you. You can't see it from the outside but they're poisoned.'

There was movement: someone came around the side of the boatyard and stood, but neither of them turned. Jennings was watching her like a dog waiting for the ball to be thrown.

'Sometimes they're born into it,' she said. 'Sometimes it comes down from a single incident, sometimes it grows, over years. Battered wives, jealous sons.' Accidents, she thought, remembering the Marshall's baby dead in its cot of smoke inhalation. 'Love can do it. Hate can do it. Not giving a shit can do it, too.'

Then she turned, and Jennings with her. Cathy Watts stood behind them on her patch of grass with her arms folded.

'Can I have a word?' said Sarah Rutherford.

Chapter Thirty-six

She was out, she was gone, she was running.

Bare feet, and the blue dress had gone under the arms. As she clambered through the wire towards him Alison had felt the old cloth pull, the ancient seams giving way. Now as she ran it loosened, opened and the cold wind crept inside. She was a bird, it beat her, it lifted and flung her, out to sea.

She counted her breaths, eight-beat, her feet slapping sore on the road. *One* two three four. *Five* six seven eight. A snicket between cottages presented itself, she took it and she was on a long, dead straight concrete path between high hedges. She could smell the water treatment plant on the edge of the marsh, its gate stood far ahead at the end of the weed-sprouting concrete. The hedges blocked her view, it was a route she had retraced in dreams for half her life and she found it again blindly, by touch, by smell, cow parsley, cut grass, mud and shit. Here. Now here. She reached the peeling gate to the sewage works and sidestepped: a fence. A stile. On the other side a great shaggy horse shied and lumbered away on tufted hooves and she kept going.

Her glasses jiggled and slid on her nose but stayed on. Underfoot the grass and mud were soft after the tarmac but every graze, every scrape and bruise the road had left felt sound and healthy to her. She found her path in a dream but her body was awake, it reminded her: she was alive. Esme lived.

Danny had held on to her as she climbed through the wire fence, his hands on her arms. He didn't let her go even when she was on the other side, only stared, his tanned face inches away.

Why had she fixed on Martin Watts? Danny could have done it. Danny could have come to her house that night. His hand was hard and tight on her arm: Alison looked down at it.

'I came to get you,' Danny had said as he pulled her closer. She resisted, but didn't break loose.

'It wasn't you,' he said. 'It wasn't you I saw out there, waiting for Bray.'

Gina had been behind her under the trees, watching. She hadn't responded when Alison had said to her, *Hold on.* Her mouth hard. Alison had gone to him anyway.

'Where's your brother?' she said, now close up against him, her wrists in his hands. 'Is he all right? I thought it might have been him at the church.'

'With Mum,' said Danny, and then he relaxed his grip but still she didn't pull away. 'He's all right when he's with Mum.'

She held his gaze. 'The night my family was killed,' she said, no longer surprised by how level she could keep her voice. 'Where was your brother that night?'

'We saw you riding up the high street on your bike,' said Danny. 'You saw us.'

'Later,' she said. 'Where was he later?' The heads turning in the market square. Danny and Martin. Which one? 'Someone brought Dad back to the house in a car.' Not Martin. Not a man. Her head ached: the night was full of blanks. The car.

304

Something jumped in her mind, something that had been compressed so small she could hardly see it as it sprang open, jack in a box. A woman.

Screaming. A woman screaming insults. The information was unstable, it danced and dodged in her head like dust in sunlight. A car. A woman. How long after that had the noises begun? She grasped for certainties. 'Someone broke his glasses,' she said. 'Where was Martin?'

'He was with me,' said Danny, and his eyes narrowed like his mother's, gleaming like metal reflecting the slaty sky. His voice was sad. 'It was true, more or less, what we said at the inquest. He took a handful of pills, I heard him making noises in the bathroom. We sat up with him, making him throw them up. Me and Mum. Tell them that and they'd put him away again, self-harm, they'd say.'

She thought of what Paul had said, the silent villagers, the bodies of the dead hidden in the high valley. Closing around the thing that might give them all away. She heard a sound from the Carters' garden, a soft rustling, then a burst of laughter and voices as though a flap had opened in the tent, but she didn't turn to look. Her thoughts ranged wild, but she tried to bring them back in, to sound calm.

'You could all be covering up. Your mum, taking care of old Mr Bray all this time. When he saw me in the pub with Paul that night did he think the time had come to tell what he knew? Who he saw.'

At the mention of Paul's name Danny had gone still, his face stiffened into resistance, close to hers. His feet were sockless, in trainers almost disintegrating, splashes of mud up his trousers.

'All these years,' she said, only sad now. 'Bray must have said something about that night. You must have heard something.'

Slowly Danny shook his head. 'Only Mum would talk to him,' he said. 'She'd shut the kitchen door. We'd hear him

305

mumbling away, for hours. Martin would go upstairs with his hands over his ears.' He looked down. 'He wasn't always nice. He didn't always make sense.'

The old man trotting out his dislocated thoughts, sometimes bitter, sometimes mad. Sometimes sharp and clear and true. Who would have killed him?

'If you weren't protecting your brother then why did you tell the police it was me you saw going out to meet Bray?' He said nothing but she held her ground. 'Your mum lied to the police,' she said. He looked down, stony. 'She said I arranged to meet him.'

He made a choked sound. 'She doesn't lie. It's what he told her, he got a message.' Rubbing at his face with a ragged sleeve. 'I thought it was you. I did think it was you. It was only later, when I saw you again. Then I thought maybe I'd been wrong.'

'Knew you'd been wrong,' she said fiercely. 'What changed your mind?'

'I didn't know at first,' he said. 'A woman, that's all I saw, it was late, it was dark. Small, like you. Then that scarf. That's why I said . . . because I'd seen you in it that morning, in the same place. Mum said I had to tell them what I saw.' She watched him.

'When was it?' she said, and he looked up, he looked into her face and the lines softened, and quite unexpectedly, something cleared in the air between them.

'We were out in the boat, Wednesday night,' he said, and she nodded, she'd seen them launching the dinghy as she and Paul stood on the quay. 'Me and Mart. It was late, but that funny light, nowhere to hide this time of year, it stays in the sky after the sun's gone down. Like, like a glow.' He ducked his head to see if she'd understood then went on. 'Mart was out of it, lying on the boards. Asleep. I'd been sculling and I sat down to let her drift a bit, I was knackered. It was warm. It's the only place – out there. On the water. Thinking about

306

nothing, the light all grey.' He sighed, soft. 'Drifting. I looked over the bow and I saw . . . someone I thought was you. Very late, ten, eleven. Coming out along the sea wall to the house.'

From where they stood now you could only see the other side, the tide so high it was grey-green water all the way, the marsh submerged. Power Station Beach where she'd looked at his brown shoulders, a hundred years ago, and she imagined him weathering under the sun, growing old, turning to stone. The power station was black under clouds. The crooked house was behind them, concealed by the marquee and The Laurels, and inside her the familiar impulse stirred, prodded. Run.

He was close to her, she could hear his breathing, she could smell the alien scents off him, varnish and diesel and mud. Mud under everything. 'You were in the house when it happened, upstairs all the time, you were listening,' he said softly. She could see the gleam of his eyes and she felt him step inside her head. Paul never came inside her head, he circled, he left her in peace. 'When he killed them,' Danny said, and his voice was quiet. Alison thought of Paul's silence. What had he wanted Roger to tell the police?

'I think it's only you that knows what happened that night. Somewhere inside.' He put his hand up to her head but didn't touch her, it hovered, an inch away, in her peripheral vision. If she turned, she'd see the lines in his palm. If she looked, she'd see. 'It's in there,' he said. 'You know it's in there.'

Alison didn't turn her head. 'So it was late,' she said, as if he hadn't spoken. 'You saw her from the boat. If she wasn't me, who was she? How are you so sure now?'

'You don't walk like her,' he said, and he set his hands on the solid place where her back flared out at the hip. He stepped back, and removed his hands. Drew in his elbows, made his shoulders narrow, his back bent a little over. 'She wore the scarf different. Tied under the chin.'

The image moved in her head, like a shape in fog, it shifted.

A figure bent into the wind, in her scarf. 'How did Stephen get the message?' she said, half turning, seeking Gina under the trees behind her, turning further, scanning the spindly trunks but there was no sign of her. The marquee gleamed pearly white: she saw a flap open in it, a slight figure in a smudge of flowered silk emerged, back to the white wall, edging along it jerkily as if trying to escape. The woman's hands fluttered, her calves against the marquee wall were spindly. Narrow-shouldered.

Alison looked back at Danny Watts, who had his arms folded across himself, watching her. He knew she was about to run.

She leaned and pulled off a sandal, shook her foot out of the other. She still had the stupid little bag under her arm and she stared at it.

'Someone called the pub and asked to talk to him,' he said. 'He said to Mum, the Grace girl's at the house, she's waiting. Something like that. Just before closing time. Stephen came straight over to tell Mum, then he was off, she said. It'll be about her dad, he said.'

Somewhere under her ribs the stone formed itself, it dug in. It hurt. 'He loved my dad,' she said.

Danny held out his hand and without a word she put the stupid little handbag in it. He gazed. 'Where you going?'

She'd taken a breath then, ready to tell him, but found herself only smiling, because if he was in her head then he'd know by now, there was only one place left for her to go. She looked back at the marquee but the woman had gone. Lucy Carter had gone. And Alison began to run.

As she came around the back of the compound, the end of the garden where the trees thickened, she heard something in the dense undergrowth as she broke away but she only headed down, to where the estuary spread out grey-green and patterned like a maze.

The slope flattened out below her to sea level and in the

low light the hedge leading away to the dyke looked black. The silky reddish grass on the landward side swayed and whispered and suddenly, blindingly low, a broad shaft of sun flared from below a huge bank of cloud, opening a slit in the grey and illuminating the flooded landscape. The water had risen almost to the foot of the sea wall: it was like the end of the world.

As if all the air in her lungs had been abruptly used up Alison juddered and stopped, half falling against the new fence. She smelled pine and creosote, she felt the roughness of the new wood against her cheek. She looked.

In the low-slanted light she saw something. Someone. A stick girl, all thin legs and arms, capering black along the sea wall as the water rose, leaning down into the wind then throwing her body upright, hair streaming out behind her. She saw herself. Esme.

PC Stuart Jennings looked around the pub tables, sidestepping with a jump when he felt something around his ankles: he leaned down to retrieve a crisp bag. The tide had begun to creep over the quay. Sarah Rutherford saw him eye the grey horizon in dismay as he straightened up. First chance he gets, she thought, he'll be back in Surrey.

'What?' she said.

'Gone,' he said. 'Kid's gone again.'

Sarah turned to look, she crouched in case the girl had secreted herself under a table but then the back door of the pub banged open and she recognised the landlord, Ron Thwaites, standing on his threshold. He was unshaven and red-eyed, half feral. Shit, these people, Sarah thought, depressed. They drink too much, they stay up too late, they can't even keep themselves clean.

'Where's the girl?' she said to Thwaites. 'Gina's girl.'

But she'd come to ask him something else.

All I know's what old Bray told me, Cathy Watts had said. *He thought she was going to talk to him about her dad. Esme Grace. He'd been waiting for her to come back, he said, he wasn't going to tell no police.*

And then Sarah had found her patience running out, the woman's flinty face staring at her over folded arms.

'And of course you told him it was his duty to tell the authorities? If he had evidence. Of course, you'd have told him that.' They faced each other, both women with the same stance, feet planted, arms across their bodies. Sarah could feel Jennings standing nervously behind her. 'The longer it goes on, the easier it is just to say nothing? Perjury is one thing, you were never cautioned, neither of you. There are other charges, withholding evidence. Perverting the course of justice.'

'You talked to him.' Cathy Watts's voice was a soft hiss as she stood her ground. Sarah couldn't help but see the sag of her cottage's roofline behind her, the grime at her windows. 'Your job, to get the truth out of people? Pity you a'nt no good at it.'

'Or did you just think, let them get on with it? Outsiders, the lot of them?' Cathy Watts hadn't bothered to answer that.

'And what about her?' Rutherford went on, softly. From behind her Jennings moved from the gravel to the grass, and he was beside her. 'Did you ever think of the girl that survived? When you sent your boy to us to say he'd seen her.'

'Her mother's daughter,' said Cathy Watts, but something slid and shifted behind the watchful eyes and involuntarily Sarah Rutherford took a step forward and abruptly she was in the old woman's space. Watts didn't flinch.

'That's enough,' said Sarah. '*Enough*. That girl. Esme Grace. That girl. You know what she was like when we found her? She'd held her sisters in her arms. She saw her brother with half his head off. You think she loved them any less than your boys loved their brother? She thinks – Esme thinks – Alison . . .'

310

Cathy Watts was staring at her now, really staring. 'She *knows* her father never did it. We've let her down.' She moved her head, from Jennings to the horizon to Cathy Watts. 'I have. You have. Something bad came into that house. Something terrible. We thought it was gone, but it isn't.'

Her jaw felt as though it was seizing up. She felt the cold through the thin polyester of her jacket. 'You know what it means, her coming back here, if her dad didn't do it? Do you know where she is now? Is she safe?' Sarah Rutherford didn't even know if she was making sense any more. She could feel Jennings's eyes on her, could feel his incredulity. 'Is that child *safe?*'

And in front of her Cathy Watts had collapsed, out of nowhere, her knees just seemed to give way and if Jennings hadn't been quick off the mark as Sarah only stood and watched, she'd have fallen.

In his back doorway Ron glared at them now.

'Gina's girl?' He turned to speak to someone behind him in the door: 'I knew she'd heard.' His jowly chin showed flushed through patchy stubble, ginger flecked with white. A girl with rusty-dyed hair appeared behind him in the doorway and he scowled at her. 'Christ,' he said to all of them. 'This place, no place for a kid.' The barmaid looked sullenly back.

'I never knew she was listening,' the girl said, sulky. Behind them the public bar was gloomy and quiet, a smell of sour beer.

'Who?' said Sarah Rutherford, impatient. 'Who heard what?'

'May,' said Ron, and she saw a tremor in his hands, the broken veins on their backs. 'Casey here,' and he jerked his head angrily in the barmaid's direction, 'was giving us the benefit of her thoughts on May's biological father.' The girl stepped back abruptly. 'Pervert's all I said,' she muttered, turning on her heel, and she was gone, back into the beer fumes.

Ron gave Sarah a hard stare. 'And I haven't got time to go

311

after her.' He swept the horizon with bloodshot eyes, to where the brown water of the estuary ruffled white in the wind. 'Do I look like anyone's childminder?' He looked at Sarah again. 'What? She'll just have gone looking for him. Her dad. Hates her mum just now, 's why Gina leaves her here.' He snorted. 'Father figure.'

Shit, thought Sarah Rutherford, the kid another little unwanted blip on her radar, moving in the wrong direction. She watched him. First things first. 'I've been talking to Cathy Watts,' she said, and something changed in Ron's face. 'She told me something. Thirteen years too late, but she told me.'

'Oh, yes,' he said, wary.

'Something she said maybe you'd be able to confirm.'

She'd stared at Cathy Watts when she came out with the name Stephen Bray had given her. The car he'd seen John Grace climb into that last night. *And why should I believe you,* she'd said, *after all this time?*

Ask Ron, Cathy Watts had said back, holding the hard stare.

At her side Jennings shifted uneasily, and spoke.

'It's not too late,' he said to Ron, with an urgency that surprised Sarah. He must have been listening, after all. 'Just tell us what you know now, and it won't be too late.'

'She says you saw John Grace leave with Stephen Bray the night his family were killed.' Sarah kept her voice soft, and Ron nodded, cleared his throat. 'Yes,' he said. 'I followed them out. Pretended I had crates to shift.'

They'd talked and talked to Bray, all that time ago. There'd been plenty who'd said, bring him in. She'd seen them look at him disgusted, the twenty-five-year-old constable flinching from the black nails, the scurfy hairline, gagging at the smell of him. Doesn't make him a killer – she'd held that line – but Bray had felt the crush of the mob against him, he'd zigzagged and babbled about everything from lights at sea to number plates and eventually had clammed up. None of it usable as evidence

312

– and Sarah Rutherford wouldn't be party to putting a man with mental disabilities inside, not for perverting the course of justice. Not for murder, either. Stephen Bray wasn't a killer.

'She says,' and Jennings took a step to flank Ron on the other side before continuing, 'Bray walked with him to the end of the quay then John Grace leaned down to talk to someone in a car.'

Sarah's turn. 'He wanted John Grace to come back with him to the boat,' she said gently. 'Bray said Grace had told him his wife wanted a divorce, it's why he'd come to the pub, and she'd start up about it again if he went back, so he wanted to stay away.'

She scanned Ron's face for a reaction but saw none: then he spoke. 'Some blokes kill their wives for asking for a divorce,' Ron said. 'Don't they? Kill their wives and their families.'

It had nagged at her all these years. 'And some women ask for a divorce, if they've got someone else to go to,' she said.

He shifted his head slightly and she saw he was looking across the marsh to where it stood, like the dead stump of a tooth: the Grace house. 'We never dreamed he'd have done that. Not John. I remember the night he came asking about a gun in the pub. The place went quiet.'

She could imagine it. That night still came back to her even now, those long moments on her knees on the bloody carpet taking his pulse, trying to look anywhere but at John Grace's face.

'We knew it wasn't rats. It was for him, he got that gun. The faces, all watching him.' She nodded, just barely. The murmur would have gone round the village, the consensus reached. 'It's a decent way to go, see,' said Ron, his voice low, face averted. 'Not a cry for help, no going back, quick. Done.'

Decent, she thought in disbelief.

Meeting her eye finally, he said, defiant, 'Their mess. None of our business. None of it.'

313

'So someone came up with a gun for John Grace, and when it turned out he didn't just want to use it on himself, you all clammed up.' She was talking to herself but when she looked up Ron's flush told her it was true.

'Why didn't he go back to Stephen Bray's boat with him that night, sleep it off there? Bray wanted him to. Who did he lean down to talk to in the car? Whose car was it took him home?'

'That was what did it,' said Ron, and it took Sarah a minute to realise he was still stuck a way back in her interrogation, the night John Grace asked for a gun. 'I remember being glad I told the kid, you only work Sundays, little Esme. Bad enough locals seeing him like that, listening to him go on about rats like a total fucking basket case – it was a busy night, too, a weekend, people up from town. Outsiders. Staring at the man like he was a freak show, like he was there for entertainment. Bad enough.'

Bad enough. And another blip came up on her radar: it sat there, this one wouldn't move, even as she asked the next question on her list it sat and waited. *Outsiders*. Like who?

'Whose car did he get into, Ron?' she said softly, and at last he turned his head and his eyes slowly came into focus. She thought the word he murmured was *bitch*.

'Who?' she said.

She hadn't got a ticket. Ten minutes in a queue that didn't move while she watched the next train's time get closer, four minutes, three and then Kay had given up and had broken away to go tearing round, batting through the milling crowd, Liverpool Street on a Saturday lunchtime, the smell of fast food, oil and metal, and stinking tracks, searching for the platform, shoving through a barrier and she was in the fusty train, pressed against the smeared window.

Rosa had turned slowly towards her under the high ceilings of her white-painted flat, barefoot, polished toes, everything about her neat and shining and perfect except her face. Her pretty face, sulky with having done wrong, ugly with resentment. Some people, Kay thought in disbelief, had no idea. No fucking clue.

'Alison said he had a gun,' she said, feeling suddenly sick at the thought, and Rosa tipped her head back, knowing. 'Some kind of Second World War memento Saunders gave him. Did you know about that?'

315

Rosa had smiled, a wide lazy smile. 'Saunders?' she said, and leaned her head back. 'I don't think so. Not what he told me. He showed it to me too, you see, he made me hold it. He wanted me to know there was still something between them. He was like that.'

Kay tried to understand. 'Not Saunders?' she said.

Rosa's smile hardened. 'He told me she gave it to him,' she said. 'That bitch.'

She'd tried to phone. It rang and rang and rang. She tried again, and again, and left a message, sent a text, another. She imagined Alison's phone in long grass. She saw it arcing out into grey water, sinking.

Could she phone the police? And say what? Say, *He's a liar.*

Kay sat pressed against the grimy window and watched East London crawl past: tenements, parks, kids playing. Saturday afternoon. It chuntered in her head with the sound of the wheels on iron track. Too slow. Too slow. Too fucking slow.

A woman's voice.

Esme has heard the car coming, reckless over the bumps, revving, wheels spinning free. It's still light outside and she's looking at the clock to see the time, tick, tock, just as well Joe's got those headphones. Hears the engine turning off. Silence. Whoever came hasn't got out of the car.

Early for Dad to come home. Not yet ten. Is it him?

Don't go out. She wants her mother to stay in the kitchen. Don't go out, don't shout at him, don't start. In your heels, swaying back from the kitchen counter like a dancer to look when Esme got home, that arch in her back, that lipstick that's not for him.

Her mother blinking as she meets Esme's eyes. The last time Esme sees her mother alive.

316

The car door opening at last and a woman's voice and Esme can't stop herself, she's at the high window looking down, the sad balding place on the top of her father's head in the summer twilight as he stumbles away from the car door. The other door opens and she sees a sharp ankle, painted toes. A woman. Getting out after him.

The woman's voice says something but he doesn't turn, he hasn't heard. Doesn't hear these days, doesn't listen. Cautiously Esme pushes the catch of her window, feels the cold air and sees the gleam of the woman's calf emerging now from the driver's door.

The woman hisses sharper and then he turns, at last he turns, steadies himself.

The woman stands, hands on her hips, body bending forward to scream at him. A woman Esme doesn't know. Didn't know.

The back door. Kitchen door. Mum's going to come out. Her best shoes scuffed in the yard. The woman.

Esme prays. Joe stay inside under his headphones, the girls watching TV. Turn up the sound. Never tell.

He's not coming. Never coming, whore, can you hear me, whore? You little fucking bitch, I'll see you dead first.

I'll see you all dead.

Bitch.

Face down in the pillow, hands over your ears.

Chapter Thirty-seven

The house was at her back now, warm as though it was a
living thing, and Alison didn't want to open her eyes.

How did I get here?

The last stretch – a hundred yards? five hundred? – a darkness had come up to either side of her, as though her peripheral vision was going. She had told herself, it's what the brain
does, you're not breathing properly, that's all, you're hyperven-
tilating and the brain is prioritising. You need to stop, you
need to kneel, head between your knees.

But the thought of kneeling made Alison feel sick, dizzy as
if the sea wall had become a mountain ridge, at the thought
of her neck exposed under the wide sky and the darkness
either side of her. Was that how Stephen Bray had felt, before
he died? He'd seen the darkness.

Had it been May she'd seen running along the sea wall?
Where had she gone?

The darkness was real. Her brain was turning to darkness,
it crept in. It stank. Breathe.

Listen. Eyes closed.

The wind whistling in halyards, clinking against masts in the fairway. The distant lazy whirr of a light aeroplane. Something rose and sobbed and was caught in the gust, a light, high-pitched sound from far away.

Then something else, close, so close. Her eyelids trembled, her throat closing up – and the sound halted. It was her own lungs Alison heard, her own blood pounding in her ears and cautiously she let out a slow breath but her eyes stayed shut.

Lucy Carter had come creeping out of her daughter's wedding, edging along the white tent like a gatecrasher, a thief. Those fragile calves gleaming under the smudged floral, ankles like a foal's, so pretty, so delicate, Morgan the great strapping child, all her father's genes, how strange, Alison found herself thinking in the blood-dark behind her closed eyes, strange to give birth to anything, let alone something so unlike yourself.

It was Lucy Carter who had climbed out of the car after Esme's father that midsummer night; it was Lucy Carter who'd screamed at him, at all of them.

Scream all you like, no one will hear.

Hands over your ears and never tell.

The police long gone now, and the house's seams coming loose behind her back. Cracks finding their path through the mortar top to bottom, window frames loose in their apertures, the black inside showing through.

It was Lucy Carter Danny Watts had seen coming out across the marsh, her hair tied under the scarf, coming to stop Stephen Bray saying anything, ever again. Fragile Lucy Carter, bird-boned and narrow-shouldered: she'd hit the old man until the blood flooded his brain, and left him to drown in mud, because he'd seen her open the door of her car and let Esme's father inside.

Folded against the house Alison felt her heartbeat. She had slowed it by sitting, by controlling each breath, but it was only waiting: a bird in a tree, it hopped from branch to branch to evade her.

Not safe, it pattered. This wasn't safe, this was the last place, the very last place . . .

It was Lucy Carter who'd taken the scarf from where Alison had left it tucked inside a jacket sleeve on the big flounced marital bed, and it was she had returned it, slipped it back under the seat of Paul's little car to lie beside the brown envelope, the dead family photographs. The scarf with the orange and lemon trees and the bright blue Italian waves that someone not her father had given to her mother, the scarf her aunt had snatched up from all the heaped dark chaos of their abandoned house. How had Polly even dared enter the place to find it, thought Alison, her eyes still closed as she listened, brave Aunt Polly, brave as a lion, ducking under police tape.

How long had she been here, her eyes squeezed shut? She should have stayed, she should have risked it, all the hats turning towards her, Morgan and Christian, waitresses and godparents, she should have climbed on to one of those tables in among the placemats and floral arrangements and shouted, *I am his daughter, the murderer's daughter, I am the child, I am the sister.* She should have found Paul and said, *It's time to go to the police.*

A soft sound, the weight of a footstep. It crunched.

Someone was there. Her eyes flew open and she scrambled upright, holding on to her glasses with one hand, steadying herself against the wall with the other. Cursing the sound of loose stones under her feet.

She was in the yard. The rear of the crooked house looked down on her and in one sweep she took it in: flat kitchen roof, tilted drainpipe, window above with a shard fallen out of it. Another sound, breathless, a high nervous giggle, and skidding on the rubble. Alison followed it.

As she reached the blistered wooden door that led out of the yard a different sound, further off, the one she'd heard high on the wind before, was blown by some eddy in her direction and she recognised it as a siren. Police or ambulance?

Go away. She should be pleading for the siren and the flashing lights to come and save her from the whispering, the giggling, from the darkness that was drifting lazily in across the marsh towards her. She had no phone, no shoes, no coat. *Go away.*

A sharp pain stabbed at the soft place of her instep and unbalanced her. Leaning back against the wall she put her hand down and felt wetness, the iron smell of blood was in her nostrils and she heard the soft giggle somewhere out of sight and in that moment the house seemed to topple towards her. The dead weight of her sisters in her arms, too heavy for her to hold, pulled her to one side. She put out a hand to save herself and it skittered over the rough brick, she felt herself go and she closed her eyes, she surrendered to the fall. But something snagged her dress: it tore.

Staggering, she was upright again, a tatter brushed her from a rip down the side of the dress, but she was upright. Limping, she shoved herself through the yard door that hung from its hinges and underfoot she felt the soft mud through fine marsh grass.

'Who is it?' Alison shouted, and heard her voice loud here in the lee of the building, everything around her muffled, the grass bright under the dustbin-lid sky. She came around the blind flank of the house to the front and there was the porch, with the plant sprouting above the door; blood leaked from her foot and unthinking she wiped it to and fro on the soft grass.

'Where are you?' No one answered. She strained to hear but the siren had disappeared too, there was only the monotonous clink, clink of rigging in the bobbing tide out in the creek. The big bay window was at her side, the crumbling stone of its lintel invited her and she leaned against it.

The black-painted boarding gave a little under her shoulder and she turned to its blank face, she spread her arms and felt around its edges with a loving touch. Her face was against it but it was too close to see the words. *Joe.* She worked her fingers in the crack where it met the stone sills and tugged – it came away, just a little. She heard her own intent breathing in her ears. This was it, this was the answer. They were all inside, they were waiting for her.

Planting her feet square in the mud she pulled, as hard as she could. There was a loud crack and a splinter came away in her hand, no more, it scored a deep cut alongside the veins of her wrist that she saw and felt in the same moment and then she fell back hard and landed on her backside, jarring her spine.

And from above and behind her on the sea wall came not a whisper, not a ghost, but a hard angry laugh. From where she'd landed in the mud Alison scrabbled around to look and saw only the fringed grass on the top of the dyke, and then it sprang up from its hiding place, a spiky shape, all elbows and knees, standing up against the grey sky in a T-shirt too short in the arms, grubby miniskirt, a wristful of cheap bracelets jangling on the arm she raised in triumph. *Hahahahaha*.

Alison was on her feet now and it seemed to her that the figure was pointing. And calling, jeering still but telling her something, showing her something. *Up there. There. That's how, there.* Standing still, her hand stretched out steady, her head thrown back and her sharp little face a white blank. Alison turned to see what she was being shown.

Above the porch, the spray of leaves nodded in the stiff wind, and it was pointing to the same place. From the flat roof of the porch, a drainpipe led up to the window above, and what Alison had thought was black board in its frame was emptiness, a pane smashed right through, a hole.

She turned back but May was gone, as if she'd never been: bright spots danced before Alison's eyes, like sparks or fireflies.

She set her bloodied foot against the porch, and climbed.

Chapter Thirty-eight

Sarah Rutherford hated weddings at the best of times, but it was apparent to her straight away that there was something more than usually fucked up about this one.

Not all the guests seemed to know it yet, but the staff certainly did. A panicked-looking waiter in a cheap tailcoat gestured to a marquee and Sarah was aware of people – a woman in a pastel suit hastily draining a glass, waitresses, an usher – falling back to either side as she strode through towards the hubbub from inside the marquee, Jennings behind her trying to keep up. Even if they hadn't seen the patrol car, even without the uniform, people knew. Thing was, she didn't know if she was bringing the bad news or if it was already here.

'Lucy Carter,' Ron Thwaites had said, stepping off the pub's threshold towards them. 'You know what? That Dr Carter's an arsehole: just because he wouldn't lower himself to come in here from one year to the next he thought we never knew? I saw him, at the sailing club one time, watching those little girls on the beach. His daughters. Very pleased with himself, he looked, like it made him quite the man even if he wouldn't give them the time of day, even though she'd followed him here with the whole family in tow. Kate Grace. Thought he could get away with it, he thought the little wife'd do what he told her to.' He spat, with feeling, a gobbet landing on the concrete. 'But she's a piece of work all right. Some couples deserve each other.' And again, uneasy now, 'None of our business.'

She'd be here.

Inside the marquee half the tables were seated: Sarah heard a cork pop and a burst of uneasy laughter but at the back of the tent there was an ominous huddle of morning coats and hats beside a flap in the heavy nylon canvas. Right, thought Rutherford, scanning the room, top table, and there it was, a whiteboard beside it holding a seating plan. A long rectangle where all the other tables were round, it was empty save for the man who'd brought May home the day before, neat in pale grey, looking down at his mobile phone with apparent unconcern. The groom.

The noise changed again, a ripple of whispers moving round the room and dying away. Rutherford saw several things at once: she saw the groom quietly lay down his phone; she saw the crowded morning coats part and shift a little to reveal the bride's father in their midst, Roger Carter, his sandy hair dishevelled and his mouth slack; she saw the bride, his daughter, in the far corner, towering bare-shouldered and staring as a woman beside her spoke into her ear, as the woman raised a finger and jabbed her bare shoulder to make her turn and listen. The woman wore a waitress's uniform, she had straggly hair and a booze-reddened face, and Sarah Rutherford knew her straight away: Karen Marshall.

Back to Roger Carter, because where Carter was, his wife would be. But she wasn't. Searching the faces Rutherford threaded between the tables, heads turning to watch her in her cheap suit that was shiny at the elbows, unhesitating. She

saw Carter quail, she saw him step backwards, an usher steadying him at the elbow.

Out of the corner of her eye she saw Karen Marshall register
her presence, saw her step away from the bride, and saw the
bride's hand move to stop her.

Lucy Carter. Inside Rutherford it set up, it started pumping,
where is she, where is she, where is she. *Where is she?*

She stopped suddenly and felt Jennings come up short
behind her, his breath on her neck. 'Can you see the girl?'
she said urgently. 'Come on, come on. The girl. Where's the
girl?' In the middle of the tables they turned, looking. 'Esme
Grace, or whatever she's called. Alison. You see them on the
way in? Her or the boyfriend?' Jennings began to shake his
head.

A flap opened in the back of the tent and a voice broke
loose, a stifled scream from somewhere that rose above the
uneasy murmuring, a clamour rising with it.

'Why?' she'd said to Ron Thwaites, all out of understanding.
'You never said.' Flat. 'None of you spoke up. The Carters and
the Graces could rot together.'

He'd stared back at her and sullenly his expression shifted,
panic entering his eyes. 'I never, I never thought . . .' and he
was choked, the barmaid stepping into the threshold behind
him. 'It wasn't *her*?' He'd jerked his head round and the surly
girl had disappeared again. 'Lucy Carter? I still thought it must
have been John did it.' His bloodshot eyes bulging with alarm.
'I thought it was over and done. We all did. No one left.'

'And what about the girl? What about Esme?'

'What good would it have done her?' he mumbled. 'To
know Lucy Carter pushed her dad over the edge? Fucking
mess.' But he went still, as though he'd remembered something
else.

'Out of sight, out of mind? We all thought she'd never come
back, but she did. We thought it was done, but it wasn't.'

In the marquee people were standing up at the tables and all looking in the same direction. 'There he is,' Jennings began to say but something stopped him. She turned to where he was staring and saw a tall man, tall and spare with a high forehead, not Esme Grace's boyfriend, this was someone she knew better than that. Bob Argent, standing tall with outstretched arms, burdened with a thing in sacking from which legs dangled from one end, paint-spattered trousers and a shoeless foot. Stiff colourless hair. Chatwin.

The whispers moved around the tables. *Hanged himself.*

As they watched, Bob Argent turned slowly towards Roger Carter, the doctor, holding out his burden but Carter stepped back so fast he stumbled.

'Ambulance,' barked Sarah Rutherford without turning her head, but Jennings was already muttering into his walkie-talkie.

'You think a woman could have done it?' Ron Thwaites had said numbly. 'You think she could have killed them all?'

'Who else?' she'd said, and the blood had drained from his pouchy face.

Where is she?

She heard the ambulance again from where she crouched, on the landing in the dark.

She'd dreamed it so long, the house had metamorphosed in the dark behind its boarded windows. Climbing through the narrow window on the first-floor landing Alison smelled the change, latrine and damp, mould spores with something other underneath, something fishy. Bare feet first in the dark she slithered in a litter of magazines splayed across the damp carpet. She was next to the twins' room: she couldn't turn her head in case anything was left. Their soft hair, their bath-warm skin. She squatted with her back to their door among the torn pages and looked down in the narrow shaft of light from the broken window she'd climbed through. More dirty magazines.

326

Stealthily the house was taking shape again around her in a grey darkness, the fogged outlines of things broken and sagging and abandoned. The splintered banister, the stairs she'd sat on with them in her arms; the door, out of sight, into the sitting room where Joe had sat, legs apart, headphones holding what was left of his skull together. Up. Up. She crawled to the stairs and as she climbed, on hands and knees, she felt a draught follow her, cold poking through the house's cracks and openings.

There must be other places to get in. The village children would have found them, they would have covered their traces as she and the twins and Joe might have done, clambering in and out, whispering, agile. Carefully replacing board or corrugated iron, heaping leaves and rubble. At the top of the next flight of stairs she stood, on shaky legs.

The ceilings were lower on the second floor. Bathroom; Joe's room. She set her cheek against the doorframe, she let the door move a crack under the weight of her body. The shape of a bed in there, the tatters of a poster hanging from the wall and as she registered the tiny sound the door made as it moved she realised the siren had stopped.

It had been an ambulance siren; she recognised the sound as she felt the wood against her cheek, the years were gone and she was back there crouching frozen against the rotted jetty. An ambulance, only this time it had stopped far off and she visualised the village ranged above her, impossibly distant. *Make all the noise you like.*

Lucy Carter had said she'd heard the shots from her patio, she said they all heard the shots together, her and Morgan and Paul, but it wasn't true.

A woman. A woman had killed them. A woman who'd given birth to a child of her own, both of them monsters. How did that happen? Alison stared up the attic stairs into the darkness. Lucy Carter, as Esme lay face down on her bed and waited, the doctor's fragile wife in the house below her, moving from room to room, struggling with Dad in the yard, his glasses falling. She tried to make it fit.

Alison looked down to the landing below and saw the gleam of the spread magazines: she listened. Something shifted and breathed, she wasn't sure if it was inside or out: there it was again, a sigh; a rustle. The wind. It circled the house, rocked it, testing its strength. She looked up. The last flight of stairs waited for her, they only led to one room, her room, under the roof. She could hear the slates lifting as she climbed. The banister Dad had built felt flimsy under her hand. She was going back up, back inside, nowhere else to go. End of the line.

A slate fell below her, a slither and sharp crash at the back of the house into the rubble of the yard and then distinctly she heard a swear-word, softly spoken. She scrabbled backwards, shuffling on her backside into the attic space, into the corner, behind the door.

The room. Her room. There was more light up here, the boarding at the casement under the eaves had half fallen away but no one had bothered to replace it. Her heart swelled to fill her chest as the familiar space enfolded her, so intimate, so terrifying, every corner, every angle laid down in her head, and she crouched, tight and tighter.

No.

She didn't know where the whisper came from, she squeezed her eyes shut. *Look. It's coming.*

It came from inside her. It said, *Look.*

And then she was up, unsteady, and down the years she heard it. *BOOM.* On her raw feet, crossing to the window, raising herself to look down. She was on tiptoe trying to see and then it came. Not whispering or laughing this time, not the pleading or begging that had clamoured to be heard in the dark.

328

A grunt. A crash.

From the front of the house this time. In two places at once.

She had heard someone at the back. Lucy Carter, dislodging a slate, trying to climb? Now someone was at the front, but the sound was wrong, it was too loud. Too big.

It was huge, it enfolded the house with her inside, the sound that came with the darkness, not human. She curled herself, her face pressed between her knees, and then at last she remembered those human sounds, or fractions of them, that had come to her, up the stairs, through the timbers. The scream that was stifled in a soft small mouth, Joe's exhalation of disbelief as he raised his head to look, a high heel skittering, a gasp, a thud. Begging. *Don't.* At her back she felt the vibrations coming up through the house along with the inhuman thing that was battering to get in, now.

Now.

It splintered and crashed and pounded. It wouldn't stop.

Her father's voice, deep, slurred, a crash as he fell against the wall, not believing. *BOOM.*

It stopped.

Wait. Hide. Wait. Behind the door and wait for it to come.

But then Alison wasn't hiding. She was half crawling out of the horrible dust and clutter of her dead bedroom, she was on her feet. She was on the narrow staircase, the banister gave under her hand and she was sliding, falling, she landed, staggered: she stayed up. Across the landing. She was running towards it. Fight.

What had Lucy Carter hit Bray with? What was she using to batter the front door downstairs now? I can fight, thought Alison, not knowing if it was true. I'm younger, I'm strong. *Where are you?*

'Where are you?' She didn't wait for an answer, she felt the stair carpet loose under her bare feet as she skidded down, she saw the light where the rotted front door sagged inwards, now

329

swinging on broken hinges. A grey light that flooded the hall exposed the fur of dust and wallpaper stripped and peeling, the filthy kitchen floor where her mother had lain and she stumbled and fell, into the arms that were waiting to hold her.

My darling.

Chapter Thirty-nine

He wasn't dead.

Jennings was leaning over Simon Chatwin and administering CPR. Having set down his burden Bob Argent was standing silently with his arms folded, his back to the outside of the marquee. Most of the guests had found their way out through the flap like sheep and had formed a half circle around Jennings and the man lying prone under him on the grass, his head fallen back and his neck raw. The rope was still around it, blue nylon, frayed, a textbook noose. You could trust this lot to tie a knot, at least, thought Sarah Rutherford grimly. They could hear the ambulance coming, at the end of the lane.

'Where's Mother?' Rutherford turned at the sound of Morgan Carter's savage whisper and saw the doctor's glazed eyes, saw him shake his head dumbly, the flesh slack under his chin. The wedding veil stood stiff off the back of the bride's head, just mad fancy dress with that face under it.

From his place behind Sarah, Bob Argent spoke. His eyes held steady on Morgan: Rutherford saw her avoid his gaze.

'Mother of the bride?' he said. 'She were watching him

331

string himself up.' He looked down at Chatwin then back at Morgan. 'Talking to herself.' He almost smiled. 'Pissed.'

'You were watching him too,' said Rutherford, feeling sick.

'I cut him down, din't I?' said Argent. 'Enough's enough.'

At the far side of the house the ambulance gave a final loud whoop and Jennings sat back a moment on his heels, gasping. On the grass Chatwin's head moved, from side to side; his eyes were opaque.

'Where'd she go?' said Sarah Rutherford and she saw Morgan Carter and her father turn to her together. 'And the girl?' she said, taking a step towards them. 'Esme Grace?'

The doctor shifted at the name, unsteady on the grass, and he put out a hand towards his daughter; Morgan looked down at it as if she didn't know what it was. 'Paul . . .' said Morgan Carter, looking around the faces. 'I need Paul.'

And then there was a commotion inside the tent and two fluorescent-vested paramedics pushed their way through the opening with holdalls and were kneeling on the grass to either side of Chatwin. Karen Marshall in her black apron had come out of the tent behind them and was standing to one side. Moving closer Sarah smelled cigarettes on her, and would have killed for one.

'She went off down after the girl,' Bob Argent answered Sarah's question, and he stepped into their circle, uninvited: Sarah next to Karen Marshall, the Carters reluctantly completing it, Jennings on the outside, looking down at the paramedics, who were putting a mask over Chatwin's face.

'Down the field,' said the bargemaster. 'Girl was running.' He lifted his head, admiring. 'No shoes nor nothing. Looked just like her mother, I said.' He looked at Roger Carter. 'Nice-looking woman,' he said.

Sarah saw Morgan Carter's hand fasten tight on her father's forearm. Esme Grace and Lucy Carter: one young, barefoot, fast on her feet; the other drunk. Crazy. She shot a glance between the Carters at Jennings, jerked her head to summon him. Slowly he got to his feet.

'Your wife picked John Grace up in her car the night he shot his family,' she stated. Clarified. 'The night he is *believed* to have shot his family.'

'She never . . . I didn't . . . I knew nothing about it,' Roger Carter said, his mouth moving oddly. Morgan Carter's knuckles were white on the hand around his wrist, but she didn't seem to be able to stop him babbling. 'Paul said I should tell you,' he went on. 'About Bray, the headscarf, about the girl, Lucy wore the scarf, I . . . I . . . had no idea. She has these moments, it's her age. Time of life, that's what I thought, women—' He broke off: his daughter was staring at him blank with fury, a child used to getting her own way. 'Mud on the carpet in the morning is all I knew. Morning after Bray died. Mud on the carpet and a bottle of my best malt missing. That's all.'

Sarah Rutherford disregarded what she didn't understand. 'What time did your wife get home the night of the shootings?' she said, and his mouth went slack. He began to mumble but Morgan Carter had stepped forward, shouldering him out of view.

'You are very well aware that you can't ask him these things here,' she said, chin up. 'Under these circumstances. This is in contravention—'

'Lucy was on the patio when I got back from the patient,' said Roger Carter from behind her shoulder. 'I can say that, can't I? She'd been drinking.' His daughter turned her face away but Sarah heard her make a sound in her throat.

Sarah felt Jennings step up at her shoulder, waiting. 'I shall need to take you in for questioning,' she began, but felt the form of words get away from her, the first time in twenty years that had happened. Karen Marshall had moved inwards: the circle tightened.

'You was at the Plough with him,' Marshall said in her

333

smoke-rough voice, looking at Morgan Carter. 'That night, I knew I'd seen him before. I couldn't make sense of it, back for her wedding with the other one.' She turned to Rutherford. 'You know they was an item, them two? The one staying with Esme Grace at the Queen's now. Him.'

'She means Paul,' said Roger Carter helpfully, instantly paling under the look Morgan gave him. Karen Marshall didn't look at him, only at his daughter.

'You was with him at the Plough eating the night John Grace done it.'

Morgan Carter's jaw was clenched. 'Were we?' she said stiffly. 'I don't remember.'

The paramedics were lifting Chatwin on to a stretcher: they'd fitted him with a neck brace and an oxygen mask covered his face. The circle shifted and compressed to allow them by and behind them the guests murmured, pretending sympathy.

'Why would he come here to top himself?'

It was Jennings. Sarah saw Karen Marshall exchange a look with Argent, a flat, dead, weary look, a smile on both their faces that said, *if you need to ask.* Sarah just lifted a hand to gesture at all of it, the marquee, the big brash house rising behind it, the gilt chairs.

'Some people get away with it,' she said. 'Other people never do.'

'Get away with murder,' said Bob Argent, and she turned to him.

'You followed Chatwin up here,' she said. 'Did you know what he was planning?' The man regarded her, quite expressionless – there was no point asking him if he felt guilty. Not now, not ever: there were men like that. 'It was you left him for dead out there on the marsh the night of the shootings.'

'Chatwin said that?' Argent only raised an eyebrow. The stretcher was disappearing inside the tent, a sudden gust of wind behind it pelting them all with rain. The guests eddied and formed a new shape, following the paramedics back inside.

Without being asked Jennings had moved closer to Morgan Carter. She had her father by the elbow and was trying to edge him out of the circle but he just stood there, stubbornly immobile. His expression was vacant. Sarah had the flicker of a thought about Jennings: maybe the boy knows what he's doing, after all.

She shook her head. 'Of course he didn't. True though, isn't it?' The smile settled on the bargeman's face. 'Hear anything while you were out there on the marsh?'

'You got a call,' said Karen Marshall suddenly. Morgan Carter didn't look, didn't speak, but they all turned towards her. 'You hadn't finished your meal and a call came for you. You paid up and you left, you and him, there and then, desserts coming out of the kitchen already but he put cash right down and left 'em. It *were* him, weren't it?'

Again her eyes rested, just a moment, on Bob Argent's face – a mild look now, peaceful, exchanged between them. 'Bartlett, booked in at the Queen's as Paul Bartlett, and the Plough too, same name. All them years ago. That very night.' Not looking at Morgan any more, nor Argent, Karen Marshall was looking at Sarah. 'Funny thing him going with that little girl now, don't you think? The Grace girl.'

Morgan stumbled backwards, a sudden jerky movement and Bob Argent's hand shot out to grip her. She pulled away, but he held on.

Karen Marshall was patting her apron down, she pulled out a pack of cigarettes and put one in her mouth while Roger Carter moved in half-remembered protest. She bent her body to light it.

'I remember thinking, he's one of them,' she said, straightening, blowing smoke back. 'All that time back but it sticks. Some people stick. One of those, likes sorting out the little woman,' she said. 'He had a look in his eye, marching her out. Gets off on it, I thought.'

'Who was on the phone?' Sarah spoke quietly.

Karen Marshall tipped her head back, blew the smoke straight up. 'A woman, hysterical. It was her took the call,' nodding to Morgan, 'then she says to him across the room, I can't talk to her, and he goes over. Him being the big man and her gazing up at him. "We'll deal with it, Lucy," he says, all sweet and lovey-dovey like.' She spoke scornfully. 'Then he hangs up and next thing we know they're off.'

'Where did you go?' said Sarah Rutherford and then they all turned to her but none of them seemed to have actually heard, Morgan paler than her dress. Only Argent spoke, and he wasn't answering her question.

'Do you know, I did see something,' he said, and his voice was soft, no more than ruminative. 'I'd been out there, just an evening walk, you know.' He gave Sarah a humorous look, as if to say, all harmless fun. 'I'd come in off the barge. It was a cold night, I went for a nightcap to warm myself up, Ron'll tell you. He said John Grace'd been in earlier, 's a matter of fact, it was all they was talking about, the state he'd been in. Anyway, I walked up a ways, just clearing my head, into the village then I passed the lane, you know, down by where they've just built the new houses now.' Argent paused and they all gazed, silenced by the length of his speech. 'I heard it.'

'Heard it?'

'Gunshots,' he said, light and musing. 'Who shoots at night? Even ducks is early morning. Funny, though, the whole village must've heard it but we never done nothing, not a one of us. Shots is what I heard, and I could tell where it was coming from.' Sarah made herself wait, holding her breath. 'So I stopped, end of Swains Lane and there was a car parked up there, almost missed it, parked like it was trying to keep out of sight, half in the hedge.' Karen Marshall stood intent, one elbow tucked in at her side. 'Closest you can get in a car to the old Grace house, I reckon. Never liked that house. Why'n't they bulldoze it after?' He looked around, but no one had an answer.

So he went on. 'There was a girl sitting in the car, see,' he said. 'Woman.' He looked down almost in surprise to see that he was still holding on to Morgan Carter's pale arm, goose-pimpled in the cool blue air. 'It was her,' he said and she looked back up at him, mesmerised, almost besotted. 'Who was you waiting for?'

'Paul,' said Morgan, her head held high but turning, right and left. 'I need Paul.'

Chapter Forty

His arms held her so softly. Paul.

Thunder rolled and cracked somewhere inland. Beyond the door the air darkened and suddenly it was raining hard, slanting across the rectangle of outside light. She could see the water glinting, high.

A hand came up and stroked: it was on her hair, it was on her neck. Alison held herself still inside his arms. She could smell his sweat, she could feel the heat of his body through the dress shirt, she could see the texture of his skin inches away and all she wanted was to lean and set her face against him. To be his. But she held her head back and listened.

'She's here,' she said in a whisper, and above her he looked up too. Something dripped in the house, something rustled. A creak. Another. Footfall.

He nodded in silence, still looking up.

'First floor,' she said.

'She followed you,' Paul said, and looked down at her, thoughtful. 'The boy wouldn't tell me where you'd gone,' he said.

'Danny,' she said, and Paul's expression barely changed but he took up her hand, stroking the fingers one by one. Then he stopped and looked back up the stairs into the darkness. 'Just a boy,' he said.

The soft footsteps overhead were distinct now. She was moving, light as a feather. The twins' room. Landing. Mum and Dad's bedroom.

'I had to let you find out for yourself,' he said, examining her face. 'I talked to Roger. I tried to make him see, he needed to go to the police about her.' He kept looking, to make sure she understood. 'About Lucy. But when I saw her heading off down the field and I couldn't find you anywhere – I had to come.'

'Did Roger know all along?' She tried to reconstruct those evenings at The Laurels, hearty Roger at the fireplace, Lucy moving around nervously. Lucy drinking. Living with it thirteen years and Esme turns up on her doorstep.

Paul shook his head. 'Roger?' he said, almost impatient. 'Roger's not clever enough.'

'But Morgan,' she said, and the certainty settled. 'She knew.' He just shrugged, yes, an eye still on the stairs, but doggedly she went on.

'And when you and Morgan got back,' she said, swallowing, 'the night of the . . . shooting. She wasn't at home?'

But he only held up a finger, head cocked. Upstairs something crashed: a door flung back and suddenly Paul was gone.

'Lucy.' His voice echoed oddly on the stairs: it sounded menacing. He softened it as if he'd heard too. 'Lucy, darling. Come on.' In the hall Alison froze. She couldn't move. His footsteps receded. The landing creaked overhead.

Darling. It hung in the air after him.

Inside her chest Alison's heart squeezed and expanded, *boom*, and she was back up the stairs after him.

On the landing she stepped across the scattered magazines

on her cut feet, heading towards a murmuring of low voices but at the slithering she made they stopped. Ahead of her was the door to the twins' room. A stone had grown inside her now, it was hard and cold and it left no room for breathing. She pushed and saw grey light leaking around a window that showed her the room's empty corners: they weren't here. She backed out. She could have called for Paul but she didn't. In the gloom she stepped back across the landing and straight in there, into their parents' room, through the door they had always had to knock at, without knocking.

The bed her father had built was there still but its shape had changed: one post was gone and the mattress was sagging sideways on collapsed springs. On it Paul was sitting, close against Lucy Carter, his arm around her shoulders. They looked up at her, united. Lucy's cheek was against his.

'She's sorry,' he said, and looking up at her his eyes gleamed in light shed from somewhere she couldn't locate. 'She's very sorry.' There was a warning in his voice.

Alison looked from one to the other but in the same moment she was moving towards them, propelled by the hard thing that had gone on growing inside her, that would split her from top to toe. She felt Paul shift out of her way and as her knee came down on the rotted mattress and all the way through it to a metal edge she felt a sharp pain that righted her and she stopped. Her hands were round Lucy Carter's throat.

Beside her Paul did nothing; she couldn't even hear him breathing.

'You killed them,' she said, but even as the words came out of her mouth they sounded wrong. Lucy Carter's eyes were wide. Alison took her hands away, and tried different words.

'I saw you from my window,' she said. 'I heard you.'

Lucy Carter's head began to move from side to side. The mattress shifted as Paul changed his position beside them. 'You told my mother you'd see her dead.' Alison swallowed, to keep the thing down that rose in her throat. 'You were screaming. All dead, you said.' She curled her hands to keep them still: she had to stay level, she had to think clearly. 'Where did you get the gun?'

They must have come inside, Lucy and Dad, they must have argued, all of them. But that part refused to come back to her.

She was half kneeling over the older woman on the bed, but with her hands pulled back the power shifted – Lucy Carter began to draw herself up.

'That woman,' she said, triumphant. 'She telephoned! She called our home.' An outrage Lucy Carter had repeated in her head over the years. 'I'd already told her, if she came and made another scene at the house . . .' Her head moved, fractionally, towards Paul, and in Alison's head it ticked down, into place. 'I told her if she made contact again I – we – wouldn't be answerable. It was harassment. Trailing out here after him, she couldn't understand it was only a stupid fling, a silly girl in a shop who flattered his ego. Just because she let herself get pregnant . . .' Her voice wavered, reedy, but then recovered, the doctor's wife almost brisk. 'She couldn't force him to have the test.' Drawing herself up further now. 'Just because her own husband was a . . . a . . .' But Paul bent his head to her, leaning across Alison: he held a finger to his lips.

'Shh . . .' he said, gentle, confiding, and Lucy Carter's face turned up to his, and fell still.

Alison set a foot down from the bed, backing off. As she retreated, the other two moved closer together.

'You were there the night my mother went to The Laurels,' Alison said wonderingly to Paul. His arm was around Lucy Carter again. 'She said they'd had company, when she came back.' He said nothing. 'The night the boy was killed in the hit-and-run, the night she brought Joe home drunk, the night she went to tell the Carters the twins . . . the twins . . .'

341

Looking up at her Paul was waiting, patient. 'Mum said they had company.'

In the kitchen with Dad, white-faced with panic, Joe vomiting upstairs.

'You do look just like her,' said Paul, and his voice was so soft. Disregarding Lucy in his embrace he leaned forward, upwards, closer to her, she felt his breath. The rain had stopped, the wind had fallen, it was quiet. Higher up in the crooked house something dripped, something creaked, easing. A tiny slithering, a snap. 'She was a beautiful woman.' Lucy moved on the bed like a restless child and Alison felt her anger stirring, a thread between them that turned her head from Paul to the woman.

'Stephen Bray,' she said, reaching for the thing she was sure of. 'You arranged to meet him. You took the scarf.'

And even as she said it she remembered, down the years, the scarf had come from a customer at the art shop where Mum had worked. Lucy Carter's portrait in oils.

'You hit him with something,' she said. 'You killed him.'

Lucy Carter's voice rose and wavered. 'We went to Amalfi, of course,' she said. 'Second honeymoon. Lovely. He bought me a necklace there, you know, he went off on his own and bought it. Not some nasty cheap scarf.' She gazed, her eyes liquid. 'I didn't mean to hit him. I had the bottle in my hand. I told him, he only had to promise not to tell. He wouldn't promise.'

Alison looked down, pitiless. 'You came to our house that night,' she said, and Lucy Carter looked back up at her, hunched and silent. 'Did you only mean to kill *her*?'

Her voice came out strange and choked, the air in the room was crowded, as though dark shapes were slipping silently back into the house and taking up positions they knew of old. Against the kitchen cabinets downstairs, curled on the floor, at the foot of the stairs, upright on the sofa. 'I can't . . . I can't understand. You wanted her dead. Letty and Mads, because they were his? And Dad? And Joe?'

And why not me? Unspoken in the foster family's front room, if he'd known you were there, Sarah Rutherford had said, *You'd be dead too.*

A head turning in the market square to watch her pass.

'And why didn't you come for me?' she said, and it was Alison's head that turned, seeking him out. A tall man in the market square, pale eyes. A stranger watching the girl on her bicycle standing in the pedals.

Lucy's eyes were huge and starry in the gloom, hypnotised. 'I did . . . did . . . I . . . didn't . . .' she faltered and she looked for Paul, past Alison. 'Tell her, Paul,' she said, gazing at him. 'He's been like a son to me,' she said and her hand fluttered up towards him, a moth in the gloom. 'I don't know why they couldn't have got married.' Her face fixed on his. 'There's never been anyone else for Morgan. Like a son to me. His own parents . . . think of that. They killed themselves with him in the house.' Her voice rose plaintively but she was a child feeling sorry for herself, it was concocted, it was a sob story for both of them. 'Like a son. I always wanted a son. He'd do anything for me.'

In the gloom she saw his hand come up to cover Lucy Carter's mouth; she sagged sideways against his neck; and above her face Alison saw the cool stare of a boy alone on a cliff.

'We haven't got long,' he said, over her shoulder. The words settled soft and comfortless as dust.

'Did she say you were in the house,' Alison said, wondering, 'when your parents killed themselves?' His free hand came up to stroke her cheek.

'They were very worried about the trauma, when I got back to school,' he said lightly, almost amused. 'About *damage*. How stupid my father was, to wait for the holidays.' But doggedly she pursued it.

343

'That wasn't what you told me . . .' And his hand stopped. 'You said you were away at school.' In the gloom she couldn't see what his face was doing: it seemed to her he was smiling, but that couldn't be right. He said nothing.

Lucy was moving restlessly under his arm and he seemed to lose interest, releasing her. 'I called him, you see,' she murmured, to no one. 'I couldn't let that woman . . . Roger never stood up to her. That woman.' Her head bobbed foolishly. 'I think she'll understand,' she said.

'A woman in distress.' He sounded wistful; he sounded cruel. 'Your mother, in her heels. Nothing more beautiful than a woman in distress. And Lucy is very dear to me.' For a moment his hand grazed Lucy's breast, and then he was on his feet and his body was pressed against Alison's, all stone. His hand was on her waist, it had found its way through the torn dress. Behind him on the bed Lucy Carter sat mute, submissive, abandoned. Lovingly his hand explored.

Alison stood motionless, and still looking into her face he reached down casually to take hold of her under the skirt of the dress he'd bought for her. She saw the stranger's face, turning to watch her as she rode through the village. It rose like a poison creeping through her veins, paralysing, burning.

'You,' she said. His hand turned hard between her thighs, all knuckles and nails, it felt like metal, like some contraption of steel and springs meant to open and expose her. She stayed quite still, her face turned up to his, and his hand stopped and slowly, insultingly, withdrew.

Beyond the walls of the crooked house the world was spinning, spinning and the faces in it blurred as they were flung away from her: Danny; Gina; Kay; Sarah. Sarah the policewoman with her anxious eyes under the straight fringe. They gazed forlornly back – this was where Esme belonged, in here with the loving dead.

344

She could hear the water lapping: she could smell the rising sea.

'You always wanted to know,' Paul said, and took her hand. She felt the force of his grip even before, sharp and vicious, he tugged her alongside him to the door. 'I'm going to show you.'

This was where the world ended.

Chapter Forty-one

She hadn't had her seat belt on. Sarah Rutherford lifted herself off the dashboard and put a hand to her temple – she registered a shocking pain in her head and Jennings staring white-faced from the driver's seat. Tried to shake her head to tell him to stop looking at her like that, but it hurt too much.

'Boss . . .' he started to say, 'Sarah . . .' but she was already climbing out of the patrol car to work out what the fuck had happened.

She'd never been in a collision before, though she'd heard enough accident victims' disjointed reports to know they often had no clue about the moment of impact. She stared. A knackered brown Volvo sat slewed across them at the junction with steam hissing from the bonnet. Unlicensed taxi. A pasty middle-aged man at the wheel in shock and a girl in the back seat, woman, short dyed hair, eyes dark and staring with panic, her shoulder at the crumpled door trying to shove her way out. Sarah Rutherford had no idea who she was.

Late arrival for the wedding, though not dressed for it: too fucking late. *Get out of my way.*

They were no more than half a mile from The Laurels and the patrol car blocked in. With Jennings behind her struggling to get the car into gear she strode up to the Volvo and kicked the driver's side front wheel, savagely. 'Get it out the way,' she said, fighting to pull the badge out of her jacket pocket to show him. The cheap fabric tore. 'Out the fucking way.' The cab driver only stared, wobble-chinned.

Morgan Carter's husband had still been seated at the top table when they came back in, talking to the elderly couple, his mobile phone held loosely between his hands. He seemed entirely calm. His bride, with Sarah holding her hard by the elbow, hadn't even looked at him as she was led up to the table: he might have been a waiter, or a perfect stranger.

She'd had to leave Morgan Carter there, in the end: she needed Jennings. She didn't know how long it was going to take for another officer to get there, Saturday afternoon and someone had set fire to a shopping centre, a drunken man was holding his pregnant wife and in-laws hostage after a family barbecue. But she needed Jennings. She couldn't take any chances.

Accessory to murder, at the least obstructing the course of justice; young and strong, with access to funds, a trained lawyer. Morgan Carter could still abscond. She could harm herself – that was what they called it, meaning, top herself. *Fuck it.* Rutherford took the bride over to her new husband who looked up at them calmly.

'I charge you with holding her here until we return,' she said, and saw confusion pass across the faces of the old couple. The bridegroom showed no surprise, only courteous compliance. 'If you allow her to leave I will hold you responsible.' Sullenly Morgan Carter sat down, and Sarah Rutherford saw his hand, with its bright new wedding band, leave the mobile phone and settle on his wife's knee below the table.

The woman in the unlicensed taxi had got the car door open and was standing in front of her. 'I'm looking for The Laurels,' she said, and she seemed quite heedless of the situation, the police car revving in front of them in the lane. She wasn't dressed for a wedding: crumpled shirt, boy's trousers. No make-up, no fascinator. 'I'm looking for my friend. She's . . .' And finally she registered the flashes on the side of the police car. 'She's . . . her name's Alison now but she was Esme Grace,' she said, falling back against the car. 'I'm Kay. I work with her, I found out . . . it's the boyfriend, you see.'

Rutherford was having trouble with her head: she felt as though something had been shaken loose in there, she should know this girl, this woman. She knew Esme Grace, after all, and the name was secret. 'The boyfriend,' she said with difficulty. 'Paul Bartlett.' Her tongue felt thick.

Standing out there with Bob Argent's words blown away in the wind, they had all looked at Morgan Carter. 'He left me there,' she said, her chin obstinate. 'I wanted to come with him but he told me to wait in the car.' Her father started to say something, a warning, but he didn't seem to be able to get it out and Morgan's colour heightened, spreading up her neck. 'When he came back he was sweating, he smelled . . . he smelled strange.' She smiled, satisfied. 'He said, he'd dealt with it for Mummy, he said, it's motiveless, they never catch you. Our secret, just ours.' She looked around at them and she didn't seem like a lawyer or a bride, she seemed like a vicious playground tormentor, ruling by shock tactics, driven by greed. 'We did it in the car afterwards,' she said, triumphant.

She seemed oblivious to her father in his morning coat at her side, his face appalled, on the point of collapse, but Sarah Rutherford had been obliged to register his response. To file it under *No Fucking Clue*.

She hadn't read Morgan Carter her rights, was that why she'd stood up and crowed it over them? Accessory, for sure. Witnesses, at least: Karen Marshall, Argent, even if the father would say he'd heard nothing. But twenty years of doing everything by the book seemed to have deserted Sarah Rutherford. Behind the Volvo's smeared windscreen the driver appeared at last to have worked out that he was under some kind of imperative, bent over his ignition. There was a strangled sound.

'It's the gun, you see,' said the woman who'd climbed out of the car, the woman who called herself Kay. She seemed uncertain suddenly. 'He lied to her about the gun. He brought it with him, you know. He's got it here.'

'The gun.' Morgan Carter's words took a different shape. Jennings was looking at Sarah anxiously and she put a hand to the bruise on her temple. Was she bleeding into her brain?

Kay took a step towards Sarah Rutherford and put out a hand to her. 'Are you all right?' she said.

'Gun,' said Sarah with difficulty.

'She gave it to him,' Kay said. 'Morgan Carter.'

'Of course, after that, we had to cool off,' Morgan Carter had said, pretending carelessness. 'We agreed. Our secret, though. Mummy had drunk a bottle and a half on the patio by the time we got back, she didn't see a thing, never mentioned the phone call again. Our secret forever. He liked that, he even wanted me to get married and all the time we'd have our secret.'

A disbelieving sound had come from somewhere at that, and Morgan Carter had looked around the circle, settling on Karen Marshall who'd looked back at her, lips set in a line.

'I gave him a gun for his birthday, that year. We'd broken up by then, in public of course, but he knew what it meant.'

Nobody asked the question: Morgan didn't need a prompt. 'It took me for ever to find the bloody thing, the one the

349

Germans fighting in France would have used. It had to be right. And of course it had to be fully functioning.' That smile again. 'I mean, what good's a gun that can't be used?'

Behind them the knackered Volvo's ignition caught at last and the car jerked backwards into the ditch.

Chapter Forty-two

The yard dripped and when she stumbled on some broken brick in her bare feet his free hand was there, solicitous under her elbow. She had to put a hand up to her glasses to stop them falling. 'Careful,' he said.

It stank in the rain. Reeling, she looked up at the house. Lucy Carter was still inside, still in the bedroom as far as she knew. Alison had stopped at the foot of the stairs, expecting her to have followed them, but the house above them was silent, she'd stayed there obedient as a child sent to her room.

Filth on the coated kitchen surfaces. Cupboard doors open, one hanging askew from a broken hinge, ancient remains inside, like Pompeii, she thought as he led her, courteous for the moment, through the narrow space towards the back door. A beautiful woman, my mother – the words repeated themselves as she didn't look down, at the floor where her mother had lain.

'They were in here when I came up to the house,' he'd said, stopping abruptly at the door, turning to explain as if he was a teacher and they were on an educational tour. 'I came round here and I saw them drinking.' Two glasses on the draining board, she thought, Mum and Dad. 'Arguing. She was winning, your mother. At least . . . he looked beaten.' Paul looked amused, the kind of teacher who likes to show how much cleverer he is.

'If he hadn't come outside . . .' he went on, musing, standing at the back door but still his hand was hard around her wrist. Her fingers felt numb as frozen sausages. She'd always known, it seemed to her then; she'd known since he lifted the wine-glass from her hand at the office, since he held her by the wrists just inside his front door. She'd always known there was something behind the calm and the order. It was the dark that had drawn her in.

'If he hadn't come outside I'd never have known where to find it.' And then Paul turned a key and they were in the yard. He looked back over his shoulder, pleased. 'A good hiding place. A good one to remember, just in case.'

He had stepped towards the lean-to at the back of the yard, tugging her after him. He brought her out through the kitchen as if he knew where he was going – but then, one thing she knew about Paul was that he didn't falter: once he had decided on something, he might go underground but he followed through. It ended how he wanted it to end.

He reached up now, under the sagging slate of the lean-to, and paused there, turned back.

'We could even have been witnesses,' he said. 'Morgan and I were there the night he came into the pub asking for a gun. Up for the weekend. She'd said something about him. I'd seen the way everyone looked at him.' His pale eyes rested on her, and there was a glitter in them she'd never seen before. 'I suppose you might say the idea started there.' His head tilted. 'Did you know where your father kept the gun?' And his shoulder followed the arm under the shed roof.

'I never knew he had a gun,' she said, and he stopped, his

352

hand somewhere under the tiles. 'I never saw it until—' She stopped. 'My father was a good man.' He was so close she could see the creases at his eyes but there was nothing left in the hard, handsome face of the Paul she'd invented, no kindness, no laughter. A reel of loving gestures played in her head – food offered, a present, his hands on her – but it had all been like a picture in a magazine you set a match to, light and empty as ash. The raw mark on her father's neck as he lay on the hall carpet. She looked into Paul's pale eyes.

'He saw me out here and he came out and went straight for the gun, left her in the kitchen,' he said. 'I got it off him before he'd even turned round, and once I'd knocked his glasses off he was helpless.' And shrugged. Smiled. 'I even thought to put both his hands to the trigger. Not straightforward, blowing your own brains out with a shotgun.'

Needs determination. She stared, dumb.

'You spent so much time covering your tracks,' he said, and the smile hovered, his eyes greedy for something she couldn't see. 'I always knew where you'd been. You didn't even wonder this morning, though, where I was, where I might have gone on my run. Did you? You didn't know I'd come back to use your father's hiding place.'

She stared. His hand came out from under the shed roof and it wasn't empty any more. He held it out to her. 'I knew we'd come back here together,' he said. 'I believe in preparation.'

It sat in his palm, dull and heavy and ugly, a lump of scratched metal, the only other gun she'd ever seen. *Herstal Belgique.*

Then suddenly, brutally, he shoved her with the heel of his hand, the hand with the gun in it, she felt it connect below her ear and, unbalanced, shocked to the roots of her hair, she fell sideways. He was over her.

'Run,' he whispered, low and loving, but he was between her and the open gate. She raised herself on the sharp stone and glass and rubble, feeling it dig into her palms and he was behind her. He gave her a push, contemptuously light and she was down again, only this time her glasses came off and the world blurred.

'If I'd known then,' he said, and he pressed himself against her from behind, she felt his weight, she felt him between her legs. 'That you were upstairs, waiting for me. If I'd found you. That'd have given the police something to get excited about.' And she started away from him, her knees ripped and bleeding, bare feet scrabbling for purchase. As she broke free she heard the crunch, and as she blundered painfully into the jamb of the kitchen door she knew her glasses were gone but she heard a sliding on the loose stone behind her, heard him mutter something in anger and she knew, in that instant, this was her only chance.

Back into the kitchen, blindly staggering, stickiness of the old blue and white vinyl underfoot, hands wide and feeling for the doorway at the other end. Through the door into the hall, her house around her, her house. She tripped: she was down.

On her knees she smelled the freshness of the rain through the open front door ahead of her; she knew she must get to her feet and run but she couldn't move, she was stone. Dad, right here, his unshaven cheek on the blooded carpet, the raw mark on his neck where Paul had manhandled him in the yard, his dying brain flooded and all of it draining out of him, love and jealousy and fear. Dad stumbling over Mum's body in the kitchen, listening to the shots in that blur, one after another. He'd have heard more than she had, high up in her attic – he'd have heard the girls crying in fear, he'd have stumbled from room to room. Mads struggling to get free and seeing Joe. The last thing she'd have seen.

And all this time it hadn't come from the village at all, not from the place she'd feared, it hadn't bred in the cramped cottages or on the flat grey marsh: the darkness had drifted in

354

from further off. Passing over those who belonged here, it had wandered between washing lines and back gardens until it found the outsiders, in their crooked house: scenting blood and damage it had gathered itself, and rushed inside.

It washed through her, it turned her like a vast wave and sucked her down. She crawled and she was there where coats had once hung, her back against the wall, Esme.

She saw a shape fill the kitchen doorway and he was there, closer, close enough for her to see the thing in his hand and then she closed her eyes and felt it cold against her skull, there where the bone was thinnest, the nerves close to the surface. He was over her, he was all around her, she smelled his sweat, his breathing was in her ear. A small movement against her ear, his finger moving on the trigger.

She heard a woman's voice. It yelled.

And as though the wave had rolled and lifted her and spat her back to the surface she moved up and forwards, heels braced against the wall, up. She felt herself catch him off balance and as he tipped she spun and was in the doorway up against another body blocking her. A woman's body.

Lucy.

She smelled sweat and cigarettes, lank hair against her face.

Not Lucy. Gina had her by the shoulders and was shifting her bodily out of the way, sidestepping into the house, and then she was screaming.

May was a ghost running along the top of the sea wall.

She ran into Sarah Rutherford's arms, thin as a whip but more solid than a ghost, a tangle of elbows and legs and Sarah couldn't tell who the sob came from.

'Mummy,' said May, her white terrified face all angles and dark eyes turned upwards, her tangle of hair falling back. 'I told Mummy.'

'Wait,' said Sarah Rutherford, but there was no time, she

planted the girl to one side and ran. No time to make sure she stayed put, barely a glance over her shoulder to make sure Jennings was still there and the friend who'd made them bring her too. The track down here had been flooded, they'd had to drive on, as far as the sea wall. She ran: as far as she could see was grey water, the marsh drowned.

Her chest burned, her feet in heavy shoes sliding on the sodden path, heart pounding in her ears. Eyes fixed on it, the dark house, it beat a pulse inside her. Run. It was there in front of her and as she slid down the bank it blocked the sky: inside someone was screaming.

Gina Harling was screaming.

Paul Bartlett was lying where they'd found John Grace, he was curled and bleeding while Gina flailed and spat and kicked, drawing back a booted foot.

Behind her she heard Jennings's heavy footsteps, further back Kay gasping as she scrambled down the slope.

Wherewherewhere.

'Where is she?' she finally managed as Gina, still kicking, turned her clenched and raging face towards her and the light and despair flooded Sarah Rutherford's system.

'You bastard,' she hissed, no breath left to scream like Gina was screaming. 'You bastard.'

But something brushed her, soft in the shadows, she turned and saw a face streaked with dust and tears, her glasses gone, a child's face defenceless and new. Sarah opened her arms and Esme Grace entered them.

Afterword

The nurse who'd led her down the corridor was different but the room was the same, the camera blinked above the door. It watched them.

She sat as close as his twisted body and the tubes attached to it would allow. She sat so close she could smell all the chemicals his stubbornly continuing life required, she felt the loose joints of his thin hand in hers, the cool slack unexercised flesh. She leaned against him, the two bodies motionless, she waited, she listened until it came to her from where it was buried, his heart beating on.

She laid her face by his.

'*Daddy,*' she said. The word that would make her known.

Christobel Kent was born in London and educated at Cambridge. She has lived variously in Essex, London and Italy. Her childhood included several years spent on a Thames sailing barge in Maldon, Essex with her father, stepmother, three siblings and four step-siblings, which provided inspiration for the setting of *The Crooked House*. She now lives in both Cambridge and Florence with her husband and five children.